# INTO THE DARK OF THE DAY

ISBN: 1490549889

ISBN 13: 9781490549880

Library of Congress Control Number: 2013912295

CreateSpace Independent Publishing Platform

North Charleston, South Carolina

# AUTHOR'S NOTE

Though this story can be enjoyed without prior knowledge
of previous events or characters, it is the author's intent that this
novel should be read after finishing the first novel in this series,
*Through the Fury to the Dawn.*

TO ROBERT
& RENEE

KEEP THE FAITH!

To my daughter, Millie.

May you live with a thankful heart—

one full of faith, hope, and love—

and may you ever be a beacon of light

shining in the darkness.

I love you.

Blessed be your name
when I'm found in the desert place.
Though I walk through the wilderness,
blessed be your name.
Blessed be your name
on the road marked with suffering.
Though there's pain in the offering,
blessed be your name.

—from "Blessed Be Your Name," by Matt Redman

# PROLOGUE

He had failed. It had been his responsibility, and he had failed. His fixation on the dream had been too much, too lofty—or had it? The cloaked man took two shuffled steps and faltered, stumbling to one knee on the dusty ground. The sky hid from him through the barren trees, glowering down from its darkened place of power. Charcoal clouds billowed across the heavens, and thunder rumbled in the distance.

Blood seeped through the cloak that concealed his many injuries, a reminder that any normal man would have been dead long ago. But he wasn't normal. He was something else. There was something *inside*. He tried to stand, but even his own weight seemed too much to bear, as though his greater failures somehow had become more physical than they should be.

"How did this happen?" the man whispered, as the blood wept from his ruined face—a wound of melded buckshot and bone that refused to heal.

"How did this happen to *me*? *You promised!*" The large, muscular man lowered his head. He growled a string of profanities and laughed mirthlessly. "You motherfucker, I didn't fail you. You failed me. You were supposed to be bigger than this, bigger than all of them, bigger than Him. I did what I was supposed to do. You failed me, and now I've been broken. If you were what you said you were, this wouldn't have happened. You're nothing more than a fake, a powerless dream."

He laughed again—a sound devoid of any amusement. "Why don't you prove me wrong, you weak son of a bitch."

In an instant the wind picked up, howling through the dead trees like the eerie singing of a pipe organ. Still on his knee, the man pulled his cloak about him. The wind lashed about, whipping droplets of blood from his face in a gust that quickly grew to a gale. He squinted his eyes and braced himself with what strength remained, as he hovered amid the dust that flew and stung in the storm.

As quick as it came, the storm disappeared, the wind dropping to nothingness as the man continued to kneel. It was then that he heard it for the first time since it had left him. The voice. It spoke in a whisper, a sharp, lancing pain that slipped into his brain with a smooth, deathlike numbness.

*Weak human. You doubt because you are miserable and pathetic. Without me you are nothing. You're an insect waiting to be stamped out. I own you—forever. You are mine.*

The cloaked man rose and began to straighten himself. "Ah, the old adversary of the king comes with his parlor tricks and threats."

Before the man could finish, he was jerked from his feet and slammed brutally against the earth once, twice, and again. In a violent movement, he was dragged along the ground on his face before being plucked back vertically. There he hung suspended in the air like a broken marionette. Dazed and ruined, he flailed against his invisible tormentor as an oppressive weight of despair came crashing down on him. As he hung gasping, a shadow materialized. The voice spoke again.

*Words. They can only explain so much. Even if I tried, your feeble mind could scarcely understand it. I'd tell you of what is coming, what you are now a part of—the grand destiny of it all. But instead of telling you, I'll give you a taste.*

The shadow moved closer as the man hung suspended, every fiber of his being taut with fear and anticipation. A dark mist seeped into his nostrils and clung to his eyes.

*Do you see?*

The man gasped as tremors seized his body.

*Do you see?* The voice cooed with malevolence.

The man's eyes rolled back into his head. He gagged as bloody saliva spilled from his lips and small trickles of blood ran from the corners of his eyes.

*Yes. You see it now, don't you?*

Blood now poured from the man's eyes, nose, and mouth, gushing rivers of red as he groaned in agony and terror.

*I'll fix you. I'll make you the most powerful creature ever to walk the face of this planet—for a price. I told you before, and I'll tell you again. I own you, Malak—forever. It's best that you not forget that.*

☆ ☆ ☆

Kane Lorusso pushed at the large, blood-soaked patch of dirt at his feet with the tip of his boot.

"Courtland, are you sure this is where he was?" Kane asked, turning toward the gigantic, bald, black man who stood to his left.

"Without question."

The heavy cloud cover churned overhead, the result of man's ultimate violation of the earth. Though complete, it was beginning to show the slightest weakness in its facade, as tiny bits of light penetrated through the oppressive, marred barrier that now stood between heaven and earth. It was a scene that inspired hope for all who looked upon it.

The two comrades stood in silence for a few moments, surveying the scene where just hours ago the greatest battle of their lives had come to an end. Kane squinted and examined the blood-soaked ground again. Though a few hours had passed, the ground was still soaked. It had taken on a tacky consistency as the blood caked in the sand.

"Doesn't make sense," Kane muttered under his breath. "Maybe some of his goons dragged him off in all the chaos."

"I think we would have seen it—seen something."

"Are you sure he was dead?"

Courtland rubbed his massive hand across his brow and sighed. "I don't know." He looked up at the gaping hole in the wall of the structure, three stories up. "That's a long fall. I don't see how he could have survived it."

"You did."

"I did," Courtland said with a nod, "but the Lord was with me, and... Kane, I landed on top of him. He landed on his neck. You should have seen how it twisted on impact." Courtland scrunched up his face. "He looked as dead as a hammer."

Kane pondered this for a second. "It is true...God has been with us. But after seeing what we saw up there—what came out of Malak—I think it's safe to say that *something* is with him too."

Courtland nodded again. "Maybe it protected him, sustained him, something..."

Kane looked up and away, toward the faint outline of smoke-shrouded hills in the distance. Finally, he broke the silence. "All right, I need to go finish preparations for the burial service. Molly and the others...they deserve for it to be done right."

"Absolutely."

"You still don't mind saying a few words? I know she would've appreciated it."

"No problem, Kane," Courtland said, patting his friend gently on the shoulder. "It would be my pleasure."

"Thanks, man," Kane said as he turned to leave.

"It's just..." Courtland started.

Kane stopped, turning back. Courtland nodded, deep in thought, as he looked once again at the blood smeared patch of earth in front of him.

"That thing in him is not of this world," Courtland spoke, choosing his words carefully. "It knows neither pain nor weakness nor death. If we didn't destroy it, you can be sure of one thing. It will never stop—not ever. Not until it is drunk with every last drop of anguish and misery it can squeeze from us. Don't ever forget that."

# ONE

EMERGENCY RADIO CONTROL STATION
ON THE COAST OF SOUTH CAROLINA
NINE MONTHS AFTER THE EVENTS OF DAY FORTY

Kane Lorusso crossed the courtyard of the radio control station with the subtle, relaxed gait of a man who was in a hurry for nothing. After a few friendly greetings in passing, he began his lazy descent down the narrow, metal staircase to the subbasement of the station. Kane reached the concrete landing and knocked twice on the metal door before turning the knob and entering. The warmer air from within washed over him, and he smelled the faint aroma of heated plastic. The dim lights buzzed, giving off a false feeling of comfort.

As he entered, a portly figure sat up in his chair in the center of the room.

"Oh, Kane. Hey, man. Wasn't expecting you this time of day."

"Hey, Winston. I woke you up?"

"Naw, uh, I mean, well…" The chubby man sighed. "Yeah, I guess you did. Sorry, man."

Kane stared at Winston, his gaze penetrating the soft, round man like X-ray vision. Winston pulled his chair forward and began to clear the microphone control booth as he mumbled.

"Uh, yeah, I can't lie. I was napping a bit, but I'm a super-light sleeper, and I've got this thing turned way up, man. I mean if anyone was broadcasting anything, I'd hear it. You know, man. I'm..."

"Forget about it," Kane said, giving a dismissive wave of his hand.

"Like I said, I'm sorry. Just haven't been sleeping well lately, man." Winston nervously smoothed an unruly cowlick.

"Forget about it. Not that big of a deal. Just hear it if it picks something up."

"Cool, man. No prob. I got this locked down." Winston smiled, realizing the threat of disciplinary action had passed. He bobbed his head. "No worries. I got this."

"Good. We're glad to have someone like you, someone with a little experience with this kind of equipment."

"I dunno if being a disc jockey for my college radio metal station is experience, but hey, it is what it is." Winston unleashed a goofy smile.

Kane motioned at the console. "Mind if I do one?"

Winston stood and offered Kane his chair. "Knock yourself out, man."

Kane took a step through the small doorway and seated himself in the cozy booth. The air was warmest there, heated by the instrument panels and various antiquated electronics. The old-fashioned radio system was stored in the subbasement to make way for more sophisticated systems. In the end, it was the only equipment at the station that had made it.

The modern studio with all of its advanced computer-controlled systems was located on the upper floors of the station. It hadn't survived the electromagnetic pulse that had blasted everything during the onset of the End War. Every unshielded appliance and gadget that relied upon sophisticated, computerized technology had been completely fried. And that was just the beginning. In a brief, violent conflict, modern civilization was completely wiped from the face of the earth. Three-quarters of the world's population were destroyed. It had taken just under forty-eight hours. That was more than ten months ago.

Those who had survived lived to inherit a fate far worse—that of the new world. It was a place of savagery, greed, and basic survival, one tainted by the radioactive biological and chemical remnants from the war. Bands of violent criminals roamed the wasteland. Vile mutants called Sicks who had once been relegated to wander what was left of the larger metro areas began to stray from the cities. Massive forest fires raged unchecked. Water sources were ruined and undrinkable. Animal wildlife appeared to have disappeared from the earth. It was a nightmare.

In those first few days, Kane had lost everything that meant anything to him, but he'd gained something as well—something astounding. A light had entered his soul, and as it extinguished the darkness it found there, it turned a once bitter agnostic into a man of faith. It protected him in those early days through seemingly unsurvivable trials against evil men, monsters, and demons. It had made him a believer in the God of the universe and in his plan, which was still unfolding even now as Kane sat alone in the radio room.

He shuffled the chair closer to the microphone, cleared his throat, and moved his hand to the hot switch. Kane thought about the spirited young woman, Molly, whom he had befriended in the days after the war when everything seemed so messed up. She had been an inspiration to him, and even though she was gone, he knew he had made it this far because of her. He asked himself what she would want him to say on the radio. More important, he thought of her final words to him. They were words that couldn't be true, words that stung and elevated his emotions to a plateau of false hope.

*They're alive, Kane. Your family is still alive.*

There was no possible way. If it were true, how could she have known anyway? When the End War began, his family was in Miami, a city that was later completely destroyed. They couldn't be alive, and Kane couldn't think of such things. It wasn't fair that Molly had told him this then passed away without an explanation. Then again, "fair" was a civilized concept, one that didn't exactly have a place in the new world.

Kane clicked on the hot switch, and the radio crackled to life.

"This is Kane Lorusso broadcasting from the emergency radio control station on the coast of South Carolina, north of Charleston. A number of survivors have established a secure colony here along the coast, north of Charleston. We have resources and expertise that we are willing to share and trade with like-minded people. There is hope. There is light in the darkness. But let this be a warning to anyone who receives this message and plots to take from us, kill us, or raid our settlement. We are prepared, we are trained, and we will not go without a savage fight. That is all."

Kane snapped the hot switch down and licked his lips.

*Don't do it. Don't do this to yourself.*

He snapped the hot switch back on.

"Susan, if you're out there, and you can hear me, I love you and…if you hear this message, contact me on this frequency. I haven't lost hope."

He snapped the hot switch down again and swore under his breath.

Winston tried without success to conceal a look of pity as Kane stood and made his way to the door. Breathing deeply through his nose, Kane turned the handle and swung the metal door open, stepping out into the dark of the day.

✯ ✯ ✯

Jenna Gregory turned to the dingy cot behind her to assess the next patient, a middle-aged male who moaned and shivered under a thin wool blanket. She pursed her lips and furrowed her brow as she took inventory of his injuries. Another mauling victim. Those things were becoming bolder. Looking the man over, Jenna took it all in: an eight-inch abdominal gash held together with an uneven stitch job that was less than sterile; severe contusions across his chest, neck, and head; and a raging fever to start. He was also dehydrated and may have been exposed to radiation or some other blood poisoning. There was no way for her to know; it was all just a guess anyway. She wasn't a doctor. She wasn't even a nurse. Regardless, she was still the best chance that this man had to survive.

Jenna stooped close to the man's ear. "Is there anything I can get for you...to make you more comfortable?"

"Wa...wagga," came the man's raspy croak.

Jenna grimaced. Water. She knew he would ask for it long before he managed to croak out the request. It would be the hardest item to give freely.

"OK, I'll see what I can do. You just rest now."

In times of plenty, people forget that the human body is roughly 70 percent water—a fact that becomes all too easy to remember when the world turns to dust and every mucus membrane in the body begins to dry out.

Water, the image of which signified life and sustenance for the human race for thousands of years, was a luxury. There just wasn't enough. The war had contaminated every exposed body of freshwater as far as the eye could see. All the rivers and lakes either had dried up or turned to a chemical orange color that sent all forms of aquatic life floating to the surface.

Some water could still be collected from rainfall, but even that had to be separated from the black tarlike substance that fell from the clouds, then boiled and treated, before it was presumed safe to drink. And even then this so-called black water still made people sick sometimes. Even with black water on hand, it wasn't enough for everyone at the radio station. People lived in a constant state of dehydration with a continual fear of dying of it.

Jenna crossed the room to her satchel and pulled a plastic water bottle from her pack. She swirled the remaining two ounces of water in the bottle and sighed at what was left of her personal water ration for the day. The injured man wasn't going to make it, not with infection setting in. There was no reason to waste the last of her water on a dying man. But just as she thought this, she forced it from her mind and muttered to herself, "No, this is the work of the Lord."

She unscrewed the top, leaned down to the man. "Jim, I have a little bit of water here for you. Tilt your head up for me."

The man responded by pulling his head up from the pillow with a groan. Jenna slipped her fingers under his head to support it and brought the bottle to his lips. With small sips, the man consumed the entire two ounces then licked his lips to moisten them.

As Jenna moved to set the bottle down, the man tried to sit up as he began to stammer, "Ma...mo...more...please."

Jenna helped him rest his head again and whispered to him in soft tones, "I'm so sorry, Jim. There's no more. That's all I have."

Jim made a defeated sound as Jenna patted him softly and closed her eyes. She prayed a silent blessing over him.

Minutes later she walked through the doors of the makeshift medical bay and headed down the hallway toward her quarters. The hour had grown late. Second shift had just ended. Maybe she'd be able to grab a couple hours of sleep. Maybe not. As she walked, she thought about the circumstances that had brought her to where she was. The memories seemed so distant, as though barely her memories at all: the onset of the End War, the fuel reserve, and her late husband Charlie...Charlie. She shook her head as if to clear it.

"Not productive, Jenna," she whispered under her breath, but she was unable to make the dark history leave her.

Again Jenna's mind wandered toward the past. She wasn't a doctor, but a long time ago, in what seemed like another life, she had been a veterinary assistant. And apart from stitching up and healing her share of cows, pigs, and dogs, she also had spent numerous hours of study and research in this field. The least she could do was put her knowledge to work by taking on an eight-hour daily shift in medical.

Her heart desired to love and help her fellow human beings while sharing the gospel of Christ. This was her calling, a purpose that had become much clearer since those months when she had been held prisoner by the Coyotes, that vicious gang of bandits. The terrors she had been subjected to at their hands had been horrific, but deep in her heart, she knew the root of the problem was how desperately those men needed God. Without God to push back the darkness with the light of hope, all was lost. It was the sole reason that ruthless men did ruthless things.

Jenna was an eternal optimist. She had refused to renounce her God. Even after the death of her entire family, and the physical torture and sexual assaults that had followed her capture, she never lost hope in the future. She never lost hope in the ability of a merciful God to save even the worst people.

This last thought brought to mind on name—Dagen. He had orchestrated her sorrow and pain, turning so much hatred toward her because
of her faith. She had every right to hate him, but she didn't. It would be
easy to hate him—very easy—but she told herself that everything happened for a reason. Even Dagen's life had value and purpose. She committed herself to not adding to the enormous amount of hate already in
the world.

Dagen, a former military man, had been dishonorably discharged from
the marines. He'd become so morally corrupt that he was chosen as one
of the commanding officers of the Coyotes. When they'd met, Dagen
had been a person of unquestionable evil. But during the events of Day
Forty, he had been broken down all the way to his core—physically, men-
tally, and emotionally. Dagen survived two shattered legs and the terrible
infection that followed, thanks only to the undivided medical attention
Jenna had given him. He survived the agonizing mental and emotional
anguish of self-realization because she had been there. She had offered
her friendship in his time of need and over a period of months, the man
became a different person. He became a man broken and consumed with
sorrow over his previous life, a man searching for answers to questions
that couldn't be asked, a man in need of redemption.

This string of thoughts reminded Jenna that she had not yet checked
on him today. She knew just where she could find him too—away from
everyone who shunned him and didn't want him at the station. After the
events of Day Forty, there wasn't a soul at the station who didn't know
who Dagen was and who he had been. Sleep could wait.

Slinging her satchel behind her, Jenna climbed the steps to the
roof of the station. With her long brown hair tied in a loose knot, she
hummed a light tune, one like those she used to hum for her sweet baby

girl, Lynn. She'd be turning one next week—if Dagen hadn't murdered her.

✵ ✵ ✵

On the roof of the radio control station, Dagen sat alone in an aluminum beach chair as a toxic wind that smelled of garbage and sea salt rustled his clothing and hair. As he stared toward the darkening hills in the distance, the faint creak of the stairway door greeted his ears. He knew she had come again.

*Why do you torment me? I can never repay you for my sins.*

In an almost invisible gesture, Dagen flexed his fingers and clinched his fist. He raised his eyebrows at her approach but continued to stare into the distance.

"Hey," she said as she approached from behind.

"Hi."

"How's it going up here?"

"It's fine."

Jenna cocked her head, continuing to look at Dagen as he sat facing straight ahead, his arms resting casually in his lap. He wore a light jacket over a dirty T-shirt. His worn battle dress uniform, or BDU pants, stitched up more than a few times, were tucked military style into his boots. The crutches would be necessary for the rest of his life. They served as a constant reminder of who he'd been, up until that fateful moment when Kane knocked him over a third-story railing. They sat stacked next to the chair and the air horn he had been given to sound if he saw trouble. He was not allowed to have a gun.

"Well…" Jenna baited.

"Well, what? Stop staring at me like that," Dagen said, cutting his eyes at her.

"Why do you always volunteer for watch?"

"It's an easy job for a cripple, and it keeps me out of everybody's way. Makes everyone more comfortable—including me. Out of sight, out of mind, right?"

"Nobody ever says anything bad about you."

"They don't have to," he replied. "It's written all over their faces—Kane and everyone else. They don't trust me being here, and I can't blame them for that. You all should send me out into the wastes to die."

"Don't say that. There's always hope, Dagen. Always."

Dagen shrugged, continuing to avoid eye contact with the woman to whom he would forever owe a debt. But her eyes were as clear and direct as spotlights, probing, searching, and crawling their way across his dark, angular features. He suddenly felt agitated by her gaze, as though he were not fit to be looked upon by such a genuine woman.

"I told you to stop looking at me like that!" he snapped.

The air filled with silence. Only the stench-ridden breeze whistling across the roof on its way inland made any sound.

After a quiet moment, Jenna spoke in a barely audible tone. "I'm sorry. I didn't mean to offend you."

*You don't owe me an apology. Not for anything. Not you.*

He had never attempted any sort of penance for what he had done to her, for what he had cost her. That wasn't something he could put into words, and he wasn't fit to be the dirt under her shoes.

Dagen grimaced. "Just forget about it."

"Are you doing OK? Can I get you anything? Do you need me to get someone to relieve you?"

"I'm fine." Dagen nodded and waved his hand.

"Did you eat?

"Enough with the questions. I'm fine! I don't need to rest. I have what I need, OK? Nobody gives a damn about me up here. Just leave me alone already!"

Jenna tossed an expired military MRE into Dagen's lap. He looked down and touched the package of expired nitrogen-packed food with his fingertips.

"I'm somebody," she said, as she turned and retreated into the shadows toward the stairs.

Dagen's face burned with shame. He had insulted her—yet again. He lowered his head and hissed as he wiped his palms across the red-hot flesh of his face.

"Jenna," he managed to croak as he heard her footsteps slow to a stop. It was painful for him to even say her name.

"Thanks," he said as he held the MRE up where she could see it.

"Don't lose hope, Dagen. There are those of us who still care what happens to you," she whispered from the shadows of the rooftop behind him.

Dagen groaned as he heard the door to the stairs click shut. He had murdered Jenna's husband and her infant daughter. He had orchestrated her torture then stood by as his men raped and assaulted her. He had beaten her and humiliated her because of her faith in a God he didn't believe in. It was all his doing, and it was a burden he would have to carry alone.

Dagen wiped the sleeve of his jacket across his eyes and exhaled. It was now his responsibility to keep quiet a terrible secret, one he never could share—not ever. He couldn't tell her that in those days, during Day Forty and afterward, he had begun to love her. It had not been a joyful love but one born of respect, shame, and sorrow over the injustices he had inflicted and her response to them. His love pushed him past the beauty and forgiveness of a creation to the God who had created her in his image. And though he had no right to, Dagen found that with each passing day his love for her grew.

Deep in his heart, he mourned these emotions. He told himself that he did not deserve to love or be loved. He was a monster, unworthy of something so pristine. He also knew that because of the nature of its origin, he could never act upon this love, and she could never know that it existed.

# TWO

Kane exited the radio room and headed up the external stone stairs to ground level. The hazy, late-morning light mingled with the oppressive smog like cloud cover, disguising the true time of day. Another broadcast had gone out; another wash of static came back in response. Though they had yet to receive any communication over the radio, people sometimes showed up at the station saying they had heard the message, which meant the broadcasts were getting out.

Kane had embarrassed himself in front of Winston by begging for his wife to contact him. He'd done it so that he might sleep at night. She wasn't out there. She was dead along with his twins, Rachael and Michael, who would have been four now. At the top of the stairs, Kane raised his eyebrows as he turned to see the scavenging party returning early.

*That's either really good or really bad.*

Things had changed too much. The world had become a mere shadow of what it once was, some darker and more primal version of its former self.

They had known from the start that the supplies at the station wouldn't last, especially with the growing number of survivors taking refuge there. It had become a settlement of sorts, with Kane reluctantly occupying the position as their leader. It wasn't something he had asked for, but then again none of it was. Maybe it was his ability to command respect and to act decisively without acting like a dictator. Or maybe it was his eleven years of experience as a police officer that led people to want him to call the shots. Whatever it was, he was up to his eyeballs in it.

The group had resorted to scavenging the surrounding area for supplies, food, and water. They also traded with other small groups of survivors they encountered. Hunting was out of the question, as wildlife appeared scarce. Farming hadn't worked out well due to the toxic combination of the absence of direct sunlight and an abundance of polluted rain.

Parties sent into the wastes to scavenge always traveled light and in groups of four or five. There was no telling what they might find. Sometimes they encountered other survivors, some friendly and others not. An unfortunate rule pervaded the new world—kill or be killed. Gangs of bandits and highwaymen had become prevalent. Many would murder at first glance, maybe for a good knife, a lighter, or some other trinket. Kane's group had been forced to kill plenty of these bandits in self-defense.

An interesting detail differentiated this world from the one before. Before the war, killing and murder were often considered synonymous, and many times society criminalized even those who killed justifiably. In this new world, just as in ancient times, murder was not acceptable, but killing another in self-defense or in defense of a group was sometimes necessary for survival. It wasn't something any of them liked, but it was necessary.

Sometimes one of Kane's groups went out into the wastes and scored something valuable, like a working vehicle or medical supplies. Other times they found nothing but the toxic ocean breeze blowing inland and the scattered remnants of burned and broken homesteads, neighborhoods, and small towns—a sorrowful reminder of what had been.

With a series of quick steps, Kane approached a battered Chevy Silverado, a rusted grate bolted to the front.

"Is everybody okay? Is anyone hurt?"

"We're good. Everyone's fine," Jacob said, stepping out of the truck bed. "You worry too much."

Kane made a face at the teenager. "Then why are you guys back so soon?"

"We scored a good one today. Check it out," Jacob answered, as he whipped back a tarp to reveal a dirt bike that appeared to be in good condition.

Kane nodded. "Nice. It runs?"

"Oh, yeah. Purrs like a kitten." Jacob spat a black stream of tobacco juice onto the dirt. "We also picked up some food, a load of canned goods, a camping stove, some road flares, a pump shotgun with a few boxes of shells, and some empty plastic water jugs. Some other junk too."

"Well done. No encounters of any kind?"

"If we had, I would've handled it," Jacob drawled with his chest out in a way only a seventeen-year-old kid can.

"Sure thing, tough guy," Kane huffed. "Just don't press your luck. You're not invincible."

"Says you."

"Kane, we did see a few of 'em at a distance," Jay spoke up, as he, Shana, and Mico handed items down from the truck. "The way they moved, you could tell they didn't quite seem human."

"Yeah?" Kane grimaced as if he could taste the flavor of unpleasant memories. "How many would you say?"

"Just a handful here and there. We didn't go close to them."

Kane nodded, frowning in contemplation. Long ago they'd decided as a group not to enter the larger metropolitan areas. This was one rule that remained constant. Whatever goods or valuables they could get there weren't worth the risk. Kane knew this from personal experience.

The creatures were former humans who had been infected by the combination of biological, chemical, and radiological attacks during the war. While it killed a lot of people, some became something else. They tended to congregate in the metro areas where the population density had been highest. Some people referred to them as zombies, but that was a ridiculous and Hollywood-fueled concept. They didn't rise from the grave, and they didn't have to be shot in the head to be killed.

Molly had called them Sicks, which was accurate since they were sick people, mutated, starved, and driven mad by an airborne concoction called Chimera that had doused many of the cities. And though it had been designed to kill, the amazing resilience of the human body allowed some to live and adapt.

Recently several groups of scavengers had encountered and been attacked by what they described as small packs of Sicks. These packs seemed more organized and less like the maddened horde that Kane and Molly had encountered as if somehow they had evolved into something else, something more intelligent. This final thought gave Kane a cold shiver, which he shrugged off, as he attempted to remain focused on the task at hand.

✲ ✲ ✲

Jenna leaned forward and rested her gloved hands on the shovel in front of her as she ducked her head forward and wiped it across the sleeve of her shirt. She sighed, the weight of death and mortality heavy upon her, like a constant burden. With a flick of her head, she cleared the hair out of her face.

"Fourteen," she whispered.

"Huh?"

Jenna remained silent, her mind far away from the dusty gravesite.

Rob cleared his throat. "Did you say something?" he asked, throwing the last shovelful of dirt onto the small mound.

"Jim. He makes fourteen since we've been here. It feels like so many when you know them all."

They stood in silence for a minute, neither sure of what to say.

"We don't know if Jim had any religious preferences?" Rob asked, patting the dirt mound gently with the flat underside of his shovel.

Jenna shrugged. "I didn't know him that well, but I don't mind saying a few words about him anyway."

Rob nodded. "Should I put this in?" He motioned to two sticks of rebar he had wrapped together with ten-gauge wire to form a cross.

"Sure, Rob. That was very thoughtful."

Rob nodded again and pushed the rebar cross into the dirt at the head of the mound, sinking it deeper with a few strikes from the shovel. He stepped back, pulled his cap off, and held it over his heart as he bowed his head.

"Heavenly Father," Jenna began, just above a whisper, "we send you another one of our own, Jim Burrleson. I think he was a heavy-equipment operator from Charleston, back...before." Jenna took a deep breath and pulled the shovel to her side. "I don't remember him mentioning any family or anyone else. I'm sorry I didn't take the time to get to know him better. I don't know the condition of his soul, and apart from my few moments with him in medical toward the end, I can't say where he will spend eternity. But I will say this. He was a good man, a hard worker around the station, and he always gave freely of himself to help others. I can only hope that in his heart he knew your grace and the eternal freedom of your forgiveness. We pray that you pour your mercies upon him and make him your own this day. And go with us as we continue on without him. In your holy name, amen."

"Amen," Rob echoed, as he pulled his baseball cap back over his balding head. After a moment he looked at Jenna and asked, "Need anything else from me?"

Jenna shook her head as she swung the shovel over her shoulder. "No. Thanks for your help, Rob, and for the cross."

"I just hate to see this. Like enough of us haven't died already. Do you know what it was? That did Jim in, I mean."

"Severe abdominal injury, infection, blood loss, dehydration. Take your pick."

Rob made a face. "Terrible way to go, being attacked by one of those things."

"We've all got to go someday. So many have gone before us."

"Then what's the point, Jenna?" the older man said, a strained look on his worn face. The question seemed to gnaw at his will to go on. "Why do we struggle on like this when everything seems so hopeless?"

"Because it's never hopeless, my friend." Jenna smiled and patted him on the back. "God told us it wouldn't be easy. So we struggle. We struggle with the weight of that responsibility, and we'll do it for him, just because he chose to love us. In the end, when he welcomes us to glory, and we know it's because of his goodness and not ours that we stand there, who will be able to say that there was a better cause to have lived and died for?"

✡ ✡ ✡

Courtland Thompson lumbered through the doorway into the mess hall, turning sideways and ducking to squeeze through the gap. At more than eight feet tall and almost five hundred pounds, Courtland had been a professional athlete in what seemed like a former life. All blood sport and fame, his Crushball career had been short and violent, like most. Those days seemed so distant to him now that they might as well have happened to someone else. As he entered the mess hall, he passed Dagen, who was balancing a bottle of water between his fingers as he maneuvered his crutches.

"Hello, Dagen. How ya doin'?" asked Courtland, his deep voice quiet and sincere.

"I'm fine," Dagen said in a clipped tone. He lowered his gaze and moved into the hallway.

Turning and watching Dagen go, Courtland pondered the strange man and how he was somewhat of a phantom around the station. He slipped to and fro without so much as a word most of the time. Courtland knew the man had not had an easy time of it and he wondered about the condition of Dagen's soul. He knew Jenna had made an immense impact on the broken man through her acts of kindness and selflessness.

Courtland made his way to the counter. "Hey, Kris."

"Courtland. What can I do for you?"

Kris was in charge of rations at the station. Everyone received a daily allowance, which included a liter of water, two canned items, and two handfuls of stale crackers or other starch. People decided when to receive their rations. As they received them, Kris marked them off the list for the day. A decent barter system had been put into effect, and individuals could trade daily rations for other necessary items, meds, or ammo.

"My stomach is growling," Courtland said, smiling.

"You want one and one?"

"Yes, sir. Please."

"Here you go, pal. It's your lucky day today. Cold SpaghettiOs and stale Wheat Thins."

Courtland's stomach growled again. "Sounds great." He paused as he gathered the items. "Kris, is there anything I can pray for on your behalf today?

Kris slowed his writing and looked up from his list. "I'm not really a religious guy."

Courtland nodded. "I respect that and don't mean to push. Just so you know, though, some of us meet in the mornings in the courtyard to pray. You're welcome anytime," Courtland said, as he smiled and turned toward the tables.

Kris winced. "Hey," he started, "I have been having nightmares, you know, about my family. Maybe you could pray for some peace for me, or comfort, or something."

"Absolutely, friend. I can do that." Courtland smiled as he took a seat at a nearby table.

"Thanks," Kris said, trying to look busy as Kane entered the room.

"Hey, big man," Kane called to Courtland. "Hungry?"

"Starving." Courtland sighed as he pried the metal lid off the canned food with his fingers. "SpaghettiOs today."

"Perfect." As Kris crossed him off the list, Kane gathered his items and moved to the table with the gentle giant.

"Can you open mine? I don't have super strength or stone fingers."

Courtland smiled, pulling the metal top away from the can as if he were lifting a sheet of plastic wrap.

"What do you miss the most?"

"Huh?" Kane said as he sat down.

"Cold SpaghettiOs are good and all, but what meal do you miss the most?"

"Ah." Kane rubbed his chin. "A hot cheeseburger and fries with an ice-cold chocolate milkshake. No contest."

"How American of you."

"Yeah. What about you?"

"I'd have to say slow-cooked, fall-off-the-bone, barbecued baby backs with baked beans soaked in brown sugar."

"Okay, stop. You're killing me." Kane huffed.

"How are you holding up?" Courtland mumbled through a mouthful of food.

"I'm doing fine, man."

Courtland gave Kane a penetrating look. "I don't want your generic answer, brother. You're the best friend I have, and I want to know the condition of your heart."

Kane smirked as he stuck his fork into the reddish slop. "Can't hide much from you, can I?"

"You should stop trying," Courtland said, smiling back.

"The truth? I'm sleep deprived, dehydrated, and stressed out. How's that? I also can't stop thinking about my family...and Molly, however counterproductive all that is."

Courtland nodded as he chewed. "I get it. There's nothing wrong with loving and missing the people we've lost. It keeps us human."

The two chewed in silence for a moment.

"I know you've been busy and all," Courtland began, "but I think it would do you a lot of good to come and pray with us in the mornings. Get everything back in perspective."

Kane seemed to ignore the statement. "What about you?" he asked. "How are things in your world?"

Courtland shrugged. "The visions have been growing stronger, but I'm having a hard time understanding them. I worry that if I can't figure them out, I might miss what they're trying to tell me."

Kane wiped a drip of sauce from his stubbled chin as the giant continued.

"I also think a lot about my daughter Marissa and her mother. Sometimes I wonder if they would've made it in this world, even if they had survived to see it."

"Yeah," Kane mumbled. "True."

"We can't survive here forever, Kane. What happens when we scavenge every available resource? Or meet more opposition to our cause?"

"I know."

"I'm serious."

"I *know*. I think about it all the time. I just don't know what it is we're supposed to do next. It's as clear as mud."

"Have you had any dreams, any word about your purpose? Anything?"

"No," Kane said without looking up.

"Are you looking to God or yourself for the answers?"

"Courtland, ease up," Kane blurted out. "God hasn't revealed anything to me. I've got no idea what he wants us to do now, Okay? Take the light into the darkness? What the hell is that supposed to mean anyway, and how does that look in real life? I can't answer your questions, and my waiting on God doesn't make decisions that need to be made. These people are looking to us."

"Maybe, but first you have to listen. Only then will you begin to trust and find the strength to obey," Courtland said, looking up to catch Kane's glare.

They sat in silence, neither of them eating, for what seemed like a lifetime.

Courtland finally spoke. "Breathe. I'm not trying to anger you."

"For not trying, you're doing a decent job," Kane said.

"Just pray about it, brother. That's all I ask. Take it before the Lord."

"Okay," Kane said, softening. "I will. I appreciate your support and your counsel, as always."

"That, my friend, is *my* purpose." Courtland raised his water bottle in a toast. "For as long as my heart beats in my chest, I'm your man—until the bitter end."

"Until the bitter end," Kane repeated, raising own his bottle with a weathered smile.

✡ ✡ ✡

On the darkest of nights, by the light of a small fire, a lone mother sat cradling her two children against her thin frame. She'd done what she had to do. It was not a position she would have put herself in had it not been for her two children. In a desperate move to survive and to ensure her children's safety in a world of fear and uncertainty, she had given herself to another man outside of her husband.

Since the end began, her husband was no longer in the picture. The hope of ever seeing him again had vanished along with every last shred of her pride and virtue. All that now remained was the fear laced certainty of an unknown future.

The events of the past year had shaken her faith in a terrible way. She loathed her new position, living among these strange people, these survivors, as they made their way north along the coast like a band of gypsies.

They were well into Georgia, now. She took a moment to recall the arduous journey that had brought them there.

She closed her eyes and once again felt the assault on her senses. The sound of the missiles as they struck the city had driven her in a panic from her hotel room, her children dangling in her arms as she fled. She didn't know where she was going, but she had to get out, screaming down the smoke-filled stairwell. Her world came crashing down in those fiery, early-morning hours. It was only by chance, by grace, that she and the children had encountered the hotel manager in the lobby who directed them to the underground shelter.

It had been weeks, months, what felt like years since she and her children had emerged, clawing their way from an underground shelter in the basement of the Fenris Tower Hotel in downtown Miami. They did so only to find the ugly ruins of their collective lives strewn about in disarray like the rubble-filled streets before them. She knew then that everyone she had ever loved, save her precious children, had died. It was this realization that changed her, breaking her down to the real parts inside, making her both a little more and a little less the person she was before.

After the initial days of chaos and fear, her group had organized with the other hotel survivors. They headed out of the dangerous, burning city, fighting off the growing number of infected as they went. She couldn't view the sick as people anymore. A denial that was key to doing what had to be done. They had gone crazy, mad with fever and disease, hungry for anything that moved—even other survivors. Few of their original group had survived, and even fewer had survived unscathed. The surgical mask she wore over her nose and mouth served as a constant reminder of the danger of exposure and the urgent need to get out of the city.

Their movement was slow, but they had managed to stay together, traveling north up the East Coast, following the former hotel manager, the man named Garrett, who wouldn't let her forget that she owed her life and the lives of her children to him. Like a tribe of nomads or a herd of cattle, they never seemed to settle for long. Garrett said they had to find the truth of what had happened. He said they would not rest until they found out why. That was nine months ago—nine months of fear, hope, and a woman's desperate need to protect her children.

The young boy made a whimpering sound, and she soothed him by gently running her fingers through his hair. It was for him and his sister that she did this, that she had done any of it. It was the only way to protect them from the animals, human and otherwise, that now prowled the wastes. The fire popped, sending a shower of sparks flying into the cool night air like fireworks that begin so vibrant, before fading to nothing. A man approached the fire from behind her. The light glistened on the blue war paint that covered his face. The paint and his knotted ponytail made him look like a misplaced extra from the set of *Braveheart*.

"Garrett wants you in his tent."

"I'm with my children—"

"Garrett wants you in his tent now, sweetheart," the man named Saxon said, an evil smile cresting the corners of his lips.

She lowered her head. *Wherever you are, don't watch me now.*

She wiped a shameful tear from her face and covered her children with the blanket as she stood. Her angels were fast asleep. They had been so resilient, even from the start, enduring every moment of fear and terror this new existence proffered. Trying to explain to them that their daddy was gone had been the worst moment of her life. They would all have to survive, she told them, and move on without him.

With the fierceness of a mother bear, she turned and locked eyes with Saxon. "Nobody touches a hair on their heads, or Garrett will hear about it."

In a flash, he slapped her across the face and grabbed her under her jaw. His smile cold in the warm light of the fire. "You don't get to tell me *shit*. If you're lucky we'll leave them alone for a while longer," he whispered, licking his lips.

She burned with anger as she wrenched her face from his grasp and shoved him back. They stood in a silent showdown for what seemed like forever. Finally, she turned to walk with proud determination toward the tent at the center of the camp. There were men who desired the company of young children—Saxon was one of them.

*Filthy bastard. I'll kill him if he ever touches them.*

She had given herself to Garrett to keep her children from the clutches of such men. While she lived and breathed, her children would not suffer that way. Not them. Her life became consumed with their survival, no matter the cost.

As she walked past the ramshackle tents, a symphonic blend of the camp's noises followed her: low murmurs, the scraping sound of a blade being sharpened, the distant whine of someone crying. Then she heard a different sound. As she walked she slowed her pace to process the noise as she neared Garrett's tent. Two men were talking in hushed tones.

"Stop it. Stop right there. Did you catch that?"

"Catch what?"

"A broadcast of some sort. Go back."

"Okay, okay. Hang on."

A blaze of static could be heard, followed by a fading and fuzzy voice. The voice slowly became clearer. Before the first word was finished, she recognized the voice. Her mouth dropped open as a stroke of lightheadedness consumed her from head to toe, causing her knees to tremble.

"Kane Lorusso…shhhhh…broadcasting from the emergency radio control…shhhh…coast of South Carolina…We have resources…shhhh… There is light in the darkness…shhhhhhhhhhh."

"You lost it!" the man cried.

"I did not. This radio is junk!"

"Well, keep trying!"

She clutched her hands to her face, trying to suppress the swelling of hope in her chest. The signal came through once again.

"Shhhhhhh…Susan, if you're out there and you can hear me, I love you…shhhhh…I haven't lost hope…shhhhhhhhhhhh."

Tears of joy cut paths down Susan Lorusso's face. Somehow her husband was alive. He was out there somewhere. But her moment of joy was interrupted. The tent flap flew back with a jerk, and there stood Garrett, the roguish leader of the outfit, half naked in the doorway of the tent.

"What are you doing standing around out here? Get in here and do your thing."

Susan hardly heard a word the rough man said as she wiped the tears of happiness from her face.

*Thank you, Jesus.*

She could do this. She could hang on for just a little while longer. There was hope. Kane was alive, and one day, when she saw him again, she and her children would be safe. Susan stepped inside the tent and pulled the flap shut as she let her clothes fall to the ground in a pile at her feet.

✼ ✼ ✼

*Gather our men. Steal their minds and enslave their souls. They will call for*
*their champion, and we will rise to show them the way. All that stands between*
*us and what we must do are the followers of God.*

Malak stepped through the narrow doorway and leaned against the
balcony railing of his eighth-floor seaside condo. He smirked as he
thought of how the former residents might feel knowing he and his gang
of savage marauders, the Coyotes, now inhabited the building. Condos at
the Reeds at Colonial Pointe had been expensive, exclusive and very hard
to come by. Back before the end began, the condos were considered a hot
spot along South Carolina's coast, a destination for wealthy retirees seeking luxury in a resort-like atmosphere. Now it served the needs of Malak
and his group. Malak ran his hand over the metal railing and looked out
over the darkened sea, an occasional star twinkling through the billowed
clouds on the horizon beyond.

He was so close to them, and they didn't even know it. Less than five
miles separated his current base of operations at the Reeds from the emergency radio control station where Kane and the others lived. He was right
under their noses, and they didn't have a clue. His men had even gotten
close enough to view the station with binoculars. It was true—he could have
attacked by now and retaken the station. He had salvaged some of his men
after Kane's assault during the events of Day Forty and had recruited plenty
more, those who had shown the proper drive and skill set for his purpose.

But taking back the station wasn't the point. It wasn't necessary for
him to achieve the objectives that the darkness set out before him. What
was important was that Kane and every last soul at the radio station had
to die. This would enable Malak to realize his vision, his dream, and the
final coming of the voice. This too could have occurred months ago, but
the destruction of the Christians had become something of a game to

Malak. It was a prize to be gained, a victory to plan and savor. In the end, he would hold this as his triumphant moment, an emblem of his arrival as the leader of the new world.

Malak sought to outdo the centuries of genocide experienced on the African continent. These pathetic, groveling maggots would get the opportunity to die in the name of what they believed. Any captive who did not believe as the Christians did would be offered a choice—join the Coyotes or die a slow and agonizing death. The choice for many would be simple. He would not rush this. He would not act until all the pieces had fallen into place.

"Malak," one of the men called from behind, breaking the bandit leader's train of thought.

"What is it?" Malak spoke without turning.

"There's a big group out front. They're armed, and they say they want to talk to the person in charge."

Malak half turned. "Why?" he asked a snarl on his lips.

"Didn't say."

Malak nodded. "Round everyone up. Tell them to hold cover and wait for my order."

The man acknowledged Malak's command. Malak walked past the greasy, bearded thug into the hallway then entered the stairwell. He took the stairs two at a time, because it was easier for him, given his large form. He was not in any hurry. He knew what was happening. An example would have to be made.

At the bottom of the stairs, he crossed the trash-strewn common area and passed between two armed, masked bandits at the front entrance. He went down the steps and into the drive, his men murmuring in fear and parting like the Red Sea as he passed between them.

Malak stopped in front of the strangers, taking a moment to analyze the group, a sizable force of about forty men. In front stood what appeared to be their leader, a solidly built man with salt-and-pepper stubble and a long shock of thick, black hair. Two men flanked his left and right, both holding assault rifles. Behind them stood a group of about ten men. The man in charge must have had some military experience, as not all his forces stood in front of Malak. Armed groups assembled to his right and left, groups of ten or so each. A smaller group waited across the street, stationed on the roof of the trashed Marathon gas station, acting as overwatch.

"What do you want?" Malak growled in a disinterested tone, one so low that it was almost inaudible.

"I want to have a conversation."

"You people…always with words. Words solve nothing."

"*You people?*" the leader snapped. "What's your problem?"

Malak smiled a sinister grin. "My problem is that I have a bunch of heavily armed paper tigers on my door step."

"What the hell's that supposed to mean?" the leader spat, as he reached into his waistband and pulled out a Kimber Ultra Covert handgun and clasped it in both hands in front of him. "You know, we were going to just come over here and have a little chat, seeing as we seem to be like-minded groups. But now that you've showed your fuckin' ass, I'm not sure I want to do anything but burn all your stupid asses right here, right now."

"Is that so?" Malak smirked, his scarred face hidden by the dark hood that fell in rumpled layers around his head and shoulders.

"Yeah, that's so!"

"And who are you all supposed to be?" Malak said.

"I'm Cortez," the leader barked, "and these are my regulators." He held his handgun high in the air as his men howled their encouragement.

Malak laughed a throaty rumble of amusement. "That's cute."

"Oh, yeah? Well, how about this, big man? Right now we've got you outnumbered, outflanked, and outgunned. I could turn you into a dripping meat bag with the snap of my fuckin' fingers."

Malak said nothing. These regulators and their leader had no idea that Malak and his Coyotes outnumbered them three to one. Malak's crew was poised behind cover in the openings of the building, ready to unleash hell on these unsuspecting guests. But Malak wouldn't need the firepower of his men to end this. He took a step forward.

Cortez raised his weapon. "Whoa, whoa, big dog. One more step and I smoke a hole in your ugly face."

"A gun? Is that your true power?" Malak said.

"Powerful enough."

"Let me show you *my* true power."

"Nah, I don't think so."

"Then shoot me."

"What?" Cortez looked over his shoulder at his boys. "Are you guys hearing this? This guy's bat-shit crazy!"

"Worship me or die. Those are your options."

"What about option three? You suck my—"

Malak took another step forward, and with a crack, Cortez fired the gun in his face—only it didn't matter. In Malak's mind's eye, Cortez was moving in slow motion, or Malak's own body was moving faster than the speed of sound. Whichever the case, the bullet missed Malak's face by what might as well have been a hundred yards. Malak sidestepped and wrapped his hands around Cortez's skull. The man's head came apart, popping like a boil. The blood and brain matter sprayed a splash of crimson into the air. Snatching away the remaining fragments of the man's skull, Malak tore Cortez's spine from the quivering body and flung it through the air.

The two men standing behind what remained of Cortez tried to raise their assault rifles, their faces frozen like masks of horror. With a raging snarl, Malak stooped low then swung his arms open, sending dark tentacles from his wrists that slashed through the men. The goon on the right was torn in half, his legs tossed into the air like broken twigs. The man on the left cried out just as the black tentacle tore his right arm from his body and cleaved his rifle in two. With a backward swipe, Malak knocked the thug's head free from his body, sending another crimson jet spraying into the air. With a lunge, Malak slammed into the group of ten. Arms wheeling, his tentacles slashing, he tore through the group, eviscerating their helpless human forms in a shower of gore and flying body parts.

And as quick as it started, the destruction was done. Malak came to a stop and slowly pulled the hood of his cloak back from his head. Drops of blood, brain, and body clung to him, falling in a fine, pink mist around him. The wailing was deafening as the gravity of what had taken place landed on the shoulders of all who looked on. The entire event had lasted for less time than it takes a cobra to strike.

The regulators dropped their weapons and fell to the ground in terror. He flexed his massive shoulders under the blood-drenched cloak and marveled at his work. The remains of the slaughtered regulators were scattered in bloody perfection before him. In their arrogance, these men had not been willing to accept his command. As a result, Malak had shown them the power of the darkness. The rest of the visitors lay prostrate in fear at his feet.

No more sickness. No more weakness. Malak had been purged of all impurity and imperfection. All that remained was the clear and uncompromising sound of the voice as it drove him onward. It was quite simple. He had been defeated during his first encounter with the warrior Christians for a reason. He had underestimated them. His human weakness had handicapped him and kept him from becoming what he should have been. Since Malak had been set free and the owner of the voice had revealed himself, everything had begun to make sense.

Malak's purpose was clear. He was to rule and enslave the new world, and in the process of this great upheaval, he was to strike down the high king of heaven from his lofty throne. The cost? His soul—a small price to pay to become a god. The time had come when every mouth that sang or whispered the name of God and every scrap of paper that taught his message should cease to exist. Those who carried God like a plague in their hearts, spreading his disease, would be violated and savaged. In time no living soul would remember or even know the name of God. Those who claimed to have no faith would be forced to join Malak's cause or die.

Malak's purpose had never been too lofty. He just needed to be reminded of the dark power that flowed within his veins. This power had corrupted him so completely that he had lost the point where his own being ended and the dark power began. His was a true power, the power of the gods.

The ridiculous group at the station posed no real threat to him or his plan. They were like gnats that flew in the eyes and the nose, nothing more than a nuisance. But if Malak had been honest with himself, he would have seen that he had made things personal. He needed them to die—especially Kane—as slow and as painfully as possible. This was a necessity. They had opposed both him and the will of the voice. What's more, Kane's group had stolen a fuel tanker from him on Day Forty, one of the two he'd captured. The tanker remained at the radio station, and it might as well be filled with gold. Malak could use that fuel where he was going.

Taking the tanker and destroying the survivors wouldn't be difficult. With the loss of his family and the murder of the girl, Kane had become demoralized; Malak could sense it as if it were a poison in the man's soul. The dark giant was distracted with the care of the people at the station. And the Indian boy and his beast were all but aliens to the others. They were all weak and struggling to survive. When Malak's growing army became strong once again, he would move in against them.

The Christians had achieved their insignificant victory over him. Now it was his turn, and in time, when the timing was right, Malak would show them his heart of darkness.

# THREE

## BEFORE
## CANINE COGNITION AND BEHAVIOR LABS
## COLUMBIA, SOUTH CAROLINA

The two scientists sat together in the stark-white, sparsely furnished concrete-block room. One monitored a computer screen, while the other scribbled in shorthand. The air vent above them whistled as it forced the recirculated air through the room.

The man taking notes stopped, looked up, and touched his face. His ID badge read *Dr. Eric Glenn* and included a picture of the man's lean, confident smile and broad forehead. He squinted his eyes and peered through the one-sided mirrored glass in front of him, where a black-and-tan Rottweiler paced in a broad circle.

"Any change with that last one?" Glenn muttered almost to himself.

"Nah." The other scientist sighed as he leaned back in his chair and stretched his arms over his head. "Just like all the others."

Glenn cracked an indulgent smile. "Relax, Harper. We're on the right track. Our patience will be rewarded. You'll see."

"Maybe, but there's an infinite number of tonal combinations to explore. None that we've tried has elicited any response from Brutus. His ears have barely twitched."

Cupping his hand over his mouth, Glenn propped his elbow on the table and leaned over to examine the computer screen. "I was so sure those last few, especially that D chain, would elicit a definitive response. Not sure why it didn't. All my theories point to it."

"Humph," Harper said with a sigh, his eyebrows raised in amusement. "That's why they're called 'theories,' Dr. Glenn."

Glenn, undaunted, ignored his cohort's last statement. "I can't help wonder if we're in the right spectrum."

"Everything we know about canines responding to tones depends on the tonal range that humans can't hear. That's how dog whistles were developed. It's the right spectrum."

"No, maybe that's the problem. Everything we know comes from working with this spectrum, but where has that gotten us? Maybe we need to bring it down."

"To what?"

"To the human spectrum."

"Dr. Glenn, you need to get some sleep. Bringing the chain down into the human spectrum won't alter how it affects the canine. This is basic—"

"But what if it did? We've fine-tuned the delivery down to a thousandth of a single note. What if it made no difference whether or not the human ear could hear it? What if it worked anyway?"

"That's absurd. No one has ever tried that because—"

"Because they're stuck in what others have done," Glenn interrupted his face flushing with excitement over this realization. He stood and continued. "But I'm not interested in standing on their shoulders. I'm interested in success. Sometimes greatness requires thinking outside the box."

"Yeah, fine." Harper sighed again, exasperated. "So how do you want to do it?"

"Run the same chain again. Start from the bottom."

"OK…" Harper said with a slight tone of irritation. He began to hack at the keyboard, plugging changes into the tonal formulas. After a few minutes, the computer gave a faint blip, signaling the conversion of the entire spectrum. He turned to Glenn. "We ready?"

Glenn pulled out his smartphone. It displayed a photo of him and a vibrant young woman, her arms encircling his waist, her long, flowing hair framing a smile that could warm the Arctic.

"My dear, Gabrielle," he whispered to himself, "this is for you." Glenn waved his hand at Harper without looking away from the photo before him—that slender, delicate frame; his engagement ring so natural on her finger. It had been the happiest day of his life. And then, like a cruel joke, the accident. He shook himself from the moment. "Go with it."

"Going with the freeze command," Harper responded, as he initiated the first sequence.

As the sequence of tones played over the speakers, Glenn watched, his pen at the ready. For an instant, he thought he saw a shudder of hesitation in the animal's step as it paced, a momentary physical indicator of some cognitive process.

"Increase the volume and proceed."

Harper nodded. "Volume up. Playing number two of seven."

A second tune played over the speakers. Glenn straightened himself and dropped his notepad on the desk. His eyes widened. "There! He changed pace. He slowed. Did you see it?"

Harper nodded.

"Jump to four and initiate."

Harper adjusted and pressed the "enter" key then immediately turned to watch the dog as the tune began to play.

In an instant the large dog became rigid. His muscles grew taut, and his neck extended as if he were a German shorthaired pointer locked on a covey of quail.

"Ha! Ha-ha!" Glenn yelled, throwing his arms into the air.

"I can't believe it. You were right," Harper muttered in disbelief.

"Of course I was! It was the D chain. I knew it would be. What did I tell you? You've got to think outside the box!"

The two men stood in disbelief, staring at the taut animal. They could just see the slight in and out of its rib cage as it continued to breathe, the only indication that it wasn't a stuffed replica.

Glenn spun, putting his fingers to his lips as though trying to make some difficult internal decision. "I want to know. I want to see what else we can do."

"Well, we'll need to—"

"No, no. I don't have time for all that protocol nonsense. I want to know now."

"But..." Harper started as he watched Glenn move to the computer and access a restricted file. His fingers jabbed at the keyboard and a new window opened. Harper spoke the words to himself. "Meddleson Surge Systems. Is that like a power backup or something?"

"Hardly. This is a system I had installed back when this place was built. I've had to keep it under wraps. It's...controversial."

"So what is it?" Harper asked.

"The floor under Brutus, as well as a few others, have electrical conductors running beneath them. This program controls the electrical output of the conductors."

"Wait, wait. Are you saying the floor in there is electrified?"

"Not right this second."

"But it could be."

"Of course."

A look of disgust appeared on Harper's face. "Why the hell would you have something like that installed?"

"Because sometimes science requires testing the limits—even when it's not popular to do so."

"That's not humane. PETA is one of our biggest contributors, for God's sake."

"PETA's not going to know shit about it."

"But Brutus—"

"Sacrifices must be made in the name of science."

"I'm not going to be a part of this," Harper said, beginning to stand. Glenn firmly pushed him back down into his chair. The air vent's whistle seemed to grow louder given the deafening silence and penetrating gaze of Glenn.

"You're already a part of it," Glenn spoke, "and I can't have you tearing my house down over some trivial notion of what's humane—especially now that we've reached the cusp of greatness."

"I—"

"You'll do what you're told, and you'll keep your fucking mouth shut about the rest. I'm an ambitious man, Mr. Harper. Bad things happen to people who cross me." Glenn smiled, relaxing a little, and patted Harper on the shoulder. "We're onto something incredible, something that could change how man and animal interact. Don't you want to be a part of that?"

"Well, yes, but—"

"Good." Glenn dismissed Harper's last protest and moved back to the computer. "We're about to find out what's possible."

Harper remained silent as Glenn adjusted the electrical current running in the floor under Brutus. The needle climbed: one thousand volts, five thousand volts, ten thousand volts. Brutus began to twitch just slightly, but his body remained rigid, locked in position as if he were under hypnosis. With a flick Glenn knocked the dial to thirty thousand volts, eliciting a shriek from the Rottweiler as it began to jump around the room, attempting in vain to escape from the stinging, electrical floor. The threshold had been broken. Harper sat back in mild horror as Glenn, moving faster now, activated the G set of tones.

As the tones played, the dog howled then became silent and still, once again hypnotized by the song. Glenn watched as the thirty thousand volts of electricity stung the legs and feet of the animal, its muscles quivering under a glistening black coat. Glenn moved his hand to the mouse and over the voltage meter.

Harper squirmed. "Haven't we seen enough?"

"No," Glenn said, as he dialed the voltage past fifty thousand and watched the dog's muscles jump and pop as the creature remained in place, frozen, impervious to the pain.

"Enough electricity to knock down a grown man, yet there Brutus stands. The mind—even the canine mind—possesses amazing powers of control."

"Please, stop. I don't know how much more he can take."

"Not yet. I want to try the aggression chain."

"While you're shocking him? We don't know if it'll work. If it does, it could—"

"It'll work. Shut up and dial it in," Glenn ordered.

Harper pulled up the aggression chain and moved to play the first sequence. Glenn stopped him.

"G. Play the G chain."

"The seventh? You can't possibly know what to expect from that level."

"Do it!"

Both men eyed the quivering, moaning dog as Harper initiated the chain. As though a lightning bolt had struck it, the animal came free of the trance. The electricity sent the dog flying from its once stationary position. Harper cried out and leaped away from the glass as Glenn stared in astonishment. Brutus, all two hundred pounds of him, slammed face-first into the wall in front of them. Again and again, blind to the pain, numb to the fear, and with an unbridled rage coursing through his body, the dog crashed again and again into the glass.

"Make it stop!" Harper screamed.

But Glenn didn't stop. The animal slammed again and again into the glass, the force deforming the creature's head, reducing it to a spattering of blood and bone as the animal willfully destroyed itself under the spell of the song.

Just audible over the whining of the air vent, Harper's moans, and the beast's labored death gurgle, Glenn whispered a single word.

"Perfection."

# FOUR

## NOW

Dagen watched through the cracked door in the station hallway as Jenna raised her water bottle and drained the last of her daily ration. Pausing at the top of the tilt, she shook the empty bottle and licked her lips as the remaining drops hit them. She sighed and examined the bottle thirstily before setting it back on the table next to her.

Dagen took a deep breath, closed his eyes, and willed himself forward. Using his shoulders, he pushed through the doors to the medical bay, maneuvering his crutches with care. It was Jenna's shift. He knew he'd find her here. From the doorway he could just make out her slender form as she tended to a recent victim of a Sick attack on one of the scavenging parties. She glanced over her shoulder at Dagen before turning back to the wounded man, patting his shoulder.

This gentle display of affection stirred Dagen's blood—how she cared for this man as if he were family to her and how she had done the same for him. He felt himself flush but recovered as she made her way toward him. In his right palm, hidden from view, he clutched a small, silver cross on a thin, silver chain. Limping forward he tried to think of how he would say it, how he possibly could put what he felt into words.

"Dagen, to what do I owe the honor?" Jenna spoke with a genuine smile.

Dagen faltered, and for a split second, he almost turned and left without a word. Looking down toward his ruined legs, he struggled to get the words out.

*Why is this so damn hard?*

"I...uh...I..." Her eyes pierced his soul and lanced his last remaining resolve. He couldn't do it. "I just...uh...thought I left something in here."

*Stupid! That's the best you could think of?*

Jenna cocked her head, an inquisitive look on her face. "Really? When was the last time you were in here?"

"Been a while, I guess. Just thought I'd check."

But she kept on. "What did you lose?"

"I think it was a...you know. Just forget about it." He turned on his crutches to leave.

"Well, nice to see you too," Jenna said in an easy tone to his turned back.

"Oh, yeah. Sure," he said, glancing back at her.

Before Dagen could reach the door, he heard a desperate cry for help from somewhere in the facility. He looked at Jenna, confusion visible on both of their faces.

"You first, Doc," Dagen said, holding the door open for Jenna, who rushed into the hallway. "I'm right behind you."

✵ ✵ ✵

Tynuk approached the front gate of the radio station and waved at the guards as they opened the gate for him. Azolja, his wolfish companion, was not with him. Instead, the huge creature watched inquisitively from the rise of a nearby hillside. Tynuk understood, of course, why people were afraid of the monstrous beast, who appeared to have been yanked straight from the pages of an ancient text on shape-shifting. As a result, he had Az wait for him outside while he conducted his business at the station. As the boy entered, his decorative necklace, animal skins, and breechclout left no question as to his Native American heritage.

"Can you tell me where Courtland is? Have you seen him?" Tynuk called to one of the guards.

"Over by the trucks, in the motor pool."

"Thanks."

Courtland was the boy's second closest friend. Early on they recognized a likeness of purpose in each other, the touch of the Great Spirit, something that was difficult to describe in words. They'd agreed to be allies and comrades should either of them ever need help.

Tynuk also had become acquainted with Kane and a few others at the station, but they didn't seem to understand him. Most of the time, they kept their distance from him and his beast. Tynuk felt that Kane viewed him as just a boy, even though he had more than proven himself during the events of Day Forty. This, more than anything, irritated Tynuk.

The warrior boy crossed the courtyard toward the motor pool, receiving an occasional glance or a nod from the station residents as they went about their day. It was next to impossible for a twelve-year-old boy covered in animal skins and carrying a war club at his side to go unnoticed in such an environment.

He arrived at the motor pool and called out, "Courtland?"

"Here," came the reply. "On the other side of the tanker."

Tynuk crossed around the front of the big rig. There he found Courtland on the ground, bolting a makeshift, ten-gauge steel grate to the front. Courtland sat up as the boy approached, and gave a hearty, "Tynuk! How are you, my young friend?"

"I am well. How are you, sir?" The boy smiled. Even in a seated position, the giant was taller than him.

"I'm blessed this day to have air in my lungs and a smile on my face." Courtland grinned a big, toothy smile. "What's up?"

"If you have a minute, I'd like to talk to you about...things."

Courtland's smile faded. "Everything okay?"

"Sure, yeah. We're fine. It's just..."

"What is it, my young friend? Speak freely."

"I...Az and I can't..." Tynuk paused. His bronze skin, flat nose, and round face showed a distinct likeness to his Central American ancestors. "What I'm trying to say is we're committed to you, but—"

With a piercing shriek, an air horn sounded across the complex in three short blasts—the signal that an emergency had occurred.

"Tynuk, I'm so sorry. Can we talk later? I have to see what's going on," Courtland said, as he scrambled to his feet.

Tynuk lowered his head. "Yes. Of course."

Courtland ran off as everyone's attention turned toward the station. No one noticed Tynuk as he slipped through a small gap in the fence and disappeared into the haze-shrouded hills beyond the station.

✱ ✱ ✱

Kane burst into the commissary and drew his Glock from a leather holster on his right hip.

"Ah," the man behind the counter scoffed, pushing a short, lock-blade knife farther against Kris's throat. "His majesty arrives to tell me what to do."

"Drop the weapon!" Kane yelled.

"Just like I said. Always giving orders but never listening."

"Drop the weapon, or we'll be forced to shoot you."

"Is your aim that good?" the man said, shuffling behind Kris.

Courtland and a few others stormed into the room. Jenna, who was one of the first to enter, stood next to Dagen and waved her hands at the armed man.

"Hey, Jeff. It's me, Jenna. You remember? I took care of you when you had that bad stomach bug a few months ago."

"I remember. I almost died of dehydration because Kane wouldn't release any more water to me."

Jenna continued. "Look, you don't want to hurt anybody. Just let Kris go. He doesn't deserve this. It's not his fault."

"I want more food and more water. *He* said I couldn't have either."

"He doesn't make the rules."

"Yeah, but Kane does."

"So what is it you want?" Kane said.

"Drop your gun," said Jeff.

"Can't do that, but I'll lower it. How's that?" Kane asked, lowering his weapon.

"Fine, whatever. Look, I want more food and water, and I want it now, damn it!"

"Shoot him, Kane," Dagen murmured.

Jenna furrowed her brow and looked sideways at Dagen

"It's not worth giving him more of our rations. Shoot him and be finished with it," Dagan said.

"Just like that, huh? Gonna shoot me?" Jeff stammered.

"No, no one's gonna shoot you," Kane called back. "Hey, Dagen, I think I've got this. Why don't you go find somewhere else to be?"

Dagen paused and glared at Kane.

"Like right now," Kane said, the dislike for the man heavy in his tone.

"Fine. The mess is yours anyhow. You clean it up," Dagen said, as he turned and hobbled on his crutches into the hallway.

"Jeff," Kane began again, "you want more rations? We'll see what we can work out. Just let Kris go, and we'll talk about the details. Fair enough?

Jeff faltered. "That was too easy. If I let him go now, you'll shoot me anyway."

"We won't do that, Jeff. I promise," said Jenna. "We're all hungry and thirsty. There's no reason to hurt anyone over this."

"You promise?"

"Yeah." Kane nodded. "You won't be shot."

The man lowered the knife, and Kris scrambled to get away as the blade clattered on the floor. Kane holstered his gun and strode forward with purpose toward Jeff, who now had his hands raised.

"Kane…" Jenna started.

"You said you wouldn't hurt me!" Jeff cried, as Kane approached him with a scowl.

He punched Jeff hard in the face. The man's nose cracked under the force, sending blood down his chin. He blacked out and fell to the floor.

"I said I wouldn't *shoot* you, you reckless son of a bitch!" Kane shouted, as the others approached to secure Jeff and make sure Kris was OK. "Take him out front."

"Kane," Jenna pleaded. "You're angry. Let's be reasonable."

"We're going to nip this in the bud right now. We're going to eliminate anyone's doubts about what happens if you act violently without cause toward anyone at this station."

"OK. Just be reasonable, that's all."

"I agree," Courtland started. "No one was hurt bad. Let's make sure the punishment is fair. If he had murdered Kris, I might feel different."

"Fair doesn't exist anymore, Jenna. We need to set an example," Kane hissed as he wiped his brow with the sleeve of his shirt.

"Maybe so," said Courtland, his face grim, "but not like you mean. Put a bullet in his head, and you're no different than those bandits out there. We have to maintain our humanity here, our identity as free men and women—as Americans. This is why the justice system existed, and you, more than anyone, should respect that."

Kane took in a deep breath. As cooler heads began to prevail, he took in a second long draw of air before turning to Courtland and nodding. "OK," he said at last. "Take him out front and rally everyone. We'll be fair."

Jeff was dragged out into the courtyard, where the inhabitants of the station gathered around. There he sat on the ground with Kane and Courtland on either side, his wrists bound together as the blood from his nose began to dry, smeared across his face.

"Everyone, listen up!" Kane yelled. "There's something very important that needs to be addressed here." He nodded at Courtland, who nodded in return.

"Everyone here is allowed a daily ration of food and water. Everyone receives the same amount. No one is considered special, and no one gets more unless extreme circumstances dictate. I don't get more, and neither does Courtland. None of us do. This is the only way we can survive. We're all hungry and thirsty, but if you want to live here, you have to obey the rules, taking only what you're given. As always, if you salvage something apart from the group—food, ammo, extra water—you're not required to share it with the group. But anything that is collected as part of an official scavenging mission is to be shared equally with everyone. Does everyone understand this?"

A murmur of acknowledgment rippled through the crowd.

"This man broke these rules and tried to take more than he was allowed. In the process, he took Kris hostage in the commissary with a knife. I don't mind people carrying their own weapons here. We live in an unsafe world. But you must understand that the consequences for this kind of violation will be swift and severe. If you want to call your own shots, you're free to go and make your own way. If you want to stay, you will follow the rules and do your part."

Kane and Courtland helped the man to his feet as he started to come to.

"Wha...what happened?" Jeff groaned.

Kane and Courtland walked Jeff to the gate. As it opened they cut his bonds with a swipe.

"The penalty for such crimes," Kane yelled to the group, "is exile."

"Wait!" a voice piped up from the crowd as a woman and a skinny young boy came to the front. "Please," the woman said, holding her hands up in front of her. "Please, that's my husband. He only did it for our son. The boy cries himself to sleep at night because he's so thirsty."

A look of shock spread across Kane and Courtland's faces. Neither of them had considered whether or not the man had a family. The information landed like a punch in the stomach as both men began to question a judgment they already had set in stone.

"Please," the woman called out again, "show mercy."

"Honey," Jeff called back, "it's okay. You stay. I'll go. You'll be safer here." He turned to Kane. "They can stay, can't they?"

Kane nodded. "Of course."

"But I can't…" Jeff started.

"Not after this," Kane said, looking away as the wind whipped at his hair.

Jeff nodded. He and everyone else at the station knew that while he had a chance, being sent out alone into the wasteland was almost the same as being given a death sentence. The woman and child shuffled forward to the man and hugged him. The woman let out a gasp. "We're going with him."

"No, dear. You can't…" Jeff said through tears.

The woman looked straight at Kane, her glare accusing him of pulling the trigger on all three of them. "If he goes, we go with him."

Kane clenched his jaw and paused. "If that's what you want," he said.

"Are we really doing this?" Jenna whispered.

The man hugged his wife and son, pulling them close. Kane gave the signal for the guards to shut the gate behind them. Courtland and Jenna hung their heads as they and the others at the station watched the small family meander slowly toward the hills and into oblivion.

A heavy, drinkable shadow cast itself over the gypsy camp, as an endless cover of churning charcoal clouds roared above the desolate landscape. This group wasn't a civilized group by any stretch, but they weren't completely barbaric either—at least not in the flesh-eating sort of way. Most of the members held to a basic code of conduct that was enforced by the leader of the group, Garrett.

There were those in the group, like Saxon and his crew, who were definitely unbalanced, doing well just to follow the rules. Garrett kept these mercenaries in check through the careful and limited application of bribery and power. He needed their help. They were valuable to him as a defense force.

The basic rules were simple. Mind your own business. Don't harm other members of the group without cause. Don't steal from each other. Apart from that, members could scavenge and trade for what they needed—or provide some service, as was the unfortunate case for Susan Lorusso.

In her previous life she was an elementary teacher. But among other harsh realities, that vocation no longer existed. Now life consisted solely of survival with little room for comfort or leisure—and much less room for a traditional educational system.

Her children, four-year-old fraternal twins Rachael and Michael, had survived the collapse of civilization. Their education consisted of the most basic knowledge and skills, training meant to keep a person alive, even a four-year-old person. They learned what was safe to eat and drink, how to listen to their natural instincts and fears, basic woodworking and other utilitarian crafts, and which types of items and tools to keep an eye out for when scavenging.

The hard truth was that the new world didn't care about age. If you didn't know how to survive, you wouldn't survive. Many times survival meant something far more than the physical act of living and breathing. Survival as the desire to thrive and to continue on centered on one thing—hope. Hope for the future and for a better tomorrow. Something.

Anything. Hope was critical to Susan Lorusso's current condition. And even though the world seemed dead and everything she had ever known was gone, Susan knew her husband was *alive*.

She stopped within earshot of Garrett and Saxon as they argued over some topic that didn't concern her. Spying, she bent and pretended to pick up some scrap metal out of the dirt.

"Are you serious?" Garrett was almost yelling. "You want to mess with the Coyotes?"

"Look, they're the real deal, and they have serious firepower—firepower we could use. To ally with them would ensure our survival."

"You've lost it. If you've heard what I have, then you know they're nothing more than bloodthirsty killers. They'll murder us all and steal what we have before they'll have anything to do with us. I've even heard their leader is possessed or something. There's no way we're dealing with them."

Saxon lunged at Garrett, yelling in his face. "They're either our allies or our enemies, and they aren't enemies we want to take on. I don't need your permission!"

"Yes, you do! As long as you want to stay here, you do!" Garrett met Saxon nose to nose, spitting with the effort of speaking each word.

Maybe they'd kill each other. If they did, Susan's life certainly would improve—at least it wouldn't get any worse. She turned her thoughts back to the problem at hand. Her problem. How in the world would she and the children be able to get out of here to locate Kane? She was something of an indentured servant, and she definitely wasn't free to just go. Garrett viewed her as his property, property to be summoned at his beck and call. She had to do something, for her sake and for the sake of the children.

It seemed so impossible, so ridiculous that Kane should be alive, especially given the condition of his heart. But it was true. She had heard his voice over the radio broadcast from the coast of South Carolina. The realization brought with it a truckload of emotions: hope, fear, love, doubt, strength, and shame. Shame at what she'd had to do so that she and her children could survive. If she saw Kane again, would he ever understand? It was a question that haunted her more than his death ever had.

Maybe she was delusional. Maybe there wasn't any real chance that she'd get through, but she had to try to get out. She would wait until nightfall when there were fewer people moving about camp. Then she would make her move and pray that no one noticed her.

✷ ✷ ✷

The dark trees appeared twisted against one another, eerily hunched, as the thick ash fell in clumps across the alien landscape. The land appeared backlit by the distant fires, always burning. Kane stretched his arms out in front of him, grasping at nothing. In the darkness, he struggled to comprehend his surroundings as the shadows laughed at his confusion.

Kane wiped a clump of ash from his forehead, and it smeared across his face like silver war paint. He rubbed the remnants of the ash between his fingers as he listened to the many distant cries in the darkness. As he began to walk, he squinted his eyes at the dancing shadows, his boots leaving perfect impressions on the ashen forest floor.

A man, a woman, and a small boy appeared ahead of him, walking toward the distant fires. It was Jeff, the man who had been exiled with his family the day before.

"Jeff!" Kane called out to the group. "Hey, Jeff!"

They continued to walk away, oblivious to his calls.

"Jeff! Jeff, I'm sorry!" Kane yelled, as he watched the family catch fire at the edge of the trees. Kane gasped as he heard their cries and watched them fold and wither into ash before his eyes.

"I'm…I'm so sorry," he said, the weight of responsibility heavy across his brow.

"Kane! Help us!" came a shrill cry in the distance.

"What? Susan?" Kane looked about, desperate. "I can't see you, sweetie. Where are you?"

The sound of muffled cries in the darkness brought Kane to a jog as he moved toward his wife's voice.

"Susan, just tell me where you are."

"Help us, Kane. We need you. Why haven't you come?"

"I…Where are you? I can't find you."

"Kane," came another voice, this one close by.

Kane spun in surprise to see the shadowed form of a woman. His heart beat faster. "Susan?"

The woman came closer, and he began to distinguish her face among the drifting shadows. "No, Kane," she replied. "It's me."

"Molly?" he whispered.

"Who are you looking for, Kane? Why are you in this place?"

"My wife, my children…You said…"

"They are alive, but because inability to stay true to your purpose, they will die."

"No," he blurted out.

"Yes, Kane. You will get them killed, just like you got me killed."

A gasp caught in his throat. "Molly, please. Please don't say that. I tried so hard. I did my best."

"Your best wasn't good enough then, and it won't be good enough for them," she said, her voice cold.

Kane lowered his head and shook it from side to side as the weight of this thought fell upon him. The raw ache made his spirit falter.

"You failed us," Molly whispered in the darkness. "You've failed us all. And now your family will pay the price for it too."

"Please, just tell me where they are, and I'll try—"

"You're too late. We're all gone now, burned up, added to the ashes of the world."

"*No*!" Kane lurched forward on the small cot, his lungs heaving, his mind racing with the words of his late friend. A sharp pang ran through him as his heart ached in his chest. He pushed his palms against his chest and pinched his eyes closed against the pain. "Not this again. Come on, damn you! Just let me find them before it's too late. I can do this."

✲ ✲ ✲

This was going to get her killed. She was quite sure of it. Susan crouched by the sidewall of the small, beat-up Nissan Sentra and waited for the best time to move. She would have to move quick, crossing an open area to the diesel tractor that was equipped with a radio of some sort. She had seen Garrett use it before. She wasn't sure whether it operated on the same frequency as the one the radio control station used, the one her husband's message had come through on, but she had to try. It was the only way she might be able to make contact.

Susan glanced over her shoulder at the children, who were sleeping soundly on a bedroll by the fire. Their faces looked so sweet, so pure and innocent as if they were dreaming good dreams of places far away from the hellish nightmare that had become their lives. Susan blinked her eyes hard and lowered her head. She would take this chance to save them.

Glancing around one final time to make sure the coast was clear, she flew across the open space in a low crouch, traveling about fifteen yards to the side of the truck. Pressing her back to the truck, she slowed her breathing and tried to control the banging of her heart in her ears.

Getting the keys to the rig hadn't been an easy task. The vehicle was Garrett's after all, and the keys were always with him. Though it had disgusted her, she'd seduced him by her own volition, and when he was sound asleep, she'd pocketed the keys on her way out.

She had thought about getting the kids, loading them up in the truck, and taking off, but the thought terrified her. First off, Garrett most likely would catch them all, and then he would have her killed. Who knew what terrible things would befall Rachael and Michael with Saxon around? But even if Susan were to escape, where would she go? All she knew about Kane's location was that he was somewhere on the coast of South Carolina. Nothing more. Add to this the fact she and her children would be murdered if they encountered mutants or other bandits. The risks involved with fleeing at this point were too great. She had to make contact first.

Susan pulled the keys from her pocket, singling out the large truck key. Sliding it into the door keyhole, she turned it with a solid *thunk*. She removed the key and pulled the handle, opening the door with a slight creak. At once Susan froze, her paranoia telling her that everyone in camp had heard the squeal of unoiled hinges. A quick glance around told her she was overreacting. The camp remained still and quiet.

Moving into the cab, she pulled the door closed until the latch engaged with a click. Lying low on the seat, she inserted the key into the ignition, checking to make sure no exterior lights would come on, then turned it one position to activate battery power to the vehicle. A few dim interior lights blinked to life, and she moved her fingertips to the power knob on the radio. With a snap the backlit panel illuminated, and the fuzz of static came over the speaker. Taking hold of the tuner knob, she adjusted it in single-point increments, trying to find the right frequency.

Ten minutes of careful work in the silence of the cab had rendered nothing. Susan was beginning to believe that the attempt had been a stupid and dangerous waste of time when, in a crackle of static, she heard the faint sound of a voice.

"Shhhh...Radio control station on the coast of South Carolina, north of Charleston...shhhh."

Susan listened as pure hope welled up in her chest. It wasn't Kane's voice, but the location was the same, and the message that followed was almost identical to the one she'd heard from the lips of her husband. She would wait until the message was over then try to make contact.

When the voice finished, Susan waited a moment before picking up the microphone and raising it to her lips. Anticipation coursed through her as she formulated what she would say to the voice on the other end. Just as she keyed up the microphone, the door of the truck flew open to reveal the wild, blue face of Saxon, grinning with evil satisfaction.

✵ ✵ ✵

In the stillness of the starless night, the sounds of the whipping wind, punctuated by the occasional skitter of a hungry rodent were the only sounds in the otherwise quiet control station.

Courtland mouthed some small bit of scripture to himself as he sat in the low, sterile glow of a fluorescent solar lantern. The tattered and worn pages of the old Bible had seen better days, but instead of feeling worn out, they felt comfortable, like an old friend who's never too busy to give a few words of encouragement.

He smiled as he turned the page and touched the ragged photographs of his wife and daughter. He wished that they had been afforded the opportunity to all live together. He had lost his dear wife, Teshauna, to a fatal hemorrhage during the birth of his darling girl, his only child, Marissa. His two ladies had only a moment to meet. It was the best and worst day of his life.

Courtland sat deep in thought, brimming with admiration and love for his two loves, one he'd lost years ago, the other lost in a terrible accident just before the civilized world had ended. He caressed their pictures with a heavy finger, nestling them safely in his worn and tattered Bible.

"I miss you both so much," he whispered in the silent glow of the lantern. "You were the best parts of me. It's so hard to keep going sometimes, but I'll praise the Lord and rejoice that he gives me the strength to do so."

Unannounced, Kane appeared in the doorway to the common room. "Am I interrupting something?"

"No." Courtland shut his Bible and set it on the couch next to him. "What's bothering you?"

"How'd you know?" Kane leaned against the doorframe and sighed as he ran his fingers through his hair.

"You're up in the middle of the night, just like me. Can't sleep again?"

"Nah. You either?"

"Not too much these days. How are you faring?"

Kane shrugged. "The nightmares are a little too much to bear sometimes."

Courtland nodded. "What was it?"

"I had a dream about Molly and..." Kane paused to exhale deeply then looked up. "...that guy Jeff and his family." He looked at Courtland. "Did we do the right thing? Did we do what was best for everyone? I mean, should we have given him another chance?"

Courtland considered this and shook his head slowly. "I don't know, brother. My heart says yes, for the sake of his family, but if he was willing to do something that drastic, who knows what he might do in the future. Besides, think of the message that not punishing him would send to everyone else here."

"Sure, but we didn't exile Dagen after what he did. Somehow that dirt bag got to stay."

Courtland made a concerned face. "I don't know, Kane. We made a choice. We did what we felt was best for the group, and now we'll have to live with that choice. There's no way we could have known about the man's family."

"Yeah, I know." Kane sighed. "My brain is just full of...so much these days."

"Your family?"

"Yes," Kane said, rubbing his eyes. "My dreams are filled with their memories—accusations that I've failed them."

"You never failed them," Courtland said. "You couldn't help what happened."

"She said they're alive. The last thing Molly said to me was that my family is alive. How am I supposed to sleep with that in my head? Knowing that they might be out there while I'm here doing nothing?"

"You're not doing nothing. You're doing what you're supposed to be doing."

"Tell that to my family who likely thinks I'm dead, and who might be in danger."

"Kane, be careful. If you try to make this thing your own, to control it, it could ruin you. And that's just what Satan wants—a foothold in your life."

"Enough with the sermon, man," Kane said, his face darkening as he stepped back into the hall to leave. "I'm serious about this."

Courtland gestured with his Bible. "So am I."

Kane waved his hands. "Yeah, I know. Courtland always knows just what to do," he said, as he exited back down the hall to a cramped room full of restless dreams.

"I'm sorry, brother. If only I did," Courtland whispered, lowering his head in the faint, glow of the common area. "Lord Jesus, help us."

Susan clutched for something to hold on to as she was snatched from the cab of the truck, falling four and a half feet to the ground. She landed face down, the brutal impact with the earth flexing her rib cage as it absorbed the blow. She cried out as the wind was knocked out of her. She immediately rolled onto her side, pulling her legs up into the fetal position. Before she could regain her breath, she was grabbed by her hair and yanked to her feet. The hand in her hair moved its way to her throat and pushed her against the side of the big rig. The blue of Saxon's ugly mug snarled just inches from her face.

"And just what the fuck do you think you're doing?"

"I...I..." Susan wheezed, still trying to fill the void in her chest.

"You were going to steal Garrett's truck, weren't you?"

"No, I swear—"

"Garrett! You'd better get out here!" Saxon called at the top of his lungs. "You're going to want to hear this!"

Torches ignited around the camp as people rose and gathered by the truck. Garrett exited his tent in a huff as he threw on a shirt.

"What's going on?"

"My dear Garrett," Saxon gestured to the group. "This is what happens when you let your little sex slave have free reign of your tent."

A few people laughed. Garrett turned red.

"What the hell is going on here?" he spat.

"I caught your woman here trying to steal your truck."

Garrett looked into the truck and saw the keys in the ignition. His rage began to blossom.

"It's not true, Garrett," Susan said gasping for breath. "I wouldn't steal from you."

Saxon slammed her against the truck again. "That's bullshit! This bitch is lying," he barked over his shoulder.

Garrett didn't make a move to help her.

"Tell the truth, or I'll cut your head off!" Saxon growled, pushing a knife to her throat.

"I was just...curious about the radio. That's all," Susan mumbled unconvincingly.

Saxon pushed the knife harder against her throat as the skin began to split.

"Sheathe the knife, Saxon," Garrett said. "Sheathe it. She doesn't care if you kill her. But there is something else," he said, motioning for one of Saxon's men to come forward.

In the flickering torchlight, Susan saw the man step forward. With a baleful smile on his face, the man held her son, Michael. Cupping his hand under the young boy's chin, he pulled the boy's face skyward to expose the soft, fleshy parts of the child's neck. The light glimmered on the blade of the knife that rested there.

"Momma?" the boy whispered, terror pouring from his quaking features like a dripping mask.

For an instant Susan almost fainted, the sheer and overwhelming sight of a knife at her son's throat causing her to go weak in the knees.

"You should choose your next words very carefully," Garrett intoned. "You're going to tell me everything, including who you were trying to raise on the radio."

Susan whimpered as Saxon released her, snickering.

# FIVE

## BEFORE
## WESTERN NORTH CAROLINA

The thin, seven-year-old boy with long, brown hair and smooth tan skin stood at the edge of his bed, stuffing the last of his schoolbooks into his canvas backpack. The school bus would arrive any minute. The boy took two steps toward the door of his small room and stopped, glancing over his shoulder at the closet to his left.

"Get out here! Miss that bus again and I'll beat your ass!" came the raspy smoker's voice from the living room.

"Yes, Momma. I'm coming," the boy called back.

He moved to the closet, digging through the junk on the floor of the small space. He grabbed a few items then stuffed them into the backpack. He would need them if he went to see Grandfather Nuk'Chala later.

The hiss of air brakes as the school bus pulled away from the curb brought him to full attention.

"No!" he yelled as he ran for the door. "Wait!"

He flung the flimsy trailer door open and saw the bus round the corner and move out of sight. His shoulders slumped and he half turned toward the living room.

"Momma, the bus—"

With a violent movement, the woman crashed into the boy, shoving him against the wall, her long, painted fingernails digging into the flesh of his arm. He cried out in shock and pain as her whiskey-soaked breath washed over him. At seven fifteen in the morning, and she was already drunk—again.

"What the hell is wrong with you? What did I say? What did I *just* say to you?" she screamed.

Tears welled in the boy's eyes as he stammered, "I'm sorry, Momma. I'm sorry."

"Yeah, you know what? You *are* sorry. Just like your damn father. You're a sorry piece of trash, and you'll never make anything of yourself."

"Momma, please!"

She slapped the boy hard across his face, her fingernails taking small chunks of skin from his cheek, just beside his ear. He cried out in pain.

"You shut your damn mouth, and show me the respect I deserve!"

The boy pinched his lips together as tears dripped from his chin.

"Do you understand me?"

The boy nodded.

"You will run to school, and you won't be late. If the school calls and says you're late, or if you don't come straight home afterward, then God help me. I swear, Reno Yackeschi, I'll beat you within an inch of your miserable life."

"Yes, Momma," the boy murmured, the look of fear plastered across his face.

"Now get the hell out of my house," she said as she released him.

The boy ran from the trailer crying, fleeing from a woman who no longer played the role of mother.

It took Reno forty-five minutes to get to school on foot, even though he ran faster than all the other boys in his class. He was still late and would receive the beating his mother had promised after the school called to tell her he hadn't arrived on time. Reno went straight to the front office to apologize. As he walked in, Vice Principal Staph stepped in front of him and blocked his way to the front desk.

"Why aren't you in class, Reno?"

"I couldn't help it. I—"

"Oh, you can't help it now?"

"Please, don't. You don't understand," Reno squeaked.

"I understand perfectly well. Ms. Pounds, get Reno to his class. Ms. Gertie's room, please." The vice principal directed a stern gaze at Reno, wagging a meaty finger in his face. "I've had enough of your shenanigans. I'm calling your mother right now."

It was as good as a death sentence. Reno lowered his head and walked from the office as Ms. Pounds led him to class. The kids snickered as he came in, disheveled, sweating, and led by the arm. Reno didn't care. It was over for him. And although Ms. Gertie was asking him a question, he wasn't listening. All he could think about was how bad he didn't want to go back home to that trailer.

The day went by too quick. Reno finished loading his backpack and walked down the hall through the front doors of Valley View Elementary. At the bus loading area, he squinted his eyes in contemplation as he waited for the bus.

He loved his mother, and she *had* loved him…once.

Everything changed on a snowy January night two and a half years ago. His dad, a full-blooded Comanche Indian, was a drinker, and while he'd never been a loving man, he had been there. Just a few unceremonious moments would forever be etched in Reno's mind. His dad told them he was leaving to go in search of the wandering spirit. Though Reno and his mother begged him not to go, he said goodbye with a wave, not a hug, and walked out into the cold night, leaving Reno and his mother to fend for themselves.

Reno's mother changed that night too. In the blink of an eye, the woman who had been loving and attentive became cold and distant. Her anger toward her husband, now redirected at her son. Every time she looked into Reno's eyes, she saw the eyes of the man who had abandoned them. The daughter of a Cherokee woman and her Mexican husband, Reno's mother was prone to alcoholism and took to the addiction with ease. Her cold and distant demeanor soon turned violent and oppressive. Everything and everyone that young Reno had loved in his life disappeared. The two and a half years that followed his father's departure were full of terrifying, fearful lessons taught to him by his now abusive mother. Reno's life was hell.

The one bright spot that remained was grandfather, Nuk'Chala, who lived in the same neighborhood. The old man was actually Reno's father's uncle, though he might as well have been Reno's grandfather. For a long time, Nuk'Chala was the only person in Reno's life who offered any consistency. In the last few years, the old man had taken an even greater interest in the boy, sensing that Reno was experiencing hard times.

"Nuk'Chala meant *lonely wolf* in the ancient tongue. He knew the old ways of the Comanche and still practiced some of them. He spoke to Reno of how the white man had brought war and ruin upon the Comanche. But in the end, he told the boy, the Comanche nation had destroyed themselves by forsaking all that was most important and accepting the lazy nature and addictions of modern society. Reno sometimes spent hours after school listening to the stories and legends of the great lords of the plains. These tales stirred something deep in his heart. A fire had been kindled inside him, an ancient fire that burned of war, courage, and noble purpose. Reno hoped that one day Grandfather Nuk'Chala would teach him the ancient combative arts of the plains warriors.

The movement came so fast that Reno didn't have time to react. The fist struck him in his left side, sinking beneath his floating ribs, forcing him to fold in half.

"What do you think about that, redskin?" the boy named Sam shouted into Reno's ear.

Reno tried to breathe, as the void in his left side seemed to pull all the air from his lungs. What felt like an eternity passed as the hooligans laughed and danced around, towering over him. They pointed fingers and yelled insults. The school bus was gone. He had missed it—again.

"I said, 'What do you think of that?' " Sam said, glowering.

Reno was coming back now, pulling himself together, taking in his first shuddering breath, when one of the boys slapped him hard across the face. He winced and instantly remembered the slap his mother had given him that morning.

"I think," he said, the anger mounting within him. "I think Sam punches like a girl."

One of the boys chuckled but was silenced when the bigger boy started to scream.

"I'll show you who the girl is, Injun!" Sam punched Reno hard in the stomach a second time. Reno hit the ground and pulled his knees to his chest. He rode out the rest of the assault, which lasted only a few seconds as the boys kicked him and dumped his books on top of him. Reno's backpack also contained a few cured animal skins and a half-finished dream catcher he'd been working on.

"Well, look at this," Sam said, picking up the dream catcher.

"Just stop, please," Reno managed.

"Yeah, we'll stop," Sam said, as he pulled the dream catcher apart and tossed it onto Reno's head. "See you tomorrow, Tonto."

As the boys left, Reno sat for a quiet moment, wiping the tears from his face. He collected his things and made it to his feet. He couldn't go home now.

The walk to Nuk'Chala's place took a while, but Reno felt numb to the pain and the hate. Time seemed to move at a crawl as he walked, his thoughts, fragmented and heavy. He arrived on the rickety porch and knocked on the flimsy door.

Evening had just begun to set in, and the insects hummed the chorus of their usual song. The old man opened the door in a fluid gesture. Though easily into his eighties, he moved with the grace of a cat. He smiled at his young friend but upon seeing Reno's face, he took on a more serious expression.

"What is it, boy?"

"Help me, Grandfather."

"What is it that you desire, boy?" the old man replied with an air of wisdom.

"Please. Teach me everything. I want to be a true blood like you, like our ancestors."

The old man shook his head. "I'm sorry, Reno, but the old ways are dying. The wheel of time has choked them out. There is no reason to teach them any longer."

Reno shuddered and brought his hands together. Tears welled in his eyes.

"Please, Grandfather. I have nothing. I need something to believe in. Teach me to fight, to survive, and to honor the Great Spirit as you honor it with your heart. There is nothing I want more in this life. I will give up everything I have and everything I am for this. *Please*, Grandfather."

The old man looked the boy over, taking note of the desperation he saw in his face and the physical wounds on his body. "You know what you ask?"

The boy remained silent. The old man sighed.

"You must understand how serious this is. This will be harder for you than anything you've ever known. Many did not survive the old trials, but if you do, your mind will become as calm as flowing water, your spirit flexible and strong like bound cords of leather, and your body as hard as stone. You must do everything I say without question. And if you choose to abandon this journey, you will never speak to me again."

The boy swallowed as this last charge sank in. He paused. "I understand," he said in a whisper.

The old man gave an almost imperceptible nod then stooped to meet the boy's tear-streaked face. "From this moment forward, you are no longer Reno Yackeschi. That name is one that you wear for the outside world. But your true name, your warrior name, the name that you will carry in your heart from this moment until you take your final breath on the field of battle will be this—*Tynuk*. In the ancient tongue, it means *wolf born.*"

# SIX

## NOW

The morning scouting party—Mico, Rick, Shana, and Cody—loaded up in the bed of the rusted Chevy Silverado and pulled the tailgate shut. They slung their rifles and took their positions. The sky was just beginning to lighten on the eastern horizon as they all checked and double-checked their gear. Each member carried a rifle based on his or her familiarity with a given type and what was available. Several of the members also carried handguns stuffed in their waistbands, and all of them brought makeshift pikes, bats, knives, or other close-quarter weapons.

Kane approached the truck in the semi-darkness and greeted the truck's occupants. They responded in turn.

"All right, guys," Kane began. "Today you're all going to Crestline Heights. I'm sure you're all familiar with the area. If for some reason you're not, Cal can brief you."

Mico, the team's leader, asked, "Haven't we hit that one already?"

"Yep." Kane nodded. "You're right. We have. Last time, though, we ran out of daylight and had to leave half the subdivision unchecked. We pulled a solid load of goods from the sections we did cover, so it's worth our time going back to scout the rest."

Mico nodded with understanding.

"Again, Cal is familiar with the area, so if you have questions, make sure you get with him, Okay? Cody is the only new guy here, so even though I'm sure the rest of you know the rules, I'll go over them again. First, don't engage with any unknown humans unless first engaged—no exceptions. Highwaymen will set traps designed to evoke your sympathies. Don't stop for anyone, not for women and children and not for old ladies. Clear?"

The group gave their verbal acknowledgment.

"Second, steer clear of anything that even remotely resembles a Sick. If you have to take one or two down, get close and use your melee weapons. As we discovered in the past, if there are more in the area, they'll converge en masse if they hear loud noises like explosions and gunfire. Fire your weapons only as a last resort.

"Third, no one goes anywhere alone—ever. If you've got to relieve yourself, then I hope you like company. Groups of two at all times. This goes for male-female groups too. Safety trumps modesty here. Cal will stay with the truck, so keep him and each other informed about where you are and where you're searching. Keep your personal walkies close by for this."

Cody nodded.

"And last, always, always, always be back at the station before dark. You don't want to be wandering around out there when the sun goes down. If you get into any trouble, break contact and get back here ASAP. Any questions?"

"Negative, Kane. We're good to go," Mico replied.

"Good. Jacob and I will be out there as well today doing some hunting. If you need us, try channel five.

"Hunting?" Shana asked. "As in wild game?"

"It's looking that way. Saw some deer tracks yesterday."

The team in the truck exchanged smiles and high fives.

"We'll see how it goes. You guys stay safe."

Kane slapped the side of the truck a few times and signaled for the guards to open the gate. Cal gave a thumbs-up out the window of the truck, and the team responded in kind. Kane waved as the truck cranked up and pulled forward through the gate, the red taillights disappearing down the gravel road into the early-morning light.

✫ ✫ ✫

The truck came to a stop along a side street in the subdivision. Trash and debris littered the streets, covering the burnt yards where happy, naive children used to run and ride their bicycles. Four team members jumped over the side of the truck and into the street.

"Walkies on," said Mico, pulling out his radio and turning the knob on top of the device. It came to life with a chirp, followed by a succession of three more beeps.

"This is the last grid. We've pulled a good load so far today so don't take any chances. It's easy to forget that a rusty nail followed by a bout of tetanus can be the end of you out here. Don't be stupid."

Shana rolled her eyes. "Spare us the speech, Mico."

"Yeah, fine. Shana, you're with me. Rick and Cody, partner up and let's get it done. We only have a few hours of daylight left."

Mico gave a thumbs-up to Cal, who switched on his radio and gave a thumbs-up in return. Cal then stepped out and pulled his rifle from the passenger seat. He shut the door and took his position as overwatch in the bed of the truck.

The two groups split up to cover different sides of the street. Coming back had been a good idea. They scored various types of fuel, batteries, firearms, ammo, and a solid load of canned goods. They even found a few pallets of bottled water, which was almost unheard of. Rick, Cody, and Shana guzzled two bottles each on the spot. Always the stickler for the rules, Mico frowned at this, though he eventually drank a bottle himself. What the others didn't know wouldn't hurt them.

Two houses down on this grid and they'd picked up nothing of real value. Mico grabbed his radio and keyed it up. "Mico to Cal. Everything still look good?"

"Street is clear," came the reply.

"Mico to Rick. You guys good?"

"Yeah, we haven't found much of anything."

"Roger. Carry on. We're going to continue up the block on the right side."

"Gotcha."

After Mico and Shana checked four more houses, a wash of static came over the radio, followed by a splashing sound. Mico frowned at Shana as he picked up his radio.

"Mico to Rick. You guys Okay?"

"Yeah. Did you hear that too?"

"Yeah. Hang on. Mico to Cal. Everything good?"

Silence.

"Mico to Cal. You copy?"

Again they heard nothing but silence.

The former Army National Guardsman swore and glanced at Shana. "He's probably taking a piss," Mico said, "but we need to check on him."

Shana nodded. The two made their way out through the unhinged front door of the ruined house. Mico peered down the street and held up his radio.

"Cal, if everything's cool, now's the time to say so."

Nothing. Mico saw that the truck and everything around it appeared to be clear.

*What the hell are you doing, Cal?*

"Mico to Rick. Rally on the truck. I can't raise Cal."

"I gotcha, man. We're headed that way."

Shana and Mico jogged at a brisk pace down the center of the street. It took just a minute to reach the truck, and as they approached, they smelled the rusty scent of fresh blood.

"Rick, where the hell are you guys? Respond!" Mico yelled into his radio, as he and Shana moved around to the back of the truck. At once Shana gasped and turned away. Blood poured from Cal's headless corpse, trickling off the open tailgate and splattering on the ground.

"Oh, my God! Where's his head?" Shana cried. "It's Sicks, isn't it? They got him. They got him!"

"No." Mico hissed. "If it was, they'd still be eating him right now."

"Then what?"

"Shut up for a second, and be ready to fight," Mico growled. "Rick, come in, damn it."

Mico's radio came alive with a wash of static. He held the device up to try to get a better signal. A voice spoke in a whisper through the static. "Rick ain't gonna be able to take this call. Would you like to leave a message?" Mico listened to the wheezing laughter. "So are you two gonna stand by the truck all day, or are you gonna make this fun?"

Mico swallowed hard and slowly turned to look at Shana. His expression told her everything she needed to know.

"Run," he whispered.

"The truck," she choked out.

Mico slowly shook his head. "They have the keys. Run. I'll cover you."

"I can't—"

"Lock that shit up!" Mico hissed. "One of us has to make it back. I'll cover you as long as I can."

Shana wiped at her face, checked her rifle, and nodded.

"*Now!*" Mico yelled, as he spun and raised his AR-15.

They came from everywhere, more than he could count. The furious bandits converged on them, sounding wicked, bloodthirsty howls. The rifle blazed in front of Mico as he dropped his targets. Just a glance over his shoulder told him that Shana wouldn't make it far. The thugs were chasing her up the street.

Mico ducked and moved to the front bumper as a hail of bullets struck the truck. His training taking over, Mico stayed low, engaging target after target from behind cover. He turned, firing at the men closest to Shana, taking four of them down. Mico dropped his empty rifle magazine and grabbed another from his cargo pocket just as something slammed into the side of his head with a spine-jarring thud.

The world seemed to reel as Mico fell to all fours. Shana screamed as the thugs began to rape her in the street. They swarmed around Mico now, laughing and yelling at him to get up. Mico tried to stand but was struck with another violent blow to the head. Consciousness left him for a moment, fading back in like the dawning of the day. He pulled his arms under him and tried to push his body up when something warm cascaded over his head and dribbled down this forehead. Urine. He remained still, trying to get his bearings. He was pulled to his feet and pinned against the truck by the angry mob as blood and piss trickled from his hairline. Shana wasn't screaming anymore.

One of the thugs pushed the others aside and got into Mico's face. The man smiled, his swollen features, all mashed together as if he were a villain from the *Dick Tracy* comics.

"Whatcha doin' on Coyote turf, shit stick?" the man asked as the other thugs around him laughed.

"You and your clowns don't scare me."

The men laughed harder.

"Everyone's a tough guy until the pain starts. The boys call me 'Shank,' " the thug slurred, bubbles dripping wet from his puffy lips. "You wanna know why?"

"I can't wait to—" Mico groaned, his words cut short as he felt a blade enter his guts. He groaned in agony.

The thug with the knife laughed. "Now you know!" Shank giggled as he pulled the blade out and jammed it into Mico's midsection again and again giving a brutal twist each time. Time slowed, and the world began to spin and blur as the bandits laughed at the tortuous murder of a fellow human being.

"Night-night," Shank slurred.

As the darkness closed in on him, Mico felt the blade sting as it pushed deep under his chin with a scraping sound, and all the lights in the world went out.

✳ ✳ ✳

The warrior boy, Tynuk, sat without a sound beside the small fire, his eyes gazing into the flames, watching them jump and disappear in a shower of sparks. He rechecked the pot that contained boiling bits of horsehide and sinew. It was ready. He dipped a small, wooden ladle into the gray glop and drew out the solid parts from the hide glue. The heat from the fire continued to refine the mixture.

Once the solids were removed, Tynuk dipped a small horsehair brush into the mix then pulled it out. He examined the stinking gray goop that clung to the bristles. Then he grabbed a yellowish, long, wide, flat bow rendered from a beautiful piece of Osage orange wood that he'd collected in the forest. The wood exhibited the perfect combination of weight, strength, flexibility, and durability under stress. The outer bark was scorched, but the heart of the wood appeared clean and supple—ideal for a bow.

Tynuk brushed the glue liberally along the back of the bow where most of the stress in the draw occurred. He then wrapped the handle as tight as he could with crisscrossed strips of sinew. He applied glue and sinew to the tips and notches of the bow to strengthen the points where the bowstring would hang. He then began to bind the sinew into a suitable bowstring while the bow hardened.

When he had bound a cable of suitable length and width, Tynuk moved on to finishing his arrows, beautiful ash stalks he had salvaged from the blackened woods. With great care he glued and bound a few pulled turkey feathers to each shaft. As the boy worked, his senses remained alert, but his mind began to flow into the past, to that fearful moment that set his destiny along its course.

The banging on the trailer door had been sharp. One, two, three, four, five—the knocks came, rousing the boy from his slumber. He threw back the sheets and took a moment to gain his bearings. He'd have to answer the door, since his mother had gone to bed only a few hours ago. She was still intoxicated.

The knocks came again, sharper and faster. It was still dark.

"Okay, okay," the boy mumbled as he made his way down the narrow hallway of his mother's trailer, the smell of cigarette smoke still lingering in the air. He unlatched the door and cracked it open to see who was outside.

"Tynuk! Come quick!" came the urgent voice.

"Grandfather? What—"

"No time!" came the old man's hastened reply. "Throw on your clothes, grab your survival bag, and meet me at the edge of the woods by the Ash Mountain trailhead."

The boy heard a tinge of fear in the old man's voice, which caused his heart to drop. He never had seen grandfather show fear.

"Okay," the boy managed, but his grandfather was already gone.

In a matter of minutes, Tynuk had slipped into lightweight clothes that he could move in easily. He grabbed his survival bag, which held several items essential for living alone in the woods. Bursting from the trailer, he sidestepped the stairs and launched off the porch, breaking into a swift and silent run across the trailer park. He slipped into the woods and made his way to the Ash Mountain trailhead.

As Tynuk moved, he heard the slight crackle and distant boom of some faraway explosion. Glancing up he heard the sound of jets flying overhead. They flew across the expanse of the heavens, their condensation trails like cotton candy littering the early-morning darkness.

Something wasn't right, and the more he thought about it, the more it felt wrong. Grandfather never came to his house, and the fear the boy had seen in the old man's face told him that something was definitely wrong.

At once a hand snatched hold of Tynuk's arm, shattering his train of thought. The boy cried out and spun to face the dark figure, the hand gripping his arm like an anaconda.

"Calm yourself, boy!" came the familiar voice.

"Grandfather!" Tynuk yelled. "Calm myself? You're scaring me to death!"

"I know, and I'm sorry, but something terrible is happening."

"I heard the explosions and saw the jets."

"Not jets, boy, missiles. The enemies of this nation are trying to finish us. I heard on the radio that several major cities have already been completely destroyed."

Tynuk's mouth dropped open. "But...we're safe here in the mountains, right?"

"I fear that won't be the case for long. The attacks are spreading, covering large areas. Much of the forest is already on fire. When panic sets in, people will begin to turn on one another. I'm afraid that few will survive this. You must go now, up the trail to the Ash Creek cave to hide. The spring inside the cave will provide water, and you have your survival bag. This is your final test."

"My mother—"

"No, you must go now."

"But—" the boy began to cry.

"You will not be able to wake her, convince her, and move her in time. You will both die—and you, my son, cannot die. You are the future of our people."

"What about you?" the boy choked out, tears spilling down his face.

In the darkness, one could begin to see the glow of spreading fires. The old man smiled wearily and placed his hand on the boy's shoulder.

"I am an old man. I will only slow you down."

"*No*! You must come with me," the boy cried.

"I cannot. I won't be able to make the dangerous trek in time. I have lived a long and full life. I have taught you everything you need to know. You are strong and wise, and...I love you as my own."

The boy lunged forward, smothering the old man in a bear hug. He buried his face against grandfather's bony chest. The old man held the boy tightly for a moment before pushing him away, the warmth draining from him.

"You are *Wolf Born!* There are no more childish tears to shed over this," the old man rasped, as he pushed a worn and beautifully ornate belt into the boy's hands.

"Grandfather, your belt. I can't—"

"You can. And when the time is right, this is how our people will know you. Remember what you have learned. Your destiny awaits you and the Great Spirit goes before you. *Now go!*" The old man nodded with one last wink of approval. Then he turned and trudged down the path, disappearing into the smoke.

The journey up the path was long and arduous. Though Tynuk had been there many times during his training, the landscape looked different this time. The forest appeared only as an outline, backlit by the raging fires that had begun to consume it. As a light sweat beaded on his brow, Tynuk pushed thoughts of his mother and Grandfather Nuk'Chala from his mind. Those thoughts would only slow him down. He moved with precision up the treacherous trail toward the cave, and as he climbed, the floor of the burning forest seemed to drop away below him.

After several hours of difficult climbing, the boy reached a plateau covered with boulders and pine trees. He hoisted himself up onto a ledge just as a blinding flash of light burst above. He squinted his eyes as he looked up at the sky, which appeared as bright as day for only a moment. Something exploded, sending an ear-shattering blast into the atmosphere above. Flopping to the ground, Tynuk pressed himself hard against the rock as the earth shook like an enraged titan. Fire fell from the sky as an orange glow bathed everything in smoke and flame. The boy hoisted himself up and began to run as the world burned around him. He scrambled up the path, his young limbs aching with the effort as he ran at a pace that would tire the most seasoned of adventurers.

A sharp cry caught Tynuk's attention in the fiery morning darkness. He slowed his pace to listen. It was an animal, but the sound was so curious that it broke the boy's concentration, causing him to pull away from the path. Nuk'Chala's voice echoed in his ears, telling him not to stray, but he had to know. He had to see what would make such a noise. He felt drawn to the creature.

Tynuk moved to a ledge as the cry came again, a mixture of howl, bark, and hiss. As he peered over the edge, he caught sight of a small, black animal the size of a large possum. Through the burning pines, the boy saw a pack of coyotes surrounding the animal, baring their teeth in the orange glow. The small creature was backed up against the rock wall, showing his pup fangs, like little translucent daggers, as the crafty coyotes closed in. The wolf-like creature snapped at a coyote as it came for him, catching the edge of a foreleg and creating a long, bloody gash. The coyote howled and leapt back. The pup was holding his ground, but he was outnumbered and outmatched as the pack of scavengers continued to close in on him.

Tynuk pulled the war club from his satchel, steadying it in his hand as he crouched on the ledge.

Dropping low, he flung himself over the ledge with a fierce cry. When he landed he used his momentum to roll forward. As he righted himself, he used the club to strike one of the coyotes in the head, knocking the creature lifeless against the ground. Tynuk spun to his right, swinging the club in an arc to knock another coyote away into the darkness. He then hit a third as it leapt toward him. The coyotes were beginning to scatter, fleeing down the mountainside, howling in pain. Typical of scavengers, they'd wanted easy prey, not an open fight.

The boy stood, baring his teeth as he gripped the club in his right hand. The light of approaching fires flickered upon his face.

"Kip!" came a call from behind him. The sound was much different than what he had heard before. The boy tried to get a better look at the small beast.

"Kip!" the animal barked again, a hopeful sound.

Tynuk put the war club back in his satchel and showed the beast his open, empty hands. "I'm not your foe, little one," he said, as he stretched his arms toward the creature.

The animal looked at him with silver eyes that cut through to his soul—eyes that seemed to harbor an unexplainable wisdom. The creature took a cautious step forward but showed no sign of fear as he moved toward the boy.

"Come on. We have to go before we get caught in these fires."

"Kip!"

"You can trust me. I'm your friend." The pup moved within arm's reach, nuzzling his head against Tynuk's hand.

"Okay. I have to pick you up. We have to go."

The wolfish pup turned his head as though he understood. Tynuk scooped him up and placed him in his satchel.

As Tynuk climbed back up the rocks to the path, the pup didn't make a sound. His oversize head and front paws hung limp from the opening of the bag. Tynuk stepped back onto the trail and took up a quick pace once more as the mouth of Ash Creek cave came into view.

The rising smoke stung his eyes, making it difficult for him to see. He climbed over the last few boulders and traversed a dangerous narrow ledge to the mouth of the cave. There the air was cleaner, and he heard the faint rush of the stream in the back of the cave, just like his grandfather had told him. He would take the time to fortify his camp later. Tynuk rested the satchel on the cave floor and lifted the wolfish pup, cradling him in his arms. He looked closer at the creature and noticed that he was unlike any animal he had ever seen. He had a long, noble snout surrounded by a shaggy, flowing mane of jet black hair. A patch of silver in the center of his chest stood out like a morning star in the midnight sky. The creature's paws were thick, with sharp claws, more like the claws of a cat than a dog. The boy marveled at the animal.

"What are you?"

"Kip!" the animal responded, tilting his head up to lick the boy in the face.

"Okay," Tynuk said as he patted the wolfish pup. "Well, for starters, you've got to have a name."

The boy thought for a moment as he stepped to the mouth of the cave. Flashes of light bloomed on the horizon, and he frowned, knowing in his heart that each beautiful blossom of light meant the death of millions. He sat with his new friend and thought about what so many people were experiencing at that very moment. In the back of his mind, Tynuk wondered whether the world would ever be the same again. Would people continue on after such an event? Tynuk frowned again and looked at the pup.

"Looks like all we have is each other. The Great Spirit knew I would need a friend, so he sent you to watch over me. We'll call you *Azolja*, which means 'vigilant one' in the ancient tongue."

The boy smiled and patted his new friend.

"We'll be all right, Az. You'll see," the boy whispered.

The two sat in silence, watching the flashes pop and swell along the horizon. A thick blanket of ash fell across the landscape, and from their tower of safety, they looked on in shock and amazement as the world below them died.

✡ ✡ ✡

The two figures lay still against the barren hillside, watching for any signs of movement along the wood line. The teenage boy was growing restless. He pinched his fingers into the dirt and squirmed. They'd been in the same position for quite a while.

"Stop moving and lie still," Kane whispered.

"There's nothing going on here," Jacob whined. "We're wasting our time."

Kane motioned for the boy to be quiet. Jacob rolled his eyes but kept his body still. They needed to be sure, absolutely sure before they pulled the trigger. As Kane searched, moving his eyes left and right, he drew his jacket up around him. The temperature was dropping, and the cold earth stealing away his body heat. A twitch of movement. Kane perked up and pointed his hand to the wood line.

"There," he whispered, beginning to smile. "All good things come to those who wait."

The boy guffawed and pulled up a pair of cracked binoculars, which he used to scan the edge of the woods. At once he froze.

"No way, man! I didn't think any had survived."

"I bet they've done better than we have. They know all the good hiding spots. I told you I saw the tracks. You can't mistake deer tracks. That's why you're here learning from me and not the other way around, Jacob."

Jacob nodded to acknowledge this fact, even though doing so appeared to injure his pride.

Kane met Jacob shortly after the events of Day Forty. Like many of the children that survived, the teen became an orphan when the End War started. Kane noticed that children of a certain age had a higher survival rate than adults during and after the end of the world. He wasn't sure whether this was due to their ability to better adapt to change, or whether their young minds couldn't grasp the full magnitude of what had happened. Many adults who survived just gave up and died. Kane had almost been one of them. The children, on the other hand, viewed the events as just the next thing in life. They seemed to take the devastation in stride.

Beyond the loss of Jacob's family, Kane didn't know much about the boy's past. Jacob refused to talk about it. He just appeared one day with a scavenged emergency radio in his hand. He'd had heard the broadcasts and walked up the coast until he found the station. It surprised everyone when he arrived alone and without supplies—that he could survive that way. Jacob was one of the hardest workers Kane had at the station. He was always lugging something heavy or offering to give someone a hand, and he was always first to volunteer for scouting or scavenging duties. At his core, the boy was a survivor. But one look in his sad eyes gave away the pain in his heart and the tragedy that he already had endured.

Kane had taken the young man under his wing, even though the teen's incessant bravado wore him thin at times. Kane knew that his machismo was simply a defense mechanism designed to distract others from his vulnerability. But to hear Jacob tell it, there wasn't an ass in the world that he couldn't whip.

Kane rolled onto his right side and brought the scoped Marlin lever-action 30-30 up in front of him. He removed his jacket, wadded it up, and placed it behind his elbow to support his shooting position. Looking through the scope, he watched the wood line and saw a slight movement in the brush. He estimated that they were no farther than one 115 yards or so from the wood line.

"Okay. When he comes into sight, we'll give him a kill shot behind the shoulder, and everyone gets deer stew for dinner. How's that sound?"

"Sounds great," said Jacob, noticing the slight rumble in his stomach for the first time that afternoon. Deer stew would be a treat. Jacob pulled the binoculars up again and waited for Kane to shoot.

The thick yet skeletal brush rustled again. Kane and Jacob both gasped as a beautiful six-point buck pushed its way out of the thicket, pausing as its ears twitched.

"He's huge! What do you think he's been eating with everything burned up?"

"Your guess is as good as mine. He must have a secret oasis somewhere," Kane whispered.

Kane took a deep breath and let it out halfway before holding his breath. With a slow, steady squeeze, he began to depress the trigger as he took aim on the great buck. The wind picked up just as the crack of the Marlin echoed across the small valley. The buck flinched and stumbled before darting into the brush.

"You missed! How did you miss him?"

Kane was up and moving, pulling his belongings together. "I didn't miss. The wind threw the shot off. He's hit in the gut."

"We've got to get him. We can't let him get away!" Jacob yelled, jumping to his feet and tearing off down the hillside.

"Jacob! Wait! Don't rush off. We'll have to track him."

"You missed him. Now I gotta clean up your mess. Keep up if you can," Jacob called over his shoulder.

"Jacob, I'm serious. It's not safe to go alone!" Kane yelled, as he pulled the rest of his things together and started down the hillside.

If the teen heard him, he didn't acknowledge it as he disappeared into the woods.

"That impulsive little jackass is going to get someone hurt," Kane swore under his breath. He stomped down the hillside, muttering, and finally reached where Jacob and the deer had disappeared into the thicket. Kane knelt to observe the blood spoor on the ground. At least the round had made a solid hit. The wound was a bleeder, which would make the animal easy to track.

Kane glanced up at the darkening sky and estimated that they had about an hour and a half until nightfall. He needed to find the boy and the kill and get them both back to the station as soon as possible. It wasn't safe to stay out after dark.

Kane had just entered the edge of the dead woods when he heard the hair-raising shriek of the seventeen-year-old.

In the silence and smoke of the dream, the warrior boy stood still before his teacher. The old man looked him over, determining his value. With a tone unaffected by any favor or emotion, his teacher spoke.

"What is it you have learned, Tynuk?"

"I have learned to honor my people and their history in word and deed. I have learned to face my fear and to remove it from my heart through diligent training and meditation. I have learned that the greatest honor is to lay my life down in the name of the Great Spirit. And I have learned to nobly stand and fight against evil, wherever it may lurk."

The old man paused, considering the words of the boy.

"Do you understand that your calling is unique to you? Even our ancestors did not possess the knowledge that you do now—the knowledge of the Great Spirit. This is the source of your greatest strength and the cause that you must defend to your final breath. When the Great Spirit moves in you, you must follow it."

"I understand, Grandfather," Tynuk replied.

"I can tell that you do," said the old man with a wry smile. "Now," he said, as he moved into a defensive stance, "show me what you can do."

A scream in the darkened woods brought Tynuk out of his meditation with a jolt. He sat forward and strained his ears to determine where the noise originated. It had sounded human. Tynuk glanced at his monstrous, shaggy, wolfish companion sitting by his side. The creature's ears perked, twitching as they drew in every sound.

"What is it, Az?" the boy whispered.

Azolja shifted and glanced at the boy before turning back to listen to the woods. The powerful muscles of his torso and legs were visible beneath a flowing mane of black hair that glistened in the light of the fire.

Silence.

They were outsiders—he and the beast. They always had been, and though they frequented the radio station to see Courtland, Kane, and their other friends, they never belonged there. But here, in the silent woods, they found a measure of peace. Here, isolated from everyone else, they both felt at home. Tynuk could sense the Great Spirit moving and pulling him away, but to where he could not yet be sure. He knew that somehow his destiny and those of Courtland and Kane were intertwined, but he also felt that there was something else he had to do. He couldn't yet be sure. It would take much more meditation and a calming of his mind before that purpose could be revealed.

Another sound pulled Tynuk from his thoughts. Someone or something whistled a sharp tune, one that went from high to low, then high to low again, followed by what sounded like a long groan. The sound lingered for a moment before it disappeared into the smoke-shrouded trees.

"Come, Az. Let's have a look, shall we?" said the boy, pulling on his knee-high moccasins and retrieving his newly hardened bow and trusty war club. Tynuk pushed a mound of dirt onto the small fire then patted his fearsome companion on the neck as they both slipped like ghosts through the darkened woods.

# SEVEN

## BEFORE
## COLUMBIA, SOUTH CAROLINA

"Gabrielle!" Dr. Eric Glenn screamed into a poisonous wind as it thrashed his clothes around his thin frame. "Gabrielle, my darling! Where are you?"

Clawing his way across the rubble, where the hospital stood just hours before, Glenn began to sob. He hurled pieces of concrete and brick, digging into the smoldering pile of rubble.

He'd gotten up to use the bathroom. That was the last thing Glenn remembered. He had stood, the warmth of his bed clinging to him as he rose in the early-morning hours, and stumbled his way to the bathroom. As he stood at the toilet, sleep still clouding his eyes, the initial flash blinded him. lightning? His mind spun as he tried to figure out what was happening. Then he heard the sound, a sound like the earth itself had been torn open, swallowing everything from above into its hellish depths. It was the sound of overwhelming destruction.

Glenn had taken one lunging stride toward the bedroom and half of a second step when the blast wave struck the house. Then he was flying, the surface of the floor falling away as he rose, spinning into the fray. Then nothing. He awoke to the pain hours or maybe days later, half buried in the remains of his house with a nasty gash near his rib cage. He emerged into the catastrophe. He could hardly comprehend the sheer devastation of the city around him. Why Columbia? There was nothing in Columbia worth an attack of that scale. Without delay, Glenn gathered his bearings and shifted focus. Nothing else mattered. He had to get to the hospital to find his dear wife. It was for her that he had striven so these last few years. It was all for her. He had emptied his personal savings and had come dangerously close to ruining his professional career only for her.

They were married only three weeks before, the white-hot fire of their love still burning strong when, late one evening, after too many drinks at a colleague's party, they'd plummeted down an embankment off the highway into Willowhatchee Creek. The car was destroyed. Glenn emerged with only a few bumps and bruises, but his dear Gabrielle had sustained significant brain damage and had fallen into a coma—an endless reminder that he shouldn't have been driving in the first place.

Glenn stopped climbing the pile of hospital rubble below him. There were so many bodies, and they all looked the same. The distinction between hospital scrubs and hospital gowns appeared indiscernible amid the dirt, dust, and fire.

"Gabrielle! Gabrielle, where are you?" he sobbed, standing to look in all directions. "Where is everyone? Why isn't anyone helping? There are people in here!"

Scrambling across the debris like a wild animal, Glenn became frenzied, flinging planks and bricks as he searched in desperation for his wife. He continued to cry and call out her name.

He had been close—so damn close. He'd perfected the song with Brutus as proof. The many other trials that followed had all been successful. He had developed tonal commands for action and inaction, commands that stirred the blood and those that calmed the nerves. Glenn could control man's best friend through song. And there were indications—if not evidence—that these songs might work on the feeble or deranged human mind. He hadn't been able to wait. He had to know.

Glenn had gone to her, his Gabrielle. He had known that he could communicate with her, that her fragile mind, despite the brain damage, would understand. If nothing else, he would let her know he was there. She had so loved music. Sitting beside her in the hospital, into the late hours of the evening, he had played the song for her. Waiting until no one was watching, he'd held his phone close to her ear and let her listen to a tune, almost screaming out loud when she shifted in the bed. Adjusting quick he played a soothing melody and saw the corners or her lips turn upward ever so slightly. It was a magnificent revelation. He'd been so close to getting through to her.

Glenn snapped from his train of thought and wiped the tears from his face, turning toward the screams behind him. From a crouched position amid the rubble, he watched as a woman tried to flee from several deranged people. They chased her down and overtook her, beating her into submission. They tore at her clothes and began to rape and abuse her.

It was no longer safe to stay out in the open. He swallowed hard and took one last look around, his heart still aching over his inability to find his wife. But it was time to be realistic. Gabrielle was dead. Even if she weren't yet dead, how could he possibly take care of a comatose woman under such conditions? She would have to sleep wherever she lay. He could only hope that she knew nothing of what had happened. Her temporary rest, uninterrupted, would evolve into eternity. He had to take some measure of comfort in that.

Turning, Glenn slid down the far side of the rubble and picked up a brick to use in self-defense. Going forward, nothing mattered but survival. He had to get to his lab. Everything, all he had left in the world, was there.

☆ ☆ ☆

Glenn stopped just on the edge of a deserted intersection. He scanned the street, looking back and forth. Surveying the area with caution, he pulled himself away from the row of vegetation and crouched low, near the edge of the street. He gave a bout of coughing then vomited a thick, green stream of slimy fluid onto the concrete and wiped his sleeve across his face. He felt as if his guts were dissolving inside him, his organs rearranging themselves in a mad attempt to escape whatever was in his blood.

It had been two days since the attacks, and he was getting sicker. Everyone he saw was getting sicker. Some wandered aimlessly, while others retched green vomit and floundered in the streets. There was something in the air, and a dirty, poisonous ash fell from the sky, burning the skin upon contact. The soot made his skin tingle and his eyes burn. His head, cloudy from the effects of exposure.

The street was clear, its only occupant the endless, drowning smoke of a thousand burning fires. In a movement half concealed by the smoke, Glenn dashed across the street. His torn and tattered clothing whipped against his lean, athletic frame as he ran. He had to get to the lab.

A few minutes later, he made his way up the long drive to the front of the Canine Cognition and Behavioral Labs, or CACOBL, as it was known. Some of the most advanced theoretical medical canine research in the world had been conducted there just weeks prior. Now the formidable structure loomed, a ghost of its former self, partly in shambles though still intact thanks to modern concrete-and-steel construction.

Slipping through a shattered window, Glenn paused to vomit again, his head reeling from a strong wave of dizziness. His health was deteriorating rapidly. His window to act, narrowing. He had to get help and knew where he could find it.

Stopping by his office, he unlocked the fireproof safe and extracted a blue folder that contained copies of his most important research notes and trial data. He stuffed the folder into a satchel next to his overturned desk. After pulling a desk drawer open, he rummaged through some miscellaneous papers and business cards to extract a single photo of his wife. He stroked it with his thumb and placed it in his pocket.

His whole world spinning, Glenn stumbled from his office and down the long corridor. Tiny streams of grayish light pushed through cracks in the walls, his only guide in the darkened hallway. He walked to the end, passing offices that belonged to the company's more abstract, developmental, and theoretical sectors, then entered the medical research wing. He pulled a large, heavy key from his pocket and inserted it into the lock beside a steel door at the end of the hall. His master key—one of the perks of being the facility director—opened every door of every wing in the building, a precautionary measure in the event of total power loss. The bolt slid free, and the massive steel door released and creaked open. It was quiet in the darkness. Glenn stopped and gave his eyes a moment to adjust. This was where they performed medical research in an effort to advance canine development and health. This was where his friend, Dr. Stroph, had been working on something special.

Slipping through the workspaces and past the glassed-in testing facilities, Glenn found himself standing in front of the facility's cold storage.

Another turn of the key opened the door, and a rush of frigid air followed. Despite the pain, Glenn couldn't help smile. Even though the power had been out for a few days and the emergency generators were down, the unit had maintained a near-freezing temperature.

Searching among the glass coolers that housed row upon row of labeled vials, Glenn searched for Stroph's baby. Dr. Stroph was one of the ranking scientists in the facility. He and Glenn had become friends—more like drinking buddies. A few beers after work was usually enough to get Stroph talking about his pet project—a highly advanced protein found only in the brain of the Atlantic shortfin mako shark. Stroph, giddy like a child at Christmas, explained to Glenn how the protein (which he'd nicknamed MAK47) could be synthetically modified and appeared to stop, and in some cases reverse, severe inflammation in canines, especially inflammation of the brain. Stroph claimed that with a little more research they might be able to cure cognitive dysfunction syndrome and encephalitis in canines. He stated that the future potential of the protein appeared extraordinary. He had only just scratched the surface as to how it might be used to help both canines and humans in the future.

Glenn stood in the darkness of the cool room, Stroph's words echoing in his mind as his fingers hovered over the row of five vials marked "MAK47." Whether or not the protein worked on him was irrelevant. He'd die anyway due to exposure to whatever was in the air. He had to do something, and this was his only plan. Maybe, just maybe, the serum would have some positive effect.

Glenn removed the vials from the rack and pulled an injector from a nearby drawer. Taking a deep breath, he locked the first vial into the injector and placed the tip against the side of his neck. At once he injected the protein mixture, as he gritted his teeth against the sting of the needle. A strange numbing sensation spread across his face. He shook his head and looked at the remaining four vials.

"What the hell," he whispered to himself as he ejected the empty vial and inserted the second. Nothing else mattered. He had to survive.

# EIGHT

---

## NOW

Courtland set the small box of scavenged medical supplies on the counter in the makeshift medical bay and glanced around. He had been in that room only a few times since they'd taken up residence at the station. He surveyed the room, noticing that ten of the twelve cots were occupied. Life in the wasteland wasn't easy.

"Hey," Jenna said, interrupting his thoughts as she patted him on the shoulder.

"Jenna. How are you holding up, dear?"

"One day at a time," she said with a small smile. "What do you have for me?"

"Looks like a few boxes of sterile bandages, some antiseptic, painkillers, wound closures, and a few bottles of black water straight from the purifier."

"You're an angel, Courtland. I've known it since the first day we met," she said and kissed his cheek.

"It's not my doing, miss. Can't take the credit. I'm just the deliveryman," Courtland responded, showing a smile of his own. "But pretty girls are allowed to lay a kiss on an old man's cheek any time they like."

"Oh, yeah?" she said, moving to check on one of the patients.

"Yeah," he said, waiting for just a moment before beginning again. "Hey, how's Dagen doing?"

"Dagen is…Dagen. He can be difficult sometimes," she replied. "Why do you ask?"

"I don't know. He's kind of a strange fixture here at the station. To be honest I don't think I've ever spoken to you about him…and what he did…" Courtland trailed off. "I guess I'm asking if you're okay. You give so much, Jenna."

Jenna looked at Courtland with a strange little smile, one that reflected both joy and pain. "I'm okay, Courtland…most times."

"You're an amazing person, and I don't think you hear it enough," Courtland said with a warm smile. "I think it's a wonderful testament to God's love, but don't be surprised if some people don't understand why you look out for Dagen."

"I don't expect anyone else to understand. And it's okay if they don't. I just think he deserves another chance, that's all. Everyone deserves a second chance."

Courtland nodded, running his fingers over a few items in the box in front of him. "I just wanted to check on you. You know, if you ever need anything, you come and get me."

She smiled. "You bet, Courtland. I appreciate it."

Courtland headed toward the door but paused and turned. "Oh, have you heard from Kane or the scavenging party today?"

Jenna shook her head as she checked on one of the female patients. "Not since they all left this morning."

"Right. I just thought they'd be back by now."

Jenna looked up from the woman she was treating. "None of them are back? I thought the scavengers were going to one place while Kane and Jacob went to another?"

Courtland shrugged his massive shoulders. "Neither group has reported back. Nowadays that's not a good sign."

☆ ☆ ☆

Kane forged ahead through the dead brush, branches clawing at his face and tearing at his hands in the fading light. "Jacob!" he called. "Jacob, where are you?" Kane burst through to a small clearing and called out again. "Jacob, if you can hear me, respond!"

"I'm here. I twisted my leg," Jacob called from the bottom of a nearby embankment.

Kane made his way to the ledge and peered down the slope. He saw the teen covered in dirt, lying on his side. "What happened?"

"My knee. I think it's twisted or something. It hurts to try to stand. I've got good news, though," Jacob said.

Kane huffed, making his way down the slope. "What could the good news be?"

"I found our kill," the boy said, pointing off to his left.

The buck was just visible through the trees, the blood loss having forced it to lie down due to exhaustion.

"All right. Come on. Let's get you up," Kane said, as he reached the bottom of the slope. He was in the process of pulling Jacob to his feet when the sound of a snarl caused him to freeze.

Several people, who looked dirty and haggard, entered the clearing on the far side. They moved with caution, focused on the wounded buck. Behind them, several more appeared through the brush, a few of them loping on all fours like gorillas. Kane heard another snarl, followed by a high-pitched whistle. The sound went from high to low, then high to low, followed by a third snarl.

Kane's eyes were wide now as he and Jacob held their position. These weren't people. They were Sicks who had organized themselves into a disciplined group, as though they somehow had come to master their new forms. Moving in an organized pack like this, these mutants seemed a far cry from the madness of the creatures that Kane and the others had encountered in the metro areas less than a year ago.

In a flash, the Sicks converged on the dying animal. The buck cried out in terror and thrashed about as they came at him. With slashing claws and razor-sharp teeth, the Sicks tore the beast apart with an unnatural strength, stuffing greedy handfuls of deer guts into their mouths.

"Oh my G—" Jacob started as Kane clamped his hand over the teen's mouth.

"Quiet! Don't say another word. Get up slow make your way up the hill and back to the Jeep. *Move slow*. If they spot us, we're dead. Do you understand?"

The boy nodded in understanding.

"Now go. I'll cover you," Kane whispered through clenched teeth.

Kane grabbed the Marlin and took a few cautious steps backward up the hill. But the boy was already moving too fast, hopping on his good leg and clawing at the earth. The fear had taken hold, and there was no stopping it now as Jacob scrambled up the hillside. Kane motioned for the boy to slow down and be quiet, but the ear-piercing shriek told him it was already too late.

Kane spun as the Sicks came fast through the underbrush, loping toward him on all fours, hybrids of man and beast. Halfway up the hillside, Kane raised his rifle and fired from his advantageous elevated position. Another scream followed the smack of the brush-busting 30-30 round as it made contact with flesh and bone. The creatures were moving fast, much faster than he remembered.

"Run, Jacob! Get to the Jeep!" Kane screamed, the sound of his own voice lost in the heaving of each labored breath.

Working the rifle's lever action, he took aim on another Sick and fired just as it reached the base of the hill. The round blasted through the front of the mutant's skull, leaving a ragged, red hole the size of a man's fist on the rear side as it exited the creature's brains across the blackened floor of the forest.

There were too many of them. Kane would be overwhelmed if he tried to hold his ground. Turning, he trudged as quickly as he could up the hill before wheeling and firing several inaccurate shots from the hip. In an instant the rifle was empty, and he knew he'd be ripped limb from limb before he had a chance to reload. Reaching the top of the hill, he flipped the weapon over, gripping the hot barrel like a baseball bat as the creatures continued to dash up the hill straight toward him. He bent his knees and bared his teeth, preparing to go up to his eyeballs in them, as his mind began to drift.

*Don't wait for me, Jacob. One of us has to make it back.*

The first Sick cleared the ridge just as Kane slammed the rifle against the monster's head, caving in its skull. As a second reached the top, Kane swung from the left, but his strike was too slow coming from his weak side. He struck the Sick in the chest, causing the monster to howl and latch onto the weapon, tearing the rifle from Kane's grip as it went down. Disarmed of his rifle, Kane drew a straight-blade knife from the sheath on his belt and held it at the ready. A Sick on his left and another on the right cleared the crest of the hill and came at him. The mutant on his left opened its sharp claws as it rushed forward. Kane parried the clawed hand away and swiped at the monster with the short blade. The blade sliced through its neck and lodged in its spine with a crunch, as the beast gurgled and fell to the ground, tearing the knife from Kane's hand. Kane pivoted just as the one on his right slammed into him, sending them both flopping hard against the blackened earth. The creature raised itself up over him, digging with its claws into Kane's flesh as he closed his hand around the mutant's throat and tried to push it away. The Sick snarled a ferocious sound, its gray lips peeling back over sharpened teeth. Saliva foamed from its lips, as the overpowering stench of rotting flesh washed over Kane in waves.

*After everything…this is how it happens.*

Straining, the muscles of his back screaming, Kane pushed the monster away with everything he had, pinching his eyes shut as the vicious, feral mutant bore down upon him.

✫ ✫ ✫

The dark wine cellar had a pungent, rotten odor, much more like death than wine. Shana detected murmurs in the darkness—a laugh, people sweating, the pungent odor of death. Her bare thighs rubbed against each other, and she realized she had been stripped naked. She shook her head and closed her eyes, trying to tell the difference between the darkness of the cellar and the blackness behind her eyelids. The darkness slid over her, causing a shudder to crawl across her skin.

*Where am I?*

"Where…" Shana whispered, beginning to speak her thoughts.

"Shhhhhh," came the reply through the darkness. "Boss wants to talk to you. Until then you keep your pretty mouth shut."

"But—"

Without warning, a slap struck the side of her head, sending a sea of stars across her eyes. She cried out in pain, whimpering in the dark.

"Shhhhhh," slurred the voice again. "I told your stupid ass to be quiet."

Minutes passed—or hours, she couldn't be sure. She clenched her jaw to try to ease the ache. She heard more laughter in the darkness, unseen devils planning their next bit of amusement. After a while, she heard shuffling, followed by a snap and the small fluorescent winking of a battery-powered torch. As the light brightened, Shana began to make out forms, shadows in the musty void around her. The blood-and-brain-soaked floor of the cellar looked brownish red and was covered with a gooey film that stuck to the bottom of her bare feet. Broken skulls and bits of meat littered the floor around her chair.

Shana let out a gasp. "Dear God…"

A massive frame stepped forward. Others instinctively moved away to give him plenty of room, as though they were afraid of what he might do. She could just make out the tattoo of a large, coiled viper in the center of the huge pectoral muscles that hung heavy like cinderblocks in front of her.

"No, God isn't here," spoke the man, his voice like gravel scraping over vocal cords. "And if you even whisper his name again in my presence, I'll tear a hole in your chest and drink what's left of your fragile spirit."

Shana sputtered in terror.

"Got your attention? That's good. You are a prisoner of the Coyotes. How long you remain that way is up to you. I'm going to ask you a series of questions, and you're going to tell me the truth. Any deviation will result in pain and humiliation like you've never imagined. Nod if you understand."

Shana took a moment, breathing in the foul stench of the cellar as she attempted to collect her thoughts. It was coming back to her now—the bandit ambush, Cal without his head, and Mico too. She had not been able to flee.

She shifted in the small, metal chair to which she'd been bound, and her insides revolted. A searing pain worked its way up from her groin and burned into her guts. She had been brutally beaten and raped and was now their prisoner. She took another deep breath then nodded.

"Tell me about where you came from—the radio station."

"Just please don't hurt me anymore. I can't stand the pain."

Malak's lips stretched tight over his teeth, forming a hateful smile as he nodded to the ugly mush-faced man next to Shana. She gasped out loud as Shank giggled and gently traced the outline of her ear and the contour of her jaw with the tip of a knife.

"Then you should answer the question," Malak whispered.

Shana swallowed and wet her lips. "Okay, please. Please. There's about eighty of us," she started, trying to compose herself. "We mind our own business, scavenge what we can, and broadcast to other survivors."

"Who's in charge?"

"A guy named Kane. He's a former cop. He and his friend, Courtland, they kind of run the show together."

"This Courtland is a very large black man?"

Shana nodded.

"Security?"

Shana nodded again. "They have it pretty buttoned up, and they're willing to fight."

Malak smiled. "Oh, I do hope so. How many weapons and resources have they stockpiled?"

"A lot. Just enough water to get by, but a good bit of everything else. Working vehicles, canned goods, fuel, weapons, ammo. It's all easily accessible."

"Good," Malak said, his voice like stale air escaping from a grave. "Now how are you going to help me get in?"

"I...I can't," said Shana, lowering her head. "I mean, you won't get in. They're armed to the teeth. You'll lose a lot of men."

Malak leaned closer, the sinister features of his ruined face becoming more visible in the dim light. She choked back a sob as the tip of the blade slightly entered the skin of her neck, just below her ear.

"Men and *women*...Didn't you hear? You're with *us* now, so I think you'd better find a way to make it happen. Well, it's either that, or I'll let Shank here deglove the skin off your face, and we'll all take bets as to how long you can survive without it."

The crowd snickered.

Shana swallowed hard, but she didn't hesitate. "I'll do it. I'll do whatever. Just don't do that. Please."

"Then accept my blood and worship me as your god," Malak said, as he cut his hand, the wound beginning to heal before he'd finished cutting. He made a fist and squeezed some of his blood across Shana's face. It splattered there, and though she found herself disgusted for a moment as she licked the liquid from her lips, she somehow knew this was her only way out. *Nothing else remains*, she thought, as her eyes began to glaze over with fear and despair.

"I'll worship you, my lord."

✕ ✕ ✕

*Shuck, shuck, shuck, shuck.* The sounds came in rapid succession, mixing with the pitter-patter of fluid slapping onto his face and chest.

"Aaargh," Kane managed as he snapped his eyes open. "What the...?"

The ghoul lay over him, motionless, more like a limp, leather sack of blood and bones than a vicious monster. Its black blood had splashed onto Kane's face and chest. He looked up and saw a roughhewn arrow piercing the creature through its eye and protruding from the back of its skull.

"Get off me!" Kane groaned as he shoved the monster to the side, looking for the one who had delivered him. Three other Sicks lay around him, all dead with arrows protruding from their skulls.

The rest of the mutants crested the hill with a strange, premeditated precision. They seemed to be surrounding and protecting a central figure. Each creature stopped at the hilltop, some swaying, others crouching in anticipation. Kane struggled to see the figure in the center. He scrambled backward, wiping the blood from his face. The creature appeared half-clothed in a primal, savage sort of way. Its eyes were wild, orange slits set into the mottled, gray flesh of its face between pointed ears that jutted away from its domed skull at forty-five degree angles. A strange, carved object of bone—like a flute or a whistle—hung around its neck. Kane saw its sharpened teeth as it let out a vicious growl. The creature pointed right at Kane and its minions turned their whole focus on him.

*Shuck, shuck,* came the sound of two more arrows released in succession as the creature blew a quick tune on the flute. Two ghouls stepped in front of the Sick, each shielding their leader and intercepting an arrow through the skull.

Just as Kane gathered himself and made it to his feet, he heard a wild battle cry. Tynuk, his lean figure clad only in animal skins, dropped from a tree branch above. With his bow slung over his shoulder, the boy slammed his war club into the skull of the Sick below him, launching a spray of black blood into the air.

The group cleaved in two and turned on the boy in a whirl of screaming rage. Kane searched for a weapon but found himself transfixed by the boy as he watched him work. Tynuk moved with incredible precision, ducking and leaping like a cat as he delivered blow after crushing blow to the ghouls with his club. With broken femur here, a shattered jaw there, Tynuk flowed like water among them, moving so fast they could scarcely track him.

The head ghoul flashed a wicked grin of bloodlust as it charged the boy, fast and primal, like a shark on the hunt. It was faster than Tynuk, faster than any creature Kane had ever seen. It caught the boy off guard, tearing a jagged gash through the flesh of his shoulder. Tynuk barely spun away from the worst of the creature's clawed swipe. It slammed into him again, knocking the boy back and into a nearby hillside, where it cornered him.

"Tynuk!" Kane called out, as he snatched his rifle from the ground.

"Go!" the boy yelled. "Get to safety!"

"But—"

"Just go!" the boy shouted.

Using his fingers, Tynuk blew a sharp, high-pitched whistle and braced himself against the hillside. The monstrous, black form of Azolja leaped from the top of the hill and cut through the group with one swipe of his a razor-like paw. Azolja snapped his massive jaws shut just as the mutant leader dove down the hill to avoid the beast.

The battle in full effect, Kane was up and moving, stumbling, dragging himself through the underbrush as fast as his legs would carry him. The skeletal branches tore at Kane's clothes and face as he blindly fled from the horror behind him. Bursting free into the open, he broke into a full run. Jacob and the Jeep were nowhere in sight.

"Jacob!" Kane yelled as he ran. "Jacob!" The Sicks were closing on him from across the field.

Gears grinding, wheels spinning, the Jeep Wrangler, with Jacob in the driver's seat, launched into view, crossing the field toward Kane, fishtailing as it went. Kane was losing ground. The mutants were almost upon him when the Jeep collided with the two closest behind him, carrying their gray, rubbery flesh across the front of the vehicle as it slid to a stop. Kane vaulted into the passenger seat and pulled a Beretta 92FS handgun from in-between the seats.

"Go, go, go!" Kane yelled, as the tires of the Jeep spun and several Sicks slammed into the vehicle's sidewall and tailgate, clinging with wild screams. Kane fired as fast as he could acquire each target. Each muzzle flash briefly illuminating the scowls of hatred on the mutant's faces as they struggled to pull themselves up and into the vehicle in the growing darkness. Kane dropped the magazine and began to reload as the last visible creature crawled through the back hatch of the Jeep.

"It's behind me! Shoot it! Shoot it!" Jacob yelled in hysterics.

"Shut up and focus on getting us out of here!" Kane responded, as he dropped the slide and took aim on the Sick, which looked like an angry goblin as it scrambled toward the front seats. Firing as fast as he could pull the trigger, Kane shouted in victory as the monster's head came apart, its limp frame tumbling backward, sliding lifelessly into the road behind the speeding vehicle.

The bitter wind bit at their faces, and Kane breathed a sigh of relief as he settled back into the passenger seat, dropping the gun across his lap.

"That was close," Kane murmured.

"We did it!" Jacob yelled. "Hell, yeah! That was awesome! We kicked their asses!"

"Just keep driving and don't let up," Kane grumbled, his brow furrowed as he pulled the emergency walkie-talkie from the dashboard and watched the road ahead. "This isn't a damn game, kid."

Courtland lumbered across the open courtyard as the setting sun dipped below the horizon casting the world around him in a murky twilight. The unyielding cloud cover had a way of distorting the time of day, making days appear dim and nights black like pitch. With no moon or stars to travel or work by, and to save resources such as fuel, just about everything at the station came to a screeching halt once night fell. Only a few solar-powered lanterns and torches remained on in the medical bay and with the station lookouts.

Courtland was on his way back from checking the water levels of the purification cisterns. The black-water levels were low, but they were always low. That wasn't the real reason he was wandering about. Courtland knew he should head inside and grab some sleep, but he was worried about the scavenging party, not to mention Kane and the boy, Jacob. There was no reason they should be gone for so long unless something had happened. Courtland couldn't shake the notion that they could have been attacked and injured, or stranded in the dark somewhere. He didn't like it. A true giant, with the superhuman strength of heaven coursing through his body, Courtland Thompson feared little, but at this moment, he feared the loss of a close friend, and that fear gnawed at his guts from a place deep within.

The radio on his waistband blipped and began to fuzz and crackle.

"Cour...shhhhhh...not much...we...shhhhhh..."

Courtland fumbled with the radio, which disappeared in his massive palm, and pulled it from his belt.

"Hello? Kane? Can you copy?"

"Shhhhhh...Court...secur...shhhhhhhh..."

Courtland struggled to adjust the volume, his thick fingers bumbling around the small knobs for a moment before he keyed the radio again.

"Kane, are you OK? You're not coming through. Repeat your last transmission."

With a squawk, Kane broke through with crystal clarity. "Courtland, can you hear me?"

"Yes! Yes, Kane. I've got you. Go ahead."

"We've had a situation," came Kane's breathless voice.

"What's going on?"

"We're coming. Open the gate, and be ready to bar it shut after we get in. Prepare the station to repel an attack!"

"An attack from who?" Courtland replied, the concern heavy on his brow as he waited for an answer. Dagen was blowing the emergency air horn from the roof of the station. Courtland realized he was holding his breath as he listened to Kane's voice break in a wash of static.

"Sicks. *They're coming.*"

Courtland's voice bellowed into the heavy night air as the residents of the station scuttled about, their confusion transforming to fear upon their hearing the words of the giant man.

"All capable men and women, take up position along the fence line. Grab a pike on your way to your position. Children and those incapable of fighting, take cover inside the station."

Frantic, the people moved from the station doors as one of the men handed out makeshift spears and pikes. Jenna, followed by several older women, herded a group of children back toward the station as the headlights of the speeding Jeep crested the hill and descended toward the front gate.

"Open the gate, then prepare to close it!" Courtland yelled, as the nervous guards began to pull the gates open.

The Jeep hit the bottom of the slope with such force that the suspension completely bottomed out. The vehicle bounced and jostled as it shot through the gate, sliding to a stop inside the compound. Kane got out, securing his handgun in the front of his pants, and took a pike from Courtland. Both men headed toward the fence line.

Waving his arm over his head, Kane yelled, "Get all the floodlights on. I want this place to look like it's daytime!"

A moment later the emergency floodlights came on with a snap and a buzz, bathing the entire station in white light.

"Everyone hold your position on the fence. We may be about to repel a group of mutants." Kane was still trying to catch his breath.

The people in the courtyard squirmed at this news. A few swore under their breath. Many at the station had encountered had past experience with Sicks, and most hadn't enjoyed the experience.

"These things can climb like crazy, so we can't let them get over this fence," Kane said. In demonstration he rammed his pike through the chain link several times in succession. "If just one of those things gets in here, it's going to be a major problem for everybody. Keep an eye on the person next to you and give that person a hand if they need it. Use firearms only as a last resort. We don't want to attract any more attention than we have to. That's it. Now tighten up!"

Silence fell over the compound as the group waited with bated breath. Some of the men and women along the fence line fidgeted, wringing their sweating hands. Kane and Courtland watched as several darkened forms came into view, standing on the low ridgeline in front of the station in the fading light. Hunched and feral, the silhouettes swayed shoulder to shoulder, about a few hundred feet up the embankment from the gate. Kane estimated about fifteen of them total. Though fifteen didn't sound like a lot, he knew his group didn't consist of many trained warriors. Those fifteen monsters could tear Kane's people apart if they got inside the walls of the compound.

Kane found himself thinking about Tynuk, hoping that the boy and his companion were alright. Kane resolved to offer his deepest thanks to the boy for saving his life—if he ever saw him again.

A minute passed and then another. The two groups observed each other in total silence, waiting for all hell to break loose. The piercing shriek of an odd whistle broke the stillness. The ethereal sound went from high to low, high to low, a pattern Kane instantly recognized as the same sound he had heard in the woods earlier. The call reminded him of the mutant leader with the bone flute around his neck. It was a battle call, some form of communication.

One by one, at the edge of the light, the shadowed figures drifted from view until only one remained. It was taller than the rest and stood just a little straighter. In fact it resembled a man much more than the rest, and Kane knew it was the same creature he had encountered in the woods earlier. He squinted his eyes at that last dark figure, which stood for a moment longer before disappearing. A collective sigh of relief rose from the crowd.

"Yeah!" the guy named Erickson called out. "They knew not to screw with us!"

The crowd murmured; some laughed while others slapped each other on the back or gave each other hugs. They had avoided bloody conflict with the monsters, and the resulting sense of relief was nearly palpable.

"Well," Courtland said, looking at Kane. "That could have gone worse."

"I don't know." Kane paused as he mulled the scene over in his head. "For a bunch of deranged mutants, that was way too organized, too calculated. They don't act like that—at least they didn't *used* to."

"What do you mean?"

Kane took a long measured breath before he answered reluctantly. "I think they're testing our defensive measures."

# NINE

---

*Chained up like a dog.*

Susan had thought her life couldn't get any worse, but now she knew she'd been mistaken. She moved into a sitting position and adjusted the shackles around her ankles. Though primitive, they were solid steel and were connected to a diesel engine block. The abrasive metal bands constricted and cut small, bloody grooves into the flesh of her ankles when she moved. She leaned to her right and picked up the ceramic bowl, tipping it to her face and probing with her lips for any remaining drops of water. Nothing. She licked her lips and tossed the bowl in frustration. She was chained up like a thirsty dog. At least before, she had maintained some freedom, access to necessities, and most important, access to her children. She hadn't seen them in days. Knowing that Garrett had locked them up somewhere caused her stomach to cramp with nausea.

It had been only a few days since Saxon caught her trying to call for help from Garrett's truck, but it felt like an eternity. Seeing the knife to her son's throat had caused her to squawk like a parrot. Now her captors knew everything. They knew about the radio station just up the coast, that the group there controlled significant resources, and that Kane, her husband, was with them. And now that she and her children had become prisoners, Susan feared they somehow would be used as leverage against Kane, used in some plot of extortion. Her future was becoming bleaker by the moment, and now she had endangered her children and her dear husband, who didn't even know they were still alive. She had no idea how things would play out. What she did know deep in her heart was that Garrett had no intention of releasing her. Not as long as he lived.

✲ ✲ ✲

Kane pushed through the doors into the medical bay and made his way across the room to the teen lying on his back on a cot. Kane smiled and gave Jenna a wave as he passed. Jacob roused at his approach.

"How's it hanging, tough guy?"

Jacob smirked. "Shouldn't you be watching for monsters?"

"I've got plenty of people on watch for now. The Sicks seem to have taken off, so I figured I'd come and check on my stubborn teen. What's the status?"

"Knee hurts, but I've been worse."

"Yeah, well, considering you could have been mutant food, I think you're doing all right." Kane chuckled and patted Jacob's shoulder. "Still ugly as sin, but all right."

"Whatever," said Jacob, rolling his eyes.

"It would've been nice to bag that buck, though."

"Too bad you screwed up the shot."

"Sure, sure. You stumbling into a drooling pack of vicious mutants had nothing to do with losing that kill."

Jacob shrugged and smiled.

"Better luck next time, eh? I just wanted to check on you and wish you a speedy recovery, bud."

Kane turned to leave but was stopped by Jacob, who grabbed his jacket. "Kane, we mess with each other a lot and don't say a lot of serious words…"

"Yeah."

"I screwed up today. I shouldn't have run off like that. I could have gotten us both killed."

"Yeah, you're right," Kane smiled and tousled the teen's hair. "But one thing about being a kid is you can do some seriously stupid stuff and get away with it."

"It's just…" the boy started, his words tangled in his throat. "You fought those things so I could get away…and…that's about the best thing anyone ever did for me."

Kane rested his hand on Jacob's shoulder. "That's what friends are for."

"No, that's something more. And if you ever need me, I'll be here for you too."

"I appreciate that, buddy." Kane winked. "Now get some rest."

"I will—if you get some target practice."

"Yeah, sure." Kane rolled his eyes and turned to walk over to Jenna.

"Hey," she said, as he walked up. "I put Jacob on ibuprofen for the swelling. I think his knee is just twisted."

"Yeah, well, his snarky little attitude is still intact."

"What do you expect?" Jenna said, smiling. "He's seventeen."

"I know, right?"

"Did you need something else?"

"Yeah, I do actually. Courtland and I would like you to sit down with us to talk about a few issues tonight. Would you be up for that?"

Jenna made a face. "What kind of issues?"

"Just stuff that affects all of us here at the station. We'd appreciate your opinion."

Jenna nodded. "Well, yeah, sure. I can do that."

"I'd appreciate it," Kane said, as he made his way to the medical bay doors. "The main office in ten minutes."

✵ ✵ ✵

Kane entered the main office to find Courtland already seated in the warm glow of a multi-fuel lantern. Courtland was busy cleaning his pocketknife with a ragged handkerchief. As Kane approached, Courtland kept his head down, continuing to focus on the blade in his hands.

"Hey, big man," Kane said as he sat down.

"Mr. Lorusso."

"Look, I feel the need to apologize for the other morning when I snapped at you about always having the answers...or something. It was rude of me. I'm sorry."

Courtland looked up from the knife. "What brought this about?"

"I dunno. I guess since I almost got killed today, I realized I would've died having been a jerk to one of the only people in this world who still cares about me."

Courtland smiled. "It *was* a little rude."

"Well, I'm done groveling, so take it for what it's worth."

"You were stressed. Fair enough. Apology accepted," Courtland said, folding his knife up. "Speaking of almost getting killed today..."

"Yeah?"

"What happened?"

Kane sighed and rubbed his eyes. "Long story, but I was with the kid—"

"Jacob."

"Yup. And we had a buck, man. A buck! He was gorgeous. Who knows how it survived, but it was there, right in front of us. I took the shot, the wind gusted, the buck flinched, and it took a bullet in the gut. The kid is impulsive, so he took off after it, slipped down a hill, and twisted his knee."

Courtland huffed.

"Yeah, so we stumbled right into a bunch of Sicks. Right into them. And man, these aren't the monsters I remember. They've adapted or evolved or something. They're more organized and methodical and more...human—if devolving and re-evolving again is a thing. I sure as hell don't know."

"Humph," Courtland mumbled, deep in thought.

"I don't know, Court. I was scared to death. There was one that was leading them or controlling them or something. It was very strange. And they had us, man. They had us..."

"Well, what happened?"

"Tynuk happened," Kane answered, his tone matter-of-fact.

Courtland smiled. "The boy is impressive, isn't he?"

"I almost didn't run—I was so busy watching him work. That kid has to be seen to be believed—that beast of his too. Those two are something else."

"Sounds like it. Are they okay?"

"I sure hope so. They saved our skins. I need to thank them for that."

Courtland nodded. "I'm sure they're fine. Like you said, he's pretty incredible."

"I remember when I met them for the first time when you and I were captured that time," Kane began, a smirk on his face.

"With Vincent's group?"

"Yeah, man. I didn't know what to think of them. And now here they are, saving my life."

"And what was it you said about the Sicks being led or...controlled?"

"I can't explain it. They all protected this one like he was a commander or something. And just now, up on the hill, he was there. He was the last man standing on the ridge, with the whistle and all."

"Whistle?"

"Right. That whistle we heard when they took off, I heard it before in the forest. It was some sort of bone flute or whistle. He uses it to communicate or to control the others, to get them to form up or attack or retreat."

"But weren't they like zombies?"

"Yeah, but don't use that term. It's misleading. They're nothing like Hollywood zombies. Plus now they've changed like I said. Evolved or mutated into something else."

"Like what?"

"Man, I don't know. I guess more like feral ghouls...or like—and I'm being deadly serious—goblins out of one of those *Lord of the Rings* movies."

"You're kidding."

"No, definitely not. I can't explain it to you."

The two men sat in silence for a long moment before Courtland spoke again.

"And you think tonight they were testing our defensive measures?"

Kane nodded. "I do."

"Why?"

"To hit us later, when we're weak, sleepy, distracted. I don't know."

"You think they're that calculated about it?"

"It scares me to death, but yeah, I do."

"Only time will tell, I guess. Let's hope you're wrong, for everyone's sake."

Kane nodded. "And what was the deal with Mico's search party?"

Courtland shrugged. "They never came back."

"Nothing? No radio contact? No idea at all about what happened?"

"I did send a scout, Greg, out on a dirt bike. He checked the area but couldn't locate anyone. No truck, no goods, no Mico, no group. All Greg found was a pool of blood in the middle of one of the streets, but no bodies or anything."

"Could be anything—bandits or Sicks—but that doesn't mean the blood even belongs to our people."

"Sure. But what if it does?"

"What are you getting at?" Kane said, adjusting his position in the seat.

"I can't shake the feeling that the blood is theirs—or what's left of them."

"And...?"

"Kane, have you considered that it could be the Coyotes?"

Kane's eyes grew wide. "Malak's Coyotes?"

Courtland nodded.

"Oh come on, Court. I don't think so. That freak show and his goons are gone."

"You think so, Kane? He was a gangster. We wrecked everything he built. Not to mention the fact that he had some sort of demon living inside him. You've got to think he'd want revenge for that kind of offense, for what we cost him."

"Assuming he's alive somehow."

"He's alive. We never saw a body."

Kane chewed the thought over before shaking his head. "I don't think that's it. It's much more likely that if something happened to our people, it was totally random."

"I just can't shake it."

"You actually think it's him—or them? The Coyotes?"

"Kane, I have this unnerving feeling that Malak wants us. Like he's going to come for us again."

"How do you know?"

"I don't know. I just…I feel it, like an ache in my bones."

Kane remained silent.

"When I tangled with it, with him, upstairs, I could feel Malak's desire like a sickness in my heart. It wanted to corrupt, to destroy. More than anything, it wanted to see us dead—or worse, to make us slaves to the darkness. I just think that if he is alive, he wouldn't give it up that easily."

"I understand what you're saying, but right now I'm not sure it's really a concern. We've got other priorities—"

"Other priorities? This is the guy who murdered Molly."

Kane froze, the blood draining from his face. He felt exhausted, frustrated. "You think I don't remember that?" he said. "She died in my arms! You think I forgot? That I could ever forget *that*?"

Courtland put up his hand, an act of submission. "Look, brother, I'm sorry, but we need to consider this to be a serious possibility."

Kane took a few deep breaths to compose himself. "Sure," he said, glancing over his shoulder as the office door opened. "We'll talk about it later." Kane turned toward Jenna and Dagen as they approached.

"Hey, um…" Kane motioned toward Dagen with a questioning look.

"I invited him," Jenna said.

"Okay, but we're going to talk about some sensitive stuff. I don't think Dagen should sit in."

"Why not?"

"I just don't want him to sit in on this, that's all."

"Hey," Dagen broke in. "You can talk to *me* since I'm in the room. Talk to my face instead of behind my back like you usually do."

Kane's tone darkened. "Yeah, fine. So I don't trust you. You've been allowed to live here because certain people vouch for you," he said, glancing at Jenna. "Why? I have no earthly idea, especially after what you did."

"Kane—" Jenna started when Dagen stopped her.

"No, no. Let him say it. It's what everyone's thinking anyway."

Kane looked around the room then raised his hands. "Am I wrong? This guy is a sadistic piece of scum, and you want him here with us. Nobody else has a problem with this?"

The room was silent except for the droning, constant hiss of the lantern.

"I'm not that person anymore," Dagen said quietly.

"Come on," Kane scoffed, rolling his eyes.

"You can trust me. I can help. Give me a rifle on the roof. I'm an expert marksman, and if we get attacked by—"

"Give you a rifle? Are you serious?" Kane all but shouted. "You want me to give a known sociopath a rifle and set him loose so he can—what? Kill and abuse more women and children?"

"What the fuck is your problem?" Dagen snapped.

"My problem is you didn't die when I knocked your sick ass over that railing!"

Silence. The usually insignificant creaks of the station seemed deafening amid the heavy silence. The weight of the moment threatened to crush them into non-existence until, with a whisper, Dagen spoke.

"You're right," he said, his dark eyes surveying shattered legs. He gripped his crutches with white knuckles, turned, and hobbled toward the door. "Losing my legs wasn't enough. I should have died. I *wish* I had died. I'm sure that would have made life a lot easier for everyone."

The door squeaked open and hissed shut, closing behind Dagen. Jenna wheeled on Kane in a flash of anger that caught him and Courtland by surprise.

"What *is* your problem?"

"What?"

"You. What is it with you?"

"Why are you defending this guy? After he—"

"He what?" Jenna flushed, her eyes welling up.

"Look at what he did—"

"You have no idea what he did, what he took from me! You don't get to talk about it!"

"I just—"

"I bet you think people can't change. How's that for a stereotypical cop perspective, huh? Criminals don't change. They can never change."

Kane was flailing, grasping at straws when he realized he'd begun to smirk. By then he couldn't stop the words that came out of his mouth. "Seeing criminals reform hasn't exactly been my experience, sweetheart, no."

"But you can change, can't you?

Her words stung. He felt his face burn in shame.

"Isn't that right? You can be saved. Take on a mission from God and be the guy with all the answers. But you can't give another human being the chance to become something better—maybe not perfect, maybe still broken, but better."

"I—"

"No!" Jenna jabbed her finger inches from Kane's face. "No. You think about your words before you talk to me again," she said, as she turned and pushed through the office door and into the hallway.

The hissing of the lamp grew louder as the pressure waned and the fuel ran low. Kane looked at Courtland. "Did you just see that? I've never seen her so...What am I supposed to do with that?"

Courtland rose with a groan from the table, a great sadness blanketing his features. He lumbered toward the door. "I don't know, boss. I don't have all the answers, remember?" He squeezed through the doorway and into the dark hall.

In the dying light of the lamp, Kane lowered his head.

In the hallway beyond, a desperate, crippled, ex-sociopath clinched a small silver cross in his fist and wiped a tear from his face as he turned and hobbled toward the lonely, windswept rooftop of the station.

# TEN

---

"We're leaving."

The voice to Courtland's left caught him by surprise as he exited the side doors of the station and moved into the courtyard. Courtland had been so deep in thought that he almost hadn't heard the young voice.

"Tynuk? You're okay. The gate is barred. How did you...?"

Tynuk pointed to the fence line. "It's not as secure as you think. There are ways in if one knows what to look for."

Courtland frowned.

"It's true, and it's something you should look into if you don't want unexpected visitors."

Courtland nodded. "I'll have the fence checked." he paused. "I heard about you helping Kane and Jacob today in the woods. That was a noble thing to do."

Tynuk nodded. "They were in a bad spot. To not help would have meant the death of them both."

"Kane was very grateful. You should probably hear it from him, but he wanted to thank you."

The boy gave a curt nod.

"So what is this, about leaving?"

"We are, Az and I."

"But why? Where will you go?"

"It's hard to say exactly, but the Great Spirit is calling us west to find my people."

"Your people?"

"My father's family. They are Comanches. They never abandoned the old ways. The Great Spirit has told me they still live, west of here in the home of the ancients."

Courtland didn't try to hide his confusion. "But...I thought you were of the Shoonai warrior tribe?"

Tynuk's face blossomed red as he shook and lowered his head. "I made that up."

"Oh. Well, then, where did you learn—"

"Courtland, can I be honest with you?"

"Of course."

"You can't tell anyone this," Tynuk said, giving him a stern look.

"I promise."

"I grew up in a trailer park in North Carolina. My dad left us years ago, and my mom was a drunk. My father's uncle was the only one who was ever good to me. He taught me the old ways, how to survive, how to fight, and how true men carry the Great Spirit in their hearts."

Courtland's surprise was visible.

"I have to go and find the rest of my family if they're still alive. It's all I have left."

"So what does this mean for all of us?" Courtland's smile had a tinge of sadness.

Tynuk took a deep breath. "It means eventually we must all leave. The rest will be revealed in the journey."

Courtland put his hand on the boy's shoulder. "Such faith and wisdom for someone so young. How long until you go?"

"We'll leave in the morning. I just wanted to tell you I consider you a true friend, Mr. Courtland. And I'll continue to honor our agreement," the boy said, his head barely reaching the big man's waist.

Courtland knelt and looked into Tynuk's dark-brown eyes. "We'll miss you terribly. You and Azolja are invaluable friends to have in times like these."

Tynuk looked up at Courtland. "Tell everyone goodbye for us."

"Not goodbye. We'll see each other again."

"I believe we will, sir, for as sure as night leads to dawn, our purposes are connected," Tynuk said, placing his hand on Courtland's arm. "I am sure of it."

The boy gave a wink and turned. Courtland nodded with a smile of assurance then directed his eyes upward.

"Go with them, Father, and be their shield, for they go in your name and for your sake," Courtland whispered, as he watched the boy's silhouette disappear into the solemn night. "To God be the glory, forever and ever."

☆ ☆ ☆

Dagen stood at the edge of the station roof, his thoughts far away, his clouded eyes surveying the horizon as though he were lost, searching for a way back home. The toxic sea breeze picked up, whipping across the roof and cutting through his clothes. A tremor shuddered through him.

They were right. Dagen had tried to reform himself, and even though he felt different, his heart was still broken and in need of something. The sick person he had been was gone, though his once dark heart haunted his dreams and threatened to steal him back.

*Don't stray too close to the edge.*

Dagen stood dangerously close, but it wasn't a fall from the roof that scared him. He feared what would happen next. What would be waiting for a man like him? A man for whom there was no such thing as true redemption. The hands of the grave—of those who had acted in violence against the innocent, the hands of those who had gone before him—reached up to pull him down to where he belonged.

Dagen hated Kane, but he understood him and why he had said what he did. He took a deep breath as he peered over the edge. He knew he was a monster, and the only way to cure a monster was to destroy it. He closed his eyes and slowly shifted forward, leaning out over the chasm.

"Stop," spoke a voice from behind him.

"No," came his mumbled reply as he shifted farther forward. Dagen felt calm, serene, better than he'd felt in a long while. He let his crutches fall and felt gravity begin to take hold, as he moved into nothingness.

"Stop it!" came the voice from behind him. A hand grabbed him by the collar and jerked him backward and down.

"Don't stop me!" Dagen yelled, furious, as he slid on his back across the gravel.

"This isn't funny, Dagen!" Jenna cried from above him.

"Do I look like I think it's funny?" he yelled, tearing her hand from his jacket. "Let me go! I'm not worth saving."

"It's not that easy. You don't get to just give up."

"Why not? It's my life. You can't choose what I do with my life."

"*Yes, I can!* You owe me a life—three to be exact—and you're going to repay me with yours. But not like this."

"What are you saying? Why do you even care? Kane is right. After what I've—"

"Stop. We're through talking like that. Yes, you and the rest of them took everything from me. It's not a secret between us. But now…the rest of your life begins now. God loves you, Dagen. I told you the day you shattered your legs—his son died for you."

Dagen laid his head back on the rooftop and pursed his lips. "I can't accept that."

"I'm not asking you what you want. I'm telling you what the God of the universe wants. And what he wants is your life, your devotion."

Dagen blinked hard as he sat up.

"No, I don't believe in God. I can't repay you—"

"You're right. You can't pay for what you've done, but you can trust in a God that is big enough to save even you from yourself. This is the only way. You have to trust me."

"I said no!" Dagen's voice rose. "Now get away from me! You and God can go pity someone else!" He shoved Jenna back and turned his face away.

The salty ocean wind whistled across the rooftop. Jenna wiped her face and made it to her feet.

"Okay," she whispered. "I'll give you some space, but you're not going to kill yourself."

"Try and stop me," Dagen muttered, as he continued to look away.

"I will." Jenna gathered the crutches and set them down next to him. "I haven't given up on you yet."

"I'm a monster."

"You're a man. You're the only man I have left," she said, turning toward the rusted stairwell.

Dagen raised his hand as if to stop her, but he was unable to find the words. Jenna opened the door and disappeared down the stairwell. He gathered himself and pulled his crutches beside him, struggling to return to a seated position. A strange, foreign feeling came over him. It came on sharply, the warmth of it spreading across his belly like a shot of whiskey. And though he never had felt it before, his instincts told him what it was.

*Hope.*

Dagen winced at the strange sensation and placed his hand on his chest as the bizarre warmth flowed over him, causing his skin to tingle. It was just a single word, a seemingly insignificant spark, the fewest embers of hope kindling in the darkest of men.

# ELEVEN

Tynuk yawned as he jammed the last few items into his satchel. With a thin stick, he stirred the coals of the fire. His fierce, shaggy companion still slept, making small purring sounds like a house cat dozing in the warm sun. The beast had a faint tinge of crimson around its jaws, an indication that he'd recently killed and eaten something.

*Whatever it was, he didn't save any for me.*

The boy winced as he touched his shoulder. It had swollen up a bit. The gash wasn't as deep as he first believed; it was deep but it wasn't to the bone. Tynuk had neither the materials nor the desire to stitch the wound closed. Instead, he rubbed a thick coat of sticky salve from a chewed-up Echinacea root into the wound. Grandfather taught him that his people used echinacea for its anti-inflammatory and antimicrobial properties. Tynuk had identified the nearly barren stalks of a few charred flowers. Digging into the soil, he'd located several intact roots that would serve him well.

The mutant had nearly gotten the best of him. Tynuk knew he was faster, smarter, and better trained than those freaks. But that one, the leader, had seemed more...human. The speed with which he moved was nothing short of stunning. The attack had been so unexpected that Tynuk had been on the defensive right from the start. He hadn't expected that kind of speed and skill from a mindless mutant, and it made him question how mindless the creature actually was. Had it attacked out of some animalistic need to kill? Or was it something else—something more calculated?

They had prevailed. That was what was important, not the details. A person could go crazy picking apart every shortcoming, every misstep in battle. The point was they had been victorious. The Sicks, as Kane called them, had fled. Tynuk worried, though, that the creatures would press the fight and attack the station. If he and Az weren't around to help, the people could be in great danger.

Tynuk shook his head. "No," he whispered to himself, "their fate is not your responsibility. You must follow the Great Spirit and trust that the rest is accounted for."

He lay down on the pallet, his bed for the night, and placed the war club by his side, where it would be easily accessible in the event of an ambush. In the light of the dying embers, his eyes began to adjust to the darkness. The occasional bit of starlight twinkled beyond the thick cover of clouds above, specks of light shining for just an instant before being snuffed out again. It lifted Tynuk's spirits to know that no matter how thick the clouds appeared and how much they suppressed the earth, the stars continued to shine above. No amount of darkness could stop the shining of the light.

The warrior boy's eyes grew heavy as he listened to the light snoring of his wolfish companion. He tried to remember his mother's face. He had loved her so, but in the end, he had abandoned her to die with the rest of the world. He wanted to tell her of his sadness and to see that she understood. He had acted on grandfather's wishes. He had done it for the future for his people.

As he drifted off, he began to dream of his relatives, imagining what they must be like. The boy slid away into the realm of dreams and fantasy, his distant family appearing before his eyes.

There they were, their skin golden, their chests proudly pushed forward as they stood atop the ancient stronghold, the Caprock Escarpment. The one-thousand-foot sheer cliff face extended for two hundred miles and separated the Llano Estacado, the plateaus of West Texas and New Mexico from the lower eastern plains. An almost impregnable fortress of stone, it had been used for centuries by the Native American tribes of the region, especially the Comanche.

Tynuk waved at the noble warriors, men he had never met, as they beckoned him forward. He took one step and then another, a great smile spreading across his face as he began his great homecoming, a reunion of blood, family, and purpose.

Screams echoed in the dark, the cries for help driving Kane forward in wild, reckless strides. The dark forest burned around him, the ash falling in clumps, obscuring his already poor night vision. Kane raised a hand in front of his face to shield himself from the heat, the smoke pulling tears from the corners of his eyes as he ran.

"Where are you?" he yelled into the flickering flames and smoke. "Susan, Michael, Rachael, if you can hear me, I'm here."

Muffled sobs were choked out by the burning forest as it closed in on Kane, smothering the light of hope in his heart.

"Susan!" Kane screamed as the ash fell like dirty snowflakes, covering the black, fiery landscape.

"Answer me! I'm here! *Please!*" He cried in desperation, as the burning trees appeared to reach toward him, their bony fingers digging at his soul as he tried to preserve the dying light of hope inside. "I haven't forgotten you!" he screamed, as the burning forest finally smothered him, blocking out all hope.

Kane woke, calling out to the empty room, "I'm here!" but the silent room refused to answer, the silence echoing words unsaid. His frustration and fury erupted like molten lava and ash launched from its crater into the atmosphere as he shot from the bed and grabbed his cot and slung the metal frame against a nearby wall.

*"Get out of my head! I can't take this anymore!"*

A shock of pain sent Kane falling to the floor. His heart wrenched inside him. Kane grabbed at his chest and gritted his teeth.

"Argh! What is it with this? Why now?"

The pain slowed and subsided, and Kane stood, huffing labored breaths as the cot rattled against the wall. "Why is the pain coming back?" he whispered to himself, standing alone in the dark.

Kane heard more screams echoing in the night. He shook his head and exhaled as they continued. It took him a moment to realize that the sounds weren't in his head. The cries for help reached out to him from outside the station, where the night guards kept watch.

*The night watch!*

Before he knew what he was doing, Kane had grabbed his Glock, stepped into his boots, and flown from his room down the dim hallway. "Courtland!" He yelled. "We have a situation!"

Kane burst through the fire exit and onto the metal catwalk of the second floor, scanning the courtyard below. He saw shadows struggling in the dark and heard muffled cries for help, followed by a gurgling sound. He ran for the stairs, jumped to the landing, and spun to take the last set in one leap. He hit the turf, and the scene unfolded before him, the night playing tricks on his eyes, causing him to question what he saw.

Thin lines of fresh blood littered the courtyard, ribbons of red in stark contrast to the dirt. One sentry was down, a long balloon of red leading from his throat. The sentry's eyes locked upward toward the unforgiving sky, his deathly silence begging for mercy that wouldn't come. As Kane neared the center of the commotion, his eyes centered on the form of one man hunched over a second man. The cries for help, replaced by a wet, slurping sound.

An air horn sounded in three short blasts as a generator cranked to life and the lights snapped on with a buzz. In the growing light, the hunched form froze. Its clothes appeared torn and ragged by time and abuse. At once the creature spun and locked eyes with Kane. It was a Sick, the blood of the dead men pouring down the gray flesh of its face. The monster snarled, flashing its bloodstained teeth as it released its victim and leaped at Kane.

In an instant Kane's many years of police training, intended to develop his combat motor skills and maximize his efficiency in moments of critical stress, engaged. Before even he knew what had happened, his weapon was in front of him, the mechanics of point shooting automated by his hardwired muscle memory. The handgun blazed in a fast and devastating three-round burst, at the end of which he settled into a combat shooting stance. The rounds had a zipper-like effect from abdomen to chest to head as each landed a critical strike. The freak fell limp midair and tumbled against the earth, sliding in a trail of black blood that ended at Kane's feet.

As the light continued to swell from the compound's floodlights, Kane took two steps away from the creature and resumed his combat stance. He swept his eyes and his weapon left and right, scanning for possible threats. He heard a howl of anger followed by the hiss of a Sick as it launched from the shadows, fleeing through a hole in the torn fence.

Kane fired his weapon as he tracked the monster, but it was moving so fast that he had trouble getting a bead on it. Rounds zinged over his head as men fired their rifles from the catwalk and the inhabitants of the station poured into the courtyard.

"Don't let it escape!" Kane yelled, as he took several more careful shots, the cacophony of gunfire rattling his eardrums.

After a moment Kane raised his hand, signaling for the group to cease-fire. He stood, loaded a fresh magazine, and holstered a ready weapon. He looked at the people of the station; their eyes were wild, sleepy, and distressed—a look that comes from being torn from one's place of rest by a moment of violence.

"I got him," a man with a rifle called from the catwalk. "Think I just winged him, though."

Kane nodded and gave a wave of his hand as he nudged at the dead Sick before him. He took two steps over the creature and moved to the side of the downed sentry, its victim. The man shivered and clutched at his throat and chest as blood poured from his wounds.

Kane took the man's hand. "Eric, right?"

The man gave a slight nod.

"I'm sorry, bro, real sorry. Can you tell me what happened?"

"Gup...ugh," the man sputtered. "Caught us by surprise..."

"Go on," Kane urged, gripping the man's hand.

"Don't know...out of nowhere...all over us."

"How many?"

"Two, maybe. I couldn't...save...Jeremy."

Kane glanced to his right, to the first man he'd seen, as Courtland and a few others approached. "You did your best. You did just fine. They're gone now."

"I'm sorry, Katie...sho...shorry..." The man gurgled, then grew still, his grip on Kane's hand loosening.

Kane lowered his head and patted his free hand against the man's chest. "Rest easy, friend."

Courtland spoke from behind Kane. "Do we know who Katie is? Is she here?"

Another man watching shook his head. "His wife. I think she's been gone a while now...since the beginning."

Everyone nodded in silent understanding.

"They got in through the fence," Kane said as he pointed. "Over there."

"It's my fault," Courtland muttered. "I knew about it. Tynuk was able to get in and out unseen. I told him I'd have it repaired in the morning."

"An costly oversight," Kane said, rubbing at the aching center of his chest. "Well, it looks like no sleep for us tonight. We need every able-bodied person out here. We have to properly fortify this place right now."

One of the men standing close by spoke up. "But this was just an isolated incident, right? I mean those things don't think. They can't reason, right?"

"I'm afraid you're wrong," Kane said, taking in a deep breath. "These two were scouts. They're testing us."

The man faltered. "But...I mean, what do they want from us?"

Kane looked the man square in the face, his tone grave. "Friend, they don't want anything *from* us. They want *us*."

✳ ✳ ✳

Dawn broke over the gypsy camp in shades of gray. Bits of light strained to breach the thick canopy, the flicker so brief it hardly seemed to exist. Susan sat up on her pallet on the floor of Garrett's tent. As she tried to swallow, dust mixed with her saliva and stuck in her throat like a spoonful of peanut butter. She pressed her tongue against the roof of her mouth, trying to release the blockage. She coughed and righted herself, attempting to remember the last time she had left the tent. It felt like an eternity. The bucket of her stale urine and feces sat in the corner of the tent, a sour reminder of her imprisonment.

The tent flap opened to reveal Garrett's roguish form. He stepped into the tent and glowered at her, his long, black hair hanging loose, partly shielding his eyes and bearded chin.

"Up and at 'em, woman."

"My name is Susan."

"Not anymore. Now you're just 'woman.' You don't have feelings, or a family, or a life. You don't have that stuff anymore. You are my property, and that's all you are." He moved closer to her, crouching. "You know, I thought we had something…good. Turns out you only care about yourself and those bastard kids of yours. It seems you like to spit in the face of my generosity."

"Garrett, where are my children?"

"Where are my children? Where are my children?" he mocked her in a girlish tone. "That's exactly what I'm talking about. Selfishness. You never ask me what I want, do you?"

"That's because you just take what you want. You always have."

"Aw, sugar. You know you like it. How about a quick one?" Garrett said, stroking the outline of her face with his fingertips.

"How about you go to hell?"

Garrett grabbed a handful of Susan's hair and a vicious yank backward, as she cried out in pain. At once he was close to her, whispering in her ear.

"You should show me some fucking respect, woman. I'm the only thing that stands between your kids and Saxon—and the things he would do to them. I personally don't approve, but I suppose every man has his vices."

"Please, Garrett, please…I'm sorry. Don't let him hurt them."

"Don't worry, honey. He won't hurt them. He *loves* children."

"Please, please…I'll do anything."

Smiling, Garrett released her hair and stroked her face again. "That's better."

"Tell me they're okay, that you'll keep them safe."

"They're okay—for now. How long they stay that way depends very much on how…compliant you choose to be," Garrett said, a lusty smile pouring over his face.

Susan nodded as she wiped a tear from her face. "Alright. I'll do what you want. Can I please have some water first?"

Garrett tossed her a plastic water bottle that contained a few ounces of lukewarm water. As she gulped it down and coughed, he surveyed her with indifferent eyes.

"Now tell me your name."

"Su—" She paused, glancing at him before lowering her eyes. "Woman" she whispered ashamedly.

"That's my girl." Garrett leaned in and licked the side of her face. He pulled down her shoulder strap and slipped his hand across her breast.

At that moment Susan knew with poignant clarity that there would soon come a day when she and her children would be free, and the blood of this disgusting man would be on her hands.

# TWELVE

## BEFORE

Dr. Eric Glenn crouched low, hunched over the form of the man he'd just killed. He'd stashed his belongings in the corner of the ruined Jeffy's gas station, thinking they'd be safe. After all, he had been gone only a few minutes to scavenge the area for goods. When he returned he found this stinking, feral piece of shit going through his stuff. The ambush happened like a predator on the hunt, and he'd overpowered the sick man with his superior speed and strength right away, crushing the violator's head against a wall.

*Not the hands. Don't hurt the hands.*

Glenn stroked the dead man's long, slender hand and lifted it to where he could see it better. Yes, the third metacarpal bone, the longest bone of the middle finger, would do just fine. Glenn reached for a knife next to his satchel, picked it up, then dropped it immediately. He tried again, his deformed hands failing at trying to hold on to the thin knife. His body was changing.

It had been two months, and as far as he could tell, Stroph's protein mixture, MAK47, had taken some effect. He could still think and reason, and apart from a growing haze concerning his memories, his recollection abilities seemed intact. The serum also had given him great strength and speed, heightened abilities he hadn't known before. Some remnant of the mako shark now lived within him.

The other infected hadn't fared so well. Some element of the exposure had caused their brains to hyperinflame and degenerate. At best they were capable of only the most basic, primal mental functions. Most had resorted to shuffling around and chasing down the poor bastards who couldn't run fast enough.

Glenn did experience some negative side effects. Some days were better than others. The fog of old memories and bits of hard-earned knowledge seemed to remain, but his mind became more clouded with each passing day. Glenn feared that he might have slowed the effects of the infection but not stopped them. Such was evidenced by the grayish flesh of his body, which continued to deform, each day becoming more grotesque.

"Hungryyyy," he spoke in a voice like a churn of gravel, foreign even to his own ears. Instinctively he slashed a strip of bloody meat from the back of the dead man's thigh. He stuffed it into his mouth, chewing with methodical strokes of his jaw as he resumed inspecting the corpse's hands.

Cutting into the flesh, Glenn pushed the tip of his knife under the metacarpal bone and raised it to the surface. After cutting through the connecting joints, he pulled the bone, which was covered in a reddish-black, clotted goo, from the top of the hand. With a grunt, he sliced off another chunk of thigh meat, stuffed it into his mouth, and moved on all fours to a nearby wall. There he sat, wiping off the bone as he chewed. He began to carve the ends of the bone, scooping out the marrow with the tip of the blade. Though he somehow knew the ultimate goal, Glenn's body and brain appeared to be running on autopilot. After some time and with a delicate patience, he finished carving the short, whitish flute. Admiring his work, he blew a few quick notes using the row of carved holes across the top. He gave a hiss of satisfaction and set the flute beside him.

Forcing his deformed hand into his tattered pocket, he extracted the picture of his wife, the photo's edges worn and abused. He cooed, tracing the picture with his deformed finger, the tip of which was forming a claw.

"Ghabreeeeellle," he groaned, his twisted vocal chords still trying to sound her name.

A ruckus outside the gas station snapped his attention back to the present. Grabbing the flute, he moved to the rear of the building and ascended an external ladder to the decrepit roof. Crawling low, he made his way to the edge and peered over. Below him, three infected humans gnashed and fought over the remains of a dead dog.

*The song.*

It was a perfect opportunity to test his theory against subjects with diminished cognitive abilities, precisely the type of consciousness that might be controllable. Raising the flute, the tune ingrained in his memory, Glenn blew hard, mashing his deformed fingers over the holes. The song began to fill the air.

In an instant the group froze, rooted in place, and their feral eyes opened wide. Glenn surveyed their stillness for a long moment before he spoke. He stretched his arms toward them and shouted, "You vheil kaall me fah-ther! You vheil doo vasht eye sayyy!"

Glenn began to play the second tune. As he did, two of the Sicks turned to face the third. As the song concluded, they leaped onto the third Sick, tearing it into pieces as it screamed.

Glenn lowered the flute and smiled, the gray flesh of his lips peeling back over broken teeth as he laughed. After a moment the two mutants stood and turned toward him, blood and filth dripping from their faces.

Their bodies swayed in delirious anticipation. Glenn raised the flute again and blew a final tune, long and low like a sad lullaby. The mutants moaned with ecstasy, raising their hands toward him, their voices calling out in unison, "Fozzer!"

# THIRTEEN

## NOW

The inhabitants of the station worked without complaint through the night, repairing the twelve-foot security fence around the station. The task wasn't an easy one, but working together as a group they'd done a decent job—having moved several disabled vehicles to block off weak areas and strengthened the lower half of the fence using whatever scrap metal they had available.

Courtland wiped a heavy hand across his brow and squatted to pick up the last sedan, a Buick LeSabre, to be placed along the fence. The rusted vehicle creaked as the giant gripped the frame, dropped his butt, and looked upward. With a groan, he locked his arms out, thrusting the vehicle wheels up, above his head the way a powerlifter snatches a barbell. He smiled as he began to walk, the vehicle suspended overhead. As he crossed the courtyard and neared the front gate, people stopped what they were doing to watch the spectacle. Like a circus strongman doing his act, Courtland commanded the attention of his audience. The station fell quiet in observation. As he neared the fence, he dipped just a little and dropped the car into position to help fortify the gate. Still smiling, he slapped his hands together as the dust began to clear. It took a moment for him to sense the silence and realize all eyes were on him. He waved a meaty hand and chuckled, enjoying the looks of shock on their faces.

"Okay. Show's over. Let's finish up and rest for a while."

The crowd murmured in acknowledgment. Courtland turned to Jenna, who was working along the fence line with Winston, the man who usually manned the radio room. They were talking and weaving strips of sheet metal through the chain-link fence. Courtland lumbered over just as they finished their task.

"Hey, guys," Courtland spoke, towering above them.

"Hi, Courtland," Jenna said, wiping her hands on her cargo pants.

"Hey," Winston began. "I was just asking Jenna how you do that. I mean, I've never seen anybody do anything like that before."

Jenna shrugged. "I told him I didn't really know."

Courtland knelt, a pleased look on his face. "Well, I've always been a big man. By the time I was twelve, I was six foot four and weighed two hundred and fifty pounds—and that was *before* I hit puberty. I was diagnosed with a rare condition. My growth hormones were overproducing. They've slowed a lot now, but technically speaking I'm still growing."

Winston was interested, starved for conversation. It was evident that the poor man spent too much time alone in the radio room.

"Fascinating! What's the name of the condition?"

"It's called gigantism. You remember Andre the Giant, that wrestler? He had the same condition."

"Don't a lot of complications come from something like that?"

"Yes. Most people with my condition live with a significant amount of pain their entire lives, but somehow I escaped that curse."

Winston nodded and held his hands up. "But just because you're big doesn't mean you should be able to press a car over your head."

"You are correct. I do have something else. It's a long story, but suffice it to say that God chose to give me a little extra something under the hood, so to speak. I don't know why exactly. His reasons are his own. All I know is that I must use my strength for his glory, or that power will fade."

"That's amazing! I mean, uh…how…" Winston stammered in excitement.

Jenna patted him gently on the shoulder. "Hey, Winston. How about you let us finish up here so you can get back to the radio?"

"Oh, no. This is far too interesting. Besides, Marcus is there."

"Yeah, but does Marcus really know what he's doing?"

"Well, he…" Winston trailed off and lowered his head. "No, I guess not."

"Why don't you relieve him, and I'll come down and visit you there in a little while?" said Jenna.

"Okay," Winston responded, flashing a nerdy smile. "But don't dilly dally. I'm a stallion, and if you wait too long, some other pretty lady will snap me up!"

"That would be so sad," Jenna said, making a fake pouty face. Winston turned and made his way to the stairs.

"You didn't have to do that. I don't mind talking about it," Courtland said.

"I'm sure you don't mind, because you're a saint, but actually I needed to talk to you for a sec."

"Oh, yeah? What about?"

"Last night."

Courtland made a face. "Which part? Last night was a doozy."

"I kind of lost it," Jenna said quietly.

Courtland nodded in agreement.

"I never blow up like that. I guess it was just a perfect storm."

"I'm not sure you were out of line. Kane pushed everyone too far."

"Yeah, and that's what I wanted to talk to you about."

"What about it?"

"I dunno. It's Kane. I'm worried about him."

Courtland met her gaze and nodded. "How so?"

"Back when you guys came here and rescued me, he was fine. He was...more reasonable. He acted like a man of God. Recently he seems like he's on the edge. He doesn't seem like the same man."

"He's had a lot on him. He's—"

"You're making excuses for him," Jenna said, cutting him short. "You always do. Why?"

Courtland's gaze shifted. He pulled on the back of his neck and took a deep breath.

"Courtland, what is it?"

"I've felt it too. I think his faith is slipping."

Jenna nodded.

"When we first met, his faith was like magnesium burning. It was so fresh and burned so hot." Courtland sighed and caught Jenna's eyes. "Recently I think he's tried to make this more about him and his plans instead of listening to what God wants in his life. I think he mourns his family. I think he's angry about how Molly died and how close he was to saving her."

Jenna touched his arm. "I get all that—I really do—but he can be so difficult, so destructive, and he's the one in charge. How do we stop him?"

Courtland pulled his arm from her and looked at her. "Stop him? Jenna, we encourage him or even help redirect him. We don't try to stop him. God has plans for that man."

"It doesn't seem like God is working in him."

"He is. It may be hard for you to accept, but we're all here to assist Kane in his purpose. It's the only reason we've come this far. We have to trust that everything happens for a reason."

"That's crazy talk. We're supposed to just stand by while he goes off the deep—" The look on Courtland's face stopped Jenna midsentence.

"You've got me all wrong, Jenna. I made a promise to God that I would stand against the darkness. It was revealed to me that I would do this at Kane's side. This is the reason my heart still beats in my chest. I won't abandon it—or him." Courtland stood and turned to walk away. "I won't ally with you against him."

"That's not what I want, Courtland. I'm just…scared. I want to know what's going to happen."

Courtland half turned to look at Jenna from the corner of his eyes. "I don't know what's going to happen, but I do know that all we've got out here is each other. We're a single flicker of light in a sea of darkness."

"And if our light goes out, Courtland? What then?" Jenna whispered, her lip quivering.

Courtland stopped but did not turn. "You don't want to be around for that."

✧ ✧ ✧

Tynuk was capable of traveling on foot, but it was tiresome, and he had many miles left on his journey. There were no working vehicles to be found. Even if there were, Tynuk couldn't drive. He viewed the use of motorized vehicles as something the world would one day be better off without.

He adjusted his handhold on the beast's mane as he rode bareback. Larger than a full-grown Bengal tiger, the beast didn't seem to mind or even notice the weight of the boy as it moved. Its muscles pushed and pulled like steel pythons beneath its flowing coat. Tynuk patted the beast on its flank, and it slowed at the top of a rise. They were making their way North then West, being sure to avoid high-traffic areas where bandits and other outlaws would be prevalent.

The boy slid off the beast, his lean, muscular form more like a man's than it should be at his age. He arched his back, stretching, reaching his hands toward the blackened ceiling of the world. Hearing a sound in the distance, he stopped, arms still raised, his senses calm, his reflexes poised. The warrior boy knew all too well that letting down his guard, even for a second, could mean doom. After a moment he relaxed, lowered his arms, and reached for his satchel to get his waterskin. He shook the container and frowned.

*Too light. Time for a little detour.*

"Come on, Az. Help me find water."

The beast lowered his head and sniffed the dusty ground. The boy headed down the opposite side of the hill, his war club at the ready. After a few minutes of foraging, Tynuk dug up a few sassafras roots to chew on, but he hadn't yet found a water source. The heavy, dry air clung to him, making him more aware of his thirst. He drank the remaining water from his skin.

Azolja continued to sniff the ground, moving further into a nearby ravine. The boy followed behind. He knew that Azolja had very keen senses. The creature had found them water in the past simply by smelling it in the air. The beast stopped midstep, lifted his head high as his nostrils flared, and sampled the moistened air of the ravine. Tynuk froze, his muscles wound like a spring. He prepared himself to snap into action at the slightest indication of danger. After a long pause, the beast drew his pink tongue across glistening fangs and chattered his teeth together. Tynuk had come to understand that this meant the beast sensed no danger.

Tynuk crept up next to the Az and pointed to the floor of the ravine. There, a narrow, twisting creek bed snaked through the dark forest. Water no longer traveled the path, but the boy knew there was a good chance the dusty floor would produce something.

"There," Tynuk whispered to the beast.

Azolja huffed and moved toward the dry creek bed, its nose inches from the charred turf. With a thud he dropped onto the soft sand. The boy followed, sinking into the earth in his leather moccasins. He stepped to the lowest point of the bed, on the inside bend of the creek bed, and bent to dig his fingers into the sand. After a few handfuls, he scooped his fingers deeper and pulled up a clump of dark sand. He held it up to his nose, and closing his eyes, he inhaled the thick, moist, earthen scent of the granulated earth.

Tynuk looked at the beast and smiled as he dug more, then a little faster, pulling greedy handfuls of the moist sand into a pile next to him. With a creeping slowness, brownish water filled the hole as the sand there collapsed in on itself. Tynuk dug out a few more handfuls then pulled a blue handkerchief from his satchel. He dipped the handkerchief into the small pool then rung the water into his waterskin. The cloth was an imperfect method, but it provided a mild filtering element to the collection process. The water was brown and had a musty, earthen smell, but it didn't appear to be contaminated, though that possibility existed. Even so, contamination was the lesser of many evils. Tynuk knew it was a chance they had to take since dehydration would kill them before anything else.

He took his time filling the skin while Azolja lapped the dirty water straight from the hole. After finishing his task, Tynuk filled the hole back in and covered their tracks across the creek bed as they headed up the other side of the ravine. The darkness of the woods began to deepen. As the day grew long, the shadows rising, telling the warrior boy and his beast that it was time to resume their journey west, into the unknown lands of post-civilization.

# FOURTEEN

In the shade of the hill, the man called Raith lay on his belly, observing the radio station. For a few hours, he had watched as the group of survivors went to and fro, working alongside one another to fortify the entire perimeter of the compound. He wondered what had prompted their little exercise. Why, after so long, had they felt the sudden need to strengthen their walls? Had they seen him? Did they have any inclination that they were under constant surveillance by enemy forces? No. It wasn't possible. He had been quite careful—every detail accounted for, every moment structured. He hadn't given away his position, and he wasn't a man of rash or impatient moves. The world was dead, and soon the Coyotes would be the most powerful force in what was once the United States of America—maybe even in the entire continent.

Raith wasn't a stupid man. He did everything with an enormous amount of planning and thought. For this reason, he never had done a significant stretch in prison. It was also for this reason that Malak trusted him to watch the station alone. Most of the gang wasn't suited to such work. They were bloodthirsty, reckless, and prone to rash or careless decisions. That was the nature of animals, which was what most of them were.

Raith hadn't quite devolved to that level. Sure, he had his vices, and they certainly included some extreme, maybe even barbaric practices by civilized standards. But the truth was Raith still appreciated some of the finer human things, like a nice genuine conversation between two people. Without question, his favorite type of conversation was the one you had with someone just before you killed them.

Some of the most personal and intimate conversations he'd ever had with another human being had been with his victims. There was this lovely fat girl in Newark, New Jersey, years ago. He still remembered her name, Loretta Lynn Bansky. What a gem. She had such a desire to live, and at one point, she nearly thwarted months of Raith's planning. She'd come so close to escaping from the subbasement of the old house where he'd kept her. But it was because of their conversations that he appreciated her most. How she had tried to plead and reason with him. She told him all about herself and her family, things he already knew about her, but he appreciated her honesty nonetheless. He had so enjoyed their conversations that he almost had spared her. Almost.

Raith shifted his position and allowed a small, yellowed smile to creep across his face. He'd learned that you really got to know people in their final hours, in their final minutes, and especially in the last seconds. He'd determined years ago that you never actually knew a person until you killed them, which was his sole reason for carrying on the way he had. He had run the authorities around in circles, sent them chasing their own tails. All the drama, all the media attention, staying constantly on the move—it all had been worth it. Seventeen victims in fourteen states and Raith had never been caught. Not once. The police were too stupid to catch him, and he exploited their every weakness.

He picked up the binoculars and surveyed the compound again, looking for his lovely. He had spotted her almost immediately, days earlier, and knew that one day she too would be his. With her long brown hair and agile frame, she was always carrying that satchel, tending to people who needed water or medical attention—especially the lookout man on the roof of the station. She visited him often. Raith wondered whether they were a couple and whether the man would try to intervene. But Raith had also noted the crutches and the way the poor man limped about. He smiled again. Like a broken-down dog, this man just might have to be put out of his misery when the time came.

One way or another, she would be his, and when the Coyotes tore the station down to its foundation, Raith would be waiting. He would be there, ready to scoop up his pretty and take her away so that he could truly get to know her.

Entering the lobby of the Reeds at Colonial Pointe, Raith nodded to the two barbarians guarding Malak's chambers. They returned the nod and stepped aside to allow him access to the king. Raith made his way up the stairs, reviewing the details of his report in his head. He wanted to be sure his delivery to Malak went smoothly. He'd learned early on that Malak was not someone whose time you wanted to screw around with.

Raith knew better than to mess with Malak, and to be fair, this was Malak's organization. Raith was, by trade, a loner, but he also knew that in this new world there was something to be said about safety in numbers. He could still fulfill his own agenda while serving the greater goals of the Coyotes. It was a small price to pay.

Raith cleared his throat and rapped on the wall next to the open door of the grand suite.

"Come in," the voice growled from inside the room.

Raith cleared his throat again and entered. The air in the room smelled of fresh blood and despair. It clung to his skin.

*Get it over with.*

"I have the station report for the day."

Malak raised his eyebrows. "Raith, the man of mystery. And what news does the mystery man have for me?"

"Surveillance report from the station. Everything—all activity in and out of the station—has slowed. No scavenging parties today. No new arrivals. This morning they were fortifying the fence all the way around the perimeter. Everyone seems to be busying themselves with tasks, like they're preparing for something."

"They've seen you."

"Impossible. You've seen me move. There is no one more careful."

"Then what?"

"I don't know. There are no indications of anything yet, but I'll continue to observe them as close as possible."

"Take care that they don't see you. If you have alerted them to our presence, it will not bode well for you, mystery man."

Raith did not reply. He stood in silence before the big man. "If that's all, Lord Malak. I'll grab some sleep and head out again first thing."

"That is all. Keep me informed."

Raith paused, considered saying more.

"There's something else?"

"As a matter of fact, there is." Raith took a deep breath. "There's a woman at the station. When this goes down, I want her."

Malak chuckled. "Do you, now? Who is she?"

"She's...perfect. About five foot six with a very lithe frame. She's always helping people around the station. She may be a doctor or something. I want her for my...collection."

Malak didn't move. He surveyed Raith with black eyes while the man finished speaking.

"You are an interesting one, mystery man, but I like your style." A moment passed before Malak nodded. "Continue to observe the station and report back. If you can identify her when the time comes, you will have your woman...under one condition—you must spare her no pain."

Raith gave a slight bow as he turned to leave. "I wouldn't dream of it."

# FIFTEEN

In the late afternoon, the business of the compound began to slow. Dagen sat on the edge of the roof and pushed his legs over the side so they dangled over the empty space. Reaching into his ragged backpack, he searched for the singular item that would guarantee him a temporary reprieve from the war in his heart. He couldn't go on like this. He was a mess, and his every waking moment and every interaction with Jenna only served to confuse him further. He had no idea what he wanted anymore—no idea what he *needed*.

Dagen tried to hold on to some shred of his identity, to reclaim something with meaning, something that made him who he was. But to his dismay, he came up empty every time. He'd never had much. Orphaned at an early age, he had never had any family who cared about him. As a boy, he'd been the victim of sexual abuse by a Christian pillar of his community. He grew up angry, with no purpose and no faith in anything. His lack of direction continued well into adulthood. He floundered, desperate to locate something in his life that felt real. With a sad resolution, Dagen determined that he had no such thing. And now lacked the ability to walk unassisted.

He was a physical, mental, and emotional wreck. The only thing he ever had been good at was playing the bad guy. He had a talent for hurting people, and he had fed off the fear and anguish of others, allowing it

to empower him further. For a while causing such misery and running
with Malak and his gang worked pretty well for Dagen—and then Jenna
happened.

Why did it always come back to her? She and her message of God just
wouldn't leave him alone. She couldn't just let him die and go on to whatever terrible fate awaited men like him. And on top of all this, as much
as he loathed admitting it, Jenna's talk of hope and God's ability to save
him had begun to resonate deep within him. He wanted to be redeemed.
He wanted it so bad, but it was something he didn't deserve—just like he
didn't deserve Jenna. For a long while, Dagen stared at the small, silver
cross necklace in his palm. Knowing what it meant and where it came
from only twisted his spirit further. What was he thinking holding on to
such a thing?

He couldn't do this any longer. He had to drown this garbage inside
himself—this time for good. Shoving the cross back into his pocket,
Dagen pulled a liter of Popov vodka from his backpack. Drinking alcohol
was like swallowing gold. Nobody had alcohol anymore, and the bit that
was scavenged was usually distributed evenly among those who wanted
it. The bottle had cost him an arm and a leg, a leg he didn't have. In
addition to the alcohol, Dagen also had traded for a heavy-duty prescrip-
tion of oxycodone, which he intended to take with the alcohol. Maybe
the combination would kill him. Or maybe it would get him so high
that he wouldn't realize it when he fell off the roof. At the very least, the
combination would take him out for a while and hopefully kill all that
confusing nonsense floating around inside him.

Dagen popped the top off the meds and shook a few pills into his
hand. He threw them into his mouth and chased them down with three
long gulps from the plastic vodka jug. He was supposed to be acting as

the lookout for the station, but why should he? The people there had done nothing for him. They could go to hell, as a matter of fact. He might get there first to greet them when they arrived.

Dagen waited a few minutes as the toxic combination of alcohol and pills began to push through him, whipping the anger inside him into a violent storm. He groaned and, with a slur, cursed everything and everyone he ever had known. Dagen flopped back against the gravel rooftop and watched the world spin, fly, and fade to black.

Evening fell over the station compound. A few people continued to work on the fence. Others transported loads of water from the blackwater cistern into the station. Kane exited the second floor onto the catwalk. He moved to the railing then took a moment to adjust the assault rifle that hung across his chest on a sling. There wasn't any time for sleep, not tonight. Besides, his sleep wasn't especially restful as of late. Instead, Kane took a rifle and planned to spend his evening in the courtyard with the night watch. It was more than a hunch. Kane knew the Sicks would come again, under the cover of darkness. This time they would come in force. He crossed the catwalk to the external stairs and made his way down to the ground level. There he encountered Jacob, hobbling along, carrying two buckets of water.

"What's up? What's with the rifle?"

"Figured I'd do a rotation on watch tonight. Want to join me?"

"Hell, yeah. Does this have anything to do with the breach last night?"

Kane shrugged. "Not necessarily," he lied and motioned to the boy's leg. "How's it healing up?"

"It's much better, man. Still a little slow on it, but I'm getting around much better."

"Glad to hear."

"Hey, let me grab a bite to eat and check a rifle out of the armory. I'll meet you back out here."

"Deal. See you in a bit."

Kane watched the kid limp to the door with a full jug in each hand. He admired the boy's perseverance, his work ethic. Jacob could be stubborn sometimes, but he had guts and heart. Kane would be glad to have him with him on watch.

Kane made his way across the courtyard to speak with the gate guards and let them know he'd be out with the scheduled watch personnel that night. After a brief visit, he decided to do a cursory check of the entire perimeter of the station. Making his way along the fence, he thought over how much work had been done in one day. The people at the station had really come together, on little sleep, few rations, and even less water. They had done a fantastic job fortifying the station perimeter. Courtland had seen to it that they'd secured and fortified all necessary areas.

Kane walked at a brisk pace, wanting to make his rounds and get back to the courtyard, but his pace slowed as he neared the rear of the station and looked toward the small bluff that peered out over the ocean. There a growing number of crosses had been planted in the sandy earth.

*It's been too long since I've visited.*

He continued to slow his stride as he approached the small bluff. Then he came to a complete stop, the gusty sea breeze pushing the smell of salt and garbage into his nostrils. Taking a few more steps up the hill, Kane stopped before a small mound with a crooked metal cross. Lowering his head, he took a deep breath in through his nose then exhaled. He hated these moments. Stooping, he straightened the marker.

"Hey," Kane said. "Here we are again." He paused, as if waiting for the earth to speak. "Never were much for words, were you Molly?" He smiled and rubbed the back of his hand along his chin. "I was just checking the perimeter fence for any weaknesses. We've been having a problem with Sicks recently, but they're not like you remember them. They've evolved or something. I'm not sure. They attacked us last night, killed a few of the night watch…but…well, you probably don't care about all that anyway. We're doing okay. We'll make it."

Kane stood and dragged the toe of his boot across the sandy dirt. He put his hand to his chest. "My heart has been hurting again recently. I thought I was better, you know? I thought I was past that, but it seems to be returning. I don't know why. I thought God healed me. Wanted me for some purpose. I haven't gotten my head around it yet. Maybe it's not that. I guess I could be overstressed or…something. Anyway," Kane said, gesturing with his hands, "I think you would have gotten along really well with the folks at the station. We have a pretty good group, lots of hardworking people just trying to find a new start in this crazy world. Sometimes I try and picture what you'd be up to if you were here with us. I miss you a lot. It's not easy losing a friend like you. Your reassurance kept me going in those early days. Kept me…balanced. I don't know if I ever told you, but I always appreciated that about you."

Kane looked up and away from the grave, his eyes wandering out to the ocean, the nothingness beyond the horizon.

"I can't forgive myself. I forced Malak's hand. I squeezed him and he squeezed back, and you got caught in the middle. I should have done better. I shouldn't have pressed him so hard, or I should've done more to…"

The words caught in his throat as he wiped a tear from his face with the sleeve of his tattered shirt.

"I'm just sorry, Molly. So sorry."

Kane rubbed at his face, fighting back the tears. He made a suppressive motion with his hand in frustration as he turned to leave.

"There's just one more thing. You were wrong about Susan and the kids. They're dead, and they're not coming back. I can't do this anymore. I've got to let it all go, let *you* go. If I don't, it's going to break me."

Kane turned and meandered away from the small hill of graves. The darkness growing deeper as night settled in around him, he made his way toward the courtyard feeling a growing sense of dread and wondering what the night had in store. As the last light faded from his shoulders, shadows leaked into the hollow places in the sand left by his weary feet.

# SIXTEEN

The slender figure crouched low along the ridgeline as the dark of night consumed the fading evening light. A faint breeze slipped across the barren landscape, making its way inland toward the emptiness of the land and whatever lay beyond. The breeze ruffled the figure's ragged clothing as it sank lower, sliding lizard-like across the ridge to meet with the others and wait for the rest to join them.

They had grown in number; the Father had seen to that. Many gathered on the hillside out of sight from the inhabitants of the radio station. Their ways were simple: feed, survive, adapt. Complicated reasoning or thought was not prevalent. They relied only on instinct—the instinct to survive, hunt, and kill. The Father was the only one with any complex cognitive abilities. The rest lived as animals of the forest and the fields, driven by singular and simple purposes.

Atop the ridgeline, the one who called himself the Father stood in the group's center, his arms open in a welcoming gesture, summoning the many who were still on their journey to join the others on the hillside. This group had never come together before. Some came from the wastes, while others came from Columbia, Charleston, or Georgetown. As they gathered they looked to be one unit, familiar as brother and sister, all drawn to the song of the Father. How they had known to come remained a mystery. In the darkness they swayed lightly with the breeze as it cascaded over them, filling the air with a distinct and pungent stench. With their blood red eyes squinted, appearing to burn like a hundred tongues of fire in the silent night.

Though those who gathered did not possess the mental capacity for higher reasoning, but they did understand two things. First, they knew the Father was like them. By smell alone they identified him as one of their own, and they found themselves unable to resist his siren song. Second, they knew with a strange clarity that the smooth skins had to die—every last one of them. Some would be eaten. Others would be taken. The rest would be left with their guts strewn about to rot on the hot sand. One way or another, their deaths were as good as done. Though the smooth skins would fight, they were no match for the speed and ferocity of these creatures.

The painted boy and his monster were the only ones who had faced their ranks in open combat and prevailed. But even the boy had abandoned them now. It was a pity. The Father wanted so badly to fill his mouth with the boy's tender flesh. It was but a small loss for the Father. Soon they would feast on the warm flesh of the smooth skins below, creatures that cowered inside their flimsy wire wall.

No more brokenness. No more segregation. Now they functioned as one, a family group living under the Father's guidance. And as he welcomed them with open arms, he raised the bone flute with a clawed hand to his wet, gray lips. Each creature froze, hundreds of them against the slope, staring in anticipation and delirium as the first few notes of the Father's song leapt from the flute. A moaned rush of euphoria swept over the scores of gathered mutants as they raised their clawed hands to the darkened sky and screamed in delight.

✵ ✵ ✵

In the station courtyard, Kane leaned against one of the vehicles in the motor pool. He threw his head back and laughed. The kid was completely out of control.

"I'm serious," Jacob said with a smirk.

"You've lost your mind, kid."

"Come on. Just for a few hours. We'll bring it right back."

Kane laughed again. "No way. Not in a million lifetimes. You are not going to borrow a vehicle to go on a date, and you're certainly not going to use precious fuel to drive around aimlessly. End of story."

Jacob wouldn't let it go. He'd been talking nonstop about Christina, a girl who worked shifts in the commissary.

"Come on, Kane. You've gotta work with me here. She's *so* hot, and she wants me," Jacob begged like a dog in heat.

"It boggles my mind that with everything that's happened and the state the world is in, all you can think about is sex.

"Dude, she's amazing," Jacob oozed.

"Dude, she's like fourteen, and her aunt hates you. *Hates*," Kane reinforced, unable to suppress a smile.

"She'll get over it. I just need the girl and the car for a couple of hours."

"Let's approach this from another perspective. Let's say you do hook up with her."

"Yeah, yeah. I like where this is going."

"No, just hear me out. So you hook up with her. Are you going to marry this girl? Make an honest woman out of her?"

"Come on, man."

"No, I'm serious. What if she gets pregnant? What then? Where would she have the baby? And if the baby survived, would you be man enough to raise it out here in the wastes?" Kane waved his arms through the air.

"Aw, man. You're ruining this for me. I was talking about something totally different."

"Yeah, I know what you were talking about. I was a walking testosterone factory at your age too, but I'm serious when I say you need to think this stuff through first."

"Sure, sure," Jacob muttered.

Kane smiled and patted his young friend on the shoulder. "For what it's worth, I understand where you're coming from."

"Yeah, all right." Jacob looked up and smiled, but they both stopped to listen to a strange noise that was growing in the distance. It rose, wailing, like hundreds of wild voices screaming into the night. The strange sound drifted across the station, causing everyone to stop and listen. A few curious individuals inside the station came outside to see what was going on.

Kane released his rifle from its sling and headed to the front of the station, the kid hobbling behind. As he arrived at the front gate, the sound began to dissipate and fall silent.

He called out to the guards, his confusion morphing into fear. "Did you guys hear that?"

The guards nodded, their faces drawn. No one knew for sure what the sound had been, but everyone agreed that it wasn't human. Kane scanned the ridgeline but found nothing. He turned to the guards, two men, and a woman. He couldn't remember their names.

"Did you guys see anything? Any movement outside the fence?"

"We didn't see anything, Kane. We were just sitting here talking," one of the men responded.

"All three of you, keep watch on the ridge. Let me know if you see any movement at all." Kane turned and called to a woman on the catwalk above. "Hey, find Courtland and tell him we need all the station lights on. Then tell him to get down here."

The woman acknowledged Kane's request, entered the fire exit, and disappeared. Kane turned back, listening to the blowing of the ocean breeze. He scanned the ridgeline once more. Still nothing. The halogen lights clanked and buzzed, blinking to life above him and bathing the station in a pale-blue light. Kane was shaking his head and pacing along the fence when Courtland exited the station doors and approached.

"What's going on?"

"I don't know yet, but I've got a bad feeling."

"What happened?"

"There was a sound. It was loud, like the way thousands of people yell in a football stadium."

"You heard screams?"

"Yeah, but it wasn't..." Kane looked at Jacob. "Help me out here."

"I don't know either," Jacob said, shrugging. "It was the weirdest thing I've ever heard, that's for sure. I don't know what to tell you."

Courtland looked back at Kane. "So what are you thinking?"

"The sound seemed too close and too much like a whole heck of a lot of people yelling." He paused, thinking. "We still can't see the ridgeline from here, and all the light is on us. Is there any way to redirect some of the spotlights to illuminate that hill more?"

"I'll see what we can do," answered Courtland.

"OK, while you're doing that, I'll have a group walk the perimeter with torches again just to play it safe."

Courtland headed toward the station as Kane briefed a group to begin checking the perimeter. Courtland instructed two men to loosen the bolts on a few of the courtyard spotlights so they could tilt them to observe outside the fence. With their tasking under way, Courtland returned to Kane. They waited in the quiet dark, observing the hillside while the two men on the roof fumbled, attempting to swivel the floodlights.

"What's taking them so long?" Kane muttered.

"The bolts are pretty rusted."

Kane nodded. "Something isn't right. I can sense it. It feels like we're being watched."

Courtland nodded but said nothing.

As the floodlights came free, squealing to their new position, Kane squinted toward the ridge. As the light swept upward, illuminating the hill, his heart sank. Before them they stood shoulder to shoulder, hunched and feral, extending the length of the ridgeline.

"No," Kane gasped.

"Lord God in heaven," Courtland whispered. "There must be five hundred of them, if not more."

As they stared in disbelief, a new sound resonated across the darkened landscape. It sounded like scraping, a rasping sound of bone on bone. First, the cadence seemed slow, the sound soft until it grew louder and more intentional. *Shick, shick, shick,* came the chorus as it built in volume and scale like a doomsday herald ringing his bell of judgment.

"Oh, my god," a nearby man whimpered. "Why are they doing that?"

"They want us to be afraid of them. They want us to fear what's about to happen," Courtland murmured, as the noise continued to grow.

"No. My god, no. They're going to kill us!" the man cried out.

"Be quiet. You're not helping anything," Kane hissed.

"No, no. They're going to get in here, and they're going to *eat us*!"

Kane grabbed the blabbering man by his shirt. "Shut up! Get control of yourself."

*"They're going to get in here! They're going to—"*

Without warning, Courtland placed his massive arm around the man's neck restraining him in a blood choke. The man had become wild with fear, but he was unable to free himself from the giant's strength. In a moment he sputtered and passed out.

"He'll be fine." Courtland gestured as he hoisted the man's limp frame over his shoulder.

"Thank you." Kane sighed and turned back to the chorus of methodical scraping that continued to cascade down from the ridge. *Shick, shick, shick.*

"Lock him up until this is over. We don't need him adding to the hysteria we're already going to have over this."

Courtland nodded.

"Courtland, I need you to rally every able-bodied person and marshal them here in the courtyard. Tell Jenna to gather all the children and anyone who can't fight. Lock those people inside the station, down in the cellar. You got me?"

"I'm with you, Kane."

"Good. I'll open up the armory and get the perimeter set."

As they both took off toward the station, Kane looked one last time at the hundreds of hunched forms that extended down the ridgeline. There they waited, dark and ominous like messengers of death.

☆ ☆ ☆

Raith lay concealed on the south side of the station, observing the spectacle forming before him. He would have left long ago had he not noticed the mass of ghoulish mutants on the western side of the station. At first, he felt awestruck, confused even, at the odd congregation crawling and loping across the hillside. But then he watched as the leader summoned them, controlled them with his primitive flute. As minions to their master, they desired only to do his bidding. What army could stand against a man with such a force?

Raith smiled. The pathetic group of survivors at the station somehow had angered the mutant chief, and now he'd come to exact his vengeance upon them. Unfortunate for them and fortuitous for the Coyotes. Malak would be interested to hear of this news. Due to circumstances now beyond their control, the Coyotes might need to move on the station sooner than they thought.

Raith adjusted his position, preparing to leave, to return to Malak. The excitement energized him, and he wished he could stay to watch the bloody slaughter. He picked up his binoculars and peered one last time at his pretty. She, along with a few other women, had gathered the children and were ushering them into what he presumed was a cellar on the far side of the compound. He watched as they sealed the door, while to his surprise, she remained outside to help defend the station. With a twinge of concern, he wished for her to survive just a little while longer, lamenting the possibility of her death.

*So delicate, yet so spirited and brave. Without a doubt, she is perfect.*

Raith watched Jenna as she stopped for a moment, clasping her hands together and closing her eyes. He watched her mouth as she uttered some unknown incantation.

Raith whispered to himself, "Yes, pray to your god, my sweet. Beg him to spare you from the beasties, for you do not belong to them."

# SEVENTEEN

*You are disgusting and weak. You've allowed your humanity to interfere with my plan. If you desire to be great, you must abandon that which you know. Lose yourself in me and find yourself anew.*

Malak opened his eyes and exhaled, the clammy, humid night air clinging to his naked form as he sat in meditation. The voice was displeased. It chastised him for his efforts. Malak clenched his teeth, making his way to his feet. The faint glow of a lamp outlined his massive nude form as he covered himself in a robe, his movements graceful for a man his size. As he slid from his chambers, moving like a serpent, he continued down the hall to the penthouse balcony. The destroyed wall beckoned him forward to gaze at what existed beyond. Squinting, Malak peered north, up the coast, toward the radio station.

The time was coming. He would step forward into greatness, not only strengthened by the darkness but also becoming the darkness itself. He and the voice would unify, and it would cease to condemn him. Malak now knew where his journey would take him once he destroyed the fragile community at the radio station. Once they were wiped from existence, his destiny would draw him westward, to the heartland of the American continent. There Malak would bring forth the power of the darkness and rule the earth as a god forevermore.

A man entered from the hallway. "Lord Malak, the man Raith is here to see you. Another is waiting as well."

"Send Raith in. And who is the other?"

"He comes with men who desire to align with the Coyotes by submitting to your lordship."

Malak nodded and crossed his arms across his chest. Raith entered and gave a slight bow.

"What do you have for me, Raith?"

"I have news of the station. I believe you'll find it interesting."

"Go ahead."

"I discovered why they've been fortifying themselves. It appears they've become the focus of a large group of mutants."

Malak's features darkened. "What do you mean?"

"Somehow the people there have upset these creatures, and the monsters appear to be amassing along the ridge in some sort of battle formation."

"I thought they weren't capable of such organization."

"That makes two of us."

Malak crossed his arms across his chest and furrowed his brow. Raith's news was unsettling. The possibility that they could start a massacre and rob him of his moment of greatness enraged Malak. He paced back and forth, clenching and unclenching his fists. Raith took a step back and prepared to flee if necessary.

*Again your human anger controls you. Your faithlessness is pathetic. It bleeds you of the control you could have. If only you would truly believe in the power of the darkness. Trust in me. Use this. Make it work for you. Command the power within you.*

Malak stopped pacing. "Don't lecture me, Voice," he snarled.

Raith, now thoroughly confused, took a few more steps away toward the hallway. He had all but decided to leave when Malak looked at him.

"We can use this to our advantage, spare our own numbers by letting the beasts wear them down."

Raith nodded his understanding. "My thoughts exactly." He took a second to gather himself, flashing a yellowed smile.

"But we hit them on multiple fronts. There must be layers to our attack. I've waited this long. I will not fail."

"If I may," Raith said with a slight bow, "I think we should send the woman, Shana, back in. We could sabotage their operation from the inside."

Malak nodded. It wasn't a bad idea, but he needed real diversion—something that would hit them where it hurt and weaken their ability to put up any resistance. As much as he hated to admit as much, at times like these, Malak missed Dagen. He had been an indispensable tactical advisor. It was too bad he had met his end at the hands of that miserable entourage.

"We have to divide them," Malak said, "draw them apart before we hit them. Kane Lorusso must pay. His whole world must die around him."

A throat cleared from the darkened hallway as a figure stepped forward into the room.

"I couldn't help overhear, and if I may be so bold, Lord Malak…" the figure stated. He stepped forward to reveal a painted face, covered with wild, blue Celtic patterns.

"My name is Saxon, and I believe I have just the thing you're looking for."

✵ ✵ ✵

"They're moving!" the guard at the gate called out. "I think they're moving down the ridge!"

"Hold your positions!" Kane yelled above the anxious murmurs of the group. "We're well fortified and prepared to withstand the assault, but you have to hold your ground!"

Few acknowledgments came from the group as they shifted nervously along the fence line. Shoulder to shoulder they stood, men and women alike. Some fumbled with their rifles or pikes, others wiped the cold sweat from their foreheads.

"Remember to move with your line. The first line will take aim and fire on my command. If the Sicks get to the fence, the riflemen will fall back and the pikemen will take their place. Clear them away from the fence just as we practiced. Do not under any circumstances let them inside this fence. Your life and the life of the person next to you depends on it."

Kane glanced to his left and noticed Jenna approaching with a pike in her hands. She took up position in the second line back. He allowed his surprise to ebb, as Jenna met his gaze and gave a brief nod of assurance. In this moment, Kane knew that their differences ceased to exist as they stood together in defense of the group. He forced a smile and gave a nod of acknowledgment. Then, looking up, he surveyed the hillside once again.

They *were* moving. Slow and methodical, they moved in step with the rhythm of their scraping down the hillside toward the station. The piercing shriek of the bone flute filled the air, stopping the creatures in their tracks about fifty yards from the fence. The mutants stood swaying, continuing their scraping in unison. *Shick, shick, shick, shick.* The people along the fence squirmed in anticipation.

Kane turned to Courtland, who had returned from the station with his giant, black, scimitar-shaped blades. The jet-black blades glistened in the artificial light, indelible reminders of wild stories and forgotten foes.

"What is going on already?"

"I don't know, Kane. I've never seen anything like this."

"The sooner we get into this fight, the sooner it'll be over."

Courtland, sensing what was about to happen, began to bellow scripture at the top of his lungs. "Remember how the enemy has mocked you, Lord. Do not hand over the lives of your doves to wild beasts. Remember your covenant because haunts of violence fill the dark places of the land. Rise up, O God, and defend your cause!"

"Riflemen, prepare your weapons!" Kane shouted. "Be mindful of your ammo, and only take shots that will cripple or kill."

Kane glanced at Courtland then back at the monsters that stood just fifty yards up the hillside. "Ready! Take aim! Two rounds. *Fire!*"

The explosive concussion of more than forty rifles blazing in unison deafened the crowd. The landscape illuminated in a brief, brilliant flash of devastating power. The creatures shrieked, and some of them fell, clutching their wounds as the piercing wail of the flute was heard once again. They began moving down the hill, closing the fifty-yard gap that separated them from the fence.

Kane screamed again. "Two rounds. *Fire!*"

Again the rifles blazed, and the Sicks fell, tumbling toward the service road at the base of the hill. The others continued on, entranced, moving to the cadence of their scraping. Without regard for their welfare, the mutants walked directly into the gunfire. The riflemen, though effective, squirmed as they realized the shots were not stopping them. The mass of freaks continued to approach the gate, reaching thirty-five yards and closing fast. The flute sounded three sharp blasts as the mass of hundreds of creatures froze, the twisted and broken bodies of their brethren in piles at their feet.

"What the hell now?" Kane managed, just as a horrific cry rose from the ranks of mutant freaks as they swung their clawed hands in the air and rushed the fence. For a moment Kane choked, his tongue caught in his throat like a foreign object.

"Fi..." he coughed out, as the maddened creatures closed the gap with blistering speed. "*Fire at will!*"

Sporadic gunfire lit the night sky, each flicker illuminating the teeth and claws as the creatures jumped for the fence.

"Riflemen, fall back! Pikemen, advance!" Kane shouted above the uproar.

The front line shifted back as the row of men and women holding spears advanced toward the barricade. Holding tight to her pike, Jenna trudged forward into the fray, her jaw set in fearful determination.

"Holy God, stand with—" she managed, just as the howling line of freaks slammed against the fence and began to climb. Sounding a wild battle cry, she thrust her pike through the links and ran one of the maddened beasts straight through its heart. The creature shrieked and clawed at the fence as black blood sprayed across her face and hair.

The creatures jumped against the fence, clambering upward, the pikemen thrusting their poles through the gaps. The bladed weapons punched holes in the mutants like hot knives through butter, their black innards spilling over the pikemen, who thrust their weapons, again and again.

As some of the beasts approached the top of the fence, Kane stepped back and yelled above the screams.

"Riflemen, direct your fire upward! *Fire!*"

Kane raised his own rifle and took a deep breath. He squeezed his rifle's trigger, sending a few well-placed shots into the heads of the maddened creatures. Their lifeless bodies tumbled over the fence and into the courtyard. It was happening so fast. Two, three, five of them landed inside the courtyard, leaping at the defenders, red blood splashing against the dusty turf. Down the line, the fence wobbled and creaked under the weight of the monsters, the poles creaking and folding as portions of the fence collapsed in on itself.

"Courtland!" Kane yelled, pointing, but he saw that the big man was already moving down the line, closing the distance between them and the breach, his bladed weapons gleaming like ebony fire under the glare of the halogen lights.

Jenna was stabbing through the fence when the section to her left came down. She turned and saw the monsters coming through the gap, pouring in like sand through an hourglass. One dropped in behind her. She smelled the thing before she saw it, the rotting stench of death and decay heavy in her nostrils. She spun to the right and tripped over the man who had stood next to her just moments ago. His belly slashed open, his guts hanging there, exposed on the dark sand.

She couldn't stop the bladed talons of the Sick as they sliced deep across her collarbone, just missing her carotid artery. She crashed into the fence, her shirt blossoming red with blood. Jenna cried out in pain and clutched at her neck, slumping back in terror, bearing witness to the demonic menace that closed in upon her.

She had done her best. She wasn't a warrior, and there was no shame in what would come next. This was a cause she would gladly give her life for. She pinched her eyes tight and whispered words of faith as the monster approached.

With a sound like wet wood pulling apart, the Sick cleaved in two, severed with one blow by Courtland's massive blades. The giant rose and flung the creature's remains into the air like a disfigured toy. Jenna gasped, her eyes taking in the onslaught.

The station's defenses were beginning to fragment as some fled and others cowered in fear. Two Sicks leaped over the fence and landed on the dirt in front of Kane, bearing their jagged teeth as they came for him. He raised his AR-15 and fired through the chest of one of them, dropping it to the ground, as the other closed the gap and swiped at him. The subhuman creature clawed a short gash in Kane's arm as it knocked the assault rifle from his hands and sent him sprawling.

Masses of creatures now scaled the fence as the terrified inhabitants fought desperately for their lives. Courtland turned, leaving Jenna against the fence as innumerable Sicks poured through the gaping hole beyond and converged on him, threatening to overpower the enormous man with their numbers.

"Come on, you vile beasts," the giant shouted, glowing with the power of battle. He held his blades high in front of him, as he faced the masses of deranged freaks. "Come and test yourselves against the power of the Lord!"

The monsters screamed as they flooded toward him. He swung his blades through the crowd, the first swipe cleaving half a dozen Sicks in half, the back swipe splitting another eight. Spinning and dropping to one knee, he flung the blades together and eviscerated another fifteen. Swinging back and forth, up and back, Courtland tore them apart in a fury of righteous anger.

Kane rolled across the dusty ground as the Sick pressed down on him.

"Not this time!" he growled, as he hip-tossed the creature and rolled on top of it. It slashed its claws and snapped its teeth at him as he parried the creature's swipes, countering with straight and hammer-fist blows to the gray flesh of its face. The monster screamed and thrashed as Kane's rage grew to a storm.

"You wanna eat me? Eat this!" Kane yelled, as he drew his Glock from its holster and crammed the barrel deep into the dazed Sick's mouth. With a muffled pop, the monster's skull came apart under the force of the blast as black blood splattered the dusty ground. In a flash Kane was on his feet, turning to acquire new targets, advancing into the madness. Nearby Jacob screamed as his M-16 blazed, sending mutants spinning to the ground.

"Cover me!" the boy yelled, as he stripped an empty magazine and retrieved a fresh one from his pocket.

Redirecting his fire, Kane moved toward Jacob and picked up the monsters that clambered over the fence in front of them, a wild snarl of violence plastered across his face.

Further down the fence, the flow of mutants through the gate slowed, bottlenecked by Courtland's bloody destruction. He swung the blades back and forth as the remaining Sicks dodged away, keeping their distance. One came too close, and as Courtland's blade came crashing down, he sliced the disgusting creature in half. Three more appeared before Courtland in a rush as two clawed their way up his back. Another flew onto his arm as others charged him, their mouths foaming like overworked horses.

Courtland swung down to the right and found that his timing was as true as the blade. He slashed through and through, from collarbone to hip, even as the Sicks continued to charge him. As Courtland fought, the two on his back sank their teeth and claws into the flesh of his upper back, causing him to roar and drop his weapons. He pulled one from his arm like a parasite as it thrashed in the grip of his massive hands. With one swift move, Courtland pulled the head from the creature's body, tossing its parts to the side as he continued to duck and shrug the violent freaks off his back. He ducked, pulling two more screaming creatures to the ground, where he secured his grip on their throats, raised them high into the air, and slammed their skulls together like bursting grapes.

Though Courtland's efforts were valiant, the compound was falling. They were being overrun by the mutant horde. Kane knew they couldn't hold out indefinitely, and sounding any call for retreat would be useless. The momentum of the conflict had shifted decidedly in favor of the attackers. But, just as hopelessness descended on the defenders, the Sicks froze as though hypnotized. With a sharp whine, the flute piped again, the sound drifting across the air in an eerie melody as the Sicks retreated en masse. They scurried back over the broken fence, their ragged, sinewy forms scattering up into the dark hills above the station.

Kane completed a combat reload of his handgun, retrieved his rifle, and checked the wound on his arm. His hands and face dripped with black goo. The question took shape across his face before it hit his lips. "What?"

Courtland shouted from across the courtyard. "They're retreating!"

A roar rose from the surviving defenders of the station as they lifted their weapons into the air and cheered in victory. In a matter of seconds, the hundreds of Sicks that were upon them were gone. All that remained was the desperate survivors of the station, the mournful cries of the wounded riding on the humid night wind.

# EIGHTEEN

In the basement of the Reeds at Colonial Pointe, a mob of psychotic bandits cheered two of their own on as they fought each other to the death. Saxon's six men were first put to the test, and now only two remained, the blood of the others splashed across the sticky basement floor.

"Enough!" Malak growled. The room fell quiet. "You have both proven yourselves. Kneel before me, and submit yourselves to me."

The last two men were first pitted against the others—every man for himself. Then they'd been forced to fight Malak as a team, two against one. Malak told them that only one could be victorious, but in the end, he accepted both. Malak had almost killed them both, while their former leader, Saxon, nodded his painted blue face in approval.

"Open your mouths and consume the flesh of darkness," Malak intoned, as he sliced a gash in his arm. The blood sprayed into the mouths of both men as they waited, their tongues extended. As the men swallowed, the darkness clouded their spirits like ink dripping into a jar of water. They licked their lips and smiled as their eyes grew dark. Together they chanted, "We worship you, Lord Malak."

"Good," said Malak, turning his attention to Saxon. "And what of their leader? Does he wish to partake as well?"

"He does," said Saxon, stepping forward and removing his shirt to reveal a muscular, scarred torso.

"Very well, then. Prepare yourself for death." Malak bared his teeth, the words like a snarl on his lips as he stepped forward, dwarfing the smaller man.

Saxon shifted, and a flicker of fear crossed his face. He suppressed it, knowing it would, without question, get him killed. Malak balled his fists and squared himself off against the painted man. "What are you waiting for—or has your fear crippled you?"

Saxon threw himself at the larger man with a scream, his knotted ponytail whipping behind him as his fist connected with Malak's frame, the impact like punching a stone wall. Saxon cried out in pain just as Malak swung his arm in an arc, catching the painted man under the chin. Saxon flew backward. The men howled as his body slammed into the concrete floor and tumbled, the blood of other men sticking to his skin as he rolled back to his knees.

"Is that it?" Malak mused.

Saxon pulled himself up and charged again with a flurry of blows, punching Malak's midsection, throwing an uppercut to the jaw that connected, and finishing with an attempted knee strike to Malak's groin. Malak deflected this last attack and grabbed Saxon by the neck, hurling him into the low ceiling, the concrete surface cracking under the force. With a disinterested air, Malak dropped Saxon's weakened body to the floor and turned.

The crowd howled again. Everyone in the room knew that not a man on earth could defeat Malak in single combat. Those who tried were either murdered or hailed for their savagery in battle. The latter was the only means by which one could become a Coyote.

"You have yet to impress me," Malak spoke, towering over the smaller man, now on all fours, trying to catch his breath. "It's time for you die."

Saxon searched the floor with his hands for something, anything that might give him an advantage. At last, he felt the hexagonal shape of a crowbar lying at the feet of one of the thugs. Grasping for it, Saxon rose with a furious scream. The movement caught Malak by surprise, allowing Saxon to slam the crowbar into his opponent's ribs, the metal bar tearing a chunk of flesh from his side. Saxon swung back again, the blood blinding him as it ran into his eyes. He landed a lucky strike across the side of Malak's neck, a blow that forced the big man to stagger backward.

Saxon's overconfidence became evident as he charged Malak, the crowbar held high. When Saxon reached him, he swung as Malak caught the weapon midair and closed his iron grip around it. In the blink of an eye, Malak grabbed Saxon by the throat and lifted him from the ground. As Malak began to squeeze, the painted man flailing and kicking Malak's torso in what was sure to be his final moment. Then, without warning, Malak released him. Saxon fell to the floor, gasping and trying to drag himself away.

"Your bloodlust is sufficient," the demonic man mused, gazing at his side, where fresh blood flowed. "That bout would have killed lesser men."

The crowd of Coyotes murmured in acknowledgment as Saxon rolled onto his back, continuing to struggle to catch his breath.

"If you wish to become one of us, drink from my side and call me your god."

Saxon raised himself up under the wound and received the blood that poured into his mouth. Saxon swallowed the sticky, warm liquid, and as he did, it seemed to flow through him, covering his former self in a cloak of fear, hate, and despair. If his heart had known these things before, in this moment his heart knew them tenfold, as he willingly gave himself to the evil that consumed him. He wiped the blood from his face and stayed on one knee before Malak.

"My god," he said. "I am yours to command."

Malak nodded. "Now these savages will call you brother, and you will call them family."

"And you?" Saxon said as he took Malak's outstretched hand.

"You are stronger than the rest of them. I am in need of a lieutenant." Malak pulled Saxon to his feet. "I will call you 'my right hand,' if you accept."

The crowd clapped and yelped, making a path for both men as they walked toward the stairs. Saxon nodded in acceptance, finally beginning to recover from the fight.

"Now that you have proven your strength and loyalty, I am interested to hear more about this plan of yours."

"Yes, my lord," said Saxon, taking a deep breath. "I know how to hit your enemy Kane where it will hurt him the most."

"Oh? And how is that?"

"I have his wife and children."

Malak stopped at the foot of the stairs. His face darkened as he turned toward Saxon, an evil smile forming.

"Say it isn't so."

※ ※ ※

The camp was quiet. Not a soul stirred in the early-morning hours, except the two night watchmen, who laughed in coarse, muffled tones as they made their rounds. A man nearby snored, the rumbling sound like a chainsaw idling under a blanket.

Susan sat up on her pallet and looked over at Garrett, who was fast asleep. If she was caught again, she would be killed for sure—or worse, they would kill her children. She pushed the thought from her mind and swallowed hard. She looked at Garrett again and noted that he was still motionless. She wiggled her wrist against the shackle, and the metal squeaked. She froze, eyed Garrett again. Nothing.

Over the last two days, she'd spent a considerable amount of time inserting a wooden dowel between the shackle and her wrist. She then twisted the dowel, trying to separate the contact points. Though it had left her wrist quite bruised, the trick had been at least somewhat successful. If she strained, she could just barely pull her hands free from the metal brackets. Putting them back in was the easy part, and the bruises went unnoticed, as the shackles had already done that job well enough. Susan pulled her left hand free with a jingle and glanced at Garrett, her mind swarming with paranoia.

*Stop worrying about him, and do it!*

She yanked her right hand free and crawled toward the front of the tent, the flap drifting in the breeze. She pushed back the canvas and surveyed the area. The camp remained quiet. Crouched low at the edge of the tent, she listened for the smallest sound or sign of anyone approaching.

She had to put the plan in motion, and she had to do it now. She had prayed, begging God to save her and her children, but He had remained silent. Her circumstances played havoc with her faith. She wanted to trust God. She wanted to trust that He was sufficient, but it had all been so terrible. She couldn't wait any longer. Her children's lives were at stake, and she refused to be the reason that they continued to live in such peril. She would die for both of them if necessary. The time wasn't yet right to leave, but it would be soon. Everything had to be in order for the escape to work. Her skin tingled. Maybe she should go ahead, abandon the plan, just get the kids and go.

*No. It's a good plan. Stick to the plan.*

Susan blinked her eyes hard. Moving from the edge of the tent, she ran in a low crouch to the back of another nearby tent. She stepped quietly between the rows of military-style tents, picking her steps so that she wouldn't trip over a tent peg or another person. Some of the gypsies, paranoid about thieves, even had set up alarms using string and tin cans to alert them that someone was approaching. Susan stepped around the home made tripwires, taking great care not to disturb them.

At the end of the row, Susan paused and looked to where the night watchmen sat laughing over some vulgar joke. She turned her head and could just see the van where her children were held—at least it matched the description of the van she had overheard Garrett mention. With the children secured inside, there was no reason to post a guard to watch over two four-year-olds. Susan swallowed hard. The thought of seeing her children after so many days apart brought a lump to her throat. She was desperate to know that they were alright.

With a deep breath, she dodged behind the laughing men, stopping to rest against the side of the van. She heard someone shift inside the rusted frame. The van, no longer mobile, was used only as a holding cell. The windshield was cracked but intact, and the body was riddled with holes, a memento from some long-forgotten conflict. Listening through the busted out windows, she could just make out the sound of breathing from where she crouched. She worried she might startle her children or cause them to shout if she showed herself in the window.

"Michael? Rachael? If you can hear me, don't shout, okay?"

"Momma?" came the small voice of her brave son.

"Shh. Yes, sweetheart, it's me. I need you to be quiet."

"Okay," came the tiny whisper.

Susan raised herself up to the window and peered into the van.

"Momma!" Rachael whispered with excitement.

As Susan's eyes adjusted to the darkness, she could see two smiling faces in the van's interior. She couldn't control herself as her muffled sobs escaped. She stifled the sound as best as she could and leaned in, wrapping her arms around her children's necks. They leaned their heads into her but did not hug her back. She realized they were not tied down to the vehicle but to each other, bound together with an old dusty rope. She held their beautiful, dirty faces in her hands and wept. Her angels had been so resilient through the end of the world and now this. It was time for this chapter of their lives to end. It was time for better things. When she found Kane, they could all be safe again.

"Don't cry, Momma," came Michael's cheerful voice. "Jesus is with us."

"I know he is. Always remember that He is with you." Susan cried.

"But Momma, why do we have to stay in here? Why can't we stay with you?" Rachael asked.

Susan wiped her face and swallowed to compose herself. "Because these people won't let us stay together right now."

"Why?"

"Because..." Susan cleared her throat and patted her sweet children. "Because they're not very nice people. But it's okay because we're going to leave soon."

"We are? Where are we going?"

"We're going to..." Susan paused, wondering if she should say it. "I'm going to tell you something, but you have to promise me you'll be quiet, alright? Mommy can get in trouble if you make too much noise. Promise?"

"We'll be quiet as a baby mouse," Michael whispered.

Susan rubbed her hand on Michael's leg. "Soon we're going to leave this place, and we're going to go find Daddy."

The children froze. It was a name they hadn't heard in a long time.

Michael's brow furrowed as he whispered the foreign word. "Daddy?"

Rachael began to cry.

"Shh, shh. It's okay to cry. I know that's a hard thing to hear, but you know Daddy didn't want to be away from us. He had to be away. He didn't want to."

Michael's lip quivered as a tear rolled down his cheek, dripping off his chin. Susan bit her lip, feeling a sharp sting of regret for saying anything, but she hadn't known what else to do. Ambush her children by showing up somewhere to find their father? That wasn't fair either.

"It's okay to cry. Mommy cries about it too sometimes." She patted them again. "We're going to find Daddy, and everything's going to be okay."

Michael ducked his head to wipe his cheek on his shirt. Together both children nodded.

"Michael," Susan started, "I'm going to put something sharp in your hand. It's a small knife. Keep it hidden, and don't cut yourself, okay?"

"Okay, Momma."

"One night, very soon, there will be a big fire. When you see the big fire, cut yourself and your sister loose. Wait here for me. I'll come and get you. Rachael, you help your brother remember? Do you understand?"

They both nodded.

"Everything happens for a reason. God has a plan for us. I love you both so much. Be strong, my angels." Susan hugged them one last time, wiped her face on her sleeve, and pulled herself from the van to cross the gypsy camp one final time.

# NINETEEN

The bodies of both friend and foe remained strewn about the fence line. In the gray morning light, dawn began to break across the grounds of the station. The people had been working for a few hours, yet the area still looked like a war zone.

A few had been trying to repair the downed section of fence but with little success. The rest, divided between moving the wounded and clearing the area of the dead. A small contingent stood at the fence, their rifles at the ready, looking out for any further threats. The pile of the dead mutants on the far side of the fence waited to be burned. Their bodies thrown there haphazardly, like a mass grave.

"That's the last of them," Jacob said, wiping his hands on his pant legs.

"Good," Kane said, taking a sip from a bottle of black water as Courtland and Jenna approached. "Check on the progress of the fence repair. See if they're going to be able to get it back up."

"Yup," Jacob drawled as he hobbled off.

"How's your arm?" Courtland asked.

"I'm fine. It's just a scratch and I've already scrubbed it. How are you guys holding up?" Kane asked.

"We could all use some sleep, but what's new?" Courtland sighed. "Jenna needs some medical attention as well."

Kane made a face at her. "What are you waiting for?"

Jenna shook her head, keeping pressure on a scrap of cloth that covered the wound across her collarbone. "I'm all right. A lot of people need the attention more than I do. Terry already has his hands full, trying to treat everyone by himself."

Kane wasn't sure whether it was the early-morning light or the blood loss, but Jenna appeared unusually frail. He motioned for her to show him the wound, and she obliged, pulling the cloth away from the ugly wound. She winced as it stuck to the gash across her collarbone. The three-inch cut went from the inside of her shoulder to just below her neck. The ivory color of her collarbone was just visible at the deepest point.

Kane shook his head. "You're lucky it's not worse. You've got to get that cleaned as soon as possible. There's no telling what kind of infection you might have picked up from the ghoul that cut you. Plus you're no good to anyone until you get yourself fixed."

"I'll do it." Jenna said.

"Were the kids OK in the cellar?" Kane asked.

Jenna nodded again.

"Best to keep them there for now." Kane motioned to the ridgeline. "They could come again at any time."

"Yeah," Jenna said.

"I don't know," Courtland murmured. "I think they'll come at nightfall. That's when they'll have the greatest advantage."

"Maybe so," Kane said, turning to face the giant. "What sort of casualties do we have?"

"At least thirty-five injured. Fifteen to twenty of those probably won't make it."

"And the dead?"

"Another fourteen."

"That's over half our people." Kane said.

"Yes, it is," Courtland added, "and we won't survive another assault like that last one."

"Did we impact their numbers at all?"

Courtland shrugged. "We must have killed a couple hundred of them, maybe a third of their total."

"They could have taken us." Kane stroked the stubble on his chin. "So why didn't they?"

"Like you said earlier, they sent a small force to intimidate us and test our defensive capabilities. Now that they know, they'll hit us with everything. Wipe us out."

Kane breathed a heavy sigh and looked toward Jacob as he hobbled back up. "The fence," Jacob said. "It ain't gonna happen. It's wrecked."

"Yeah, I figured," Kane grumbled. "With it down, we'll have to pull back and fortify the actual station." He paused for a long moment. "Has anyone seen Dagen? He should have seen this coming sooner—if he was on the roof. We could have had more time to prepare if he had alerted us."

Jenna's face dropped as she realized she hadn't checked on him recently. Considering that he'd tried to kill himself before, anything was possible.

"I'll—" she began.

"No, no." Kane stopped her. "You get that wound taken care of. I'll go find him."

"Kane," Courtland said, "considering your feelings toward the man— and now his falling down on the job—maybe I should go find him. You wrap up down here. Make sure the station is fortified."

"That's probably best." Kane said. "Jacob, will you please help Jenna get to medical?"

"Right," Jacob agreed, moving toward Jenna.

Jenna stopped the teenager. "There's one other thing I was thinking about, Kane."

"Yeah?"

"It's about the leader of those things and his bone flute. That's how he controls them, unifies them, right? Without him and the flute, they're just monsters."

"What are you saying?"

"Well, they used to be humans, right? We all know how music has an effect on the mind and the body, just like when you used to listen to classical music to relax and hard rock to get amped up for a workout. Music can, in minor ways, impact mood and behavior in humans. On top of that, there are studies about the effect of certain tones on the animal brain—on dogs for example. The research was woefully underdeveloped at the time the civilized world ended, but there were some interesting theories on the subject. They were just that, though—theories. One study claimed that certain tones could be used to control animal behavior."

"Are you saying the one controlling them has some experience with this?"

"It's possible. That's all I'm saying. I heard you talking about how you saw the leader with them in the woods when you were attacked. You said they protected him, like he designed it that way, right?"

Kane nodded.

"It's like they revere him, like he's their chieftain," Jenna said. "I don't know if it's the flute or something more primal, like the instinct to operate in a family group or a pack. Maybe it's a combination—I don't know. What I do know is that I've never seen anything like it. That's the only rational explanation I can come up with."

"Interesting," Kane responded.

"I think if you take him down—the leader, I mean—they'll disperse and go back to being less organized."

Kane nodded. "I have to ask how—"

"What? So I learned a few things while studying to be a veterinary assistant. It happens," she said with a smile.

"Thanks, Jenna. Look—and I don't mind saying this in front of every-one…" Kane paused and looked at both Jenna and Courtland. "I was glad to see you join us on the line last night. I'm sorry if I got out of line the other day about Dagen. I hope you'll forgive my bad attitude."

Jenna nodded as she prepared to leave with Jacob. "I just want to do my part, Kane, and while I appreciate the gesture, it's Dagen who deserves your apology."

Kane exhaled. "Yeah, don't press your luck," he said, motioning for Courtland to check on the man on the roof.

As the parties separated, Kane stood in the courtyard to visually assess the scene. As he did, he wondered whether there would ever be a light at the end of this tunnel. Suddenly one of the guards at the gate began to shout. It took Kane a moment to register what he was saying.

"Shana! It's Shana. She made it back! Hey, get me some help! She needs medical attention!"

The guard opened the gate for the woman on the other side. She staggered in, covered in dried blood. A few people ran to close the gate as Kane took a few steps forward. He squinted, trying to confirm that the woman was in fact their Shana, the girl who had left with the scavenging party and never returned.

"I'll be damned," Kane murmured.

✲ ✲ ✲

Tynuk stopped short of the entrance and paused, his senses alert to something that might have been nothing at all. It sounded like the dry scrape of fabric on metal. The wind picked up, blustering through the shattered windows of Chappy's General Store, howling like some trapped spirit of vengeance. Across the street the smartly dressed Burger Boy statue rotated in the wind, his plaster burger held high, a giant smile on his face blackened by soot and dust.

The warrior boy's mouth watered at the thought of a burger. It had been too long. He relaxed a little but remained alert. The sound didn't seem to merit any response. Tynuk and Azolja had been traversing I-40 west since they'd picked it up back in Tennessee. The cracked and crumbled road was full of junk cars and other remnants of the previous era, including highwaymen who scavenged the ruins for valuables. It was not wise, even for the boy and his beast, to risk an encounter with such a group. He and Az tried to stay off the road, using it more as a compass.

The boy took a few careful steps over the broken glass at the open entrance to the store. What had once been a hub of commerce for the small town of Okemah, Oklahoma, was now as empty as the town that surrounded it. The nearby buildings along West Broadway appeared ruined, their brick facades crumbling and covered in ash. The town was not big enough to have been targeted for a direct hit. Still, the backlash Okemah received from Oklahoma City, just seventy miles to the west, had been enough to destroy it. Thanks to the windswept fires and the madness of survivors fleeing the city, this town had not survived.

Tynuk felt uncomfortable this close to civilization, but food was hard to come by without scavenging, and there was little to scavenge in the wastes. He resolved to venture into Okemah to stock up on whatever he could. Then he would head south from the town, looping well below the ravaged shell of Oklahoma City before heading back north and finally west to I-40. It wasn't a perfect route, but he had no sun or compass by which to navigate. He had only an old map of the United States, which he used as a reference to locate large metro areas they needed to avoid.

Just inside the store, Tynuk stopped and scanned the interior for threats, looking, listening, and smelling the musty environment. He glanced behind himself once more, accustomed to the beast watching his back. The creature's absence left a void in his methods. Rather than come with Tynuk into the town, the beast had elected to hunt for his own food. Though scarce and usually scrawny, the occasional hare or prairie dog remained. The beast was picky like that, always preferring a live catch over food from a can. This didn't worry Tynuk much because he knew his protector would come flying to him at the first sight or sound of danger.

The boy scanned the half-burned, ransacked store, looking for a few canned goods to satisfy his groaning stomach. Moving down one aisle, he stooped to pick up a can of ravioli and two cans of refried beans. Another grab secured a tin of fish steaks. Four cans wasn't a bad pull from one location. He decided to scan one last time and cut out. But just when he moved to leave, he heard the voices.

Without hesitation Tynuk ducked low and scurried to the rear of the store, pressing his satchel to his side to prevent the cans from clanking. He slunk to the back of the store, where he climbed up some wooden, built-in cabinets to hide like a cat above the aisles. From his position, he remained hidden, with an unobstructed view. Tynuk watched as three men with guns entered, looking up and down the empty aisles.

"I swear I saw a boy come in here."

"You've lost it."

The men laughed.

"I haven't lost it. I'm telling you, I know what I saw. A boy came in here alone."

"If he did, he's gone now."

"Yeah, but are we willing to just let it go without looking?"

Tynuk's blood chilled as he listened to the whispers among the group.

"Boys are tender. Good eating."

"Come out, boy!" one of the men shouted. "We have food, and we'll share it with you. We'll take good care of you."

More laughter followed as one of the men uttered, "We'll take good care of you all right."

Tynuk shifted, his mind working through possible scenarios.

*Cannibals. Even with their guns, I can take all three without too much fuss, but I won't try it unless my hand is forced. No windows. Nowhere to run. Maybe they'll give up.*

Any well-laid plans evaporated as six more armed men entered through the front of the store, laughing as they came. Tynuk was good, but nine to one odds weren't good odds for anyone, especially when at least six of the men had firearms.

"Scouting us out some boy for supper, huh?"

"Shh. If he's in here, he'll hear you, you stupid shit!"

At the offense, the one man grabbed the other, and they began to tussle while the rest watched. There was no organization to this group. They weren't in the same league as a gang like the Coyotes. These men had banded together out of convenience, desperation, and no doubt, because they were willing to eat people to survive.

Tynuk knew this was his chance. He dropping down like a cat from the shelf, landing without a sound in a side aisle, and moved toward the front of the store. As he neared the cashier's desk, he slunk behind it, pressing himself against the cheap particleboard shelving. He would wait for them to begin searching. When they neared the rear of the store, he'd make his move for the exit.

Tynuk waited for the scuffle to subside, finally hearing clomping footsteps spread throughout the store. He waited for the men to distance themselves before he stood but saw that the two men had stayed at the entrance. Tynuk dropped low again, his mind spinning.

*I'm trapped now. They won't leave without checking behind this desk. I can take those two, but not before the rest of them are on me. I'll be shot in the back. Think! Don't be stupid. Slow down and think.*

Tynuk was out of options, and just as he resolved to move with violence against the men, the haunting howl of his companion crept through the air and settled in his ears. A slow smile crept over Tynuk's face.

"What the *hell* was *that?*" one of the men at the door squeaked, as they both spun. The footsteps of the search party clomped down the aisles to the front of the building, the whole group muttering.

"What was that?"

"Coyote?"

"Too big."

"Shh!"

"What the hell was that? Did you hear that?"

"Are there wolves around here?"

"Not anymore, there aren't."

"Shut the fuck up and listen!"

In the silence that followed, Tynuk stood then vaulted over the counter, landing in plain view of the men.

"That's the sound of your death," the boy said. He placed his fingers in his mouth and blew a sharp whistle to confirm his location for his partner.

"Who...what the hell is this?" one of the men asked, motioning at the boy.

"I told you there was a boy."

The mournful howl sounded again, closer this time. The cannibals shook with fear. A few of them raised their weapons toward Tynuk as he dashed into the shadows of the store. Flashes of gunfire rippled through the building as the men fired their guns in all directions.

Tynuk rounded the aisle, staying low in the shadows as he watched a huge black mass of fangs and flying claws cut the stunned men to ribbons. The men screamed in terror, falling over one another as they tried to escape the blood and violence. None of the men could get a shot off at the furious creature, as they went running in a frenzied panic. It was over in seconds, long before Tynuk could get to the storefront to join in.

Running forward, Tynuk came to a stop just as the man before him gasped his last breath, blood smeared across his face in a death gurgle. The boy furrowed his brow at Az and scolded, "I hope you had a good time out there. I almost got my goose cooked."

The beast tossed his head at the boy and yawned.

"Oh, sure. It's not a big deal to you. And by the way, what took you so long?" Tynuk asked, walking through pools of blood beside the hulking, wolf-like beast with blood splattered across his mane. The creature lowered his head in apology.

"Okay. I accept, but only because you live up to your name, vigilant one." Tynuk smiled and patted the beast on the flank.

Az licked the bloody foam from his lips and drooled like a hungry dog. He bent to nose one of the dead men and looked back at Tynuk. It was easy for Tynuk to forget that the beast was still one hundred percent wild animal. To ask such a creature such as this to ignore a fresh kill while in a state of hunger—even if that kill was human—was foolish. Tynuk made a face of disgust but obliged Az with a wave of his hand.

"If you must, but be quick. I'm ready to quit this place," Tynuk spoke, as the hulking creature clicked his teeth and began to feast on the warm remains before him.

# TWENTY

Courtland squeezed his way to the top of the narrow stairwell that led to the roof of the station. With each step, the metal rivets that held each stair in place creaked in protest at the giant's full weight. Courtland mumbled under his breath, grumbling that nothing in this world had ever been built to accommodate him. Pushing the door to the roof open, he ducked, turned, and squeezed his way through the opening onto the gravel roof.

He saw Dagen immediately, the man flat on his back, his crutches scattered as though he'd lost some great struggle with himself. An empty plastic jug of vodka lay just out of reach of his open hand. Courtland sighed as he strode over to the disheveled man, whose eyes were shut, his mouth agape. The slow and steady rise and fall of Dagen's chest confirmed that he was in fact still alive.

"So many demons for one man," Courtland whispered, as he scooped his arm under Dagen and lifted his limp frame. "There are better ways to fight them, my friend. Let's get you some help."

After stooping to grab the man's crutches with his free hand, Courtland turned and headed back to the stairwell. It was a bit more of a puzzle, squeezing himself through while holding a full-grown man and a pair of crutches. After a few minutes of careful maneuvering, Courtland arrived at his destination, where he ducked his way through the double doors and into the medical bay.

Courtland stopped. The sight before him, one of utter catastrophe. Residents of the station filled the room, some on cots, others lying on the bare floor, their bodies crowding the narrow walking spaces before him. The cries and moans of the wounded filled the small space. Courtland scanned the room and located Jenna. She stood up from a chair where Terry had been patching her up, a fresh bandage visible across her collarbone. Terry, who had once been a physician's assistant at a local hospital, was the only other medic besides Jenna at the station.

Courtland caught Jenna's eyes. "Hey, I found him on the roof. He's alive, but he's out of it. It looks like he was trying to overdose on drugs and alcohol."

Jenna's face was unreadable as she nodded her understanding. "All right. Put him on the floor there. When we don't have any more critical patients, I'll take a look at him."

Courtland put Dagen down where Jenna had indicated and turned toward the door. "Do you need anything else?"

Jenna huffed and looked over her shoulder. She'd begun working on a man with a bad head wound. "We need a lot of things. You could help by generating a few prayers for us."

"Of course." Courtland nodded and took a few steps before stopping, his eyes settling on the still, blood-covered form of Shana. Her eyes open, she stared at the ceiling. Her mouth moved, forming soundless words in the low light.

Courtland turned back and called out to Jenna, "Is this Shana?"

"Sure enough. She just showed up at the gate a few minutes ago."

"Did she say anything? Did she say what happened?"

"It's all incomprehensible, Courtland. She's in shock. Whatever happened, it was bad."

Courtland watched the woman's strange, silent incantations as she continued to stare wide-eyed at the ceiling. Maybe she'd recover. Maybe the Sicks would come again in the night, and she'd never get the chance to recover. Only God could know what was in store for them. Courtland shook his head and made his way to the hallway, seeking a reprieve from the moans and the persistent smell of festering wounds.

Pushing through the doors, Courtland stopped momentarily, his bulky form blocking most of the main corridor as people came and went, squeezing past him. He turned and headed toward the front of the station, catching a glimpse of Kane, who carried an armload of wood, most of it broken furniture. Kane dropped the wood at the double doors and turned to Courtland.

"Dagen?"

"He's alive but in a drug-induced coma or something. It looked like vodka and painkillers. I don't know what his condition is. I left him in medical."

Kane scowled and shook his head. For once he refrained from speaking his mind. Not giving him a chance to reconsider, Courtland spoke, gesturing toward the busy people moving about. "What you got going on here?"

"Fortifying the station, just like we said. Any potential entry point is being barricaded—doors, windows, even air vents. We're improvising a lot. It's going to be hard to secure everything as well as we'd like."

Courtland nodded. "And what about these windows here?" he asked, pointing to the six, unobstructed, ground-level bay windows in front of him.

"Well, to be honest, we don't have enough material to secure everything. With that in mind, this is going to be our choke point. Everything behind and above us will get some amount of fortification. Just like outside, we'll set up two lines of defense—riflemen and pikemen. We just have to hope that the savage, mutant, freak instinct to go for the throat is stronger than their tactical reasoning—if they have any. This will be the easiest place for them to enter, so we'll bottleneck them here in the lobby, make them climb over their dead to get in."

"Not bad, but why don't we all just go down to the cellar with the children and ride it out down there?"

"Well, two reasons. First, there's not enough room for everyone, so we'd have to play favorites and choose who got to go in. Second, after they swarm the station, who's to say they won't make this their new home—camp out, put down roots, whatever? We'd be trapped down there with no resources. In the early days, I spent way too long in a fallout bunker. Trust me. That's not how you want to go."

"Okay, so what can I do to help?"

"Grab some of the trashed vehicles outside and move them in front of the bay windows here. That'll help restrict their ability to just pour through."

"And then?"

"We'll double-check everything inside and out to make sure it's all secure."

Kane paused as they both accepted cups of black water from Kris, who was making his rounds carrying a discolored water pitcher. Both men murmured their thanks, quickly drank the water from their cups, and handed them back to Kris.

"Do you think it'll work?" Courtland asked.

"It has to. I don't know what other choice we have."

"Then we'll do our best, and the Lord will take care of the rest," Courtland said with a smile, as he dropped a hand the size of a Thanksgiving turkey on Kane's shoulder.

Kane sighed. "I don't have your faith, big man."

"You do," the giant said, as he made for the double doors that led to the outside, "but you have to remember to trust in it again—just as you once did."

✯ ✯ ✯

Shadows drenched the camp in a murky coolness as Susan pretended to busy herself in her tent with the meaningless task of arranging her meager possessions. As she did, she listened to a conversation she shouldn't be hearing.

"And?" Garrett asked, sounding exasperated.

"And then we extort him. We have the guy's wife and kids. What makes you think he won't come for them?" Saxon replied.

"We don't know this guy, how he'll react."

"Trust me, Garrett. The guy is probably some nobody who got lucky and happened to survive. He'll come to bargain and beg for his family, and we'll take him for everything he's got."

"Assuming she told us the truth about his broadcast," Garrett said.

"She told the truth. You saw how terrified she was. Her kid's life was at risk. The guy will come, and he'll be so desperate to get his family back that he'll have to square with us. That's his only option."

"And when he's square? We can't just go and give him what he came for. I'm not giving the woman up. She belongs to me now."

Susan's stomach twisted with revulsion. She took a deep breath to try to clear the sinking feeling of nausea and hate.

"You won't have to give her up. We'll decide what to do with him when the time comes. It's no rush. This is a sure thing. You heard the broadcast. They've stockpiled resources—resources that are ours for the taking."

"Right," Garrett said, nodding. His head was just on the other side of the canvas. "Yeah, alright. Let's do it."

She'd have to move sooner than she'd thought. The last thing she needed was for Kane's life to be jeopardized because of her. Now that she knew Kane was alive, she wasn't going to lose him again. She'd have to figure out how they planned to entice and entrap him. Then she'd have to beat them to the punch and pull their leverage out from under them. It was the only way. Failure wasn't an option—not now, not after all this.

The tent flap pulled back, startling Susan and sending a wash of prickly heat flowing over her face and shoulders. She felt as though her treasonous thoughts somehow had become visible. In the entrance to the tent stood Garrett and Saxon, both with malevolent grins on their faces.

"Hello, love," Saxon mocked. "Are you ready?"

Susan surveyed the two men for a long moment before answering. "Ready for what?"

"Ready to hear the voice of your long-lost husband, of course. You do want to hear his voice, don't you? I'm sure he misses you and the children very much. Wouldn't it just make your day to hear his voice?"

Susan swallowed hard, then nodded her head. "Yes," she whispered, as a runaway tear escaped the prison of her hardened eyes. "I'm sure it would."

✼ ✼ ✼

He was good at waiting. It's what he did—wait, hide, plot, scheme, and finally, when the moment was just right, act. Ever since the first time, it had come naturally to him, like a spider waiting for the perfect moth. It wasn't something to rush. The spider was never rushed, and neither was he. He could wait as long as he needed to wait, enduring whatever he had to in order to be sure that his plan was successful, executed just the way he planned.

Raith looked through the binoculars again, sweeping the station in the fading evening light. He picked at his yellow, rat-like teeth with a jagged, dirty fingernail and pressed his lips together. Earlier they had fortified every door and window from the ground level up. Now he could see little movement outside the station. It irritated him that he couldn't monitor everyone the way as he wanted to, especially his baby-doll.

She had survived the night, as he knew she would, but she hadn't emerged from inside the station all day. It concerned him that her injuries may have been more severe than he'd first thought. A chill ran over him, and he squirmed at the thought that she might be seriously injured. That was not acceptable, not for her. She had to be perfect. Not a single imperfection. He would collect his doll and spirit her away from all this nonsense. He would take her to where he could savor her, where he could enjoy the game to the fullest.

Even at a glance, it was quite obvious that these pitiful survivors didn't have much left in them. And after the mutants hit them again, which they would, and Malak began to execute his plan, there was no way that they could hold. Not in a million years. At that moment all the waiting would be worth it. Amid the screams, the pillaging, and the fire, Raith would swoop in and secure his dolly quick, quiet, and completely without incident. Then the knowledge of what occurred would forever be shrouded in myth. Only in the dimness of some future day would some survivor say, "Do you remember that woman? The one who took care of everyone else before herself? She was so full of life. What ever happened to her?"

# TWENTY-ONE

Everything was ready at the station. They'd gathered all the necessary supplies—food, water, and ammunition—and brought them to a closer, more central location to limit the number of unnecessary trips. This would increase their combat efficiency once the fighting began.

All they could do now was wait. They had to hold fast to what little courage remained as they awaited the inevitable scraping of bone on bone and the maddened howls of the damned—sounds heralding their most certain doom. The dark of night would usher in the beasts, eyes aflame, jaws and claws poised to tear at the flesh of the innocent. And as they came, so would the final moments of every man, woman, and child at the station.

There was little chance for their survival and each of them seemed to know it. All that remained was their fortification efforts, a dwindling supply of arms and ammunition, and a few weary leaders to guide them through the madness. It was a fearful process, one that transformed every creak of the station or scratch from a gust of wind against the outer walls into the beginning of the end. Everyone seemed jumpy, some resorting to nervous chatter while others sat alone with their thoughts. Every individual dealt with their circumstances as best they could, together but alone, in the artificial light of the station lobby.

Courtland finished praying over several members of the group as they hugged and patted one another on the back. The giant stood, remaining half stooped to wander among the dirty survivors who crowded the lobby. He stopped next to Kane, who was talking to Winston. The radioman appeared frustrated.

"No, that's what I'm telling you, Winston. It's not important right now."

"Sure it is. I can—"

"Winston," Kane said in a softer tone, "I know you're more comfortable down there. Look, everyone is scared. Believe me—I'm scared too, and if I thought that having you stay in the radio room was the best thing, I'd keep you down there. But we need everybody we can spare up here when they hit us. And think about it this way. If we got overrun and you were down there, you'd be trapped down there. They could very well decide to just hang around."

Winston nodded, nervously wringing his hands. "The..." He paused, considering his words. "The last attack made me piss my pants. I've never been so scared that I pissed my pants before. I wasn't even on the front line. I don't think I'm cut out for this stuff."

Kane glanced at Courtland, and the big man nodded. Courtland leaned down toward the nervous man. "You won't be on the front line, but we could use you on support, bringing supplies, water, and ammo to people who need it. Think you can do that for us?"

"Yeah, I suppose so."

"You're a good man, Winston."

"If you say so," the sheepish, chubby man said, as he turned and began carrying crates from the armory to the lobby.

Kane sighed. "I hate the waiting. Let's just get it over with. We're as ready as we're going to be. It has to be past midnight already. It feels like they came earlier last night."

"It's somewhere between eleven and one by my estimation. And yes, you're right. They'd come and gone by this time last night."

"What are they waiting for? We're all but finished as it is."

"Don't say that, Kane. We're not finished. You can't let that resonate in your heart. The Lord is with us. We will triumph over this evil."

Kane rubbed at the center of his chest, trying to massage away the pain that had begun to swell inside his heart. *Why won't it stop aching?*

"Maybe we'll get a break. Maybe they won't—" Courtland stopped midsentence as the high-pitched whine of the bone flute drifted with the light breeze.

"Come," Kane said, finishing Courtland's sentence in a whisper. "They're coming."

"I'll protect the children and act as the last-ditch contingency we discussed."

Kane nodded and turned to address the people in the room. "Everyone on your feet and prepare yourselves. They're coming!"

The room launched to life at once. People ran back and forth, grabbing weapons and other gear. Some swore while others cried out in dismay.

"Keep calm and form up!" Kane yelled. Courtland already had begun to make his rounds, confirming that everyone was in position. Quickly three lines were formed, two compact lines of about ten riflemen with a rear line of approximately fifteen pikemen. The idea was to try to hold off the mutants using rotating columns of fire. They'd either end up victorious or run out of ammunition. If the enemy began to close the gap, the pikemen would advance in an attempt to keep the beasts from flooding the lobby. Since the monsters had no long-range weapons, they would be deadliest up close and personal. When they were that close, any real chance of victory vanished. Humans, especially those without any real combative training, wouldn't be able to contend at that range with such creatures.

Kane watched Jenna pass him on her way to the medical bay, a nagging reminder that half their people were currently receiving medical care. The previous night they'd faced the monsters with twice as many. As the lines settled and the room fell quiet, Kane glanced over the men and women before him. They were good people—some of them good friends—and while they were not warriors, they had become much stronger in the last few weeks. They would die defending one another.

Jacob shuffled up next to him and unslung his M-16A2. He performed a quick function check of the rifle, competently slapped a thirty-round magazine into the magazine well, and tabbed the bolt release.

"Whaddya think?" the teen drawled then spat a stream of tobacco juice onto the floor. He rubbed his jacket sleeve under his chin to catch the black dribble.

"I think that stuff you've got in your mouth is disgusting," Kane teased in a feeble attempt to release some tension.

"Can't scavenge it around here anymore," Jacob said, surveying the courtyard outside the window with a steady gaze. "It's about the same as chewing on gold. Probably tastes better, though." He flashed a nervous smile, spitting again. "Might as well, since I won't live to see another day."

"Come on, Jacob," Kane scolded. "Don't talk like that."

"I'm serious," Jacob said. "I've seen way too many horror movies, and you know as well as I do that the wisecracking, obnoxious kid, the one who's only around for comedic value, doesn't make it. Never does."

Kane shrugged, "fair enough."

"So whaddya think? For real," said Jacob, his voice quieter, more serious.

Before Kane could answer, a scream from outside pierced the night. Everyone in the room flinched. The sound wasn't far away. Just behind the first, a second scream was heard, this one more like a moan, long and low, like a person in terrible pain.

"Not long now!" Kane called to the group, as the rhythmic sound of bone scraping bone began. *Shick, shick, shick, shick.*

Jacob squirmed. "Why do they do that?"

"They want us to fear them," responded Kane, watching the darkness beyond the windows, the night covering the open spaces of the courtyard, cloaking it in a relentless, consuming black.

"Shit works," Jacob mumbled, and scooped the dip from his mouth, flinging it to the floor. He raised his rifle in one motion.

"Fall in line, Jacob, but stay close," Kane whispered.

"Yeah," came the uncharacteristically quiet reply as the teen stepped away from Kane, moving into the front line.

The hellish cadence continued to grow, swelling in the darkness as it seemed to scrape against every last raw nerve Kane possessed. As it grew, he thought he could make out a groan here, a hiss there. The scraping seemed to move closer and closer, as though it were a sound made by the darkness itself. Just when Kane couldn't take it any longer, the sounds stopped. The bone flute's shrill call faded and ceased. Nothing and no one moved in the silence. The people inside the station held their breath in anticipation. An eternity passed.

*"Lights!"* Kane screamed at the top of his lungs.

With a pop, the bluish halogen glow threw back the shadows and bathed the courtyard in an eerie false light. A collective gasp was emitted as the station defenders were met with hundreds of the mutant creatures, the red of their eyes like tongues of fire. In that singular moment of stillness, the flute sang once more as the Sicks snapped to life, throwing themselves in a frenzy toward the windows and the terrified station defenders.

"Rifle team one, *fire!*"

It took just a fraction of a second for the command to fire to shatter the fear-induced inaction of the group. In a deafening blast, the rifles of the front line blazed to life, the cacophony in the confined space like raw energy poured into the air. The rounds found their marks, tearing ragged holes in the freaks as they clambered toward the shattering windows.

"*Cease fire! Reload! Team two, advance and fire!*"

Like the cogs of a machine, the second line advanced through the first, their faces full of fear and determination as they raised their rifles and brought a second wave of fiery destruction. The plan was working. The beasts were so enraged that they straight into the concentrated fire, pouring en masse through the restricted opening, bottlenecking, crawling right over their fallen as they howled in lust for the human flesh inside. In wave after wave, they came as Kane and the defenders destroyed them, their broken bodies beginning to amass in piles outside the window.

"Last mag!" someone yelled.

"Me too!" cried another.

The ammunition was running out as the creatures continued to swarm. They pushed through the windows even as they were blown apart by rifle fire.

"I'm out!" several riflemen cried.

Kane stepped forward and lowered his rifle. "Pikemen, advance! This is our house! They will not take it!"

With a roar the pikemen charged forward, their lances outstretched as they collided with the beasts.

"Everyone else, fall back into the hallway!" Kane shouted, as the support personnel poured into the hall and the riflemen fell in behind them, their empty weapons raised.

"Second rifle squad, up the stairs to the catwalk! Drop whatever ammo you have left on them from above! First rifle squad, hold and protect the med bay!"

Kane watched, helpless, as the pikemen were slaughtered and pushed back, the monsters still pouring through the windows and moving toward the narrow hallway.

"Prepare yourselves," Kane gasped, as the mutants rushed forward. Shots and screams rang out in the darkened hallway.

With a deep breath, Courtland relaxed and stepped off the roof of the station, directly above the bottlenecked swarm of mutants. The free fall took just a moment, and in that brief moment, he asked God to cover him in the grip of grace. With the sound of lightning erupting from the heavens, the giant hit the earth in the center of the Sicks, obliterating several under his boots. Rising back up, Courtland used his enormous black blades to tear a gaping hole in the swell of monsters.

From behind the barred doors of the medical bay, Jenna and a few others stood facing the door. They were the last defense for the wounded, those who would not be able to protect themselves when the monsters came. The pistol in her hand trembled as she checked it again to make sure the safety was off. She heard Kane shouting commands in the hallway as the screams of his men and women reached her ears. A few of the wounded in the med bay cried out in fear. Jenna responded with soothing words. One way or another, it would soon be over.

Five of Kane's people had fallen, then six, seven, as more became trapped in the hallway, the monsters continuing to push forward. Blood splashed the walls amid a tangle of claws and rifles. The two groups flowed forward and back, like bloody waves on an open ocean. The ammunition was gone. In a blind rage, Kane screamed and used the butt of his rifle to crush a Sick's face against the wall as it lunged for him. The creatures were all over them. There was no escape.

In the courtyard, Courtland bellowed as the mutants enveloped him like a swarm of ravenous insects. For a moment he feared that they would devour him, that he would become overwhelmed by the sheer numbers thrown at him. And then, without warning, the song of the bone flute filled the air once more.

Immediately the monsters stopped, entranced by the melody. Kane's mouth hung open, his lungs heaving, his back to the wall. He sat gasping, with his forearm wedged under the neck of one beast in a desperate attempt to keep the monster from eating his face. With a snarl the creature freed itself, dragging its claws and tearing a hole in Kane's shirt as it pulled away. The Sick fled back down the hallway with the others as they climbed through the windows and disappeared into the night.

Courtland stood, anger swelling within him, as the swarm dispersed into the darkness. The giant roared to their wake, "Come on! I'm right here! Finish me if you can!"

And then silence. Once again the sound of the flute had stayed them, stopping the creatures from wiping out the station defenders altogether.

Courtland huffed and released his weapons, dropping to the ground in exhaustion as he watched the monsters disappear, fading before him into the dark embrace of the night. Inside the station, the remaining survivors breathed a sigh of relief, a far cry from the victory cheers of the night before, for they knew this was no victory. Just as a cat plays with its prey before it pounces to kill, these vile creatures were drawing out the inevitable, toying with their targets in the final hours of pursuit.

Kane, Jacob, and one other man were the only survivors from the first rifle team. The second team had been cut in half, and all the pikemen had perished, every last one. Jacob and Kane slid down the blood-streaked wall and collapsed next to each other in the darkness of the hallway. Neither man could speak as the adrenalin rushed through their bodies. Jacob reached into his pocket and fumbled with a crinkled plastic bottle of black water. He struggled to open it, taking a deep gulp that splashed over his chin. His hand shaking, he handed the bottle to Kane, who took a deep breath through his nose then held it to slow his breathing and heart rate. He then took a big gulp of the clouded water.

"Kane!" Courtland called from the windows.

Kane cleared his throat as he wiped his mouth. "I'm here."

"Thank God. I'll check on the children."

Kane didn't reply but stood and offered Jacob his hand. For once the teen had nothing to say.

"How about you? You all right?"

Jacob nodded.

"Give me a hand with the others."

A few minutes of searching confirmed that Jenna and those in the medical bay were okay, as were the children in the cellar. Those who were able began to remove and separate the bodies of friends and foe, isolating those who were wounded. Winston appeared, pushing his cracked glasses to his face. His pants were newly wet, and he shook as he spoke.

"Are they gone? Are they gone, Kane?"

Kane nodded, realizing Winston had slipped away during the fighting. *Coward.*

"Kane...I...I just couldn't do it."

"Forget about it, Winston. Just help us out, okay?" Kane spoke, his exhaustion and irritation overflowing.

"Kane—"

"Winston, just help us out, damn it."

"No, Kane," Winston stated, attempting to sound assertive. "You're going to want to hear me out."

Flabbergasted, Kane turned toward the soft, chubby man and raised his hands. "What is it?"

"It's the radio."

"It's going to have to wait. If someone is making contact, you'll have to tell them they're on their own for now."

"No, Kane. You don't understand. You want to hear this. There's a guy on the radio. He says he has your wife and kids."

✼ ✼ ✼

"Who *is* this?" The question disappeared into a wash of static that made everyone in the room wince.

"You don't need to know," came the fuzzy response.

Kane tightened his fingers around the microphone. He paused, forcing himself not to blurt out what he wanted, not to scream into the microphone. He took a deep breath and let it out slow.

"Look, I don't know what your game is, fella, but these aren't trusting times. How do I know you aren't blowing smoke?"

The reply sounded coarse, like the scratching of fingernails on a chalkboard. "Your wife is a delicious brunette. Together you have twins. The girl cries too much, and the boy doesn't talk often. Do as we say, and we'll return them all to you."

*If this is true and you have them, I'll kill you.*

"I don't believe you. Let me speak to them."

"I don't think so, big man. You're just going to have to take my word for it." The voice said.

"You're bluffing. You've given me nothing substantial to validate your claim."

"Maybe so, but if you don't come, you'll have to live with the fact that I might have had your family and you let them die. It's your choice."

"Yeah, it is my choice," Kane tried to contain the snarl in his tone. "So what is it you want?"

"Our camp is about four miles southwest of your station, off Highway Seventeen, up Steed Creek Road. Come at first light, alone. Bring a vehicle loaded with whatever you value most. Make sure it equals the value of your family and represents what they're worth to you. We'll evaluate whether the trade is fair. When you see the fires of our camp, stop your vehicle one hundred yards out. Step out of the vehicle with your hands visible. Try anything funny, and they die."

*I'm going to kill you—every last one of you.*

"First light. I got it."

"Screw this up and your family is dead."

The scratch of static made everyone wince again as the radio went silent. Winston turned down the volume. Kane stood, turning to face him and Courtland. Jacob leaned back against a nearby wall, his face covered in darkness.

"What time is it?" Kane asked Winston. Exact time had ceased to be important long ago, but Winston still possessed one of those fancy kinetic watches. He looked down to check it.

"Three forty-five in the morning."

"So with the cloud cover, I've got three hours or so before first light."

"What are you thinking?" Courtland asked, his voice a whisper.

"I'm thinking..." Kane pondered, touched his lips. "I can't believe this. How could they have survived all this time? My family is...This isn't possible."

"I don't like it," Courtland murmured. The gentle giant's usual easy demeanor seemed worn and guarded. "They're going to extort you."

Kane began to pace. "Of course they are, but what choice do I have?"

"If you go, the mutants will finish the rest of us."

With an expression raw with grief and pain, Kane turned to face Courtland. "It's my family." He clenched his jaw as he recalled the dusty voice describe his wife as *delicious*. It made his skin crawl, the familiar, prickly feeling of white-hot rage took hold. "I'm going to get my family—and I'm not trading shit for them!"

"Kane..." Courtland swallowed. "I don't like where this is going. We don't know if they have them yet."

"The guy described my family!"

"I don't like what's been happening to you."

"What's that supposed to mean?"

"It means we've all been through a lot, and we need you," Courtland reasoned. "I need you—the Kane I first knew in those early days."

"So I'm supposed to ignore the fact that a group of bandits may have my family?"

"Kane, I'm not trying to be hurtful, but what are the odds that your wife and kids survived and made it up here from Miami? We can't spare you right now. We've almost been reduced to nothing."

"Come with me," Kane pleaded. "Help me, Court. I need you in this."

Courtland dropped his head and wrung his hands. "I... can't."

Kane raised his voice. "You said you were with me. You said you had my back, always."

"I know I did, but I have to be here. I have to protect the people here—the children. What you're thinking...this is something different. Something isn't right with this."

"Of course it's not right. They plan to kill me. I know the law of the land. But if they have my family captive...What is it you want from me?" Kane yelled, causing him to wince and press his palm to his chest.

"What? Are you alright?" Courtland asked.

"It's nothing. Forget about it."

"What about when the Sicks come back for the rest of us? You're the leader of this group, and we need you," Courtland said. "When this is settled, I swear I'll do everything I can to help you secure your family—if they're alive and if these people have them. But think of how many families are here now. There are people *here* who need us."

"If you're not with me in this, you're against me," Kane stated firmly.

"Don't say that, Kane. Don't do it like this."

"It's done. I'm going,"

"Your choice will doom the rest of us. I can feel it." Courtland paused. "I already know what you're going to do."

"Oh, you read people's minds now?"

"Yeah. You're going to murder those people, whether they have your family or not."

Kane picked up a chair and hurled it across the room. "You're damn right I am! Those bastards will get what's coming to them! They're going to find out what happens when you hold my family hostage!" He stormed past Courtland and Winston, heading for the door.

"Kane, *stop*!" Courtland growled, fierceness in his voice. The sound made everyone in the room freeze, Kane included.

Kane turned slowly, his eyes betraying his fear and agony as his gaze locked on Courtland.

"You need to hear me, just this once," Courtland said. "I understand why you feel you have to go, but you've become reckless and self-absorbed. Neither God nor I can protect you in this. If you do it this way, you'll do it alone."

"I'm tired of all of the unanswered prayers. I'm tired of waiting on God to do something that he doesn't seem interested in doing. Why isn't he here now, like he was in the early days? He's abandoned us."

"No. It's you, Kane," Courtland whispered. "You've shut him out."

"Great. Thanks for the sermon, preacher. Since you've got such a great connection, why don't you talk to Him for me? And while you're at it, tell him to stop wasting my time," Kane spat as he slammed the door.

Courtland dropped his head, feeling the pain and regret of things left unsaid. Pulling away from the wall, Jacob glanced at him before pushing the door open to the outside.

"I gotta go with him, Mr. Courtland. I'm sorry. I owe him my life."

Courtland didn't respond as the teen lowered his head and left the room, the door closing with a click behind him. Winston collected the thrown chair and set it back in place.

After a quiet moment alone with the giant, Winston spoke cautiously. "What do you think? Are we going to be okay? I mean, those of us who stay here."

The giant remained silent for a long while as a myriad of troubled thoughts tumbled through his mind. He sighed as he considered Winston's question. "It seems like the world is falling down around us," he said. "We're down several more men now, including the leader of this group. He can leave, but the mutants will come again."

"But you can lead us, right?"

"I don't know, Winston. This wasn't part of the plan."

"What plan?"

"The one I swore to follow a long time ago."

# TWENTY-TWO

Kane moved hurriedly, stuffing a few items into a camouflage backpack. He holstered his Glock and slipped two extra magazines into a pouch on his belt. The man named Arrice worked beside him, preparing the items that he would need. Kane didn't know the man well. It surprised Kane when Arrice volunteered to go. The man was dark-skinned and spoke with a thick African accent. He'd been on the second rifle team and had proven himself proficient with a long gun. Arrice told Kane that no one had helped him when his family died and he wouldn't let the same happen to someone else. Kane offered his condolences and gladly accepted the man's help.

In minutes word spread around the station that Kane was leaving. The news didn't have far to travel. Only about fifteen able-bodied people remained. The rest were injured or had become ill. Kane felt a certain amount of guilt over leaving the people at the station, especially given the many wounded and the children with few to protect them from the evil that would come again after nightfall. But Kane felt he'd these people his problem long enough. He had to make a choice, and that choice had been clear. Courtland could think whatever he wanted; his family wasn't being held hostage any longer.

Jacob entered the armory behind Kane and stopped in the doorway. "I'm going with you."

"No, you're not. You're needed here."

"You can't choose that for me."

"Sure I can. You're just a boy."

Jacob stepped forward and grabbed Kane's jacket, half turning him. "This *boy* just stood shoulder to shoulder with you in that damn hallway. Besides, you know I owe you one. I'm coming."

Kane turned and pushed Jacob's hand away. The teen stared at Kane with hardened eyes. "Your call, kid," Kane responded, turning back to his task, "but I'm not responsible for you. You can't be stupid about this. You've got to pull your own weight. Grab whatever ammo you need, but we'll be traveling light. Meet us out in the courtyard. We're out of here in five minutes."

"You got it," Jacob said, as he stepped forward, taking a rifle from Arrice's outstretched hand. "I won't let you down."

✵ ✵ ✵

The three men double-checked their weapons and their equipment. Then they loaded up into the old truck. The vehicle idled in the center of the courtyard as Courtland watched from the catwalk on the second floor above. Kane gave the signal to move. As the truck pulled forward, the double doors of the station swung open, and out came a woman, walking briskly toward them. Kane motioned for Arrice to stop.

"I'm in too," Shana said, as she climbed into the back of the vehicle. Though she'd cleaned herself up some, her body and clothes were still partially covered in blood.

"Shana? But you were in shock or something. Are you okay?"

"I'm fine. I want to go," she said, stuffing a revolver into her waistband.

"Look, you're obviously competent and all, but you were missing for a while," Kane explained, "and you still haven't told anyone what happened."

"I was kidnapped by bandits who beat, raped, and tortured the shit out of me until I was able to escape. Cal, Mico, and the rest were all murdered. Does that cover it?"

Everyone sat silent, looking at Shana. This unexpected change in her condition had come out of nowhere. Kane was still trying to find the right words when she spoke again.

"All I'm saying is if you're going with the intention of wreaking havoc on some bandit scum, then I want in. I've got a personal score to settle."

Kane glanced quickly at the other two, who both nodded in agreement. "Then you're in," Kane said, leaning forward. "So here's how I'm thinking we do this."

✧ ✧ ✧

The world burned, and as it did, the moon turned to blood. The stars fell from the sky one by one, spinning and breaking apart in the atmosphere, bursting in showers of sparks that rained down upon the darkened landscape. The shadows of the dark ones gathered on the horizon as they waited for the fire to spread, sending hopelessness and despair like a cancer into all who could not fight against it. The darkness would never stop, not until the last shred of light was extinguished from the world and every last shred of hope was gone.

*This is how it ends when you allow the light to die.*

Tynuk jerked upright on his bed of wool military blankets. The light of the fire felt warm and comforting in the stillness of the cool prairie night. The boy looked across the fire to the beast, curled on his belly, snout to the ground, his silvery eyes winking in the glow of the fire. The beast rarely slept if the boy was sleeping, as though he held to an unspoken duty to watch over his friend. Ever vigilant, Azolja was indeed deserving of his name.

Tynuk pushed a blanket aside and pulled his knees to his chest, a concerned look on his face. In response the wolf-like creature raised his massive head ever so slightly. He tilted his head as if he'd been asked a question. Tynuk noticed and met the creature's gaze, one that seemed to bore into him. Tynuk felt something eternal behind the beast's eyes.

"It's the vision, Az," the warrior boy muttered. "The vision came to me again in a dream."

The beast bobbed his head.

"It's always the same. The world burns, the moon turns to blood, the stars fall, and the darkness threatens to drown out the light. There is no one to stop it." The boy stopped and looked away from the beast. "I don't yet know what this means for us. Are we supposed to try and stop this event? There is much I don't yet know. Maybe my uncle and cousin will know more. Surely they will join us in our cause."

The beast gave a light woof and rested his muzzle back against the earth. Tynuk sighed.

"I fear for the safety of our friends, though, Az. I fear for Courtland and Kane and the others at the station. Their light may be fading. If so, then it may be fading just as the darkest times are upon them. I can only hope they look to the Spirit for the strength to face the darkness of that coming day. If they do not, if the darkness extinguishes their light, as the vision predicts, I fear we may never see the rising of the sun again."

Dagen sat up with great effort, holding his head in his hands and moaning. His tongue felt like a plank of flayed wood in his throat. He was dehydrated and felt the faint introduction of a headache pulsate behind his temples. Dagen pressed back against the wall behind him as the cries and groans of agony that surrounded him hung thick in the air like smog.

Rubbing his eyes, Dagen fumbled for a moment as he tried to identify his surroundings. He couldn't remember how he'd gotten wherever he was. His eyes felt as though they were stuck to the inside of his eyelids. He groaned in frustration and cleared his throat a few times, which sent him into a spasm of coughing. The stinking, moist warmth of the room rose and filled his nostrils, the smell death and fear. A few silhouettes drifted across his field of vision, and as they went, a host of pleading arms grasped and called out for the figures. For all Dagen knew, he was in hell, right where he belonged. He closed his eyes and tried to think, to recover the last thing he remembered.

The rooftop. He'd tried to jump. Jenna had saved him. No, there was more, something else. He rubbed at his face. The pills and vodka—that was it. He'd tried to overdose on the roof. It hadn't worked, unless he really was in hell.

A slight figure appeared and knelt beside him. He felt a gentle hand rest on his shoulder blade. No, he wasn't in hell because she was here. He knew who it was long before words were spoken. Something felt different.

Something inside him felt real, like a caterpillar emerging from the darkness of its cocoon into the light of day for the first time. The emergence was painful, but something about it felt honest, as though some of the false layers were being peeled away.

"Why?" she whispered, handing him a cup of cloudy, lukewarm black water.

Dagen didn't answer and cleared his throat again. He drained the shallow cup and waited as the bitter liquid poured down his throat, giving life to his broken voice. He coughed again, dipped his fingers into the remaining moisture, and rubbed a small amount into his eyes to help clear them.

"You know why."

"Killing yourself won't change anything, Dagen."

"I wasn't trying to change. I was trying to die."

"We've been over this—"

"Yeah, I know," Dagen said, blinking a few times as his vision returned. He turned to see Jenna giving him that look again.

"I hate it when you look at me like that."

"Then stop trying to take your own life," she replied. "It's selfish, and you're obviously not any good at it." She gave a small smile.

"Okay, make jokes."

"Hey," Jenna said, looking Dagen in the face. "I'm just glad to see you're all right."

Dagen pulled his eyes from hers—eyes that seemed to know his most terrible secrets. "Where am I?"

"You're in the medical bay. Courtland found you on the roof and brought you down."

"You got any more water?"

Jenna shook her head. "There may be a few bottles floating around, but the black-water reserves are gone. No water has been scavenged recently. It's not looking good."

Dagen's vision grew stronger as he adjusted his position against the wall and looked around the room. "What's with all the people?"

Jenna's face grew serious. "You've missed a lot. We've been under siege for the last two days by a huge group of Sicks, an organized group. With you out of it on the roof, we never saw them coming."

Dagen lowered his head, the shame of yet another personal failure made real by the deaths of so many. He'd thought his responsibility as lookout had been unimportant. He couldn't have been more wrong.

"You said they're organized?" Dagen asked, deflecting the focus of the conversation off him.

"It's a long story, but there's one creature who leads the others."

"A leader?"

Jenna nodded.

"Why are they attacking now?"

"We don't know exactly. Maybe because Kane and Jacob stumbled into their group and killed a few of them.

"How many are there?"

"Hundreds. They broke through the outer fence two nights ago. Last night we fell back and defended the station. They got in here too. They stopped just short of wiping us out. We think they're toying with us. They'll come again tonight. You'll see."

"Is that where you got this?" Dagen asked, pointing to the bandage across her collarbone.

Jenna nodded.

"That's crazy. Just a few days ago everything was fine here."

"Yeah, and on top of that, Kane is gone now so—"

"He's gone?"

"No one can believe it. I heard he got a radio message about someone holding his family captive. He left with three others in one of the trucks a few hours ago."

"I did miss a lot."

"You did. There aren't many of us left. Now our numbers are mostly the injured and children. We won't stand a chance when the Sicks come again."

"What are we going to do?" Dagen asked, his face softer, the weight of his role in their situation heavy upon him.

Jenna shrugged. "What can we do?"

"We take the fight to them," came a throaty rumble from across the room. Dagen and Jenna turned to see Courtland push through the medical bay doors, a few heavy duffel bags across his shoulders. He was followed by a small group of individuals carrying weapons and equipment. Kris from the commissary stood among them.

"What's going on, Courtland?" Jenna spoke up.

"I've been thinking about what you said the other day—about these creatures being controlled by the one, their leader. He uses the song of the flute to get them to do what he wants."

"So, what about it?"

"You said it yourself, Jenna. We could kill every one of those things, and it still won't stop until he says so. They revere him. If we take him down, maybe they'll disperse like you said."

"Uh, Courtland, I, uh…" Jenna backpedaled.

"Isn't that what you said yesterday?"

"It was, but I'd been up all night staring death in the face. I wasn't exactly in my right mind at the moment."

"I think you were, and we need to be thinking outside the box right now. Look, they're attacking us at night, which means they must be sleeping during the day. They're animals, just like us. The difference is that they're the predators here. They have no reason to fear us. Attacking them is the least logical thing we could do. Which is exactly why we're going to do it."

"I'm not following you," said Dagen, frowning and shaking his head. "You want to use a handful of people to assault a much larger force head-on? That's certifiable crazy."

"No, no," said Courtland, kneeling down to their level. "Not assault. Infiltrate and assassinate. It's brilliant. We take a small force, slip in under their noses while they're sleeping, take out their leader, and while they're reeling from the confusion, we make our getaway."

Jenna shrugged. "We have no reason to believe they'll disperse if they're not controlled by their leader. They could just as easy turn on you."

"Maybe so, my dear Jenna." Courtland nodded. "But if we do nothing, they'll come here tonight and murder every man, woman, and child at this station. What else can we do?" the giant said, returning to his full height and adjusting one of the bags on his shoulder.

"That's the stupidest thing I've ever heard," Dagen said, as he gathered his crutches and struggled to his feet. "I'm in."

Courtland gave him a serious look. "And what can you do to help?"

"Well, I'm a pretty good tactician. I've had years of training. I can help orchestrate your infiltration. In addition you give me a good rifle and an elevated position of overwatch, and I can shoot a burning matchstick from your fingertips at three hundred yards. My time in the marine corps wasn't for nothing."

Dagen's cold, analytical delivery convinced Courtland and Jenna that not only was this true, but also somewhere, somehow he'd actually performed this dangerous feat in the past.

Courtland nodded and smiled. "I think I have just the weapon for you. Get what you need, and meet us out front ASAP. I'll get your rifle." Turning to Jenna, he continued, "Lock everyone down here as well as you can until we return. Even if the Sicks don't come back, you're vulnerable to bandits with the fence down."

Jenna nodded and watched Dagen take a few awkward steps with his crutches. "Wait," she called out. "I'm not sure what to say here. You're risking your lives for the rest of us. You're doing this so they don't come for us again."

"We're doing it because it has to be done," Courtland said.

"Right, and I appreciate that. It's just…this sounds like a suicide mission."

"Then it's right up my alley, isn't it?" Dagen said, the edges of his mouth turning up to form a sly smile.

# TWENTY-THREE

Tynuk crouched low and observed the scene with curiosity and caution. The camp was alive. Even at such an early hour, they didn't wait for the sun to rise to begin the day's work. Tynuk saw people, both male, and female, moving back and forth in front of the glowing light as heavy curls of smoke belched into the sky.

Tynuk had seen the fires from a long way off. He'd known immediately that they'd finally found what they'd been looking for. He and the beast had diverted south and then west as they approached Amarillo, Texas. Though he'd intended to avoid the city as usual, Tynuk also sought to stay away from the interstate. It no longer took him in the right direction. His final destination was southwest through Palo Duro Canyon, toward the Llano Estacado and above the Caprock Escarpment. There he would find the remnants of a civilization that had lived and thrived long before the one that was now dead.

As they approached Palo Duro, Tynuk and the beast saw the glow of distant fires burning along the canyon. The camp was definitely Native American. The tepee dwellings, their arrangement, the horses, and the muffled, non-English language all served to confirm his suspicion. The camp included twenty to twenty-five members, either a scouting or a raiding party. Were these people the true bloods Tynuk had been looking for? Or could they be some other tribe? It was impossible for the boy to know without making contact. He shuffled back a few paces, away from his place of observation, and patted Azolja on the head.

"I don't want to seem confrontational. I'll wait until first light, and then I'll approach the camp—alone." He rubbed his friend on the snout. "You are my brother, but they won't understand you. I must make contact alone, and you must not interfere—no matter what. This part must be my journey alone."

The beast gazed at him with ethereal, silver eyes. They seemed to convey an almost celestial understanding.

"Do you understand?"

The beast lowered his head.

"Good. Then let us rest here together for a little while longer. When the sun has risen, we will see where fate leads us."

✲ ✲ ✲

Dagen carried a satchel loaded with the last of his water ration, a wool blanket, a few makeshift squeeze bags, a pair of binoculars, a note pad and a pencil, and fifty rounds of ammunition—all that was left in the armory. He didn't know which rifle Courtland would bring or how it was outfitted, but he had been told it was chambered in 308. Stabbing at the ground with his crutches, Dagen swung his legs forward and rounded the corner. Looking up, he caught sight of the doors to the medical bay and hesitated.

*Keep going. There's nothing left to say.*

"Yes, there is," he whispered to himself. "There's still so much."

Dagen dug deep into his pocket and coiled the silver chain and cross around his fingers. He'd held on to it for too long. Moving with long strides on his crutches, Dagen made his way up to the doors and eased them open with his shoulder. He took a moment to survey the room until his eyes came to rest on the woman he loved, the woman who should never have to know how he felt.

"Jenna," he said, her name catching in his throat.

She looked up and caught sight of him dressed to leave. She gave a small nod but kept her focus as she talked with one of her patients. After a moment, she rose and crossed the room. Dagen watched as she made her way among the wounded and the sick like an angel sent from God to do His good work on earth.

"Ready to head out?" she said as she approached.

"Yeah," Dagen said, dropping his gaze, his fingers still touching the cross in his pocket. "I uh…"

*You can do this. You could die, and if you do, you're a coward if you take this to your grave. Give it to her. Tell her.*

"What's up?" asked Jenna, surveying him. She looked puzzled.

"Can you step into the hall for just a sec?"

"Okay," she murmured, her confusion deepening.

As they stepped out, the doors swung shut behind them, blocking them from the view of others in the med bay. Dagen took a second to compose himself.

"Look," he began. "I need to give you something I should have given you a long time ago. I'm sorry I didn't."

"Dagen, I don't know what this is about—" Jenna gasped and put her hands to her face as Dagen held up the small silver cross and connected chain. "That can't be," she cried, as the scooped the cross from his hands, tears welling in her eyes. "Have you had this since…since…?"

"Yeah," Dagen said, looking away. "I took it off your daughter. I… don't know why I kept it…" Dagen paused and cautiously raised his eyes to see Jenna weeping as she clutched at the small chain to her lips. The sight of which caused the stone of his heart to crumble, like the ancient facade of a forgotten fortress, darkened by self-loathing and fear. "Jenna." He swallowed. "I'll hate myself forever for what I've done to you, for what I took from you."

"Why are you saying this to me, Dagen? Why now?" Jenna mumbled through her tears.

"You rescued me—showed me the way," he responded, his voice faltering. "You told me I can be redeemed—that it's up to me to choose if I can accept that gift or not."

Jenna nodded and wiped the tears from her face with her shirtsleeve. "All I've wanted for you is to be free from what you can't change. And I thought that if I could care for you more than I hate you, then maybe you'd understand the things I've said. God has spared you for a reason. I want you to know why."

Dagen nodded and swallowed hard. "You told me that Jesus died for me, that He was enough, even for someone like me. If you're a reflection of His love, then maybe that's true. But I have to start by telling you that I'll always owe you something I can't repay."

Jenna shook her head. "No. You don't owe me anything else."

"Yes, I do," Dagen said. "I'll always owe you…something," he said, as he turned and started to go.

"Hey," Jenna called with a sniffle. "This is all so twisted, but…" She exhaled as she wiped her face and rolled her eyes. "Gosh, Dagen. Everything is so messed up. I'm just so…ugh. Look, you're all I have left. I don't want you to go, okay?"

"You know I have to," he answered. "You know why." He pushed the door to the courtyard open with his shoulder and turned on his crutches to face her once again. "You're the best thing that ever happened to a guy like me. I'm going to prove that to you the only way I know how."

"What are you going to do?" Jenna said, bringing her hands to her chest.

"I don't believe in me, Jenna, but you do. You never gave up on me, even when you had every right to. I never deserved your kindness, but you gave it anyway. I don't deserve God's love, but still, you say he loves me."

Jenna nodded, tears glistening in her eyes.

Dagen glanced down and shook his head slowly. He looked back at Jenna, connecting once more with her tearful gaze.

"It's all so hard for me to accept. I'm not even sure I *can* accept it. I don't know if we can save this station, and I'm not sure I can become that man, the man you believe I can be. But for the first time in my life, I'm not afraid to hope, and I'm not afraid to try."

✰ ✰ ✰

"They are divided, Lord Malak," Saxon said, as he bowed his head before the leader of the Coyotes. His resources and his men were organized to achieve the maximum effect against his enemies. It would not fail. Not now.

"Raith reports that Kane is en route to Garrett's camp with a few others to secure his family. It's looking like they're armed and plan to use force."

Malak turned to face his lieutenant. "And the giant?"

"He has departed as well, we believe on some mission to stop the beasts that have whittled down their numbers."

Malak smiled. "So who is left at the station?"

"Not many. Mostly the injured and the children. There is no one there to protect them or the resources they have left, including the fuel tanker that was taken from you months ago when—"

Malak snarled as he grabbed Saxon by the throat. "Are you saying I was defeated?"

Saxon gasped. "No, of course not! It was a part of your plan to leave them be so you could finish them on your own terms."

"Exactly," responded Malak. "You won't ever question my methods if you value your life," he hissed into the blue of the man's face.

"No, of course not. I would never—"

"Good," Malak spat, releasing Saxon and turning to survey the men as they lined up the vehicles and prepared the weapons. His temporary base at the Reeds at Colonial Pointe had been functional, but it was time to leave, to discover something on a grander scale. It was time for Malak to make his move and claim his destiny.

Saxon swore and rubbed at his neck.

"Stop crying like a little bitch, and pull yourself together," Malak growled. "Contact Raith and tell him to move ahead with taking the station and what's left of the people there. Tell him that when he's finished, we'll meet back up on Highway Forty-Five, north of Seventeen."

Saxon nodded, a hand still on his neck. "And what do you need me to do?"

"You and I will be moving in on Garrett's camp to take advantage of Kane's separation from that giant who follows him around like a loyal dog."

"Yes, Lord Malak."

"And tell Raith to leave nothing to chance during his assault. I have given him my consent to collect the woman he wants, but beyond that there must be no survivors. Even the children must die. Do you understand?"

"I do, my lord."

Malak glowered. "They won't know what hit them until they've been reduced to nothing. They will beg for their God to save them, but he will not for he is a cruel and unjust hypocrite, a disinterested tyrant who loves only himself."

Though Dagen had joked about the plan being a perfect fit for him, he knew it was suicidal. It was especially risky for Courtland, Kris, and the other men who would make a run for it. They planned to blitz straight into the camp of Sicks while the mutant freaks slept. They'd head straight for the one who controlled the others and hope that if they could take him down, the others would flee.

*Fat chance. Definitely a suicide mission.*

The mutant camp hadn't been difficult to locate. It sat just two miles away, due west into the hills. After confirming the location, they parked the truck and walked in to avoid detection. That had been easier said than done, especially since Dagen relied on crutches to get around.

It had taken him much longer than planned to get into position. His crutches weren't made for off-road travel. After the first coating of clay, they'd become useless. Dagen had to crawl, dragging his rifle and gear the last fifty yards up the hillside. The extensive crawling on his elbows had brought on a strong sense of déjà vu, taking Dagen back to his military days, reminding him of how exhausting the simplest tasks could be.

Finally, in position, Dagen could now see that his guess on which location to use had been correct. From his elevated position, he had a clear line of sight through the camp for approximately two hundred fifty yards. Before Dagen contacted Courtland as planned, he took a moment to analyze the best means of approach for Courtland and the others.

He observed the terrain, noting the rolling hills on all sides, and the camp's position in the center of a short valley. The scene was strange. The encampment appeared as though it might belong to some primitive culture. It had a dirty, disheveled look, which might befit any cave-dwelling or woodland creatures. But there were also structures, more like huts made of wood and clay. These were spaced at regular intervals throughout the camp, with an enlarged open space in the center. Dagen could just make out a large fire pit, the hot coals mere specks through the lens of his binoculars. Further on, he saw a larger mud hut, three or four times the size of those around it, which seemed to push its way out of the earth. Dagen watched it for a few minutes. Nothing moved in or around the camp. Courtland was right. Like any animal, they had to sleep, and since they seemed to fight and hunt at night, it made perfect sense that they would rest during the day.

Dagen pulled his eye from the scope mounted to the top of the Remington 700 bolt-action rifle Courtland had given him. It seemed an interesting coincidence that it was the same style of rifle Dagen used in the marines. Given this familiarity, the rifle felt like an extension of himself. After a quick test fire back at the station and a few minor adjustments to the glass, he felt confident that anything that landed in his sights was as good as dead. From his position, he observed everyone and everything from above much like a bird of prey, as he used his wool blanket to brace himself from the cold turf beneath him.

He caught a slight movement in his peripheral vision near the base of the hill before it registered as Courtland's massive frame, crouched among the foliage. The image of the giant attempting to hide, like an elephant behind a flowerpot, brought a smirk to Dagen's face. He keyed up his radio and listened for the transmit tone.

"Dagen to Courtland. Do you copy?"

"I copy," came the muffled reply in his earpiece.

"You look ridiculous trying to hide behind that bush."

"Tell me something I don't know. Have you got a decent line of sight?"

"Yeah," answered Dagen. "The camp is just ahead of you in the seat of the valley, approximately thirty yards up the embankment. I see mud huts, at least a hundred of them, each able to accommodate maybe four or five of those things. It all looks fresh, like they just settled there, possibly because of the conflict with us."

"Okay. What else? What's our best approach?"

"Straight up from where you are now, there's a path. It zigzags some through the structures, but it goes straight to the center of camp. Follow it and you hit an open area. Keep your radio on, and I'll try to call out strays and threats. Copy?"

"Yeah. What then?"

"There's a big dwelling, significantly bigger than the others. No question that's the head honcho's place. I'd bet anything you'll find him inside. Just be careful and move quickly. Once you're in, they'll probably start to surround you and cut off avenues of escape."

"We'll get in there and take him down. Any idea how we get back out?"

"That's the hard part." Dagen sighed. "I'd start by hoping Jenna was right."

# TWENTY-FOUR

The warrior boy and his beast watched from their place of concealment as the sky began to lighten and the small Native American camp on the edge of Palo Duro Canyon sprang to life. He was sure of it now. These were Grandfather's people. Tynuk gave Azolja a few final rubbings on the snout and looked him in the face.

"Carry my weapons and satchel for me?" He said, tying the items onto the beast like a packhorse. "I will send for you once I've made contact and all is well. Don't worry. They will know me by my grandfather's belt." Tynuk smiled at his companion. "See you soon, my friend."

He pulled the beautiful, braided beaded belt from his satchel and folded it over his palm. He hiked down the hill and made his way toward the camp. Taking slow steps, he held his palms open toward the sky with Grandfather Nuk'Chala's belt draped over his palm. This was the customary greeting of his grandfather's people.

It took a moment for Tynuk to be noticed. A few yelps rose into the air, people gathered at the edge of their tents, looking to see what was happening. One young man, a fellow warrior, strode between the onlookers and headed straight for the boy. Tynuk smiled and extended his hands farther in anticipation of the stern warrior's approach. The young man couldn't have been older than seventeen or eighteen. Tynuk quickly offered a greeting in Comanche.

"*Marñawe! Nꭒ nahnia tsa* Tynuk."

Tynuk flinched as a punch connected with his side of his jaw. The force sent Tynuk reeling as the decorative belt flew through the air, landing in the dust next to him as he crashed to the ground. He had been so focused on the young warrior in front of him that he hadn't seen the assault coming from the left. The last thing that Tynuk suspected was an ambush.

"*Mꭒi tekwarꭒ Comanche, hakai!*"

"Wait," Tynuk managed as he tried to raise himself, his world still spinning. The second punch struck him in the same spot as the first and felt three times as hard. A wave of nausea coursed over Tynuk. "Wait—*haamee*," he managed, as a third blow landed hard on his jaw. Everything seemed to fade for a moment before his senses returned, riding a flaming tongue of pain that lashed across his skull.

"Do not speak our language," the man above him yelled. "You are not fit to be our dog, outsider!"

Tynuk rolled on his side and tried to cover himself as a group of warriors, spitting and cursing, struck him with sticks. Through the dust and pain, he opened his eyes for a moment to see the silent form of his friend poised to strike, like a shadow of death against the hillside behind them. Tynuk knew that with a wave of his hand, Az would descend upon the strangers and tear them to pieces. He also knew it couldn't happen this way. This was his journey, and these were his people. He would not have them killed over a misunderstanding.

In an almost unseen gesture, the boy opened his hand with his palm down and pumped it. In response, the creature bowed his head and slunk back out of sight. The group continued to curse and strike the boy against the ground, while others looked on in silence, glued to the spectacle before them.

"*Tohpnarn!*" came a simple, firm command from behind the men. The violence stopped.

Tynuk remained in a fetal position in anticipation of another round of punishment. As the dust began to clear, he looked up at the group of fearsome warriors that surrounded him. Some looked more like boys, while others appeared older and more weathered. Common among them was the single article of clothing they wore, a breechclout wrapped tight around their waists and groin. Many also wore their long, dark hair drawn back to reveal the taut muscles of their short frames. Their sleek forms, poised like racehorses in the early-morning light.

Tynuk rubbed his eyes then watched as another muscular figure appeared from behind the others and stooped to retrieve Grandfather Nuk'Chala's belt. The colored beads were now tarnished with a solid layer of dust. Tynuk watched as the man gently dusted off the belt by slapping it against his palm. The warrior looked the token over as Tynuk held his breath. The boy knew now to remain silent. Any unsolicited outburst on his part would bring more beatings.

The man was short—as they all were—not taller than five foot five, with a lithe, muscular frame that revealed a natural physical ability. His face, worn by the wind and weather, showed creases along the brow and at the corners of his eyes, but he was far from old by any standard. After what seemed like forever, the man stepped forward and spoke in English.

"I will give you a chance to speak, but first you will hear me speak. I am Queenashano, War Eagle. I am the war clan leader of the New Comanche Nation, descended from the great ancients who once made their homes in the plateaus of the Caprock Escarpment. After the fall of all things modern, we make our home there once again. We are Comanche—survivors of the end days, and we are one with this land, the land of our ancestors."

The man paused to survey the boy who returned a fearless gaze. Tynuk, unsure of the appropriate response, gave a slight nod. The man continued, "I don't know who you are or why you have come here, speaking our language, attempting to imitate our customs. You are not one of us. Your skin is like ours, but you are not true blood, and you make our language filthy with your dog-like pronunciation. Had you come without this," he said, motioning to the belt, "I would have told these men to mix your brains with the dirt."

Tynuk did not move. Perhaps a measure of boyhood naïveté had propelled him heedlessly into such a dangerous encounter with unknown men. Perhaps he'd been blinded by the possibilities rather than the realities of the situation. Whatever the case, this was a far cry from how he had envisioned the encounter. He nodded again. Queenashano turned, considering both the boy and the belt.

"I now give you the chance to speak, to identify yourself, and to explain how you came upon this belt. Be cautious as to what you say and how you say it. Nothing is guaranteed for you."

Tynuk took a moment to compose his thoughts and raised himself up to a kneeling position, his head bent low. "Great Queenashano, I thank you for the opportunity to speak. I mean no disrespect by coming here. My given name is Reno Yackeschi, son of Noconah Yackeschi, a full-blood Comanche, and his wife, a Cherokee woman."

Tynuk thought he saw a flash of recognition in Queenashano's eyes, but as fast as it appeared, it was gone, fading back into the emotionless gaze before him. The boy continued to speak, choosing each word carefully.

"You are correct, in saying that I am not true-blood Comanche. However, I was trained in the old ways by an old man I call Grandfather

Nuk'Chala. He was my father's uncle, and he instructed me in the ways of your people."

A hushed murmur cascaded through the crowd. Tynuk tried not to seem pleased that his grandfather's name received recognition. The warriors peered with wide eyes at their leader. Queenashano did not acknowledge that the name clearly meant something to his people.

"And the belt? Where did you get it?"

"Grandfather Nuk'Chala gave it—"

A sharp glance from the clan leader brought about another surprise punch to the rear part of Tynuk's jaw, just below his ear. The strike was followed by a pressing kick that pushed the boy facedown in the dust. Tynuk coughed a few times, the woozy feeling returning as he struggled to return to a kneeling position.

"You are lying," came the emotionless voice of the clan leader. "This is a war belt. It is earned with blood, sweat, and a hardened resolve, qualities a boy like you will never know."

"I swear," Tynuk blurted out before being dealt another vicious blow. He fell back to the earth in a swarm of dust.

"You will not swear upon this place. Further disgrace will mean your death. You have come here and tainted my people with your lies and deceit."

Tynuk was growing weary of this game. He righted himself once again and spat in the dirt, the blood from a gash above his right eye dripping steadily to the ground beneath him.

"I knew a Nuk'Chala once," Queenashano spoke. "From boyhood to manhood, I knew him well. A wizened, noble spirit and a fearsome warrior, he was the best of us—until that day when he chose to abandon his name and his people. He walked away from us and from his promises. He disappeared into the eastern horizon and was never seen again."

Tynuk wiped the blood that ran down his face and glanced at the crimson smear across his palm. The clan leader began to pace as he spoke.

"Regardless of Nuk'Chala's personal shortcomings, he was true blood. A true blood would never give an item of this kind away. Never. And he would not have taught anyone—much less a frail, bastard child like you—our dying ways, which he guarded fiercely."

Queenashano stopped pacing and faced the boy. He knelt, lowering his eyes to the boy's round face.

"Which brings us back to you. Nuk'Chala has likely been dead a long time, but if by some chance he survived for a time, I am most confident that he did not teach *you* anything, which makes you a liar. And as I said, he would never have given you such a valuable item, which makes you a thief."

Tynuk squirmed at the accusations and furrowed his brow.

"There is no place here for liars or thieves, so…we will kill you. You may be run through the gut and left here to die, or you may receive hot coals on the belly. Neither will grant you a swift or honorable death. I will let you choose."

Tynuk betrayed no emotion as he wiped at his face and stood to his full height, which was still considerably less than the men who surrounded him. He locked eyes with each warrior, including Queenashano.

"I am not your dog," the boy spoke with a steely resolve, "and you will have to slay me on my feet."

Tynuk thought he saw the clan leader smile as his warriors howled, closing fast. He was ready. While Queenashano had gone about his oratory exposition, Tynuk had analyzed each man standing around him. He knew that the one to his left, the one who had struck him on the jaw, had a strong right and a weak left, just by the way the man held his arms up. Tynuk also knew that the man rushing in from behind favored his left leg, likely due to an injury to his right knee. The angry-looking young fellow, the man Tynuk had first encountered, was overconfident and therefore susceptible to a groin kick. The one crouched low would likely try to tackle him to the ground. Most important, Tynuk knew this wasn't intended to be a fair fight. As soon as the men realized he was highly trained, they would bring their weapons against him.

As expected, the man on Tynuk's left lunged in with a right cross, leaving his left side vulnerable. The boy deflected the punch and stepped up the man's thigh, punching him hard with a downward strike to the rear of the jaw. Tynuk felt the joint unhinge under the force of the blow. The man's knees wobbled; then he dropped, both hands flying to his face as he screamed out in pain.

As the man behind rushed in, Tynuk pivoted and stomped through the attacker's weakened right knee, the sound like a bundle of dry twigs snapping. Tynuk felt the man's knee tear apart under the force of his foot as his leg folded inward.

He turned to see the angry one screaming as he rushed in carrying a short spear. Tynuk sidestepped the thrust, parrying the shaft of the weapon away with a swift movement. With a skip, he kicked as hard as he could upward into the man's groin. The man's eyes flashed wide with pain just as Tynuk slammed into him with a barrage of punches that laid the man's nose flat with an explosion of blood.

Tynuk redirected his focus as the man with the ponytail shot in on him, attempting to tackle him low. Dropping his weight and widening his base, Tynuk dropped the heel of his fist in a hammer-fist blow to the base of the ponytail's skull. Doing so impaired the man's balance and vision. Tynuk then struck the man's floating ribs on both sides and finally his kidneys along the back. The man moaned and went limp, falling to the earth where he stayed motionless.

Before Tynuk could adjust, he was sacked from behind and knocked into and over the man he'd just dropped, slamming face-first in the dirt. Dust flew into his eyes and nose as he was pinned in place by the weight of many furious foes. Tynuk had become trapped under the pile of bodies.

With a violent jerking motion, a fist seized hold of his hair and yanked his head back. Tynuk bared his teeth and groaned as he felt the cold steel of a blade slip below his neck, tracing a line across the soft flesh.

"Neraquassi! Tohpuaru!"

The angry man over Tynuk froze, the blood still seeping from his ruined nose. He held the knife against the boy's neck as a small dribble of blood began to drip from where the steel already had begun to split the skin.

"Do it," Tynuk spat. "You don't have it in you."

The angry man swore and tensed his grip around the handle of the knife.

"Yellow Horse! Move that blade again, and I'll have you castrated and your better parts left on the sand of this canyon!"

The young warrior with the knife froze once more.

"I knew you couldn't do it," Tynuk spoke with a smirk. "We should change your name to Ugly Nose Can't Fight."

With a grunt the man smacked Tynuk's forehead against the dirt and released his hold on the boy's hair. The aggressor stood and sheathed his knife. Those who were able jumped on the boy and held him down. A few of the others were dragging away the injured.

"Interesting," the clan leader mused. "Well, someone has taught you something. The question is who? Your style *is* familiar. Maybe you aren't a liar. Maybe you did know Nuk'Chala, but I need more proof than this." Queenashano paused, thinking.

"I'm done trying to prove anything to you. I'll save my effort for someone worthy of it," Tynuk spoke, then blew an exasperated puff of air to clear his face.

The clan leader smiled and turned to Neraquassi, who was scowling and trying to stop the blood gushing from his shattered nose. "I like this boy. He is quite spirited, don't you think?"

Neraquassi spat a stream of blood from his mouth across the boy's back.

"The thing is," Queenashano continued, "you came to us, boy, and you did so with a sacred Comanche item in your possession. You have much to explain and much to prove. In time you will have the opportunity."

"What are you saying?" asked Tynuk hesitantly.

"I'm saying we won't kill you—for now. Instead you will have to enter the trials of the ancients to prove to us your earnestness, your worthiness, and your skill."

Tynuk had heard of the trials of the ancients through his grandfather. An ordeal long forgotten, the trials were intended to separate the pure of heart from the rest. According to his mentor, few ever survived.

Queenashano saw the boy's expression and answered the question he assumed would come next. "No, you do not have a choice. There is no other way. And yes, you will try. But like the many who have come before you, you will not be found worthy."

Tynuk exhaled and closed his eyes, whispering words of protection as Neraquassi stooped low with a hateful grin and struck the boy across the back of his head with the shaft of a spear. With a flash of pain, he suddenly felt a very real fear, as visions of the trials he would have to endure poured over him. They clawed at his spirit, dragging him down, into the embrace of the pale sister of night.

# TWENTY-FIVE

The truck rolled to a stop just out of sight of the gypsy camp. Kane took a hesitant breath as he stepped from the vehicle and grabbed an M4 rifle. He pulled his light pack from the front seat and nodded to Arrice, who exited the driver's seat to switch places with Jacob in the truck bed.

Kane shot a wink at the teen. "Stay cool, buddy. I'll see you there."

"You just get your family back," Jacob said with a stern look, the concern obvious on his face. "We'll take care of the rest."

"All right. Be careful," Kane said, slamming the door and taking off in a trot toward the camp.

The throaty growl of the old eight-cylinder engine rumbled off as Jacob and the others continued down the dusty road toward the camp's entrance. Kane watched out of the corner of his eye as he brought his speed up to a jog, lengthening his stride. He had about a mile of uneven ground to cover, and he had to do it fast. He knew the truck would beat him there as planned, but he also didn't want to be too far behind the curve. The diversion would only last so long.

Jacob rehearsed the plan as he cruised down the dirt road, listening to the gravel ping and ding off the truck's undercarriage. After a few long minutes, he saw the campfires. Approximately one hundred yards out, he slowed the vehicle to a stop and sat still in the semidarkness. Jacob exhaled as he watched a group of people exit the camp and fan out, crossing the exposed area between the camp and the truck. He estimated about fifteen total, some carrying firearms, all of them carrying weapons.

"All right," Jacob whispered, mustering his courage. "Let's do this." He opened the door of the truck and stepped out with his hands up.

✵ ✵ ✵

"You're clear. I've got no movement. Go now," Dagen's voice crackled through Courtland's earpiece. Courtland looked down and slipped two sausage-like fingers into the breast pocket of his shirt to remove a photograph of a teenage girl. He looked at the tattered picture for a long while before kissing it and putting it back.

"Courtland," Kris spoke over the giant's shoulder, "I just want to say, you know, I'm not really a religious guy, but I believe in what we're doing here. We've talked a few times, and I always thought you and your faith were a bit much. Big black preacher gonna get everyone saved." He chuckled nervously.

Courtland gave a gentle smile.

"Now, with everything that's happened, I think I'm starting to understand why sometimes people need faith in something bigger than themselves. Regardless of all that, I want you to know that I'm behind you one hundred percent until this is finished," Kris said, sweeping his hand over the other men. "We all are."

Courtland smiled and touched a hand to Kris's shoulder. "I'm proud to stand with each of you in this moment. I hope you all know in your hearts why we serve the light and why we must not allow that light to be stamped out by this evil. This is our purpose." Courtland surveyed the terrified faces behind him. "I know what you've chosen to do is horrifying. I won't diminish that. But we have to remember what's at stake here. If we don't do this now, we may not get another chance. Everyone at the station will die painful deaths, including every last one of those children hiding in the cellar. We'll do this for them. It won't be glamorous, and there isn't a man alive who would want to stand in your shoes, but listen to me when I say this. Take heart, you men of honor, and find your courage, for though it seems bleak, and we don't know what lies ahead, God has gone before us. He's already there, and he's assured us the victory. They can take these mortal shells, but they'll never claim our souls."

The men smiled, giving nervous nods of acknowledgment as Courtland turned back toward the slope. "Now ready yourselves," he said, picking up his curved ebony blades. "Forward we go, into the fray."

"Courtland," came Dagen's voice through the earpiece, "if you're going to do this, you've got to do it now—right now."

"I understand," the big man whispered. "We're moving."

In the musky gypsy tent, Susan Lorusso thought she might die of anticipation. She tried to keep her hands from trembling as she tightened her grip on the crude, sharpened spike of deer antler clenched in her right fist. She'd been ready to make her move for hours, ever since the radio broadcast. She forced herself to wait for the right moment, but that moment hadn't come. Garrett hadn't gone to sleep like he usually did. Instead, he'd been in and out of the tent all night, moving back and forth among other hushed voices. No doubt he was preparing for first contact with her husband, and it wasn't a welcoming committee. She had to move soon, or her chances of doing anything to help Kane or herself would be completely lost.

She would have to move at the next available opportunity, the next time Garrett came into the tent and came close enough. In the early-morning darkness, she strained, twisting her wrists and pulling them through the steel shackles with the tiniest jingle. She froze, as even the slight sound seemed amplified by her paranoia. Still there was no response. Susan breathed a sigh of relief and furrowed her brow.

In the hellish, frantic nature of the situation, she hadn't stopped to consider what would happen if the plan actually worked—If she and her husband and children were to be reunited again. The sheer joy of the thought caused a swell of hope to grow inside her. But as soon as the feeling came, it immediately began to dwindle. The realization of what she had become hit her like a punch in the gut. She had become another man's concubine in order to save herself and her children. She had been forced to do unspeakable things. Kane could never truly love or cherish or respect what she had become.

As the hope for the future of her family began to fail, her lip quivered. She hardened her heart to such things, thoughts that wouldn't help her now. She sniffed and wiped away the last dirty tear she would allow. All that mattered was the children, that they made it safely back to their father. She would do anything, and sacrifice anyone, to make that happen.

The thin woman closed her eyes and whispered a silent prayer, her words fading into the humid night as she gripped the bone tightly, waiting for the man who would soon be forced to remember her as more than just *woman*.

✡ ✡ ✡

"The stuff is right here." Jacob motioned at the open truck door as he backed away. "No need for the weapons. I've got what you asked for right here in the truck. Now let me see my family."

"Stop backing away!" one of the men called out. "Stop and raise your hands higher."

The teen pretended not to hear as he continued to take shallow steps backward toward the bed. "It's alight. I've got the stuff right here. Come on. Check it out. Then you can get my family."

"Stop backing away!" the man shouted, as several rifle bolts made the sound of rounds being chambered.

Jacob stopped backing up and took a large step to his right, behind the bed of the truck.

"I mean it!" the man screamed. He and the others in Garrett's security group were now about twenty yards from the front of the truck.

Jacob opened the truck bed and let it drop open, the blued metal of an AK-47 assault rifle loaded with a thirty-round magazine just within his reach. He eyed the rifle then raised his hands farther above his head.

"Move again and you're dead!"

Jacob complied and allowed the security force from the camp to come closer. He watched as they stopped about ten yards in front of the truck and fanned out into a semicircle facing him. Lights snapped to life, and he squinted as they pointed the glaring beams at him.

"There's no need for this. It's fine," Jacob continued. "I've got what you wanted right here. I just want to see my family first." He shifted his weight, nervous.

"Did you come alone?"

"Yeah, man, yeah. I just want to see my family."

"Your family?"

"Yeah."

"Aren't you a little young? That's not your family. What are you doing here, boy? You screw with us and we'll kill them."

"Okay, you got me. They're not my family," he said, lowering his hands and touching the rifle.

"You little shit. What are you trying to pull?" the man hissed.

"I'm not *trying* to pull anything, jack wagon—I am pulling it," Jacob drawled, grabbing the rifle from the bed and dropping into a low squat behind the truck. Diving out, he slid under the rear axle of the truck, screaming at the top of his lungs to his unseen comrades. *"Now!"*

The security group glanced about anxiously as Jacob disappeared from sight. Two shadows rose from their positions among the shallow hills, approximately thirty yards away from either side of the truck. The barren ground beneath the shadows bloomed to life as Arrice and Shana fired on the unsuspecting group. Under the truck, bullets pinged and zinged as Jacob cursed. He took careful, well-placed shots at the feet, ankles, and knees of the security force, the bullets finding their marks and causing their targets to fall. Once they were down, he could take a final, fatal shot.

One guard ran toward the truck, desperate to find cover. "I don't think so," Jacob muttered, as he rolled onto his side and fired, striking the figure in the foot. The guard screamed in pain as the bullet blew fragments of toes from a gaping hole in the shoe. The figure dropped right next to the truck. Jacob immediately fired two rounds into the shadowed chest.

The unsuspecting security force tried to return fire, but they were cut down, thrashing about in the open like goldfish released from a shattered fishbowl. The last one finally fell, crying and clutching at his chest.

Jacob slid out from under the truck and jumped to his feet. "Let's go!" he yelled, as Arrice and Shana made their way toward the vehicle. Jacob took two steps then called out in fright as a hand grabbed his ankle. He swung, turning his rifle on the form below him, and stopped, his eyes wide with horror. At his feet a teenage girl stared up at him, her eyes pleading for help, her mouth forming soundless words as foam bubbled from her blood-soaked lips. She was the guard Jacob had shot next to the truck just moments earlier. She wasn't any older than him.

"Jacob, get in the truck!" Arrice shouted.

Jacob blinked hard and pulled his leg from the girl's grip. He shook his head and whispered, "Oh, God. I'm...I'm sorry."

"Leave her and get in the truck," came Shana's voice from behind, her tone revealing stress and tension as she grabbed Jacob's shirt and hauled him into the bed of the pickup. Arrice jumped into the driver's seat, and with the sound of tires spinning against the dirt, the truck was off, barreling toward the front of the camp.

"I...I didn't mean to—"

"Get a hold of yourself, kid," Shana spat. "People die. It happens."

✲ ✲ ✲

"Get up, woman. My people are headed out to retrieve your hubby," Garrett growled, as he stepped into the tent and approached Susan.

Susan remained motionless, surveying Garrett's movements through partially closed eyes. She squeezed the bone spike in her fist and prepared to strike.

"I said, get up," said Garrett, reaching toward her. He stopped short as the sound of nearby gunfire caught his interest. He turned toward the sound, gritting his teeth. "What the fuck? I told them not to kill anyone yet!"

*Now!*

Susan lashed out with the bone spike and felt it strike true as it sank through the meat of Garrett's calf muscle. She twisted it and tore it back out, certain the spike had at least severed the muscle and tendon. Garrett screamed in pain and fell toward her, reaching as his wounded leg failed to support him. With a furious scream, Susan rose with a scream, thrusting the spike again, this time causing a deep gash down his forehead and nose, then across the flesh of his cheek. A bright crimson plume sprayed down Garrett's forehead, obscuring his vision. He grabbed at her blindly, and together they fell across the bedroll in a frenzied struggle. Screaming, groaning in the darkness, Garrett grabbed Susan's arm and banged the back of her fist against the ground, knocking the weapon from her hand.

"I'll kill you, woman!" he screamed, as he pulled himself over her.

*"My name is Susan!"* she snarled back, as she thrust her knee up hard into his groin. She sank the nails of her free hand into the flesh near his ribs and twisted.

Garrett groaned as she forced him off her and scrambled to her feet. As he tried to recover, she lunged forward and kicked him as hard as she could in the face, the blow whipping his head so far backward that she thought it might have snapped his neck. Without a sound, he fell, her crude and merciless tormentor now crumpled at her feet.

Susan nodded in satisfaction. "Forget my name *now*, you sick son of a bitch," she quipped, as she tried to catch her breath. Garrett wasn't moving. He could be dead. Susan took a second to catch her breath, realizing for the first time how great she felt and that she couldn't care less if he was dead or not. He'd made his bed.

She moved quick, grabbing the two items she knew she would need—Garrett's Zippo lighter and a handle of salvaged Southern Comfort, his prized possession. Exiting the tent, she looked toward the front of the camp, where the sounds of sporadic gunfire could still be heard.

In a few paces, she arrived at a pile of dead brush and logs that had been used as a walkway partition. She dumped the entire bottle of Southern Comfort, flicked the Zippo, and tossed it onto the pile. A rush of flame stretched to the sky, big enough to alert the children. The time had come for them—all of them—to be free.

# TWENTY-SIX

Courtland ran up the hill and past the first few mud huts as he entered the Sicks' lair. Though he was only jogging, his enormous stride and impressive endurance allowed him to move faster than what should have been humanly possible. Behind him the rest of the men ran and stumbled, trying to keep up, fighting to keep the terror from consuming them.

Glancing over his shoulder as he ran, he weaved his way through the huts toward the center of the camp. The men were falling behind, but he couldn't slow down. He had to accomplish the mission or it would all be for nothing.

"Courtland," came Dagen's tinny voice like a house fly in his ear. "You've got one moving in on you from the right. Don't check up. I've got him."

As soon as the transmission ended, Courtland heard the creature huffing like an angry wild boar.

*Come on, Dagen. Be the guy you say you are.*

The mutant flew into sight on Courtland's right, leaping toward him, flashing its jaws as it came. Just as the creature was almost upon him, the crown of its head opened like a rotten, gray pumpkin, the contents erupting into the air with a splash of black blood and brain. The lingering crack of a rifle followed.

"Cut it a little of close, didn't ya?" Courtland breathed into his microphone.

"I said, I've got you."

"How about the other guys?"

"They're trailing you a good bit. I'll do my best to keep them clear."

"Okay."

As the big man ran, his heavy boots pounding holes in the muck beneath, he heard the camp stir to life. The hoots, screams, and growls of the residents filled his ears, growing to a frenzy. The report of the high-powered rifle and the screams of the dying Sick assured that the stealth element of this mission was now in the bag.

"We've got to get in there and finish this, now!" Courtland yelled to the men behind him as they scrambled desperately to keep up. He heard them firing, followed by the resounding echo of Dagen's rifle.

"Go, Courtland!" Kris yelled from behind, as he fired his pump shotgun into the growing masses that had begun to surround them. "Go and finish it!"

Courtland stopped just long enough to see Kris and the others, their weapons roaring as the rabid mutants swarmed them. The giant knew he could either help these men or see the mission through. He couldn't do both. With a wince of anguish, he turned and ran toward the leader's hut, which quickly came into view at the center of camp. Behind him, Kris and the others began to scream—the sounds of men who knew their deaths were at hand.

"Dagen?" Courtland said, breathless concern in his voice.

"Keep moving, Courtland," Dagen said with a tone of finality. "No one can help them now."

From the top of the rise, Dagen fired a round and watched as it dropped short of its intended target, a disgusting freak that was making its way toward Courtland. Dagen shifted his position and gave the elevation knob on the scope several clicks up, adjusting for the change in target distance. He looked again and keyed his microphone. "Courtland, you've got a few coming for you on your left. I can't get the shot."

"I see them."

Looking through the scope, Dagen watched Courtland crush his attackers with a single swipe of the blades. The power the big man could exert was nothing short of astonishing.

Dagen held the rifle snug to his shoulder and grabbed his right bicep with his left hand to create a solid shooting platform. Breathing deep, he watched as Courtland neared the open area in the muddy center of the camp. Drawing a bead on a few stray attackers, Dagen exhaled slightly and paused his breath as the trigger yielded with an easy pull. With a resounding crack, a creature's head split open and its bony frame fell to the earth. Two more shots in succession brought down two more mutants. Dagen aimed to destroy another, further clearing the big man's path. He keyed his microphone again.

"You've got about twenty-five yards to—" A snarl from behind froze Dagen's blood to ice. As Dagen rolled hard to the side, the Sick's claws just missed connecting with flesh as they tore a gaping hole in the back of his jacket. Then it was upon him, its claws flailing, its jaws snapping as it came down upon him like a wild animal.

"Gahhh!" Dagen groaned as he wrestled with the creature, his broken legs twisting in useless movements beneath it. The thing had absolute control of him, and he knew with certainty that without the use of his legs he would soon be killed. Through his thick military jacket, he felt the creature's claws digging into his skin. It snarled in his face, its breath laced with the stench of rotting flesh.

"Dagen, come in," came Courtland over his earpiece, which had popped out and dangled like an ornament on his collar. Dagen had one shot at this. The longer their struggle went on, the higher the likeli-hood that this encounter wouldn't end well for him. In a lightning-fast movement born of struggle and hardwired military training, Dagen caught the creature around the back of the neck and pulled it in with his left hand while simultaneously yanking a combat knife from his vest. Driving the knife straight up, he sank the blade through the hypo-glossal nerve under the monster's chin, causing the creature to spasm and thrash. As the mutant bucked to the side to get away, Dagen rolled with it, riding it over, while working the knife back and forth into its cranial cavity.

"Die already, you ugly mother," Dagen groaned, pressing all his weight on the knife.

With a savage gurgle, the creature finally stopped moving. Dagen released a deep sigh and withdrew his knife. He rolled off and crawled back to his rifle, his lungs laboring.

"Courtland," Dagen huffed, as he examined the busted scope on his rifle, "you're on your own. My weapon system is down."

"Are you okay?"

"I'm…yeah. One of them ambushed me, but I took care of it. The rifle is down, though. I'll try to get it back up."

"Copy. I'm here at the hut. If you can read me, I'm going in."

Dagen wiped the blood from his face and nodded as he keyed up his microphone. "I copy. Go get 'em."

✯ ✯ ✯

In a mad dash to reach her children, Susan flew across the gypsy camp, her slender form fast and unseen against the backdrop of ramshackle tents. She ran heedless of the danger, with a determination born of fear, anxiety, and hope. Gunfire continued to erupt around the camp, and her mind spun with the possibilities. Had Kane really arrived? Had Garrett's thugs ambushed them, or had Kane hit them first? Or was it something else— some other group attacking them?

Susan wasn't about to stop to find out. First she would secure the children. Then and only then would she exit the camp and try to find her husband. With bullets zinging overhead, the last thing they needed was to stay one fraction of a second longer than necessary.

With an unexpected twang, Susan's foot snagged on a taut length of cord lashed to one of the tent pegs. With a yelp she tumbled and crashed through the side of a canvas tent. Her world spun, and in a moment of terror, she thrashed about in the collapsed canvas tarp. She felt sure she had been discovered. Her heart raced, and her mind reeled. She forced herself to be still for a moment, to allow her senses to rejoin her body. The tent was empty. Its owner likely had left to investigate the cause of the gunfire at the front of camp.

Taking a few deep breaths, Susan reassured herself and worked her way through the pile of canvas and junk, crawling toward a small opening in the front. There she gasped as she heard footsteps that sounded as though they were rapidly approaching. Several wild-looking men ran right in front of the tent, their rifles raised, their faces red with fury. One swore, grumbling something about a kid and loading another magazine. She'd had seen these men before.

As the men departed, Susan allowed herself to breathe, slowly at first and then in deep gulps. Somehow the effort seemed to increase the thundering of her heart. She shut her eyes tight, scrunching her nose. When she reopened her eyes, she saw it.

She knew she was close but not how close. The fire she'd started had taken hold. With nothing and no one to contain it, it spread across the camp. In the growing light, she could just make out the rusted van where her children were being kept. It's corroded, hulking form looked like a sleeping Goliath, a giant she dared not wake. Susan was so close that she couldn't stand it. In just a few steps and with a little maneuvering, she and her babies would be free from this hell. She raised herself from her hiding place as a nearby burst of gunfire rang out, causing her to crouch and duck, as she questioned her decision to move to the van.

*Do it!*

Cringing, she raised herself up again and scanned a full 360 degrees around herself before turning to focus on the van. Surely her children had seen the fire. Like a sprinter leaving the starting block, Susan launched across the open space toward the van, every step carrying her closer to her beloved Michael and Rachael. She slammed against the van, her euphoria turning to dread. They were gone.

"Michael! Rachael! *Where are you?*" she called, unable to contain her hysteria. The fear consumed her quaking frame. "Where did you go? Come back to me, *please!*" she wailed, losing hope that she would ever see her children again.

Just as her entire being sagged with defeat, she caught a flicker of movement behind her. Susan spun toward it, her eyes taking it in, her jaw dropping open in a breathless, silent scream.

✵ ✵ ✵

Kane moved with a rapid, fluid efficiency through the burning gypsy camp. With the primary diversion at the front of the camp, every armed idiot rushed there only to get caught in Jacob, Arrice, and Shana's ambush. The sporadic rat-a-tat-tat of assault rifles echoing across the camp told him they were still holding. They might hold a while longer or fold any second. Snapping this way and scanning the other as he flew across the open spaces, Kane was nothing more than a shadow, a messenger of death amid the fire, smoke, and screams.

Rounding the edge of a row of tents, Kane came face-to-face with a disheveled man who screamed in surprise. Knocking into him, he covered the man's mouth, jamming a knife under his rib cage and into his heart. The man squirmed, his eyes rolling in his head before Kane released him and dragged him into one of the nearby tents.

The body hidden, Kane stopped in the shade of the canvas and tried to assess where his family might be. He felt distracted, alone with his demons. He'd just murdered a man for being in the wrong place at the wrong time—the third such man since he'd entered the camp.

Without warning, a sharp pain in his heart caused him to grit his teeth. It twisted in his chest, causing him to lose his balance. He inhaled deep, his head swimming with a dizzying warmth. Something was wrong inside him, and he felt it grow like a rotting infection in his soul.

*Why have you forsaken me?*

"No," he said, pressing his hands against his chest. "I don't need you. I can do this."

He took a moment to compose himself and returned to survey the immediate area, sweat beading on his forehead. As he watched, two men ran into a nearby tent and helped a third from it. The injured man limped, cussed, and wiped at the blood that poured from a gash in his head.

"That bitch kicked my teeth out!" he heard the man slur. "She's gone to get those brats of hers. I know it. Find her!"

Kane felt a combination of relief and concern pour over him as his suspicions were confirmed. Only Susan could make a guy that mad, but the man was right. She would have gone for the children straight away. Kane saw a moment of opportunity and seized it as he stepped from the shadows and into the flickering light of the spreading fires.

"You the guy on the radio? Where is she?" he asked, his face dark with hatred.

Garrett wiped his face and snarled, "And who the fuck are you supposed to be?"

"I'm the guy who tells you how it is. Where's my wife?"

Garrett's face flashed recognition instantaneously. He smiled as he spoke. "Why should I care what gutter that bitch and her little bastards end up in? I used that little whore up a long time ago." Garrett tried to wipe the blood from his face, but it continued to stream down his face. He waved his hand in Kane's direction. "Kill this piece of shit."

The two men approached Kane, moving to either side of him. Kane's M4 rifle came up fast. He found his targets, engaging the two goons with triple-tapped shots to the chest long before they had a chance to even draw their weapons. Watching his men fold against the ground, Garrett's face went slack. He pulled a knife and swung it back and forth as Kane closed in on him.

"Where is she?" Kane said.

"Wait. Don't—"

Kane slammed into Garrett's jaw with the butt of the rifle, releasing more teeth with a sickening crunch.

"Don't what?" Kane mocked. "Don't kill the man who defiled my wife and enslaved my children?"

Garrett stumbled, falling to his hands and knees. Kane hit him again hard in the back of the head with the rifle. Garrett made babbling, unintelligible sounds as he slumped to the ground. Still, he tried to raise himself again.

"Where are they?" Kane said.

Garrett fell silent, crawling his way to all fours.

With a snarl of anger, Kane kicked the man hard in the side and felt his ribs fracture under the force. Begging for him to stop, Garrett cried out and stretched his arm toward Kane, who dropped the assault rifle and grabbed Garrett's arm, pulling it tight.

"Where are they?" Kane spat through clenched teeth.

The man's silence, either a result of stubbornness or pain, determined Kane's path. With a violent twist, he shattered Garrett's arm, eliciting a shrill scream. Kane dropped down into the man's face.

"You like abusing women and children? Huh? You like that? Not so tough now, are you?" Kane threw all of his weight behind a devastating straight punch to Garrett's face and felt the cheekbone give way beneath his fist. "Where are they?" he screamed, as his rage overtook him. It blossomed inward, like the bloom of a nuclear blast.

"They're gone. You can't save them now," came Garrett's garbled, blood slurred response.

Kane screamed as he seemed to detach from his actions, watching himself through someone else's eyes. He shook with primal, murderous rage as he felt his thumbs sink deep through the eyes of his victim.

*You've become what you hate. Why have you forsaken me?*

※ ※ ※

"They're running!" Jacob called out to Arrice and Shana as they fired at the last of Garrett's people who posed any threat. They continued their path to the front of the camp, the gypsies fleeing, scattering like roaches exposed to daylight.

"Okay, so where's Kane? Any thoughts?" Jacob asked, as he looked down and checked his rifle magazine. It was full. Since the death of the girl, he hadn't fired a single round. He had to be sure going forward. He couldn't kill another like her. That look on her face would haunt him forever.

"We split up, sweep the camp, and meet back here. One of us will find him," said Arrice, his African accent thick.

"Look, Kane isn't going to get his family back," Shana spoke up.

Jacob scowled. "I don't think you understand why we're here, Shana."

"Don't lecture me, kid," Shana said from behind him. "I know exactly why I'm here. You're the one who doesn't understand what's happening."

Something in the way Shana spoke caused Jacob to turn. Just as he did, she fired her rifle point-blank at Arrice, shooting him in the back of the head without a word. She spun, swinging the rifle on Jacob.

Jacob screamed, slamming into her, the weapon firing as it knocked from her hands. Jolting hard against the earth, they rolled, nearly equal in size and weight, struggling, groaning in the perilous toxicity of the situation.

"You crazy bitch!" Jacob yelled.

"You're either with us or against us!" she said, scratching her nails deep into the flesh of his face. "No one opposes the Coyotes!"

Jacob didn't waste any time. He punched the furious woman again and again in the head and rolled on top of her, where he secured a solid front choke.

"You murdered Arrice!" Jacob screamed.

Shana gasped. Reaching out, she picked up a sizable stone and slammed it against the side of Jacob's face.

For a moment he lost his bearings. His mind floated back to eighth-grade summer school at Gardenvale High School. The older boy wasn't going to give it up. They never did. Jacob had never been good at watching his mouth. When someone tried to push him around, his mouth caught up with him. The sun had been suffocating, and Jacob had kept getting up every time the older boy knocked him down. He had been hit so many times that he couldn't remember how it had all started—except that it had something to do with his mouth. It always did. Jacob took in the warmth, nausea, the ringing in his head like a thousand bells all chiming at once. He was coming to.

"You punk-ass kid! I think you broke my fucking nose," Shana swore, dabbing at a trickle of blood that ran down her face as she struggled to get up from the ground. She moved to secure her rifle. "Here's what you don't understand. Kane's family is already dead. And now we've got to finish off the rest of you sheep at the station."

Jacob rolled to his stomach and shook his head. "We?"

"Yeah, we. I'm with the Coyotes. Fuck everyone else. I'm on the winning side now."

"I've heard of the Coyotes. You let them get in your head. You don't remember what they did to you? You're the one who's been had."

Shana bristled. "Nobody controls me. I know the truth. You and all your weak-ass friends have to die," she continued, raising the rifle, "slaughtered like a bunch of squealing pigs. Any last squeals, little piggy?"

Jacob smirked as he brought his legs under him and dug his fingers into the dirt. "Yeah, I bet you were *that girl* back in the real world, weren't you?"

Shana clenched her teeth and moved her index finger to the trigger.

Jacob huffed, "You know, the girl who's friends with this group one day and stabs them in the back the next. No self-respect, big time daddy issues, willing to let every stray thug who comes along get some. Guess not much has changed."

"You little—"

In a flash of movement, Jacob flung a handful of dirt in Shana's face as he launched from the ground like a young hare, zigzagging as he went. Cursing, Shana let loose a wild burst of gunfire, the dirt stinging her eyes and obscuring her target as he fled.

*Great job, Jacob. Way to be diplomatic.*

Shana was tracking Jacob as he made a desperate attempt to reach the nearest row of canvas tents. Squinting her eyes, she began to regain her composure as her rifle vomited fire and lead, locking onto Jacob's movements with quick bursts. The last two of three fired rounds hit him like a sledgehammer in the back, sending him toppling forward just as he entered the front row of tents. Jacob flopped against the ground and slid, his body screaming in pain. Scrambling to his feet, he was up and running as an earth-shattering adrenalin dump rocketed him out of the line of fire.

With shuddering breaths, he touched the jagged holes in his right shoulder and upper chest. He could no longer move his right arm, and each terrified gasp brought on searing spikes of pain that seemed to swallow him whole. A wave of dizziness passed over him, and he stumbled, trying to press the feeling away into the far corners of his consciousness. He was bad off—maybe really bad—but to stop now meant certain death. Jacob had to find Kane. Kane was his only hope.

As Jacob's pace slowed, he heard Shana shouting behind him as she entered the first row of tents. "I got you! I know I did! Time for you to die, piggy!"

# TWENTY-SEVEN

Courtland stooped low and turned sideways to squeeze through the narrow opening as he entered the low structure. He waited for a moment, confronted by the pungent scent of decay, scanning for threats as he waited for his eyes to adjust to the darkness. The warmth of the windowless mud hut clung to his skin, hanging in the air like scum on the surface of a stagnant pond. His muscles tensed in anticipation of an ambush that didn't come, as he slowly stood to his full height. His brow creased, and he hissed under his breath. "Great. It's empty. What now?"

The hut was large enough for Courtland to stand up straight and still have a little clearance between him and the twiggy ceiling. With his eyes adjusted to the darkness, the interior of the hut began to come into focus. As he surveyed the rest of the space, he found something that caught him off guard. This wasn't the disheveled, bone-filled mud hole he'd expected—at least not entirely. Though the smell and feel did seem like that of any woodland animal, there was also something familiar, something human about the space. It brought to mind the way a convict might decorate his stark, gray prison cell with pictures, drawings, and trinkets. Scanning the room, Courtland noticed a cracked guitar with only two strings, a pile of quilted blankets, various tools, and useful items, and a short three-legged desk that looked as though it could topple over at any moment. He leaned in to observe several items on top of the desk.

A shuffling movement outside the hut caused Courtland to turn and scan the room again. Nothing appeared to move in the dank space around him. He knew the swelling mass of freaks should have caught up with him, but he had yet to hear their approach. It was possible that if the mutants revered the one who controlled them, they might not enter their leader's personal space.

Looking back at the dingy desk, Courtland ran the tip of his finger back and forth across the cracked glass of a picture frame. It took several passes, as he cleared the dust away, for him to realize he was looking at a doctoral degree from the University of California. The certificate had been presented to Eric Steven Glenn "for demonstrating ability through original research in animal behavior, specifically canine behavior." Wedged in the corner of the frame was the worn and faded picture of a young woman, her arms raised as though she might be dancing.

Courtland frowned and moved the frame aside to wipe the dust from the glass of a second frame. Inside was an aging newspaper article dated May 17, 2007, clipped from the *State*, a major newspaper in South Carolina. The story featured an inset picture of a thin, well-dressed man with an infectious smile shaking hands with another well-dressed, portly individual. Courtland scanned the article.

*Columbia, South Carolina—The University of South Carolina announced today that they have handpicked Dr. Eric Glenn of the University of California, Los Angeles, to be the director of their new Canine Cognition and Behavior Lab, also known as CACOBL. Dr. Glenn received his bachelor's degree in microbiology and cell science, as well as a master's degree in animal behavior analysis from the University of Houston before attending the University of Florida to obtain his doctoral degree in canine cognition and behavior. In 2004 he returned to his roots, accepting a position on staff at the University of California's universal animal studies department, where he worked for three years before taking on this newest endeavor.*

*When asked for a comment, Dr. Glenn stated, "CACOBL is the largest and most advanced canine cognition and behavior lab in the world. I'm absolutely thrilled to have been asked to be a part of this. We have an incredible group here, from top-level researchers to our assistants, all of whom will strive to break every barrier possible when it comes to the understanding of man's best friend. There is no limit to how we may be able to better our canine friends and, in so doing, benefit humankind as well." Dr. Glenn stated that he will be studying the use of tones to alter and direct canine behavior.*

"Findsssss vhat it seeeksssss?"

Courtland spun in surprise, dread crawling over his skin like thousands of mites. He had been so absorbed in the article that he'd let his guard down. Near the darkened doorway of the hut, he could just make out a wiry figure with goblin-like features wearing torn rags for clothing. The mutant's eyes appeared to be filled with blood, absent of any white. His body was sleek and predatory, with mottled, gray flesh, dagger-like ears, clawed hands, and lips that peeled back to reveal sharp teeth bared in a wicked smile.

Courtland looked down at the frame in his hand then back up at the creature, making a small gesture with the item. The mutant nodded.

"Dr. Glenn? Why? Why have you killed so many of us?" Courtland all but whispered.

The voice came back like soiled vapors escaping from a cracked sarcophagus. "Zhere isss no vhy. Zhere isss ongly zurvivallll."

"But how could you do this? You're a doctor, a scientist."

"Zhere isss no vhyyyyyy. "

Courtland looked at the picture again. "You did it, didn't you? You achieved your dream. When these poor people devolved to this terrible state, you still had something of the old Dr. Glenn inside. You knew how to use your knowledge to control them."

The mutant leader smiled with evil intent, touching the small, ivory flute, no longer than a man's index finger that hung from a cord around its neck. The white of which lay in stark contrast to the dark, ruined flesh of the creature's chest.

"Zhey ere mae chilldrennn and eye zher fozzer. Zhey do vasht eye zayyyy."

"And you tell them to murder us?" Courtland was beginning to gain confidence.

"Killssss smooth skinsss, yessss. Killssss them and eatssss them."

"There's another way. If you leave us alone, we'll leave you alone."

"Zher isss no ozzer vhey. Zher isss ongly zurvivallll."

"Please," Courtland pleaded, "I know Dr. Eric Glenn has to be in there. If there's enough of him to create that..." He motioned to the flute. "Then the man who loved animals and wanted to better humankind has to be in there too. He wouldn't do this."

Courtland thought he saw something in the mutant's face, a distant flicker of sorrow, fear, and failure. The creature snarled and flung its clawed hands open. Suddenly Courtland heard the screams of hundreds of mutants gathered outside the hut. The one they called Father brought the bone flute to its lips and blew a few quick notes, causing the clamor to subside instantly. The Father kept the flute to his lips and crept back toward the entrance to the hut.

"Leave us alone, and we will leave you alone," Courtland pleaded. "Last chance."

"Zher isss no ozzer vhey," the Father responded, his voice broken and strained. "Yur timesss hasss pasht. Now esch our timesss. Vhe vill gho aghain disss nightss and taste zhe chilldrensss fleshhhiieessss."

"I don't think so," Courtland said, tossing the broken frame at the creature's feet. As the mutant followed the frame with his eyes, Courtland made his move.

In a blinding surge that recalled his old crushball days, Courtland straight tackled the Father as they crashed into and through the front wall of the mud hut. The giant winced as a clawed hand slammed into his face, tearing grooves in his flesh. He flung the vicious creature through the air and watched as it tumbled and flopped across the ground. The Sicks moved to surround Courtland and the Father, filling the gaps, creating a menacing barrier of tooth and claw. There was no escape now.

Courtland put his hand to his face and felt the blood drip into his palm. He would have to tend to his injury later. He watched as the Father flew to its feet while groping for the flute before realizing with a howl that it was gone. Extending a fist the size of a bowling ball, Courtland dangled the flute before the group, causing the creatures to croon.

"Look at them," Courtland mused as he gestured with the object, his face dripping crimson splashes onto his shirt. "Just the sight of this thing sets them to moaning."

The Father flung its arms open in a wild rage. "Killsssss it! Eatsss itsss fatz fleshhiieesssss!"

Courtland braced for an attack that never came. The mass of Sicks remained rooted in place, some swaying, others staring with empty eyes. They were slaves to the Father's song, not to him.

"Killssss itsss!"

"They don't revere you," Courtland boomed. "They revere this," he said, dangling the object again. "No one—not you, not anyone—should wield a weapon like this." Courtland flipped the item up into his palm and closed his fingers around it.

The Father screamed and foamed at the mouth, clawing the air in front of him.

"You don't control them anymore." Courtland closed his fist tight, reducing the flute to a fine, white powder that trickled like sand through his fingers.

Whether perceived or real, Courtland sensed a shift in the crowd around him, as though a measure of resolve had just drained from them. The Father wasn't deterred. Like an apex predator, he loosed himself on the giant in a whirl of violence. Before Courtland could change his position, the mutant was upon him, its claws tearing, slashing, peeling back sections of clothing and flesh with each strike. The assault was so complete, so animalistic that Courtland found himself nearly immobile as the maddened creature slashed and climbed all over his massive frame. Courtland swung his arms in desperation, trying to fend off the vile monster, which, blow by blow, weakened his body and crushed his resolve.

The Father moved faster than should have been possible, as the screams and howls of the surrounding creatures seemed to fuel its rage, willing it to emerge victorious over the massive intruder. With power and precision, the monster swiped Courtland's lower thigh then slashed him under the arm, causing Courtland to gasp and stumble. The Sicks went wild as the giant tried to stand, his body quivering. With a cold realization, Courtland knew he had attacked the symptom and not the cause. By destroying the flute, he had enraged the Father. Courtland knew that destroying the flute had deterred the Father's power over the masses, but as long as the mutant leader survived, it could use its knowledge to create another flute. He couldn't allow this to happen.

Courtland's body was weakening, shaking, as the blood that poured from his numerous wounds began to soak through his clothes. Another flurry of swipes nearly toppled him as his heart slammed in his chest and his head swam with pain.

"My God," Courtland cried out, "do not abandon me to these wicked creatures!"

A surge of supernatural light stirred the air around him, whipping his clothes and bits of blood and flesh from his body. The giant felt the hand of God cover him. Digging deep, Courtland felt a renewed strength of righteousness swell inside of him, setting his senses ablaze. In a flash, he could see everything, track every movement, and hear every footfall, as the creature came at him again.

Raising himself up, Courtland parried away several swipes, swinging an uppercut like a wrecking ball, catching the Father by surprise, and launching the creature into the air. It flailed before smacking hard against the ground to the screams of the on-looking mutants. Wild with rage, the Father approached again, but this time the giant was ready. As the Father leaped at him, Courtland met the mutant head-on and snagged it in a bear hug, pulling it close and bracing himself. The Father wailed and lashed out at Courtland's face and chest until the giant squeezed and snapped its spine in one jarring movement. The mass of mutants howled and jumped in the air as Courtland dropped the Sick's writhing frame against the earth. Its lower body useless, the creature became wild with pain as it screamed and thrashed itself against the ground.

The Father gnashed its teeth in pain. "Killsss!"

Courtland loomed over the Father, placing a heavy boot on its writhing body.

"Killsss meeeee," the Father begged, as a look of shame covered the feral mutant's darkened face. "Killsss vasht I hasht become..."

Courtland nodded in understanding and glanced at the silent, unmoving crowd of freaks around him. "It is finished," he whispered. He reached down and with both hands tore the Father's head from its body with one deft movement. Black blood sprayed onto the ground from the Father's corpse as the giant thrust the mutant's head into the air above him. The surrounding Sicks squirmed, some continuing to stare while others began to flee.

Dropping the lifeless head with a thunk, Courtland let out a terrifying battle cry as he swung his arms open as a bold challenge to any others who dared confront him. The Sicks fled into the forest in droves, nearly climbing over one another, desperate to escape the fury of the giant. After a long, vigilant moment, Courtland let out a deep sigh and lowered his head.

"Oh, God, who hears my cries and delivers me," he whispered.

With a crackle, Courtland's earpiece came to life.

"Courtland," Dagen spoke. "What is going on down there? Can you copy?"

"I'm here."

"You're okay?"

"The Lord has given me the strength to prevail yet again."

"I don't see any Sicks. Do you still have any threats?"

"No. They're gone, scattered."

"The leader?"

"Here at my feet," the giant said, wiping at his bloody face, his wounds already beginning to mend. "We did it, Dagen. Praise God. Those at the station will live another day."

"Don't speak too soon. I just heard gunfire coming from the direction of the station. I think something is happening there. Jenna and the others may be in danger."

"The work of the righteous is never finished," Courtland murmured to himself. He keyed up his microphone. "Take the Jeep, and do what you can to save lives."

"What about you?"

"I'll go on foot."

"Are you serious?"

"Dead serious," Courtland said as he began to run. "I'll probably beat you there."

# TWENTY-EIGHT

At first as a mist and then in heavier, fatter droplets, a greasy rain fell from the blackened sky. An hour after daybreak, the sky was just beginning to show minimal signs of light. Thick, black smoke billowed in plumes from the burning gypsy camp, disappearing into the void above.

It hadn't rained in weeks, as was obvious from the way the parched earth soaked up every oily drop. Though not as thick as it had been in those early days, the rain still retained the grungy remnants of the initial fallout. The black droplets clung and slid together as gelled masses. Mother Nature had not yet purged this poison from her, a filthy reminder of humankind's recklessness.

The fires around the camp had begun to die, the shadows they cast but a fading memory in the light of the dreary morning. Jacob closed his eyes and let the thick water cascade over his wounded body. He huddled in the shadow of a rusted vehicle, long disabled and abandoned.

Shana had been relentless, tracking him through the camp, firing at every stray movement. He had done his best to stay ahead of her, to keep moving, but with every ragged breath, his chest clamped down like a vice, squeezing the life out of him. He swallowed and looked down at the bloody hole that bubbled with every labored breath. The round must have hit his lung.

Jacob raised his good arm and placed his hand over the hole, which seemed to relieve some of the pressure. He inhaled a shallow breath and pushed back an incoming tide of nausea and pain. The effects of the adrenalin were beginning to wane. He may not have long to live.

The oily rain slid down his flesh as he waited. It was all he could do. He was tired of running, tired of hiding. In an attempt to catch her off guard, Jacob had veered off the path and doubled back between the tents. He knew Shana would find him, as he had left behind a splatter of crimson droplets that had yet to be washed away in the rain. Shana would come, and he would be waiting for her. He had to warn Kane. He had to tell him what the Coyotes were doing. But first, he had to survive his pursuer.

Jacob felt so tired. Closing his eyes for just a moment, he allowed the small feeling of comfort to envelop him. The pitter-patter of rain on canvas reminded him of rainy Saturdays, which his grandma called book days. On these days Jacob and his little brothers were forbidden to watch TV or play video games. Book days were for reading books or doing something creative and quiet. At first, the boys protested, but over time, it became a ritual, a time for each of them to refocus, to curl up with a good story, or delve into a favorite creative outlet. They came to love book days and the peace and simplicity those days promised.

Jacob drifted, floating through the memories of his little brothers giggling, curled up with their cat, Sam. Grandma loved having a fire in the fireplace on book days and always whipped up some yummy treat for the boys. Jacob had not known his father, and he'd never had a meaningful relationship with his mother. She, having signed custody of Jacob over to his grandma when he was a baby. He'd had only his grandmother and his brothers, and though they wouldn't all survive the beginning of the end,

Jacob willed them back to life in this moment as he melted away into the safety and security of better times.

With a spasm of pain, he gasped and forced his eyes open. The rain continued to pour down across the permanent gloom of the gypsy camp. "No," he groaned. "Not yet."

A flicker of movement caught his eye. Jacob hugged his soaked body closer to the frame of the abandoned vehicle. With each breath, he shuddered, a few droplets dripping from his face. He forced himself to listen through the gloom and heard the steps approaching.

"I'll get you, little piggy. I'll find you," the voice whispered, as Shana came into view, swinging her rifle left and right. "You're hurt. You're bleeding. You can't make it far."

Jacob held his breath and crouched low against the frame of the rusted car. With a shudder, he realized that in his flight he had forgotten to secure anything that might be used as a weapon. He glanced around the immediate area but found nothing of use as he watched Shana creep past. He refused to move. Unarmed, outgunned, and severely injured, he didn't stand a chance. At once Jacob heard a malevolent snicker and knew instantly that he had been found.

Shana laughed quietly. "Well, how about that."

Squinting, Jacob looked up, certain he would be staring down the barrel of her rifle. But he wasn't. She still hadn't seen him. She'd stopped, crouched between the tents where she appeared to be watching someone else.

Jacob slowly pulled himself up and peered inside the rusty vehicle, where he saw a tire tool half hidden under the rear seat. He groaned in pain as he leaned his upper torso into the vehicle, secured the makeshift weapon, and returned to his crouched position.

"I got you," Shana whispered not fifteen feet in front of him, beginning to raise her rifle on someone in front of her.

Mustering his strength, Jacob crept forward on his hands and knees, willing himself to be as quiet as possible. Arriving at the edge of the car, he peered forward and around the bumper. There he saw Shana and what appeared to be two men on the ground. Jacob wiped the greasy rain from his face and looked again. One man was motionless on his back, and the other was crouched over him. The sound of the safety clicking down on Shana's rifle brought Jacob's attention back to her. It was the perfect time to make his move, but he felt so weak.

At once the tire tool seemed like such a stupid, ineffective weapon to deploy against an armed opponent. Had he lost his mind? Jacob faltered, his courage failing as he tried to determine the fastest route to get away from the madness of the situation. As he looked around, scanning the perimeter, he heard Shana whisper to herself. Her words rooted him in place.

"You aren't so tough now, are you, Kane?"

*Kane!*

With no time to think and no time to form better plans, Jacob had to move against Shana or she'd kill his only friend. Taking a slow breath, he stood on shaky legs, swallowing the bloody spittle that clung in his throat, and made his move. After only a few clomping steps, Jacob realized he wouldn't make it to her in time. In a burst of violence, Shana's rifle ripped the air with a three-round burst, and out of the corner of his eye, Jacob saw Kane drop to the earth.

"*No!*"

Hearing Jacob's wild scream, Shana spun in surprise, the whites of her eyes flashing as she squeezed the trigger again. Blinding flashes accompanied the deafening roar as Jacob felt the hot rounds pierce his chest and bury themselves deep inside him. The world blurred, and he felt as though the earth separated from the sky in a whirl of fire. He fell toward Shana, the tire tool flying with devastating force as it struck the side of her skull.

They tumbled into a muddy pile as Shana shoved Jacob off her, cursing the reckless boy and her jammed rifle. Jacob could barely hear her now as an intense warmth covered him like a blanket, consuming his quivering, rain-soaked body from head to toe.

*Grandma, I'm coming home.*

Kane scrambled for his M4, trying to stay low as Garrett's lifeless body doubled for cover as well as a shooting platform. Two shadows ahead struggled in an early-morning light that made everything gray and indiscernible. He wiped his face and aimed at one of the shadows, the one that had fired on him, just as the figure stood and began to run away.

Taking a deep breath, he squeezed off a few rounds and saw his target stumble, clutching at its leg. Firing off several more shots, Kane watched as his target ducked and scrambled out of sight.

"Damn it!" Kane swore, wiping his face again.

He did a quick check of himself and confirmed that he hadn't been hit. Kane knew that time was of the essence, but he felt compelled to check. The downed figure had stopped the other from firing. Kane wondered whether the lifeless form might have been an ally.

He raised himself and did a quick scan of the area, his hand pushing at the burning in his chest, now terrible and constant. Taking short steps while sweeping his rifle back and forth, he approached the downed figure and felt his heart sink.

"Jacob!" Kane cried, dropping his rifle and crashing to his knees next to the teen, whose life had all but slipped away. "Jacob! Come on, buddy!" he said, pulling off his jacket and pressing it over the numerous holes in the dying boy's chest.

"Kane...tried to stop her."

"I know. I know. Just relax now, buddy. I got you."

"No, you don't know what's happening, what they're planning."

"Save your strength," Kane urged, feeling a pang of responsibility for the boy's condition.

"It's the Coyotes. None of us are safe."

Kane was consumed by a fresh wave of fear. "What about the Coyotes? How do you know it's—"

"Listen to me," the teen rasped, coughing blood. "This is their plan. They have your family. They're attacking the station. We're lost."

"No, Jacob. You can't be right. It can't be—"

"It's them. They planned this all along. Kick us while we're down."

"Dear God," Kane gasped. "Not like this."

"I'm sorry, man. I tried..." Jacob gagged and shook, his young body failing him.

"I'm the one who's sorry, Jacob." Kane clenched his jaw and fought back feelings of déjà vu, as he watched another friend die in his arms. "I let this happen to you. I shouldn't have let you come."

"Yeah," Jacob rasped weakly, "but then you'd be dead." The boy squirmed against the ground, coughing and gurgling as he struggled to breathe.

"Stupid kid. Why did you have go and do something like this?" Kane mumbled as the rain came down, covering them both in a warm, dark shower.

" 'Cause that's what friends do. I have to go now," he whispered, as the last bit of life slipped away from him. "You got another chance. Make it count."

Kane gritted his teeth and swore under his breath. He lowered Jacob's head to the ground and pulled the shirt up to cover the boy's face. Sighing with despair and the weight of his failures, he lowered his head, allowing the rain to run down his face.

It was then, that Kane heard his wife scream his name.

# TWENTY-NINE

The sound of nearby gunfire brought everyone in the room to high alert. Some of the critically injured patients even tried to sit up on their cots.

"It's all right, everyone," Jenna said, waving her hands. "Just keep calm. I'm sure it's nothing." She spoke with a quiver in her voice. Every patient in the room knew the sound of gunfire never meant nothing.

She walked to a nearby drawer and removed the semiautomatic handgun, causing more murmurs among the patients.

"Hey, it's fine. There's no harm in checking," Jenna said, wincing at a fresh round of gunfire, followed by screams from outside. "Terry, you got this?"

Terry nodded, resolute.

Jenna pushed through the medical-bay doors and entered the hallway. Her mouth, dry from the combination of nerves and dehydration. She swallowed and held the handgun up to give it a function check. Just because she knew how to operate a handgun didn't mean she had to like it. The gun wasn't for her; Jenna kept the gun for the rest of them, those at the station who could no longer defend themselves.

Arriving at the front double doors, she shook her head and steadied her nerves. The mutants couldn't have returned—though maybe they had. Maybe they had overcome Courtland and Dagen and the rest. There was only one way for her to find out. With a heave, she shoved the doors open and raised her gun as the door slammed against her, crushing her hand against the frame. She cried out in shock and pain, falling back to the ground, where she cradled her throbbing hand.

Before she knew what was happening, several brutish men yanked the door back open and grabbed her. After dragging Jenna to her feet, one man held her tight by both arms, while the other mocked her. "Careful, love. You could hurt someone with this thing," he said, dangling the gun before her. Jenna whimpered, her hand throbbing while the thug traced the outline of her breasts with the gun barrel.

"You look familiar to me," he said. "Have we met?"

"Please, just take me," Jenna pleaded. "There's no need to hurt anyone else."

"Oh, yeah?" The man behind her laughed.

"Please, just take me."

"Hey, man. The lady wants you to take her. What are you waiting for?" he said with a giggle.

The thug leaned in close. "I swear I've seen you before. Wait, yeah. You were the woman Dagen brought in last year when we controlled this place!"

Jenna grimaced and turned her face away.

"Yeah, man. Let's do her," the thug said, panting. "I don't mind walking down that street again. It looks like she needs to be reminded that she still belongs to the Coyotes."

The other man laughed.

"She doesn't belong to the Coyotes," another figure said as he stepped up alongside them. "She belongs to me."

"Bullshit! We found her first. Get in line, Raith."

"Malak said I could have her. She's mine," Raith said, a dark finality in his tone.

The bigger thugs began to mock their own. "But Malak said…Malak said." They laughed. "Just because he put you in charge of this raid don't mean you get to tell us what to do."

In a move that stunned them all, Raith jammed a short knife into the side of the front thug's neck, jerking it free, wiping it on his pants and putting it away as though nothing had happened.

Jenna moaned in terror as the thug behind her cussed and backed away. A thin stream of blood shot from the wounded thug's neck. Gurgling with shock and pain, he tried in vain to cover the gushing wound as he fell to his knees.

"This one belongs to me," Raith said, raising his voice and grabbing Jenna's hair with a jerk. "You can let her go, or you can die like your friend here."

The thug released Jenna and held his hands in the air. "Yeah, Raith. It's fine. Be cool, man."

"The time for being cool has passed. Go take your ignorant ass and do what we came here to do."

The bigger thug nodded, and after taking one last look at his dying friend moved back into the station. Jenna gasped again as the thin man pulled her by her hair outside and across the courtyard while the thugs raided the station. Jenna's skin crawled, and her head swimming with painful memories as she was pushed against a truck, her arms restrained behind her back.

"What are you going to do?" she managed.

"First we watch the show, my dear. Then you and I will embark on our little honeymoon." He smiled as he turned her around to face the station.

"Jenna!" a woman named Claire called from across the courtyard. "I'm sorry! They said they'd kill me if I didn't tell them where they were!"

"No, Claire. You didn't." Jenna yelled though she knew with absolute dread the answer to her question. Moments later a line of children was herded around the front of the building before them.

"No! Don't do this, please. If there's anything human in you, don't do this," Jenna begged, as tears filled her eyes.

Raith smiled, his expression, one of sheer wickedness. "Children are so innocent, even in times like these, are they not? Look at them. Holding hands and smiling. They have no concept of what's about to happen to them."

"*Please!*" Jenna cried. "Do whatever you want to me, but don't harm them."

"You know, you're an exquisite creature," Raith cooed, looking Jenna over. "Even now you care nothing for yourself. I'm really looking forward to this—to *us*."

Jenna watched as the children shuffled toward the double doors. She couldn't contain herself any longer. "Run, children! Run away as quick as you can!"

The kids looked at her with confused expressions as they continued to walk into the building, following the bandits' orders.

"Run! Don't go in there, please!" Jenna screamed.

But her cries fell on deaf, unknowing ears, as the last of the children shuffled in and the last of the bandits came out, pouring a trail of gasoline.

"No! No, please, don't! Please!"

Raith nodded to one of his men, and the man secured the last of the doors. Several others lit Molotov cocktails.

"*No!*"

Jenna's voice cracked as a multitude of fire bombs were launched at the building. It burst into flames with a rushing *whoosh*. Jenna's legs buckled as the children screamed. She writhed and wrenched at her bonds, her body quaking in horror. The slap came hard and fast as she was dragged into the truck, buckled in, and secured.

As the truck started, Raith yelled something to his men about where to meet up. Then they were moving, the flames belching the smoke and the ash of its victims into the sky. Tears of fear and loss ran down Jenna's face as she begged God to keep her spirit from breaking. She was completely alone now.

*All is lost.*

✫ ✫ ✫

Courtland opened his gait as he crossed the hilly bluff that overlooked the station, each long stride reaching farther than the last. The black smoke of the fire gushed into view as he heard the sound of screams in the distance. They were the screams of children.

"Lord Jesus, carry me forward," the giant gasped, consuming every morsel of oxygen that made its way into his lungs as he propelled himself forward.

Cresting the ridge, Courtland could see the barricaded radio station as flames snapped and flew from all the doors and windows. Jenna, Terry, and all the sick and wounded were in there. A glance at the open cellar door confirmed his darkest fears. The children were inside too.

He was moving down the hillside, each jarring step threatening to split his healing wounds, but he didn't care. As the last of the screams began to fade, he felt the finality of the moment give new life to his inhuman strength.

"Lord God, make me your messenger of justice!" was all Courtland could manage as he flew toward the station, extending his glimmering blades. He felt his body surge as every limb bristled with an electric fury. Nearing the main gate, he watched as several trucks sped through. He caught a glimpse of a woman who appeared to be Jenna strapped into the front seat of the lead vehicle.

"Jenna!" Courtland cried as it flew past. The skinny man driving sneered as he went. Without losing his stride, Courtland ducked his shoulder and slammed into the second vehicle, a pickup with a bed full of bandits. The truck flipped, launching the flailing bodies of several men into the air. A few others rolled with the truck and were crushed beneath it, their screams cut short.

Moving with reckless abandon, fueled by the power of God, Courtland mastered his empowered form as the mass of Coyotes fired upon him. Picking up the disabled truck, he spun, flinging the vehicle into the courtyard the way an Olympic athlete throws a hammer. The truck-missile landed amidst the bandits like a meteor striking the earth. An explosion of sand and debris rained down over their mangled forms, the truck grinding to a stop above crimson streaks in the dirt.

Wild with poisonous hate, the rest of the bandits charged Courtland, their assault rifles blazing with fire. He moved toward them in righteous anger, raising his blades to shield himself as the bullets flew past, failing to strike.

"Shoot that big bastard already!"

"I'm shooting him!"

"I can't hit him!"

"How about that?" Courtland said, snarling. He bent his knees and launched himself forward, swinging his blades while crossing the distance between them in a flash. The bloodcurdling screams lasted only an instant as he tore them apart.

As the last thug ran in terror, Courtland dropped his blades and launched into the air after him. He crossed the thirty-yard gap in no time, crashing to the dirt behind the terrified goon. The man spun and tried to attack the giant as Courtland seized him in two massive hands.

"You're a big fucker, aren't you?" the man spat.

Courtland raised the thug to eye level, shaking as he spoke. "You like murdering innocent people—*innocent children?*"

"I like skinning them," the tattooed thug said, "but I didn't get to *this time.*"

"Who put you up to this?"

"We're the Coyotes, bitch. We do what the fuck we want."

Courtland squeezed the man's throat with a meaty hand. "*Who put you up to this?*"

"Gakkkk. He'll kill me!"

"What do you think I'll do?" the giant roared, as he turned the man to face his slaughtered comrades.

Flames licked at the charred windows as the Coyote shook, realizing his fate had been sealed regardless of his answer.

"Malak. He calls all the shots. No one opposes us."

"I do. Where is he now?" Courtland asked in a menacing tone.

"He's taking care of your friend Kane, and his family. Gonna do 'em up right."

"And where are they taking the woman in the truck?"

"Raith is taking her somewhere. Then we'll all meet back up and head West."

"What's West?"

"He's got something big in the works. Arizona or New Mexico is what I heard. I don't know, man. I swear."

"Swear on the lives of the children you just murdered!"

A strange calm settled over the man, and he smiled. "I enjoyed hearing them scream."

Courtland felt a sting of righteous anger as he dragged the man to the front of the building, talking through clenched teeth as he went. "You Coyotes have a sickness that has no cure. Like rabid dogs, you just have to be put down."

"Yeah, kill me. Do it. I ain't afraid."

"You should be. It's the fire that comes after these flames you should fear."

"I don't believe in that shit!" the man spat.

Courtland smoldered. "It's existence doesn't require that you believe in it!" he barked, as he flung the man through one of the flaming windows and into the blazing furnace.

As the thug howled and shrieked through his final moments, Courtland turned and caught his breath for the first time. He looked at the dust trail that still lingered from the first truck as he dropped to his knees and clasped his hands. His worst fears had been confirmed. Malak wasn't dead after all. He was exacting his vengeance against Kane at this moment. Courtland cringed with the pain of agony and failure.

"Why, Lord?" he called out, as black smoke poured from the doors and windows of the station. "What is your purpose here? I tried to help these people, these children. You entrusted them to me and gave me the power to fight for them—And for what? So they could die at the hands of these fiends? I can't believe that what we tried to do was all for nothing! We've been conquered," Courtland murmured, lowering his head and wiping his face.

The giant's portable radio crackled to life. "Courtland," a voice called through the static.

The giant fumbled, keying up the microphone. "Dagen?"

"What's your status?"

"Not good. Where are you?"

"It took a few minutes for me to crawl back to the truck, but I'm en route to the station."

"Don't come here, Dagen. There's nothing left. They murdered everyone."

"What?"

"Even the children."

A moment of silence passed. "Who did this?" Dagen said.

"The Coyotes. We stopped one monster just to have another take its place. They've destroyed us here. Kane and the others are in terrible danger."

"Is Jenna alive?"

Courtland paused and turned to look at the flames pouring from the station. "I don't know. They took her. They left before I could stop them."

He paused, waiting for Dagen's response, but the radio remained silent. After an eternal moment, it crackled to life again.

"Which direction?" came Dagen's solemn reply.

"I can't be sure. I think south on the coastal highway. Dagen, they've got a truck full of goons guarding her. I don't think you can—"

"Don't tell me what I can't do," Dagen interrupted with an iron resolve. "If they've got Jenna, I'm going after her. They'll have to kill me if they want to stop me."

✡ ✡ ✡

The rugged tires of the battered Jeep Wrangler slid across the dusty gravel. As the vehicle came to a full stop, Dagen grabbed the frame of the vehicle and hoisted his body from the seat to gain a better view of the highway below. The corners of his mouth twitched upward as he took in the lingering dust trail, a sign that a vehicle had passed recently. Dropping back down, he grabbed his right leg and placed it on the gas pedal. He shoved his hips forward, causing the tires to spin and go. On the passenger seat next to him lay a pair of military binoculars, an MP5K submachine gun with three thirty-round magazines, and the bolt-action rifle wedged between the seat and the center console.

Dagen knew all too well about the men he was about to confront. He knew he would face superior numbers of brainwashed, rabid sociopaths. Because he had almost no functional use of his legs, he knew the only course of action available to him was absolute and overwhelming violence in the form of an ambush. It was the only chance Jenna had to survive. Dagen knew the Coyotes wouldn't hesitate to skin and scalp him alive unless someone recognized him, which was unlikely considering the attrition rate for a group like theirs. For an instant, he considered the possibility of finding Malak in the vehicle and how strange and dangerous it would be to encounter that sick bastard once more, now from the opposite force.

Pulling himself forward against the steering wheel and craning his neck upward, he could just make out the rear end of the fleeing truck through the dust. He watched as it meandered left and out of sight, down the coastline. Willing the vehicle ahead, Dagen knew he had a real chance. He hammered his fist on the steering wheel and shouted, "Here we go! You can do this!"

He was familiar with this stretch of road. He knew the vehicle had passed out of sight only to follow the highway through what used to be the Francis Marion National Forest. He also knew he had a fairly straight shot along his current path. At full speed, he could come out ahead of them where the scenic highway came back into sight. From that position, Dagen would make his move.

He forged ahead, a look of determination like a permanent expression on his face. After a few minutes, Dagen slid to a stop along the bluff and retrieved the MP5K sub gun from the passenger seat. He inserted a thirty-round stick into the magazine well and slapped the charging handle down. He took the second and third magazines and shoved them into a large pouch in the front of his load-bearing vest. Resting the gun across his lap, he retrieved the bolt gun. After bending the side mirror as far down as possible, he stuffed an old rag into the wedge between the mirror and the frame to create a suitable shooting platform. Adjusting his body into position behind the rifle, he supported the rifle as best he could. After double-checking the scope, which now had a distracting crack in the glass, Dagen was ready.

After just a few minutes, the truck rose back into sight as it made the climb back up the highway. Dagen swallowed once and licked his lips, his heart hammering inside his ears. So much was at stake. What if he missed? His equipment had taken a beating, and he couldn't be sure the rifle scope was still zeroed after his tussle with the Sick.

He exhaled, took another breath to steady his heart. It was a long shot, close to seven hundred yards on a moving vehicle. He might hit Jenna if his shot was off. Even if by some miracle he made the shot, there was still a chance that she could get hurt in a crash or at the hands of her captors.

"Come on, Dagen," he whispered. "Get your head together." He watched through the cracked glass and made a slight hiss through his teeth as he began to make out Jenna in the front passenger seat. He'd have to take the shot head-on. If he waited, the truck would begin to angle, and things would become much more complicated.

Holding the rifle close against his shoulder, Dagen found his eye relief and took several controlled breaths, lowering his heart rate as he worked the action and drove a round into the chamber.

"All right, God," he whispered. "If you're out there and you care at all about what happens to this woman, I'm going to need your help with this." He took another breath and let it out slowly. "I'm begging you. I can't do this on my own."

After one final breath, he allowed the stillness to wash over him. He tracked his crosshairs where he knew his target would be, and with a final breath, he exhaled halfway and began a slow and steady trigger squeeze to the rear. With a *crack,* the rifle recoiled. Dagen continued to hold his breath as he watched through the fractured glass of the scope. The windshield of the truck spider-webbed, throwing bits of glinting glass like tiny diamonds into the air in front of the driver. Dagen watched as a crimson spray formed against the inside of the windshield. The truck began to fishtail, sliding across the dirt and tossing a few goons from the bed as it went. Catching a tire, the vehicle rolled, slid across the road, and came to a stop upside down.

*"That's what I'm talking about!"* Dagen shouted, as he threw down the rifle and cranked the Jeep. The tires spun beneath him as the Jeep took off, descending at full speed down the steep hillside. The bandits began to crawl out from beneath the flipped truck, attempting to get their bearings. In seconds, they were onto Dagen, firing their weapons, the windshield of the Jeep popping and cracking as the rounds struck it. Dagen ducked his head and made straight for a few stragglers who'd been tossed from the vehicle, hammering them into the dirt and across the

hood of the Jeep as he came. As their fire intensified, Dagen leaned down and yanked the emergency brake, simultaneously cutting the wheel and grabbing the sub gun in his lap as the Jeep began to spin. As the Jeep spun toward them, the goons all fumbled with fresh magazines, unable to engage.

Dagen was ready. He snarled as he hung out the door against the seatbelt and launched a steady stream of lead into his intended targets. He tracked the men with an arc of bursts from the MP5, expending every last round as the vehicle spun to a stop with its rear to the truck. A new barrage of fire hit the tailgate of the Jeep as the few remaining men reloaded and began to tear the Jeep apart. The fabric of the seats burst open, and something exploded under the rear axle as the bullets pinged and clanged off every bit of metal that surrounded him.

Releasing the empty magazine from the submachine gun, Dagen pulled the spare from his vest and slapped it in, charging the weapon. Crawling as fast as he could, he pulled himself over the console and made for the passenger door. The men hadn't yet figured out that Dagen couldn't walk. The instant they did, they would surround him and he'd be finished. He had to end this now. Popping from the passenger side, he fired several more rounds, taking down more thugs with vital hits to the head and chest. Taking cover back inside the vehicle, he went to change magazines a third time when he heard the last bandit call out to him.

"I know you're here for my girl! Throw the gun to the rear of the vehicle, and I might not blow her brains out."

Dagen knew the man was lying and had no intention of sparing either of them. He and his crew, shamed by Dagen's attack on them, now had nothing to lose. Malak would slaughter them when he found out.

Dagen chanced a peek out the passenger door and saw a skinny man pushing the barrel of a 1911-style handgun into Jenna's neck. Dagen noticed a jagged, bloody hole in the man's right shoulder and noted the way he held the handgun loose in his left. He was right-handed, but he no longer had any use of his right arm. This was the driver. Jenna gave a whimper, and her knees shook upon seeing Dagen's head poke out.

"Throw the weapon out *now!*" Raith yelled.

"All right. The gun is coming out. Don't do anything stupid," Dagen said, as he cleared the sub gun and heaved it over the roll bars onto the dirt. "I'm going to step out now, but I can't hold my hands up because I'm crippled."

"Let's see it," Raith said.

Dagen grabbed his legs, and they tingled with a strange sensation as he pulled them out of the door and let them fall to the ground.

"Ah, it's Mister no legs," Raith said.

"Do I know you?" Dagen asked.

"No, of course not. But I know you. I'd hoped we might meet, just not quite like this." The rat-faced man scowled and looked down at his ruined right shoulder. "That was an expert shot, I must say."

Dagen stood silent, staring holes in the skinny man that held Jenna at gunpoint.

"You must care about her."

"I owe her my life. That's why I'm here. Release her to me." Dagen said.

"I don't think so," Raith said. "I've been watching my lovely here for quite a while. You're not going to steal her from me now."

The tingling continued down Dagen's legs. A prickling sensation that stretched across the soles of his feet, as though his legs were falling asleep, except instead of losing feeling, they were gaining it.

"She doesn't belong to you," Dagen said. "She never did. Release her."

"Or what?" The villain smiled, flashing his yellowed teeth. "The legless man will fight me for her?"

"If I have to."

"How noble of you, but that's ridiculous. I won't stoop to fighting a man who can't stand on his own, and I don't want to be tardy for our little date," Raith said, nudging Jenna forward with the barrel of the pistol. "You don't mind if we use your Jeep, do you?"

"If I did, there's not much I could do to stop you." Dagen lowered his head.

"Now you're speaking my language," Raith said, as he moved with Jenna toward the vehicle.

Dagen felt strength building in his legs. Though he still held onto the frame of the vehicle, he knew he could support himself on his own, even if only for a few moments.

"Naturally," Raith continued as he approached, "I can't have you coming after us again, which means you have to die." Raith swung his gun on Dagen.

Catching them both off guard, Jenna kicked back hard with the heel of her shoe and struck Raith in the center of his shin. She turned and began to flee with her arms still pinned behind her. The gun fired as Raith jerked the trigger, and Dagen ducked to avoid the wild round as it pinged off the sidewall of the Jeep. Raith pivoted, pointing the gun at Jenna as she ran, the slide rocking with a crack as he fired with his unsupported weak hand. Her arms still bound behind her, she dove to the ground behind a small dune as the rounds struck the sand around her.

Dagen shoved himself from the vehicle with a groan, his face twisted with fury as he snarled, willing his legs forward. Crossing the gap of five yards between them, he launched himself at Raith, his previously useless legs moving with clumsy strides beneath him. With a cry, Dagen crashed into Raith, forcing the goon's gun hand outward, where the handgun struck the roll-bar support with a clang and fell into the Jeep as both men crashed against the dusty ground.

Jenna screamed Dagen's name as Raith came up fast, wielding a hidden blade. Twisting, Dagen parried the blade away and came across the skinny's man's face with his elbow, followed by a crushing headbutt. The combination split the flesh of Raith's lips against his rat-like teeth.

"I thought you couldn't walk!" Raith screamed through clenched teeth.

"Guess I'm full of surprises!" Dagen spat back, as they rolled and wrestled across the ground. Dagen felt the knife cut through his jacket, slashing him, once and then a second time across the shoulder and outer arm. Lashing out, Dagen punched hard the side of Raith's neck hard and saw the thin man's eyes flare with pain.

Hissing, Raith came again with the blade as Dagen rolled toward the Jeep and felt his legs come alive with one final surge of strength. Drawing his legs in as he lay on his back, Dagen pushed his legs up as Raith came down and the blade buried itself deep in the thick rubber sole of his boot. Lashing out with all his strength and coordination, Dagen thrust his other boot up and caught Raith under the chin with his heel, knocking the man back.

Dagen wasted no time. He rolled to his belly and scrambled for the Jeep. He had to secure the handgun. He wasn't sure how many rounds Raith had fired, but knowing that the average 1911 magazine held six to eight, he knew there wouldn't be many left. He had no other option. It was his only card left to play.

Pushing with his legs as they seethed with pain, Dagen pulled himself up using the tailgate and swung the door open as Raith approached with his knife raised. Holding onto the frame for support, Dagen drew his right leg up and stomped down on Raith's pelvic bowl, knocking him back, the man sinking the knife deep into the muscle of Dagen's thigh as he fell. Screaming, blood streaming from the puncture wound, Dagen swept his arms through the junk in the car as Raith pushed himself up from the ground.

Dagen felt his legs give way as he fell and tried to slow his decent by gripping the frame. As he hung there, his free hand touched the gun. Pulling it to him, he could already see the weapon was jammed, a misfed round causing the weapon to malfunction. Raith stood, wiped his face, secured his grip on the bloodied knife, and approached again.

"What are you gonna do now, soldier boy?" Raith whispered, noting the jammed weapon as he closed the distance.

Dagen pressed the rear sight of the gun down against the metal bumper. He drove his arm down, ejecting the jammed round with one hand as the magazine fed the last good round into the chamber with a snap.

"It's called a malfunction drill, asshole."

Raith charged as Dagen came up fast with the 1911 and saw the confidence fade from the villain's face. With perfect accuracy, Dagen fired a single round through Raith's eye socket, causing the thin man to flinch midstep, his mouth hinged open in a failed scream, as his brains scattered across the sidewall of the overturned truck behind him.

Dagen let go of the frame and dropped to the ground, his legs screaming, his body trembling. Leaning against the Jeep, he pulled off his jacket and tied it tightly around his wounded leg. He gave Raith's crumpled form one last look.

Jenna struggled to her feet and was now taking shaky steps forward, her hands still bound behind her back. She stared at Dagen, a man who just succeeded at the impossible.

"Dagen! They murdered the children. I couldn't stop them," she sputtered, dropping to her knees next to him and weeping tears of sadness and relief.

"I know. I know they did," Dagen said, wrapping his arms tightly around the woman he loved. He leaned back against the bullet-riddled vehicle. "I'm here now. I'll take care of you."

"How did you...? You risked yourself..." She cried, as she tucked her face against his chest. He reached behind her to cut her bound wrists free. "I saw you run," Jenna continued. "I saw you tackle him."

"I don't know, Jenna. I can't explain it. I asked God to help me, and then I came for you. That's all I know," he said, holding her tightly against him.

"You don't believe in God."

"I don't know what I believe. But if you say God won't abandon a bum like me, then why would he ever abandon you—his messenger of love and hope? You've got to be more precious to Him than all the stars in the midnight sky," Dagen said, closing his eyes as Jenna wept, cradled against him in the comfort of their shared embrace. "I think He sent me so you'd remember that."

# THIRTY

"Susan!" Kane screamed at the top of his lungs as he stumbled forward through the muck and downpour. The rain was subsiding. A fine veil of mist seemed to drown the landscape in an inescapable fog.

"Susan, where are you?" Kane cried out.

"Kane!" came the sobbing cry of his wife's voice. "Kane, help us!"

The words were lifted straight from one of Kane's nightmares. He stumbled onward, maneuvering through the burnt gypsy camp. Out of breath, an overwhelming fear covered him as he arrived at the far edge of the camp.

There before him stood a mass of bandits, all with their rifles trained on him. A shiver coursed through Kane. He knew he'd be shot to pieces the moment he tried to raise his weapon. He tried to compose himself, as he peered through the curtain of mist that separated him from the barbaric men before him. Eyeing each figure carefully, Kane's eyes rested on a female form huddled with his children. Kane choked on a breath as he tried to form the words to call to them.

"Suz—" he managed, taking one step forward.

"That's close enough. Do anything stupid, and we'll turn your family into hamburger meat." A voice called out from the crowd.

Kane stopped and surveyed the group again as he struggled to master the intensity of his emotions. Multiple gunmen stood behind his family, their weapons pushed against his wife's flesh as she embraced their terrified children.

He fought back a wave of unbridled fear as he clenched his jaw and swallowed with difficulty. "I don't know who you are or what your game is, but your leader, Garrett, is dead. Release my family, and I won't kill all of you."

The men laughed, as a blue-faced bandit stepped forward and crossed his arms. "Garrett doesn't lead us. You did us a favor by killing him. He was a puppet, just like you, dancing to our little tune."

"Sure thing, guy," Kane said, shaking his head. "If you people are so organized, if you're pulling everyone's strings, then who's the puppet master?"

"I am," came a menacing growl. The crowd parted, and the hulking form of Malak stepped forward.

Kane stood in shock, his face filling with terror as he recognized the monstrous, bald figure with the coiled viper tattoo in the center of his chest. There was no underestimating the imminent danger his family faced at the hands of these madmen.

"Look! It's a family reunion!" Malak mocked, clapping his hands together. "This is just perfect. Kane and his lovely wife and children separated by one terrible day. Now, after believing the other to be dead for so long, they see each other for the first time!"

Kane ground his teeth and made eye contact with Susan. The defeated look in her eyes killed him inside. The group stood at attention as though Malak were leading story time.

"Oh, but then the reality of life begins to set in," Malak continued with a dramatic flair. "Kane realizes the horrors that his innocent children have been exposed to. How his wife gave herself to another man, long before the memory of her husband had grown cold."

Susan winced and bowed her head as a blush of shame spread across her face. Kane swallowed and stared at her, but she wouldn't return his gaze.

"Oh, yes. It's true—the man Garrett, whom you murdered. Maybe you can take some small measure of satisfaction knowing your wife's lover died by your hand."

Susan still refused to look up. Kane caught the pleading eyes of his children and tried to look confident. He was so damn thirsty.

"And you, Kane. How much time did you waste hanging around that fucking station? Time you could have used to find and save your family. They were right under your nose. You could have kept all of this from happening, but you didn't. You were probably shacked up with some whore. Or maybe it was that little blonde tart I ran through. She didn't make it, did she?"

"You don't know anything about me!" Kane spat.

"Oh. I touched a nerve there. I think you had a thing for that blonde. Who are you to blame your wife for not keeping her legs together?"

"Enough! What the hell do you want, Malak?" Kane shouted.

"I want you to know this was all part of the plan. I used those freaks. I used your divisiveness. I even used your own personal weakness to ruin you. This is the bed you've made for yourself by fucking with someone—*something*—you can't possibly understand."

Kane glared at the hulking villain. "We killed you."

"No, apparently not. But maybe you'd like to give it another shot. This time we'll see what's what when you don't have that loyal black dog of yours getting in the way—that is, if you do still call yourself God's warrior."

"Malak, just let them—"

"Enough of this bargaining shit." Malak waved his hand in an impatient gesture. "I hold all the chips. You have nothing to bargain with.

Your family is now my family to do with as I please—and there's nothing you can do about it. Unless, as I said, you'd like to fight me for them."

"What am I going to do against all of you? Like you said, you have every advantage. The minute I start to win, my family and I will be gunned down. You're not the kind of men who keep your word."

"No?" Malak smiled and looked around. "I will say this now. If Kane will fight me in single combat, none of you may harm him or his family. And if he should defeat me, you'll release his family and allow them all to leave. Am I understood?"

The bandits lowered their weapons as a wave of acknowledgment passed through them. This wasn't Malak being fair; it was a very bad sign. He didn't have a snowball's chance in hell fighting Malak one on one.

Reading Kane's expression, Malak stepped forward. "How about this? I'll let you keep your firearms. I'll remain unarmed."

A feeling of newfound confidence swelled in Kane. He knew it was more than foolish. Still, he performed a quick function check of the M4. Maybe he did have a chance.

Malak smiled. "This is going to be slow and painful for you, and I'm going to enjoy every second."

"Just do what you came here to do, you son of a bitch."

Silence fell over the group as the bandits took shelter. A few of them pulled Susan and the children behind a pair of old vehicles. Malak flashed an evil grin as the dark of his eyes filled with a black fury.

"Well?" Malak growled.

*You can do this, Kane. Don't fail them now.*

Kane raised his rifle as Malak came forward and swung his arms open, the air shifting around him. Kane pulled the trigger, and the assault rifle roared to life. Malak raged, crossing the space between them in an instant.

In a moment of sheer dismay, Kane watched as each round veered away from Malak, skirting their target as if they were in the pull of oppositely charged magnets. Kane continued to fire on the monstrous man as the bullets zipped past, refusing to connect.

"Come on!" Kane shouted.

Then, Malak was upon him, snatching him from the ground like a child's plaything. Kane struck the big man's iron jaw with the butt of his rifle, shattering the plastic retractable stock. Malak smiled malevolently and flung Kane through the air. The ground soared beneath him as the empty rifle fell from his hands. His arm hit first, folding under him as he slid across the tar-like mud. He began to raise himself, but Malak was already there. Kane felt weak, underpowered, and alone, as the brute lifted him into the air again, drawing him face-to-face.

"Is that it? You disgust—"

"Deflect this," Kane said as he jammed his Glock under Malak's chin and fired. Kane fell, smacking on his back against the mud, where he scrambled backward. Malak stumbled, clutching at the gaping, crimson hole in his face as the blood sprayed from it.

Hope swelled in Kane's chest mere seconds before it was replaced with absolute horror. With a wet, smacking sound, Malak worked his jaw, and the jagged hole in his face began to mend. Kane crawled away in terror as the surrounding goons cheered and laughed. Malak moved toward Kane once more.

"No," Kane stammered. "That's not possible."

Malak's guttural laugh sounded far from human as he continued to stalk forward, the last bit of his face coming back together. "Your weapons can't hurt me. Nothing can."

In a flash, Malak lunged forward, seizing Kane by his face, suffocating him as he lifted him into the air. Kane's legs kicked franticly beneath him as he clawed at the iron fingers that seemed to stretch around his head.

"Behold! This is what awaits the followers of God!" Malak roared as the crowd cheered. Malak swung Kane down, slamming his head hard against the mud-soaked earth. Malak raised the weakened man again and again, slamming him against the earth headfirst, as each impact threatened to crush his skull.

Then, it was over. Kane gasped, his head vibrating with pain, his vision and hearing returning to him. He wasn't dead yet. He managed to swing his arm in order to roll onto his belly. A shooting pain stabbed at the base of his neck and raced to the tips of his toes. Malak laughed as the crowd of thugs cheered for their champion. Susan cried and covered the eyes of her twins.

*Don't fail them now.*

"My family," Kane muttered as he began to crawl.

"Well, make a path for him," Malak encouraged, as the goons laughed and hooted. The crowd rushed forward, lining either side of Kane as he crawled through the muck. It wasn't long before the urine and spit cascaded down on him as he dug his fingers into the mud. Pushing to his hands and knees, Kane moved faster between the rows of boots. A violent kick to the ribs sent him falling back against the unforgiving terrain. A second kick struck the side his head, and he felt himself fade.

"Let him up," Malak growled. The men immediately stopped and hauled Kane to his feet. "The man wants to see his family. Why should we deny him that?"

The thugs grabbed Kane under his arms and dragged him toward Susan and the children. As he went, Kane watched through mud-caked eyes as his feet carved a path through the filth behind him.

"Give them a minute." Malak motioned, and the thugs dropped Kane to his knees in front of his family then backed away.

"Kane? Kane, honey, are you alright?" Susan's voice cracked as she leaned in to cradle her husband's bloody face in her hands.

"Suz...I thought you were dead," Kane mumbled.

"No. We survived for you, to see you again," she said, weeping.

Kane looked up and touched his children's faces. Even under such dire circumstances, they smiled. "Hey, guys. I missed you so much. I never gave up on you."

"Did those men hurt you, Daddy?" Rachael asked with eyes full of fear.

"Daddy's okay, sweet pea. Daddy loves you."

"Kane." Susan caught his eyes as her face hardened. "I had to do what I had to do to keep them safe. I hope you can forgive..."

"I know, honey. I don't care about that. None of that matters."

"Oh," Malak said, stepping in and wiping away a fake tear. "This is beautiful, sacrifice and forgiveness—the cornerstones of the Christian faith. Why don't we see how deep it runs?"

"Wait. Just wait. Give us another minute," Kane pleaded, as the bandits yanked him from his family and his children began to scream.

"Wait, damn it! Stop!" Kane yelled, as a sack pulled over his head and a devastating impact landing behind his right ear, bursting night into day in a flurry of stars.

✵ ✵ ✵

The jostling of the vehicle woke Kane. For a second he panicked as the bag restricted his breathing and threatened to smother him. He was face-down, his wrists and ankles tied with rope. The sound of the rumbling engine didn't quite drown out the coarse laughter of the bandits, the muffled prayers of his wife, and the sobs of his precious children.

Inside the hood, Kane felt the burlap scratch against his skin and a warm trickle of blood run down his face from his right ear across his jaw. As he tried to twist against the bonds, his heart burned in his chest, the pain radiating down his arms.

"Susan, I love you so much. Always remember that, no matter what happens."

"I'm so scared, Kane," she whimpered amid the low hum of the vehicle.

"We're going to—"

Kane was interrupted as the vehicle came to a sliding stop and the doors opened.

"Everyone, be strong!" Kane managed, as someone grabbed hold of him and snatched him from the vehicle. His body fell free of the vehicle then smacked hard against the earth, the impact stealing the air from his lungs. Kane had only a moment to adjust before he was dragged across the ground to some unknown destination. He was left lying on his face, his mind reeling with the fear of things to come. He listened for recognizable sounds. He heard the sound of the ocean lapping against the shore, bandits laughing, Malak giving instructions to someone, and his wife and children as they sobbed louder.

"What the hell is happening? What are you doing to them?" Kane cried.

He was jerked upright and forced back into a kneeling position.

"You're going to be cut loose, but if you so much as move an inch, your family is dead. Nod if you understand."

Kane nodded and felt his hands and feet come free.

"Do you remember the first time we met? Right before I killed that sweet little girlfriend of yours." Malak's voice whispered in Kane's ear. "Do you remember what I told you?

Kane shook with fear and anger. "You said…"

"Yes?"

"You told me sacrifices must be made."

"Exactly. And then what did you say?"

"I said you were finished. I told Molly it was going to be Okay," Kane said, shaking.

"Yes, that part! That's what I was looking for," Malak said, as he snatched the hood from Kane's head. An overwhelming sense of dread poured over Kane. Blinking his eyes as the wind whipped his face, he saw his family trembling and sobbing before him.

"No," Kane sputtered. "Don't…do this. I'm begging you," he pleaded, shaking as his wife and two children knelt before him on the edge of a seaside cliff. Susan was tied up with a heavy hemp rope, the end of the strand trailing from her to him. Next to her, their children whimpered as they sat bound together with rope in a similar fashion, the end of their strand leading from them to Kane.

"Now," Malak spoke with a dark vigor, "tell them like you told Molly. Tell them it's going to be okay. Lie to them."

"No. I won't play your game."

"*Do it,*" Malak roared, "Or I'll cut them to ribbons while you watch."

"I…I…" Kane stuttered as tears ran down his face. "I love each of you." He swallowed. "It's going to be all right."

"Now choose!" Malak said. "You have ten seconds."

"No! Please, no. Dear God, no, no…" he mumbled, his eyes blurring with tears.

"Kane," Susan's voice reached out to him, soft amid the chaos.

Kane blinked through the tears and saw the calmness in her face, a serenity that knew no end.

"Susan, I can't choose."

"You have to. Everything I've done up to now has been to save our children. Don't let it be for nothing."

"I can't lose you again!" Kane wept.

"You never lost me. Promise me you'll do everything you can to save them."

"I...I promise," Kane gasped, as the thugs closed in on his family.

"Kane," Susan called out, "I never stopped loving you."

"Daddy!" the twins cried.

"Choose!" Malak raged, as his thugs placed their feet against Susan and the children and, in one violent movement, shoved all three of them over the cliff.

As they fell, time seemed to slow. Their screams shattered the fear that bound Kane to inaction. He threw himself forward and grabbed a strand of rope in each of his hands, clenching his fists down.

Screaming with terror, Kane dragged toward the cliff's edge as the fibrous rope burned through his hands, the rough strands carving trenches in the meat of his palms. He heard Susan and the children screaming as they fell, and he knew he had only milliseconds to either die with them or save one of them. The thought of letting it all go and taking the easy plunge with them seemed one of sweet release, but as he considered it, something surged within him and denied him that path.

His body, wrapped in mortal terror, flew toward the edge as he cried out. Forcing his right hand to open, Susan's rope whipped free and disappeared over the edge. He heard her scream again as she continued to fall, faster now, and as he placed his free hand on his children's rope and dug his feet into the wet soil, he heard the sound of his dear wife as her body struck the rocks below.

*Why have you forsaken me?*

Locking his body down, Kane slowed to a stop. He wrapped the hemp around his mutilated hands, crying as he drew his children to him. They were all that mattered to him now. He had made a promise, a promise he never would forget.

Struggling, his heart hammering with violent blows inside him, Kane labored for the lives of his children. Inch by inch he pulled them up, the meat of his hands falling in chunks to the ground. Raising them just to the rim, he lunged forward and grabbed a handful of coiled rope, dragging his children up and over the edge as they cried out. The wind blew in gusts as he pulled them against his chest and listened to them call his name.

"Shh," he cooed, as the tears streamed down his face. "Daddy's got you. Daddy's got you now."

In a movement that surprised them all, they were yanked apart. Malak's goons pulled the children from Kane and held them back, the boy and girl bawling in terror.

Defeated, Kane raised his pulpy hands, "You hateful bastards! What do you want? You've taken everything from me!"

Malak stepped forward and leaned in close. "I want you to know that your God has abandoned you."

Hanging his head, Kane wept, his body quaking.

"I want you to know that because you couldn't stop me, I'll continue to torture, murder, and enslave every oxygen-stealing Christian, Jew, and religious zealot I come across. The voice will empower me, and I will rule this world without mercy. This is the dark future that you and your God could not prevent." Malak knelt to look Kane in the eyes. "Of course, I also want you to die, and I want you to do so knowing that your children will be raised beneath the hand of cruelty. In time they will resent you for your weakness and your failure. Their lives belong to me."

Kane looked at Michael and Rachael as tears streamed down his face. "Listen to me, children," he said, shuddering. "No matter what happens, do not lose faith. I will come for you. I will find you."

Malak shrugged and motioned for Saxon to come forward. "I'm not going to waste any more of my power on this Christian maggot. Shoot him in the face and force the children to watch."

Kane raised his eyes past his sobbing children and past Saxon, who drew a crude semiautomatic pistol and pointed it in Kane's direction.

"Don't hurt my daddy!" Rachael screamed as a foul wind whipped at Kane's hair, causing the tears to streak across his face as they fell.

"It's okay, baby," Kane whispered. "Close your eyes now," he mumbled as he locked his eyes up toward the sky. "Forgive me, Father. I failed you. I failed everyone."

The flash of a muzzle preceded the rolling echo of gunfire. Kane was struck by a crushing blast of pain that seared its way through his chest. Another blast followed, then another, as the air left his lungs and he began to feel weightless. The children screamed as Saxon raised the gun to Kane's face and fired again, the blast snapping his head back with a spray of blood. Kane teetered, hanging on to the edge of gravity, as his body began to sway, and he felt a coldness descend upon him.

"When you see your whore of a wife, tell her I've got her kids now," Saxon sneered as he kicked Kane viciously in the chest and over the edge of the cliff.

Then Kane was falling, suspended for an eternity in the open air. As he fell he saw the faces of his father, his mother, and his dear Susan as they welcomed him home with open arms. He felt a sense of calm cover him as he plunged toward the rocks, the surf rising up with a mighty crash, receiving him into its loving arms forevermore.

# EPILOGUE

Momentary sparks of light danced like flecks of gold in the darkness. The smallest flare of recognition soothed the hidden fears of his heart. Something moved inside him, and his heart beat within his breast once more. With a distant hum, a grand warmth flowed over him, causing every fiber of his being to tingle. It was then that a voice, ethereal yet as familiar to his heart as the voice of his own father, spoke to him.

*Kane, my child. Why would you hide your face from me? There is nothing you could do to cause me to turn from you. My son has interceded on your behalf, and his blood redeems you. Everything has happened for a reason, from the moment of your birth, to your survival, to your place among those whom I have chosen, and all the horrors you have experienced. This pain was not my desire for you, but you are mine, and I claim you as mine. You are not yet finished.*

With a fresh blossom of overwhelming pain, Kane groaned in agony as a pair of massive hands hauled him from the surging tide and onto the rocky shore. His battered body hung like a torn bit of cloth in the enormous arms that cradled him as his many wounds continued to ooze blood and fluid.

"I've got you, brother. I found you. I don't know how, but I found you," came the soothingly deep baritone. Pulling Kane up onto the beach, Courtland dropped to his knees against the sand and cradled his broken friend against him.

"Look how the enemy aims to destroy a man whom the Lord God himself has raised up." The giant touched the bullet's entrance wound on Kane's forehead. With the tip of his finger, he traced where the bullet grooved its way under the scalp and across the dome of the skull to where it exited through the flesh on the back of his friend's head. "Your hard head is intact," Courtland muttered.

The giant grabbed Kane's shirt and tore it open, the buttons popping away to reveal the blue face of a bulletproof vest. Two rounds were lodged in the central trauma plate, while a third hit low and to the outside, just passing through the Kevlar. Courtland pursed his lips into a smile. "The Lord doesn't want you dead yet, my friend."

Kane moaned, unable to move or respond.

"Save your strength. Courtland will take care of you. I know it was Malak who did this to you. I think I found Susan nearby on the rocks. I can't tell you how heavy my heart is for you."

Courtland's tears fell without restraint as he held his brother to his breast. "They designed it this way." The big man's voice quivered. "They wanted to break you all the way down. Right or wrong, I wasn't there for you when you needed me most, and seeing this happen to you and your family is my punishment."

The wind lashed at them from a darkening sky, the storm flinging droplets of water against their huddled frames. Courtland squinted and leaned in close to Kane's ear.

"Brace yourself, brother. Now I have to carry you, and it's going to hurt."

Courtland lifted the dripping wet, near lifeless body of Kane Lorusso in his arms, causing Kane to give a weak cry. Holding him close, the way a father carries his child across his chest, Courtland trudged upward, toward the sandy bluff above. As he went, his brow bent with concern and determination, and he allowed his deep, fatherly voice to well inside him.

"Seize now the shards of your broken faith, my brother, and fear nothing, for the living God has assured us the victory," he said, the words drifting down, a hymn of encouragement over his closest friend. "We are not yet defeated. Our purpose is not diminished. And though this task may take us into the jaws of hell itself, we will not rest until your children are safe and this demon has tasted the justice of the Lord." The giant set his jaw in righteous anger.

*"This, my oath, I swear to you."*

# ACKNOWLEDGMENTS

First and foremost I must give thanks to my lord Jesus. My hero. My savior. It is because of him that I am or have anything. I, for one, am a man who is grateful for second chances.

To Kara, whose constant love, support, selflessness, and patience is an indispensible commodity in my life.

My proofreaders, David Jones and Gareth Worthington (author of *Children of the Fifth Sun*)—your thoughtful, constructive criticism has enhanced this novel beyond measure.

The editing team at CreateSpace who handled my manuscript and did a wonderfully professional job tightening the narrative and removing all the small inconsistencies that plague any creative effort.

I also owe a great many thanks to any and all that contributed to this work in ways large and small. It is because of you and your support that this project is a reality.

Finally I thank you, the reader. The sheer fact that you hold this book means you had the heart to take up this journey in the first place. By purchasing this book, you are also an instrumental asset in the war on human trafficking. Thank you for your support.

# TAKING A STAND AGAINST HUMAN TRAFFICKING

"We cannot simply bandage the wounds of victims
beneath the wheels of injustice.
We must drive a spoke into the wheel itself."
—Dietrich Bonhoeffer

One hundred percent of the profits from every physical and digital book sold in the Action of Purpose series will go toward combating the epidemic of sex trafficking in the United States.

Buy a copy of *Through the Fury to the Dawn*, *Into the Dark of the Day*, or *Against the Fading of the Light*, and an equal contribution will be made to Blanket Fort Hope and/or The Wellhouse, two faith-based nonprofit organizations dedicated to stopping the sex trafficking of women and children and assisting in the recovery of those affected by this evil practice.

Please also consider leaving a review of this book online on Amazon, Goodreads, or social media. Reviews increase exposure, and help generate more profits for these incredible charities.

For more information about other books in this series or future projects in the works, visit the series website at www.actionofpurpose.com or the author's website www.stujonesfiction.com.